MINAKAI
MONSTER TAMER

VOLUME 1

JORDAN ALLEN

Contents

Arc 1
Welcome to Harmony Tower

Contents

Arc 2
The First Hazelton Tournament

Contents

Arc 3
Building a Team

Contents

Arc 4
Zodiac Hunters

Chapter 1

Today was the day to conquer the tower. Aurin could think of nothing else as the train pulled up to the platform. He rose to his feet, grabbing his backpack from the empty seat to his right. He beckoned his short friend forward and the pair waited by the door for it to open; what was mere seconds felt like an hour. Aurin was excited to venture into Harmony Tower here in the quiet countryside town of Hazelton.

The doors opened and he burst out. He could wait no longer, and his companion followed him enthusiastically. The small green creature had spikes protruding from the back of his head along with a wooden mask featuring green markings.

The creature, Shamtile, chased after the young man who had run down the platform and leapt down the stone staircase. The reptilian Shamtile had no trouble keeping up, even though he was less than half of Aurin's height. He was a speedy little Minakai.

Minakai. Monsters from parts unknown that made their way to Aurin's world through ancient, magical towers. Some kept Minakai as pets, others battled them for fun, and some used their Minakai to ascend the towers in search of adventure. The last of those was Aurin's goal.

"No time to rest, Shamtile," said Aurin brightly as the pair quickly dashed through the streets of Hazelton.

Harmony Tower was a magnificent structure and loomed in the distance, higher than any building in the small town. Fifty floors tall was what they said, but nobody seemed to know what lay at the top. Aurin wanted to find out. He was going straight to the top this very day. He would be the first person to reach the top of a monster tower on their first try.

Less than half an hour later, Aurin stood in a small forest clearing at the base of the tower with his masked lizard standing beside him. The grey stone tower was covered in vines and moss all around the outside. At the top of the mysterious structure, was a shadowy aura that was almost reminiscent of storm clouds as they swirled and flashed, fading from sight for a short while only to reappear seconds later.

The only windows were to black voids and the only entrance was the large wooden doors. It was not a doorway that you could merely walk through, and you certainly couldn't break the doors down. The magic of the tower would not allow you to.

Aurin walked towards the entrance while reaching inside his shirt, pulling out an ornate key tied to a string. The bronze key glistened in the midday sun, without a hint of stain or tarnish. It had been a gift from Aurin's father for his fifteenth birthday a few months ago. In fact, his father had given Aurin both a key to Harmony Tower and a Shamtile egg on the very same birthday. It took many months after that to convince his mother to let him embark on this journey.

Shamtile waved his arms frantically, letting out a warbling noise as he did so.

"It's fine, Shamtile," grinned Aurin. "Just follow my instructions and we'll be at the top by this time tomorrow. I've been studying for this for years, remember? A combat-type tower like this one should be easy for us."

Shamtile clapped his hands and started jumping. Aurin was never quite sure what his Minakai was trying to convey, but he took it to mean that Shamtile was reassured by his tamer's confidence.

The young man ran his hand through his dark blonde hair and sighed, a lot had led up to this big moment. He raised the key and inserted it into the lock. It turned with little force and the doors began to open by themselves. Aurin pulled his key out and took in the sight before him. The tower doors didn't open into a room. No. The doors opened into a swirling vortex of blue and green. Aurin could feel the portal pulling him inside and he gave in, allowing it to do so. For a few seconds, everything went dark.

Light then flooded Aurin's vision and he found himself standing in a corridor. It was lit by mysterious lanterns that did not contain fire, but something much closer to glowing orbs of pure light. The walls were a dull grey stone, and the floor was covered in cream and black marble tiles, similar to a chessboard.

"We're stuck now, Shamtile," said Aurin as he turned

to where you would expect to find a door. "Now that we're in the tower, we don't get to leave until you've been defeated, I find a magical orb to use or...well, I die. That doesn't happen too often these days, certainly not on the lower floors."

Aurin and Shamtile walked down the corridor, Aurin on the lookout for treasure with each stride. Silver, gold and magical items would all be very nice, but Minakai eggs are what Aurin sought most. You could buy them on the outside, but the best ones were pricey.

"Caaaaaw," came a sizzling screech from around a corner. A tiny fireball with bird-like legs and a beak that emerged from the centre of the flickering flame and was charging at Aurin.

"A Flowl!" yelled Aurin at Shamtile. "You've got this, buddy. Go get him!"

Shamtile got down on all fours and sped towards the charging Flowl, tackling it and knocking it backwards. The angered Flowl spat a fireball at Shamtile, but the reptile slickly dodged with a well-timed leap.

"You've got the elemental advantage, Sham," called Aurin, "use an earth attack."

Shamtile nodded and waved his hands in the air, conjuring a large rock. Shamtile hurled the rock at the flaming bird-like Minakai; it was not fast enough to get out of the way. The rock collided with the Flowl and pinned the little monster against the wall. The Minakai passed out and disappeared in a burst of red light.

Aurin jumped and cheered while Shamtile started to wave his hands in the air once again, this time in celebration.

"Good job, my friend," congratulated Aurin. "Our first battle in the tower and it was a great success. Feeling better now?"

Shamtile rubbed his hands on his wooden mask and then began to clap. Aurin was confident that that was a yes.

The pair walked further down the corridor. Before long, it forked in two directions and Aurin chose to go along the left path, which led into a small room containing...

"Yes!" exclaimed Aurin, rushing to the centre of the room. "A few pieces of silver. Now we might be able to afford a place to stay for the night, Shamtile."

Aurin continued to wander the first floor of the tower, slowly taking in the different rooms and corridors as he moved. He began forming a map in his head, making every effort to remember it. He didn't run into any more Minakai, nor any fellow tamers. He considered this to be somewhat odd, having read up on how the towers worked many times over.

"It's strange," said Aurin to Shamtile. "Why is it so empty here? Is somebody here on the floor with us clearing the way? It must have been recently or new Minakai would have spawned. We haven't found the elevator to the second floor either, so there must be more ahead somewhere."

Aurin backtracked to try and find a corridor he missed and, find it, he did. He walked down the corridor and came to another room. The young man's eyes lit up even more than when he had found the silver coins.

"An egg!" he yelled and ran towards it. "It's my lucky day."

"Indeed, it is," came a gruff voice from the shadows as Aurin picked up the egg.

Aurin turned towards the voice. Before him stood a man dressed in a black shirt and boots, with a white jacket and trousers. His hair was hidden by a white hat, and he wore a star-patterned mask that covered the top half of his face; it was made of wood and painted black, save for the white dots that were the stars.

"Who are you?" asked Aurin, backing off. Shamtile started waving his arms once again—he spent most of his day doing this for various reasons.

"Ah, you must be new," said the man as he walked closer. "I'm a member of the Zodiac Squad. You'll soon find out that Harmony Tower is our territory. Anything in here belongs to us. Got it? Now, hand over that egg you've got there."

"No," said Aurin, swiftly moving the egg behind his back.

The Zodiac member laughed and raised a gloved fist with three diamond-shaped gems slotted into the back of it. One of the gems glowed a bright blue and he cast his hand out in front of him. A blue, water-like Minakai in the vague shape of an upright fish appeared before Aurin. It had two handless arms instead of fins and it floated eerily above the ground, not any less creepy for the large grey eyes on the sides of its head. The Minakai stared lifelessly at Aurin, sending a shiver up the young man's spine.

"If that's the way you're going to be, then let's fight for it. My Spritzard versus your Shamtile. What do you say?" asked the Zodiac member.

"I don't think we have a choice, Shamtile," said Aurin. "Let's get them!"

Shamtile darted forward on all fours towards the Spritzard, but it was a slippery creature and dodged with ease. It spat a jet of water from its mouth at the lizard, knocking him to the floor and out cold. Aurin ran to his friend, but the Spritzard fired a jet of water into Aurin's back pushing him into the wall and knocking him out as easily as it had Shamtile.

Aurin came to. His head was aching, but he was surprisingly comfortable. It felt as though he was lying in a bed. Yes, he was sure it was a bed. He slowly opened his eyes and light filled them. It was blurry, but he could see a ceiling above him. He blinked a couple of times and his vision started to adjust.

"You're awake," came a sweet-sounding voice from next to him. "I was worried it was more serious than I first thought."

"Shamtile?" asked Aurin, remembering what had happened and bolting upright.

He looked around and saw that he was in a girl's bedroom. A young girl, about Aurin's age of fifteen, was sitting on a chair staring at him. She had sparkling blue eyes and shoulder-length auburn hair, held back by a blue hairband. She wore a purple jumper with wide cuffs, a white skirt and a pair of boots that matched her jumper.

"He's fine," smiled the girl. "Inno, come here and bring your new friend."

A knee-height, sky-blue drake with a cream-coloured belly and a tall fin-like ridge atop his head ran into the room excitedly. He was followed by Shamtile who, true to form, waved his hands wildly as he ran. Shamtile leapt onto Aurin, almost winding his tamer. The drake stood by, smiling widely and patting his stomach while flicking his short tail back and forth.

"Good to see you, buddy," laughed Aurin as his Shamtile sat there staring at him from behind his wooden mask.

"I'm Luna," said the girl, reaching out her hand. "Nice to meet you properly."

Aurin shook it. "Nice to meet you too. I'm Aurin. How did you find us?"

Luna stood up excitedly. "My little Innogon and I were on a valiant quest to enter the tower and search for magical healing herbs when we happened upon you and your Shamtile unconscious outside."

"Of course," said Aurin, realising what had happened. "Shamtile is my only Minakai, so the tower threw me out."

"I thought as much," said Luna, nodding her head. "It's normally only the Minakai who gets knocked out. Your Shamtile came around quite quickly so the three of us carried you back here to my house. You're rather heavy, you know? I'm not sure I could have done it by myself."

Aurin gasped. "My egg! My coins!"

Luna nodded once again. "You won't see those again. When the tower expels you after being defeated, everything you've gathered is left behind, but I'm sure you knew that already. Did you get attacked by another Minakai?"

"Not quite," said Aurin quietly, embarrassed by what had happened. "We were attacked by a strange man with his own Minakai. He said he was part of a group called the Zodiac something."

"The Zodiac Squad? They've been causing a lot of trouble here lately. They're a large gang that acts like regular people in the town, so you don't even know they're part of the group. When they enter the tower, they put on their Zodiac outfits to disguise themselves and sabotage other tamers."

"Why?" asked Aurin.

"I don't know," sighed Luna. "Maybe they want to claim the treasures in the tower for themselves? It's been happening a lot lately and people are starting to get sick of it."

Aurin sat on the bed thinking about all of this. He'd met his fair share of unpleasant folks in his hometown of Buckstone, but this Zodiac guy was something else. He didn't like the thought of many more of these Zodiac Squad members walking around, hidden in plain sight, ready to attack you the second you enter the tower.

"Do you have an Orb of Return?" asked Luna. "It's a magical orb that lets you escape from the tower with everything you own."

"I know what it is," said Aurin, slightly offended. "I had an unfortunate accident in the tower, but I'm not clueless."

Luna raised an eyebrow.

"Sorry, I shouldn't have snapped," Aurin said, feeling ashamed of how he had spoken to her. "And thank you for helping me out, Luna. I haven't said that yet and I really should have."

Luna beamed. "It's okay, Aurin. You can stay in our guest room tonight, my parents won't mind, and tomorrow morning we can go to the tower together. I have an orb, so we'll have an escape route when we need it. I'll help you find an egg and you can help me find herbs."

Aurin nodded. "Okay, that sounds like a great idea. What do you think, Shamtile?"

Shamtile made an uncomfortable screech that Aurin took as a yes.

The following day, Aurin, Luna, Shamtile and Innogon walked up the forest path towards the monster tower that forever stood above the trees. Aurin felt substantially less prepared this time, despite being more prepared than on his first venture.

He knew he had been foolish in thinking that he could conquer the tower on his first try and being defeated so easily on the first floor had brought him back down to Earth. Now it was time to be serious and not underestimate the challenges that would make themselves known to him.

"Ready?" he asked, stopping by the large doors.

"Yes," nodded Luna with a smile on her face.

The young man placed his key in the hole and turned it once again, feeling the tower trying to pull him inside as the doors opened. Aurin, Luna, Shamtile and Innogon did not resist and entered the swirling vortex, ready to face the gauntlet of Harmony Tower together.

Chapter 2

Aurin and Luna landed in the tower with their Minakai, Shamtile and Innogon, standing by their side. Luna reached into her bag and put on a glove with a blue gem embedded into it. Aurin recognised it as one similar to what the Zodiac Squad member he faced had worn.

"Let's go this way," he said. "I went this way last time and it..."

The young man realised suddenly that it didn't matter which way he had gone before.

"The tower changes each time you enter," said Luna.

Aurin pressed his fingers into his temples and massaged them. "I know. I'm being sloppy again, sorry."

The duo walked forward with their Minakai in tow and followed one of the corridors presenting itself to them. Aurin instinctively wanted to turn left, knowing that the last time he faced a similar route it led him to silver coins. Perhaps, it would again, but he knew that he could not rely on his previous experience in navigating the floor.

"Don't forget to keep an eye out for traps," whispered Luna, trying hard not to sound like a know-it-all.

"Right," said Aurin, grateful for the reminder.

Aurin rounded the corner and spotted a room ahead. He cautiously approached, careful not to trigger any of the unseen traps that could be activated by simply stepping on the wrong floor tile. As he neared the room, he spotted a hunched figure rummaging around on the ground. As Aurin and Luna entered the room, the figure stood up and turned to face them.

"Good day!" smiled the young man, barely older than Aurin and Luna. He had a round face and wavy red hair. Outside of the tower, you would have presumed him to be a farmer had you met him.

"Hello," said Luna brightly.

"Are you a tamer?" asked Aurin.

"I am indeed, yes," said the young man. "My name is Gardner. Fancy a battle? This floor has been too quiet for my liking."

Aurin started to get more excited. "Let's do it! My name is Aurin and this is Luna."

"Who's going to face me? I've only got two Minakai, so I'd rather not lose them both and get booted from the tower. One versus one is enough."

Luna nudged Aurin forward slightly, but he had already decided that he would be the one to fight.

"That works for me," said the man as he raised his hand, equipped with a glove containing two green gems.

Aurin sent Shamtile to the front of the room, ready to face whatever monster Gardner was going to use.

"Ready when you are, Gardner," he said.

"Fantastic," smiled Gardner as he thrust his hand forward. "Let's go, Happynut!"

One of the green gems started to glow and a Minakai appeared upon the floor in a flash of green light. It was a reddish foot-tall nut-like creature with a face and a small shoot growing from its head that split into two green leaves. It smiled a toothless smile so wide that it was hard to see its eyes.

"Attack, Happynut!" called Gardner, suddenly seeming a lot more serious.

Happynut ran and jumped into the air. It curled up like a cannonball and threw itself towards Shamtile, who leapt out of the way.

"Conjure up some sand," ordered Aurin.

Shamtile waved his hands around and a whirlwind of sand spawned from the chessboard-patterned floor. The little reptile directed it at the Happynut and it shut its eyes even more tightly, trying to blink away the sand that had hit it in the face.

"Follow up with a rockfall," Aurin called out.

Shamtile raised his hands up, then brought them down forcefully and a large rock appeared in the air before suddenly plummeting and colliding with Happynut, knocking the Minakai out. Luna and Innogon jumped up and cheered.

"Oh no!" yelled Gardner as he ran to make sure his Happynut was okay.

"Did we overdo it?" asked Aurin.

"No, no," said Gardner as his Happynut disappeared in a green glow, "Happynut will be fine. He's in stasis for now but will be on his way back to Kyle's ranch the second I leave the tower. A little bit of sunshine and food and then he'll be right as rain."

Aurin reached out his hand for Gardner to shake. "It was a fun battle."

Gardner shook it. "Albeit far too short on my part. Congratulations, Aurin. We should have a rematch someday when we both have full teams and more experience."

"I'd enjoy that," said Aurin sincerely.

"Say," began Gardner, with a slightly puzzled look, "I noticed you don't use a summoning stone or tamer glove for your Shamtile. Is there any particular reason for that?"

"I haven't found or bought any stones yet and Shamtile is my only Minakai so it's easy just to have him follow me."

"You can only use three Minakai for each tower run, so I'd think about buying one if you don't find one in the tower soon. It'll be useful for when you expand your team. Just a little advice, my friend."

"It's good advice, to be honest. Thanks."

"I'll see you both later, perhaps in town," said Gardner as we waved and departed.

"He seemed nice," said Luna.

"Nicer than the Zodiac guy I ran into last time," laughed Aurin.

He, Luna and their Minakai returned to the corridor to try a different direction. They weaved in and out of the long hallways and across the various rooms. It took less than ten minutes to cover the entire floor, but it felt a lot longer to both of them. Along the way, they battled a couple of stray Minakai and picked up a few coins, but it was otherwise as quiet as the first floor was the previous time. Luna insisted that this was normal, but not to expect the easy ride on higher floors.

"What's the highest floor you've been to?" asked

Aurin.

"The third floor," Luna admitted, suddenly seeming shy. "I entered the tower for the first time four weeks ago and this is my fifth time in here."

"That's nothing to be embarrassed about. You know how my first attempt ended."

"What's that up ahead?" asked Luna excitedly as she pointed. "Is it what I think it is?"

Aurin squinted up the corridor to the open doorway ahead. Inside the room sat a blue egg-shaped gem, considerably larger than Aurin's head. It was embedded in a podium of ornate gold that wrapped around it, securing it firmly in place. There was a great majesty about it, radiating importance with how prominent it was against the otherwise flat tower floor.

"Is that the elevator?" asked Aurin, also growing excited.

"Yup!" exclaimed Luna.

The quartet ran into the room and admired the beautiful stone. Aurin suspected that the orb alone would be worth thousands of ounces of gold, never mind the gold content of the stand itself.

"Has anybody ever tried to remove one of these things?" he asked with no intention of trying himself.

"I've never thought to ask," said Luna, raising an eyebrow. "I don't know if the magic of the tower would even let you."

"How does it work?" asked Aurin. "How do we go up?"

"Hold out your hands and touch the gem," said Luna, moving to do just that. "Don't worry about our Minakai, they'll follow us."

Aurin copied her, holding out his hands. They both laid their palms on the large gem and felt themselves being pulled. The sensation was similar to the feeling of entering the tower through the vortex in the doorway, however, they could tell they were being dragged upwards rather than forwards.

The pair stood on the second floor mere seconds after touching the elevator. The room they were in looked different from the ones below. The chessboard pattern on the floor was now yellow and grey, while the walls were a dark green. Aurin was glad that it had changed as it would help him keep track of which floor he had reached once he rose higher and higher.

Once he was no longer disorientated on this new floor, Aurin led the way forward. Something about the corridors here felt darker, but he didn't think that it was just because of the walls. There was something that unsettled him, but all was quiet except for the soft humming of the light from the glassless lanterns.

After navigating a few looping corridors, Aurin spotted a room ahead. He walked towards it, hoping it would hold a treasure of some kind. Sadly, for him, it was empty save for a couple of large red berries.

"Wow!" exclaimed Luna. "I was hoping to find Orna berries around here somewhere."

"I'm glad the berries excite you so much," laughed Aurin.

"You can joke, but they're great for helping Minakai recover from fights once you mix them into a good meal. They work by themselves, but they can be enhanced."

The pair walked out of a door on the other side of the room and deeper into the second floor. It only just hit Aurin how difficult it would be each time he entered the tower if the layout kept changing. One floor was bad enough to keep track of, but what about a dozen floors each new tower run?

"Egg," said Aurin bluntly and with a large grin forming on his face.

Luna clapped her hands as Aurin ran into another room excitedly. When Aurin stepped through the doorway, he heard a click as four teal birds appeared in a flash of creamy white light. It was a small flock of Peekan, a flying Minakai, which were neutral elementals as signified by the colour of the light.

"Oh no," said Aurin, realising his folly. "Shamtile!"

The earth elemental lizard ran into the room on all fours, followed by Luna and Innogon.

"Inno, it's time to battle," said Luna pointing towards the birds.

The Peekan split into two groups of two, one group heading for Shamtile and the other towards Innogon. Shamtile began conjuring small rocks and tried to knock birds to the ground, but they were fast. Innogon shot jets of water from his mouth, only clipping stray feathers.

"Shamtile, wait for it to get close then summon the best boulder you can!" called Aurin.

Shamtile waved his arms in anticipation as the birds dived at him. As Aurin had ordered, he summoned a boulder and the two Peekan crashed into it, bursting into light shortly after. Innogon continued to spray water jets, rolling out of the way of the birds anytime they struck, but it was clear that he was tiring.

"Distract them," ordered Aurin.

Shamtile ran towards the remaining two Peekan and flailed around, hoping to grab their attention. When they started chasing him, Innogon was free to catch his breath for a moment. He took careful aim and shot a jet of water at one as it charged for Shamtile. It was knocked out in a watery splash and disappeared from the tower seconds later. The remaining Peekan saw that it was alone and flew out of the room, wanting to save itself, giving the quartet a resounding victory over the wild Minakai.

"Thank you," said Luna to Aurin. "I'm not much of a battler if I'm honest."

"I'm sorry. It was my fault for setting the trap off and summoning them in the first place," lamented Aurin, slapping himself lightly in the face.

"That egg definitely belongs to you. You know how to handle Shamtile so well, so I'm sure a second Minakai will be easy."

"I don't know about handling him well, but at least this run hasn't ended in disaster yet."

Aurin thanked Luna and walked over to the egg. As he picked it up, Aurin noted that it was a little bigger and heavier than a football. He placed it carefully in his backpack, not wanting to damage it, but he had the suspicion that it was sturdier than your average egg. Upon putting his backpack on once again, he found himself doubting that he could carry more than half a dozen of these easily.

"Help!" called a voice from down the corridor.

"Was that Gardner?" asked Luna. "Did the final Peekan attack him?"

"I'm not sure," said Aurin as he ran to the door.

Aurin followed the commotion and saw Gardner suddenly burst into light, now ejected from the tower. As Aurin hurried along, he heard two voices chuckling and start to talk amongst themselves.

Aurin and Luna darted around the corner and saw two individuals, a male and a female, in Zodiac Squad uniforms standing with their Minakai. The male had a green wolf cub in front of him and the female had an orange puppy dog in front of her.

"Got any eggs?" chuckled the man, tossing an egg from hand to hand. "That young lad was very kind and donated one to our cause."

"We thought we'd give him a shortcut home," smirked the woman.

"Shamtile, get them!" barked a furious Aurin.

"Back him up, Inno," ordered Luna, visibly angered and with a red face that almost matched her hair.

The two Zodiac members were taken aback by the sudden attack. Shamtile hurled rocks at the orange dog while Innogon shot jets of water at the green wolf.

"Don't just stand there, Heatpup!" yelled the woman.

"Do something, Petalcub," scolded the man.

The two canines charged at Aurin and Luna's Minakai. Shamtile continued to hurl rocks relentlessly at the orange Heatpup, utilising his earth elemental advantage against the fire elemental. Innogon's strong jets were powerful enough to knock the green Petalcub back repeatedly even without an advantage. Both the Heatpup and Petalcub were clearly already tired from fighting Gardner and the two Minakai attacking had caught them completely off guard.

The Zodiac members yelled orders and protested vigorously, but it was to no avail. Shamtile threw a particularly large rock and Innogon shot an extra intense jet of water, both of which knocked their targets out within seconds of each other. Shortly after the Minakai burst into light, their Zodiac tamers did the same—all four were expelled from the tower.

"Good job, boys," smiled Aurin, squatting low and patting his Minakai friends on the shoulders.

"Yes, well done," agreed Luna, retrieving Gardner's

egg from the floor, having been dropped by the Zodiac man.

"I think we should leave to check on Gardner. I don't want to speak for you, but I think both of our Minakai have earned a rest."

Luna nodded. "No, you're right. Come close to me and I'll cast the spell."

The young girl withdrew her Orb of Return from her pack and stood up, fixing her hairband that had gone astray in the excitement. She held the orb out in her palm and focused, willing it to return her and Aurin to the entrance.

Aurin felt himself being pulled downwards, Luna alongside him, and they found themselves almost instantaneously on the grass at the tower entrance. The Zodiac members were nowhere to be seen, but Gardner was sitting on the grass a short distance from the pathway, up against a nearby tree.

"They ran into the woods," lamented Gardner, his face filled with disappointment.

"Are you okay?" asked Luna.

"Thanks for dealing with them."

"How did you know we dealt with them?" enquired Aurin.

"They appeared out here shortly after I did and I could see you weren't ejected by a defeat. There was something different about how your teleportation looked."

"What now?" asked Luna.

"We should go back to Hazelton," said Aurin, wondering if he could come up with a better plan on how to handle the Zodiac Squad there.

Chapter 3

"There's nothing you can do?" protested Aurin.

Aurin and Luna stood in the Hazelton mayor's office with their Minakai, Mayor Boren and two detectives called Knot and Scarlett.

"We're a small town with limited officers," insisted Detective Knot. "We've been trying to keep Zodiac under control, but they're as slippery as they come. Harmony Tower keys only began appearing in the world three years ago, so Hazelton hasn't had time to adjust to the influx of new people coming to see a brand-new tower open, never mind deal with these troublemakers."

Knot was a man in his early forties with brown hair that was starting to grey and light stubble on his sharp chin. His face was more wrinkled than it should have been, no doubt from the stress of his job. His partner,

Scarlett, was a brown-haired woman in her late twenties who had a warm smile, but sharp eyes that darted about upon hearing even the faintest noise. The mayor himself was tall and broad, but he gave the vibe of someone much more laid back than his appearance suggested.

"Kids," began the mayor calmly, "I agree with you entirely that the Zodiac Squad need to be stopped. They've been growing more and more persistent, fighting people in the tower, kidnapping rare Minakai and stealing eggs...it's terrible. Detective Knot obviously agrees too."

"I do, of course," said Knot, nodding his head.

"If you see anything else or have any more reports, please don't be deterred from letting us know," said Detective Scarlett in a soothing tone, placing her hand on Luna's shoulder.

"I became mayor of this wonderful town shortly after Harmony Tower opened," said Mayor Boren. "The town has become a haven for tamers looking to enter one of the quieter towers in our fine country. It helps that it's a combat-class tower so you know what you can usually expect. I've been making many improvements to the town to try and adapt to our new way of life here, but these things take time. Perhaps it's my fault that I didn't invest more in law enforcement at the beginning of all this, but please know that I'm trying to rectify that."

"There's nothing we can do in the meantime?" asked Aurin.

"I would suggest forming a team, building their strength and I would also urge you two to stick together when you enter the tower. That Innogon you have, young lady, is one I'm sure that the Zodiac Squad would love to have added to their arsenal of monsters. He's attuned to a crystal, right?"

Luna nodded as Innogon playfully blew a bubble from his mouth.

"That's good. If they don't take your gem, you can summon him back to you."

"If you'll excuse us, children," said Knot, "we've got a few things to discuss."

Aurin and Luna thanked the mayor and detectives before leaving. Aurin was reluctant to show much gratitude considering they had been of little help, but they *had* taken the time out to speak to two teenagers they had never heard of. He knew that the Zodiac Squad's existence wasn't the fault of the mayor or the detectives, but he couldn't help but feel a little disappointed that they weren't able to do much to stop them, leaving everybody to fend for themselves.

"Come on, Aurin," said Luna, grabbing him by the sleeve and marching him onto the road towards the tower.

"Are we going back into the tower already?" asked Aurin.

"You heard them, we need to get stronger," Luna said, not looking back to face him. "We're going to Kyle's ranch just outside of town. Let's hatch that new egg of yours so we can start building up our teams."

"Who is Kyle?" asked Aurin, thinking the name sounded vaguely familiar.

"Kyle!" called Luna as she waved at a man carrying a large sack of food.

They were at a large ranch just outside of town but down a different path from the tower. There were large fences used to keep various Minakai apart to stop them from fighting. The fences were protected by bulky white monsters wearing crowns of ice called Frogre. The Frogre were constantly patrolling back and forth, likely to keep the Minakai inside safe from the outside more so than to prevent them from escaping.

"Hello there, Luna," replied Kyle as he approached. He was a tall and well-built man in his late thirties, with thick black hair and a short beard.

"Hello, Kyle. My name is Aurin," said Aurin extending his hand to greet the rancher.

Kyle shook his hand. "Welcome to Hazelton, Aurin. I've heard that you're new around here."

Aurin looked puzzled. "I've only been here two days; how did you know?"

"I know everything in this town," chuckled Kyle, "even though I live all the way out here."

Aurin reached into his pack and brought out his egg. "I was hoping that you would be able to help me hatch this."

The rancher inspected the egg and smiled again. "You've come to the right place. Hatching eggs and looking after Minakai is my speciality."

Kyle went inside his house and came back a minute later with a small device that looked not too dissimilar from a hot plate. He set it on the ground and turned it on, placing the egg on top of it.

"This is a special kind of incubator we use for Minakai that rapidly speeds up the hatching process. When activated, they'll hatch almost instantly."

Aurin glanced at Luna, then placed his egg on the incubator. Kyle instructed him to push the button on the side. Upon doing so, a small forcefield encircled the egg and within moments, the egg started to crack. A glowing red light burst from within and a small Minakai appeared. It was red, scaly and curled into a ball.

"What is it?" asked Luna.

"I think it's a Hornber," said Aurin uncertainly.

"Yes, it's a Hornber alright," Kyle chimed in.

The Minakai uncurled itself and stood up on all fours. It was a short, red dinosaur with a bone-like spike protruding from its head. It looked up at Aurin with its big red eyes and snorted out a small puff of grey smoke from its nostrils.

"Hello there," said Aurin, moving to pat Hornber's head.

The small dinosaur looked uneasy, but it allowed Aurin to touch it. The young tamer carefully avoided the spike and, after a couple of seconds, Hornber gave a warbled growl of comfort.

"Did you hatch your Shamtile yourself?" asked Kyle.

"No," admitted Aurin. "I mean, I had him as an egg, but I've never seen an incubator like that before. My dad took me to a lab in Ludonia and they hatched him for me. I don't think we have any incubators like that back in my town, Buckstone."

"I'm sure somebody does, but they probably don't advertise it unless they're running a ranch," said Kyle knowingly. "It's one of the few drivers of money in this business."

"Oh," said Aurin reaching into his pack for some coins from the tower.

Kyle shook his head and laughed. "I wasn't trying to imply anything. I don't expect any money for it. I'll tell you what...how about a battle?"

"Me versus...you?" Aurin blurted out clumsily.

"I'll play fair," said Kyle with a smile. "I'll use a couple of recently hatched Minakai that I haven't trained much. If you lose, you can stay here while you're in town and help me around the ranch. It may even help you get more familiar with Minakai up close rather than relying on what you read in books and see on the television."

"Sounds good," said Aurin enthusiastically. "What if I win?"

"If you win...you can still stay here until you find somewhere else. I'll even give you a tamer glove and a couple of summoning stones that you can link your Minakai to. It'll let you summon them to your side whenever you need them."

Aurin tilted his head, confused. "I win either way?"

"Don't question it," whispered Luna, nudging Aurin's ribs.

"I suppose so," admitted Kyle. "You remind me of a young me. I was a tamer before becoming a rancher. Are you ready to battle then? Your team of two versus one of my teams of two."

Everyone walked to a small grassy clearing in front of the ranch. Aurin's Shamtile and Hornber were by his side, but Kyle's Minakai were nowhere to be seen. Luna and Innogon stood at the sidelines, ready to cheer Aurin on.

Aurin sent forth his newly hatched Hornber. Young Minakai are not like human infants. Minakai are born to fight and are ready for battle shortly after hatching. Aurin was confident that he would be able to lead his Hornber to victory.

"Alright," said Kyle, readying his glove. "If you're using a fire elemental, I'll use an earth elemental. Pottemp!"

One of the gems in Kyle's glove glowed an orange-brown and what appeared to be a statue appeared in the clearing in a flash of light. It was also a dinosaur of some kind, yet it was made of brown stone. It looked old and decayed, however, with both of its arms broken off. It did not possess eyes, rather it had two empty sockets where small glowing green dots rested. It was hard to tell if the dots were physical objects, but regardless of what they were, they allowed the Pottemp to see.

Aurin thought that in the battle between the two dinosaurs, he had the advantage even with his elemental weakness. Kyle's Pottemp didn't even have arms. What was he thinking using this one?

"Charge straight for it, Hornber!" called out Aurin.

Hornber lowered his head and ran forward, aiming for Pottemp. Pottemp simply stood there with a goofy reptilian grin on its stone face. Hornber collided with the stone Minakai, who fell backwards to the ground, but Hornber was noticeably hurt. Whatever stone Pottemp was made of, it was tough.

Kyle didn't need to say a word. His Pottemp swung its legs and threw itself back to its feet. It leapt ten feet into the air and slammed straight into the ground, causing a shockwave that knocked Hornber over. It charged towards Hornber, aiming to do what Hornber had failed to do to it.

"Get out of the way and hit him with a fireball!" yelled Aurin.

Hornber wasn't fast enough and Pottemp ploughed straight through him, sending Hornber through the air and crashing to the ground. He was too weak to fight on, so Luna ran over and picked him up to tend to him on the sidelines.

"Shamtile, you're up," ordered Aurin and Shamtile

immediately ran in to avenge his new ally. "Use your own rocks to crack it wide open."

Shamtile began waving his arms, conjuring forth stones and then hurled his barrage of rocks at Pottemp. As surprisingly nimble as it was, Pottemp could not evade all of the rocks and a particularly large one smacked it in the eye socket. Shamtile used this distraction to grab Pottemp by its rocky tail and spin it around. Shamtile rotated faster and faster, suddenly letting go of Pottemp and it soared through the air. It crashed down on its head with a heavy thud on the grass and stopped moving.

Kyle gave a small smile and used one of the summoning stones in his glove to dismiss Pottemp. He raised the glove once more and a flash of blue light summoned forth a ball of a watery jelly-like substance with a small blue tadpole inside.

"Spaqua, you know what to do," said Kyle.

Aurin was surprised that a supposedly untrained Minakai would know what to do. "Shamtile, it's an ice elemental! There's no elemental advantage for either of you here. Use your speed to outmanoeuvre it!"

Shamtile dashed forward and Spaqua started spraying streams of solid, icy bubbles in his direction, but Shamtile was agile enough to duck and dive over the streams as he moved closer to Spaqua. As the masked lizard moved in to strike, Spaqua pointed downwards inside his jelly and sprayed bubbles into the ground, forcing him into the air above Shamtile.

"Shamtile, he's made an error. Pelt him with rocks!"

Shamtile waved his hands in the air and conjured his rocks, hurling them upwards almost as rapidly as Spaqua had sprayed its bubbles. In the air, Spaqua was helpless and the rocks collided with it. The small tadpole fell to the ground, unable to right itself, and sprayed a powerful frosty breath towards the grass in a desperate attempt to slow the fall. Its sack of jelly lessened the impact as it hit the grass, but it was too wounded to fight on.

Luna and Innogon jumped and cheered while Shamtile started performing a bizarre dance. Aurin breathed a sigh of relief. The stakes weren't high, but he knew that he wanted to win.

Kyle walked forward and shook Aurin's hand. "Well done. Your Hornber needs a little experience, but that's to be expected. You and your Shamtile are quite a good team already."

"Thanks, Kyle," said Aurin with a smile. "For untrained Minakai, your Pottemp and Spaqua are tough."

"They're untrained, but never neglected. All of my Minakai get attention, even if I don't actively battle with them."

"I think that's a good way to handle things," admitted Aurin, feeling slightly guilty for doubting Kyle's intent.

Luna ran over and continued to jump for joy. "That was even more exciting than our Zodiac fight, Aurin."

"Zodiac fight?" asked Kyle, raising an eyebrow.

"It's a long story," said Aurin. "What was it you said about a glove and summoning stones?"

Kyle laughed as he led the way into his house, eager to give Aurin his prize and hear the two teenagers' tale about their battle with the Zodiac Squad members.

Chapter 4

Aurin sat on a bench in the town square wearing his new tamer glove with Shamtile by his side. Kyle taught him how to use it the previous day, along with showing him how to use the magic of the summoning stones to bond them with his Minakai. Aurin's glove was embedded with a brown crystal for Shamtile that sparkled orange when the light hit it at just the right angle and a red crystal for Hornber—who was currently relaxing at the ranch—that radiated with fiery intensity.

"I'm here!" called Luna as she ran down the street with Innogon clinging to her back. "I'm sorry I'm late."

"I've been waiting for twenty minutes!" exclaimed Aurin, eager to hit the shops with his tower earnings, meagre as they might have been.

"I know...I know," panted Luna. Innogon hopped off

her shoulders, not out of breath in the slightest and started play fighting with Shamtile.

"Do you need a moment?"

"No, I'm...okay," Luna lied.

Aurin handed her a milkshake he'd bought for her half an hour ago. It wasn't chilled anymore, but it was still tasty.

"Oh? For me? Thank you so much, Aurin," Luna said with a large smile on her face. She began to drain it at lightning speed through the straw.

Aurin simply laughed and they all walked towards one of the many shops selling supplies for tamers that would prepare them for adventures in the tower. Aurin had decided to stock up on whatever useful items he could afford that would aid his tower runs, which was admittedly a very unspecific shopping list. He knew he couldn't afford much, but he thought it wise to reinvest what he had now that he had somewhere to stay while he was in Hazelton.

"What about Hazelton Tower Goods?" asked Aurin.

"No, they can't even get the name of the tower right," said Luna.

"Adventuring Supplies?"

"No, they'll rip us off."

"Minakai Merchandise?"

"No, they mainly sell t-shirts and mugs."

"Where do you suggest?" asked Aurin, growing frustrated.

"Right here," said Luna as she stopped and pointed to the building ahead.

Aurin followed her finger and saw a small shop with a large sign that read 'Taming Solutions' in fancy lettering. It looked like a small shop, definitely older than a lot of the ones taking up the prime real estate positions in Hazelton.

Luna walked inside, with Aurin and the Minakai following her. As the door creaked closed behind Aurin, he surveyed the shop. There was a wide variety of herbs and berries on the shelves to his left, orbs aplenty on desks to the right, and even a few pristine eggs kept in glass cabinets behind the counter. The eggs weren't tagged, but they were almost certainly out of Aurin's price range.

"Ah, little Luna. How's your father?" asked a balding man behind the counter. He appeared to be in his sixties but was well-built. Aurin suspected he was no stranger to the tower himself.

"He's good, Cedric. How are you?" asked Luna.

"Business is decent for a small place like this, so I can't complain," chuckled Cedric. "I think a lot of people are hitting the tower hard to prepare for the tournament in a few months."

Tournament? This was the first time that Aurin had heard of a tournament, but he was intrigued.

"What are you in the market for, lad?" asked Cedric, noticing Aurin for the first time.

"I'm honestly not sure," he replied, rubbing his head. "I don't have that much silver, but I'm trying to climb higher in the tower."

"If you want to get higher in the tower, particularly a combat tower like Harmony Tower, you need a strong team and the ability to get *out* of the tower to preserve what you find. Do you have an Orb of Return?"

"I have one with a single charge left," said Luna.

Aurin did not know that Luna's orb had been almost drained of its magic until now. "An Orb of Return would be great, in that case. I owe Luna for helping me out so we can use my orb instead of hers while we try and earn money."

"Very good," smiled Cedric as he walked over to the shelf and lifted an orb. "That'll be twelve ounces of silver then. Normally fifteen, but you're a friend of Luna's so I'll cut you a good deal."

Aurin counted out his silver and handed over most of what he had left to Cedric. He greatly appreciated the discount.

"This should be good for five uses, so make sure to use them wisely," advised the shopkeeper.

Luna picked up a few herbs for herself and asked about egg prices but decided against buying one for now. The pair then bid farewell to Cedric and made for the tower with Shamtile and Innogon following them.

Aurin and Luna arrived on the fourth floor with little trouble. The tamers they met weren't looking for a battle, so they were pleased, however, the wild Minakai were more aggressive on this run; particularly on the third floor. The tamers decided to make sure that each of the Minakai had a solo battle so they weren't constantly relying on each other.

Shamtile defeated a metal elemental insect, called Metaworm, with ease. Hornber achieved his first victory against a Petalcub. Innogon, meanwhile, defeated a nature elemental plant class Minakai called a Shroomlie. They weren't entirely smooth battles, but Aurin and Luna's Minakai were no worse for the wear.

"Do you think we'll be unlucky and find any Zodiac

members today?" asked Aurin.

"Don't say that!" scolded Luna, slapping him lightly on the arm.

Aurin and Luna roamed the floor, Shamtile and Innogon following as closely as always while Hornber remained in stasis. When a Minakai is summoned from the outside world, the magic of the tower forbids it to leave without its tamer. Even if it's defeated, it doesn't get ejected, it gets sent to a pocket dimension until the tamer is defeated. If a tamer banishes a Minakai willingly, the monster is sent to that same pocket dimension but can be recalled into the tower at any time using the summoning stone. It was the tower's failsafe for anyone who would try and cheat their way to the top by sending their Minakai outside to heal and then bringing them back in, thus finding a loophole in the ascension.

The fourth floor was the highest that either Aurin or Luna had been to before. The chessboard-patterned floor was now a mixture of green and gold while the walls were a dark purple. Aurin wondered who built this place and how, but he knew he would never know the answer. It was a mystery as old as history. The towers had always been here, each would open and close at random intervals. Some would remain open for fifty years, and others would be open for three. On the other hand, some towers have never opened.

"I see something in the room ahead," said Aurin, squinting. He was careful not to rush and cautiously approached, having learned his lesson.

Aurin entered the room and picked up a few silver coins, but beside them lay a long, jagged crystal. It was a bluish-tint and inside there appeared to be moving images of stars in a void of space.

"Is this what I think it is?" asked Luna.

"I believe so," said Aurin. "It looks like an Astral Shard."

An Astral Shard contained powerful magic that, when unleashed, would allow Minakai of the neutral element to evolve to a new and more powerful form. Aurin was dismayed that Shamtile and Hornber were incompatible with the shard, but he put it in his pack hoping to either sell it or perhaps use it on a new Minakai he may hatch in the future.

"Do you want this one?" asked Luna, indicating a much smaller crystal coloured a deep orange.

"Nah, it doesn't look all that useful. If it isn't money, eggs, orbs, or evolutionary shards, I won't fight you for it."

"Alright, if you're sure," said Luna, looking at the item uncertainly before picking it up.

The group continued searching for the elevator on this floor and narrowly avoided a couple of wild Minakai they could see roaming in the distance or lurking in nearby rooms. Both Aurin and Luna had agreed to prioritise egg hunting today and save training for later. They had managed to narrowly avoid another grumpy Shroomlie when Luna spotted an egg in the room they sought shelter in.

"I've got two Minakai, you've got one. It's only fair that you take this egg," said Aurin.

"You're sure?" asked Luna.

"You found it, it's yours."

Luna and Innogon jumped for joy with the egg, but Luna was careful not to let it drop. A few corridors later, they found the elevator. Aurin was excited to be reaching the fifth floor, it felt more like an important milestone than any other floor. He knew that at this point he was ten percent of the way to the top.

The duo had been exploring the tower for nearly three hours, so they decided to take a short rest. They found an empty room and Shamtile elected to stand guard while everybody sat on the floor and had a small snack.

"Nothing makes a Minakai feel better than food," said Luna as she gave Innogon a few meatballs infused with herbs.

"What do the herbs in the meatballs do?" asked Aurin.

"Oregano? It's just for flavouring," said Luna, looking confused.

Aurin laughed. "I thought it was one of the ones you found here or bought earlier today."

"Nope," giggled Luna. "The herbs from the tower come from wherever the Minakai come from. They're good for healing wounds and status conditions, but they work best when made into a dish or a concoction."

"I see. To tell you the truth, I don't know all that much about how to heal a Minakai other than food and rest."

"It can get complicated, probably even more so than with humans, but food and rest will usually take care of most wounds. Minakai can heal a lot faster than we can."

Aurin took a chicken breast from his pack and threw it to Shamtile, who danced, then sat and ate it. Shamtile and Aurin both had big appetites, but Shamtile's magic left him with a considerably larger one than his human tamer.

"I'm surprised that we've had such an easy ride this run," said Aurin.

"Will you stop jinxing things?" asked Luna, looking

concerned.

"What do you mean?"

"If you keep saying that nothing bad has happened, then the tower will conspire to make something bad happen."

"Really?"

"Well, probably not, but it's making me paranoid anyway."

"As it should," came a cold, male voice from outside of the room.

Shamtile leapt to his feet and started waving his arms while screeching, half a chicken breast hanging from his mouth and protruding from underneath his mask.

"You should pick a better watchdog next time," said the voice. Its owner walked forward into the room. He stood much taller than Aurin.

"Zodiac," said Aurin.

"I'm glad our reputation precedes us," said the man smugly. This Zodiac member's uniform was different from the previous ones. He bore a similar, but more ornate white jacket. He didn't wear a hat, revealing his slicked blonde hair, and his mask was shaped like a lion's face, exposing only his mouth.

"Who are you and what do you want?" asked Aurin, standing up tall.

"You can call me Leo. If you know of us, surely you know what we want by now?"

"You can't have the egg."

"I'm afraid that I'm not merely requesting it," said the man. "You can hand over the egg and leave peacefully, or I can take it by force and you can be kicked from the tower. I would prefer the former, but the latter is of no consequence to me."

"Luna, stay back," said Aurin.

Luna and Innogon moved to the corner of the room while Aurin and Shamtile faced Leo.

"If that's the way it's going to be," sighed Leo.

The Zodiac member raised his fist and hurled an orb of cream light into the centre of the room. From the orb appeared a large cobalt-blue lion. Its dark mane was swept back and it was crouched, ready to pounce at a moment's notice. Aurin couldn't help but notice the large scar over its left eye.

"Leonite," said Leo, "do whatever you need to do."

The Leonite leapt at Shamtile before Aurin could say a word. Shamtile narrowly dodged and immediately waved his arms to conjure his rocks, but the Leonite swept around and slammed its hook-shaped tail into Shamtile, knocking him out cold. In a flash of brown light, Shamtile retreated to Aurin's glove.

"Hornber, attack!" called Aurin, casting a red light out from one of his summoning stones.

Hornber appeared and instantly charged at Leonite with his head lowered, aiming to impale the lion. Leonite reached out a paw and swatted Hornber out of the way as though he was a mere fly. It let out a low growl which could easily have been mistaken for a laugh.

Hornber continued to try and attack, but Leonite played with the small dinosaur. Aurin's frustration grew and he ordered his Minakai to use every attack it had, but they were all too weak for the powerful Leonite. Embers were lobbed, flames were spat, but every single one was ineffective.

"Finish him," ordered Leo.

Leonite drew its mouth open and clamped down on Hornber's back. The dinosaur yelled in pain and passed out. It glowed red momentarily before being drawn back into its summoning stone, banished from the tower and into stasis.

Aurin glanced around at Luna and watched as she used the Orb of Return to flee. Aurin heard Leo yell in anger at Luna's flight, a moment before Aurin was pulled from the tower now that he had lost both of his Minakai. Seconds later, he fell forward onto the grass at the base of the tower.

Chapter 5

"Aurin, are you okay?" asked a worried Luna as she reached for his hand.

"I'll be alright," said Aurin as Luna helped him off the ground. "You still have your egg?"

Luna nodded and pointed to her bag. Innogon was clinging to her legs looking nervously towards the looming Harmony Tower. There was nobody else in sight, but Aurin felt uneasy after the battle with Leo.

"We should get out of here in case he warps out too," he urged. "For all we know, there may even be other Zodiac members lurking nearby just waiting to jump us."

Aurin, Luna and Innogon rushed to Kyle's ranch, hoping that he was already treating Aurin's injured Minakai who were now freed from the interdimensional stasis. Aurin knew there were powerful tamers around, but Leo was something else. Having a single Leonite who was able to take out both of his Minakai with such ease was frightening. Hornber was understandable, he was early in his training, but even the more experienced Shamtile was defeated in mere seconds. It was a lesson to the young tamer that he had a lot of distance to cover before he was ready for any serious battling.

"Kyle!" called Luna as the tired trio arrived at the ranch.

"They're both fine," said Kyle with a concerned look. "What happened?"

"Zodiac," panted Aurin, trying to catch his breath. "Lion mask...called Leo...with a Leonite..."

"You were attacked by a Zodiac member called Leo who wore a lion mask and used a Leonite to defeat you?"

"Yes."

"Okay, I get it. Take a few moments to catch your breath and I'll take you to Shamtile and Hornber. They're eating, so they should be right as rain within the hour."

Aurin gave a nod of thanks to Kyle while Luna flopped onto the grass to rest. Aurin was getting tired of rude awakenings about how much of a novice he was. Every time he did something that he considered an achievement, he was knocked down.

After a few minutes, Kyle led Aurin and Luna into one of the fenced-off fields. Shamtile and Hornber were playfighting on the grass with scraps of food littering the ground beside them.

"You're both okay?" asked Aurin.

Shamtile leapt up and waved his arms excitedly, while Hornber was less enthusiastic about seeing Aurin.

"I'm sorry," said the tamer. "I got so excited about

pushing higher in the tower that we haven't been training properly. That ends now. We start training hard from tomorrow. We'll work to get tougher here at the ranch, and we'll ensure that we can handle whatever powerful foes we meet."

Aurin and Luna left the Minakai, including Innogon, in the enclosure to rest. They debated whether or not to bother reporting the latest Zodiac encounter to the police, but Luna convinced Aurin that they should.

The sun was starting to set by the time the pair reached the station and were able to get hold of Detective Knot.

"He called himself Leo, you say?" asked Knot, upon having the full story explained to him.

"Do you know of him?" asked Aurin.

Detective Scarlett nodded. "We know that there are a number of elite Zodiac members that are far more skilled tamers than the regular hoodlums. I hadn't heard of Leo before, but I presume he's one of these elite members. It's a good thing you ran."

"Sadly," began Knot, "we don't know how we can find him. Every piece of information you can give us would help, of course; tone of voice, height, weight, complexion, and so on. Please fill it in the report sheet that the receptionist will provide you with."

"I don't know why we bothered," sighed Aurin upon leaving the police station.

"What else can we do?" asked Luna with a shrug.

"Get stronger and take care of them ourselves," said the young man defiantly while clenching his fists.

"I don't mean to sound harsh, but he didn't break a sweat when he defeated you. We have a lot of work to do to be able to stand our ground."

"I know. I should have emphasised the part about getting stronger. We need to get *much* stronger. I meant what I said in the field to Shamtile and Hornber."

"Are you going to ask Kyle to train you?"

"I am. He's a much better tamer than I am, so I know there's a lot I can learn from him. What about you?"

"Fighting isn't really my strength," said Luna, looking despondent. "Honestly? It scares me a little."

Aurin shook his head. "If you want to keep coming into the tower, I don't think there's a choice."

"You're probably right. I suppose the first step to having a strong team is to hatch my egg and actually *have* a team."

"I forgot you had the egg," laughed Aurin, remembering now that Luna had warped from the tower using an Orb of Return. "It slipped my mind in all the chaos."

Aurin and Luna hurried back to the ranch, eager to find out what was in Luna's egg. The sky was an orange hue as the sun started to fall behind the hills in the distance.

"I figured you'd come back with the egg, Luna," said Kyle as the duo approached. "I have the incubator by the front door if you want to use it."

Luna ran to find Innogon while Aurin brought the incubator over to the gates of the fields. Shamtile decided to follow, but Hornber stayed behind.

"Here you go," said Aurin as he placed the incubator on the floor.

Luna set the egg on the incubator and pressed the button. The forcefield formed around the egg and it began to crack shortly after. A blue light shone brightly as the egg hatched and, once it cleared, the Minakai appeared. It was the shape of a water droplet but looked like it was made of translucent blue jelly. It had two round eyes and a small mouth.

"Is that a Dripper?" asked Aurin.

"It is!" exclaimed Luna. "That's another water elemental to match Innogon."

"You're a water Minakai tamer now?" joked Kyle.

Luna pondered this sincerely. "I wasn't planning to be, but I suppose I am for the time being."

A short while later, Aurin and Kyle escorted Luna, Innogon and Dripper home. Luna insisted she would be okay, but the Zodiac Squad was weighing heavily on both Aurin and Kyle's minds.

As Aurin and Kyle walked back to the ranch, Aurin contemplated how to bring up the idea of Kyle training him.

"So, Kyle..." Aurin began.

Kyle didn't look as he replied. "When somebody starts a sentence like that, I know they're going to ask for a favour."

"Funny you should say that because that's what I was going to do."

"If you want me to train you, just say it," said Kyle with a slight smirk.

Aurin knew Kyle was enjoying this. "Will you train me to be a better tamer? I want to be able to defend myself, guide my Minakai better and keep Luna safe in the tower."

"I'm a friendly guy, but I take training seriously. You're sure about this?"

"I'm certain."

"Alright. I have my ranch duties to tend to, so you help me out each morning. That should buy us an hour before lunch each day. Sound good?"

"Sounds great," beamed Aurin.

"Get up," ordered Kyle. "You have another lap to do."

Aurin, Shamtile and Hornber lay on the ground exhausted. Kyle had made them all run laps around the ranch to try and get them in better shape.

"If you're not a good example, how can your Minakai follow you?"

"Shamtile is already a lap ahead of me," panted Aurin.

"Yes, but you're in this together. Neither of you stops, even if one is exhausted."

"What about Hornber?" asked Aurin.

"He doesn't stop either."

The little dinosaur growled and stood up. Aurin and Shamtile followed suit and the trio began to run again. Kyle ran alongside them, completely unfazed by the exercise. The final lap wasn't going to break any records, but they all finished.

"Okay, time to battle," said Kyle.

"There's more?" asked a hunched-over Aurin while the two Minakai lay on the ground.

"It's been half an hour and we have another half to go. Last night you said this sounded good. Do you want to stand up to Zodiac or not?"

"You're right," admitted Aurin. "Where are your Minakai?"

"I don't need any. Shamtile and Hornber are fighting each other. You're going to watch them and study their movements and tactics. It'll help you see their strengths and weaknesses more objectively. Got it?"

"That's not fair to Hornber, the earth element is strong against the fire element. Shamtile has a big advantage."

"Does the tower care which element is fair? Do Zodiac members? Does any tamer, for that matter? Wouldn't it make sense to be able to face your weaknesses?"

Aurin said nothing, knowing Kyle was right once again. He stood at the edge of the clearing he once fought Kyle in while Shamtile and Hornber faced each other from opposite ends.

"Fight!" yelled Kyle.

Hornber charged towards Shamtile while the earth elemental waved his arms to conjure rocks. Hornber dodged the barrage of rocks that were hurled at him. As the red dinosaur charged, he suddenly started running in circles around Shamtile and breathing smoke.

Shamtile was unable to see a thing while Hornber lowered his head and confidently charged into the thick smoke to try and bulldoze his masked ally. Hornber emerged from the other side of the smoke, looking confused. Shamtile was nowhere to be seen.

The smoke cleared and Aurin could see a small hole in the ground where Shamtile had once stood. Hornber realised what was happening too late as Shamtile burst from the ground underneath the fiery dinosaur.

Hornber was tossed aside and rolled through the grass a few times before steadying himself. He breathed in deeply and ran for Shamtile again. As Shamtile leapt out of the way, Hornber turned his head to follow and unleashed a fireball he had conjured in his mouth. It struck Shamtile on the leg and he fell to the ground, wounded.

Aurin watched on as Hornber ran at full speed to Shamtile with his head lowered to impale Shamtile with his head spike. Shamtile was unable to move and braced himself to take the hit. As he came within a moment from impact, Hornber leapt over Shamtile and skidded to a halt. He then walked over to Shamtile and tapped him lightly with his head.

Aurin and Kyle started clapping for Hornber, impressed at his victory over the more experienced and advantaged Shamtile.

"Excellent!" called Kyle. "A very impressive display from both Minakai. What did you think, Aurin? Honest feedback?"

"Shamtile can sometimes be slow to react, but Hornber doesn't always try and account for the unexpected. Those are things we can work on."

"I agree. I noticed a few other things too, but we'll go over those tomorrow. Shamtile has a sore leg, so I'll do some arm work with him for the next few minutes while you and Hornber do three victory laps."

Aurin sighed as he and Hornber started running once more. As soon as it hit noon, Kyle called them back over.

"Have you heard about the tournament coming up?" asked Kyle.

Aurin remembered that Cedric from Taming Solutions had mentioned it. "All I've heard is there was a tournament, but I don't know more than that. What's the story there?"

"It's a tournament organised by the Bretonian Tournament League, so it's an officially ranked event. The top four get to qualify for the national championships in Ludonia."

"Is that how the tournament qualifiers work? I'd always wondered."

"Yes. There are regional tournaments, usually close to monster towers, and this will be the first time Hazelton has hosted a tournament. Are you interested in competing?"

"I am, for sure," said Aurin excitedly. He had always dreamed of being able to rise in the ranks of tamers, and even facing off against the national champion one day in the future; the far future.

Kyle scratched his chin. "At your current level, you may only make it past the first or second round, but we'll have you whipped into shape in no time. You'll need a third Minakai too, it's the minimum requirement to enter."

A third Minakai? That would mean another tower run or buying one from town. Aurin knew he had better dedicate himself fully to Kyle's training.

"I'm going to ask Luna to enter too," said Aurin.

"You think she will?" asked Kyle.

"I think she will," said Aurin sounding confident. "It's a good way for her to get more experience fighting other tamers, which we'll need with the Zodiac Squad running around Harmony Tower."

"Don't be surprised if they enter themselves. Under their civilian identities, of course."

"Why?"

"There's a rare Minakai egg as the prize for winning the tournament. I don't know which Minakai, but that's a standard prize at these sorts of tournaments."

Aurin's excitement only grew upon hearing Kyle's utterance of a rare egg. He tried to hide it, but Kyle could already see that Aurin believed the egg would be his. The rancher let out a small chuckle and headed back into the pens to sort out the next feed for the Minakai.

Chapter 6

Kyle's weeklong training boot camp was over and Aurin was back in the tower with Luna by his side. The pair were eagerly hunting for new eggs to expand their teams, but Aurin was sticking true to his promise to his Minakai and explored each floor thoroughly before using the elevator to ascend.

After a lot of pestering from Aurin, Luna had agreed to enter the upcoming tournament. She was reluctant, fearing that she would embarrass herself in front of a crowd of people, but Aurin insisted she would be too caught up to notice any spectators. Innogon was more enthusiastic than Luna about the prospect, but she was determined to give it her all despite her hesitancy.

"This means you can't do most of the battling in here, okay?" asked Luna rhetorically.

"If you want to handle a battle, just speak up. I won't stop you," answered Aurin. "We still need to find more eggs and shards."

Aurin and Luna both required Solar Shards to evolve their Minakai to new, more advanced forms. Solar Shards reacted to fire, air, water and earth elementals. Lunar Shards reacted to lightning, ice, nature and metal Minakai. Astral Shards, which Aurin had previously found one of, reacted to neutral elemental Minakai.

"Who do you want to evolve first?" asked Luna.

"Hornber," replied Aurin. "I think he would benefit more from evolving than Shamtile would. It's the less dramatic change of the two so my tactics won't have to change much. What about you?"

"Dripper. I don't think I could get used to Innogon growing five feet taller."

"I understand. I can't picture Shamtile as larger than he currently is. I'm sure it'll happen eventually, but it's not a priority. He's strong as he is now and we'll work together to get stronger in his current form."

Shamtile put his hands on his mask and started slapping it. Aurin wasn't sure what this meant but patted his friend on the head anyway.

"Elevator!" said Luna, pointing down the corridor ahead.

The duo and their Minakai were currently on the fifth floor. This elevator would bring them to the highest floor that either of them had been to. It was an exciting prospect, but there was more to explore here first.

Aurin made a mental note of where the elevator was and walked down a side passage. The group walked through many rooms, collecting silver coins and miscellaneous items they could sell in town. There was nothing particularly notable until Luna called out.

"Egg!"

"Mine!" yelled the voice of a young woman as she darted past the group.

Aurin didn't even have time to take in what she looked like before sprinting at full speed towards the room where the egg could be seen. The young man quickly caught up with his opponent and they both grabbed hold of the egg.

"We found it first!" shouted Aurin, trying to wrestle the egg away from the young woman. He could see now that she had sharp features and long black hair that was dyed blonde near the ends.

"I touched it first!" she protested.

Luna caught up and whistled at the pair. "The only fair way to settle this is a Minakai battle. I'll keep an eye on the egg until the battle is over."

"How do I know this isn't some trick to distract me?" asked the young woman, her eyes narrowing in suspicion.

"She's not like that," insisted Aurin. "I'll loosen my grip on the count of three, then you pass it to her. Okay?"

"Fine," muttered the woman.

"One. Two. Three," counted Aurin, releasing his grip. The young woman passed the egg over to Luna, then stood at the far end of the room while Aurin walked to the opposite side to face her.

"I'm Aurin," called the young man.

"I'm Ilena," said the woman. She was presumably a few years older than Aurin and Luna were.

"I only have two Minakai, so it's only fair that this is a two-on-two battle. Are you okay with that?"

"I suppose I'll have to be," nodded Ilena. "Are you ready?"

"Let's fight!" called Aurin as thrust his hand forward, summoning forth Hornber.

"Take it out, Rabbacat," ordered Ilena as she threw an orb of cream light from her own glove.

Hornber stood facing a docile-looking Minakai. It was shaped like a rabbit, but more rotund. It was a creamy brown colour with a big smile on its innocent face, revealing its two buckteeth. It started bouncing in place while waiting for Hornber to make a move.

The young dinosaur stood in wait, sensing that his opponent was a lot faster than he was. Acting rashly would give the Rabbacat the edge. Aurin said nothing, knowing what Hornber was thinking.

"Enough waiting!" yelled Ilena.

Rabbacat bounced rapidly forward on all fours, then curled into a ball, throwing its entire weight at Hornber.

"Lower your head," ordered Aurin.

Hornber lowered his head, his horn ready to take the hit. Ilena looked shocked as Rabbacat landed directly on the bone spike which pierced a large hole in its side. Hornber rolled backwards, unsteadied by the attack, and Rabbacat fell to the floor unconscious. Seconds later, it was recalled through the summoning stone in Ilena's glove.

"Good job," praised Aurin as Luna and Innogon danced a goofy cheer.

"A lucky start," scoffed Ilena as she threw a red light into the centre of the room.

The Minakai that appeared looked similar to a Heatpup but larger and more aggressive. Aurin recognised it as a Dogember, Heatpup's evolved form. Its eyes narrowed upon locking onto its target.

The Dogember charged forward and began running circles around Hornber. Aurin assessed that Ilena's strategy was to use speed to overwhelm her opponents. He wouldn't let it be that easy for her.

Hornber charged up a fireball in its mouth, waiting for Dogember to make a move closer. The fiery dog leapt through the air and whipped its flaming tail at the dinosaur, who unleashed his fireball at it. Dogember twirled in the air and deflected the fireball, slamming Hornber across the back with its tail.

Aurin's Minakai climbed to its feet uneasily and roared as he engulfed his horn in fire. He was angry and Aurin knew he would get sloppy if he let the urge to strike overtake his wisdom.

"Careful, Hornber," warned Aurin. "Don't act rashly. Wait for an opening."

Hornber gave a small roar of acceptance and remained in place. Dogember meanwhile began to run in circles around Hornber once more. This time, it ran so fast that it was hard to keep track of and it began to look like a swirling orange ring.

Dogember leapt, seemingly from three places at once, using its speed to create an illusion. Hornber wasn't sure which image to attack and hesitated, giving the real Dogember the chance to strike him in the side. The young dinosaur fell down, turning into a red ball of light almost immediately and passed through Aurin's summoning stone, banished from the tower.

"Shamtile!" called Aurin while Ilena smirked.

Shamtile ran forward, waving his arms. Dogember began to repeat its trick of running in circles around its target.

"Conjure a stalagmite," ordered Aurin.

Shamtile waved his hands and pointed at a spot on the ground where Dogember was running. A large stalagmite burst forth from the tiles and Dogember slammed face-first into it; its own speed used against it.

Aurin, Luna and Innogon cheered as Shamtile squatted and beat his legs, one of his favourite victory dances.

"Chull!" called Ilena as Dogember returned to her glove. A yellow light appeared in the air and a small black bird wearing a mask of bone flapped in place. Visible on its feathery chest was a small white skull.

"What are you doing?" yelled Aurin.

Ilena merely smirked as her Chull took aim at Shamtile and flapped a powerful gust of air at the masked lizard. Shamtile, not quite realising what was happening fell backwards. The Chull burst forward, trying to charge into the unaware Shamtile, currently prone on the ground.

"Roll left!" ordered Aurin, acting as Shamtile's eyes.

The earth elemental rolled out of the way of the attack, Chull ascending out of its dive and turning around to attack again. Shamtile bent his knees, ready to take the hit.

As Chull approached, Shamtile encased his forearms in thick stone. Ilena, not learning from her previous mistake, did not stop Chull in time as the undead bird collided with the rock. It fell to the ground, barely able to push the braced and grounded Shamtile back, and was recalled.

"This isn't over, Aurin," said Ilena, as she gave a small wave before being ejected from the tower in a burst of light.

"I don't like her," said Luna, walking over to Aurin.

Aurin nodded. "She plays dirty. She wanted me out of the tower so she could take the egg from you directly."

"Innogon, Dripper and I would have dealt with her," said Luna cheerfully, as Innogon nodded in agreement.

"I know you would," smiled Aurin. "Who gets the egg this time?"

"You won the battle, Sir Aurin, so I bequeath it unto you," said Luna with a fake royal accent, as she passed the egg to Aurin.

"Thanks, Luna," said Aurin, stashing it in his bag.

"We're now down one team member, so I'll feel safer if Dripper is here too," said Luna, calling forth Dripper in a flash of blue light.

The blue, jelly-like droplet wobbled in place, looking surprised, before smiling widely. Aurin honestly thought she was a creepy little thing, reminding him of both an alien and an ooze from tabletop games he played when he was younger.

"Let's keep moving," he said, leading the group back to where they had previously found the elevator.

Aurin and Luna placed their hands on the blue orb within the pedestal and they were all transported to the sixth floor for the first time.

The tiles on the sixth floor were still in a chessboard pattern, but rotated forty-five degrees, looking more like diamonds than squares from Aurin's perspective. The bottom half of the wall now featured intricate wooden panelling with smooth red stone on the top half.

"Another new record," said Luna cheerily.

Aurin didn't want to get overly excited, recalling what happened with Leo the last time they reached a new floor. Not wanting to be too negative and spoil the otherwise pleasant mood, he guided everybody down a corridor to the left.

Dripper started bouncing wildly, seemingly very excited.

"What is it?" asked Luna.

Dripper bounced back and forth for a second, staring at her, before bouncing down the corridor at a surprisingly fast pace. Aurin and Luna followed her into a room up ahead and immediately noticed what Dripper had seen.

"A Solar Shard!" exclaimed Aurin.

"Good spot, Dripper!" applauded Luna.

"I'm surprised such a little thing like her has such good eyesight. I think Shamtile's eyesight isn't helped by his mask."

Shamtile started rubbing his mask with affection.

"What does Shamtile look like without the mask?" asked Luna.

"I don't know. I've never seen a picture of one maskless, even in a book. Shamtile doesn't mind me putting my hand on his mask, but I think if I tried to take it off, he would tear my hand to shreds."

"Come to think of it," began Luna, "when he eats, he seems to just shove the food underneath the mask rather than lift the mask up to uncover his mouth."

Shamtile began growling and held his mask tightly, worried that one of the two humans would get too curious and try to see what his face looked like. Shamtile as a species are born wearing masks and would fight to the death to keep their faces hidden.

"I have the egg, so I think you should get the shard," said Aurin.

"Not this one," said Luna. "You have a lot more experience with Hornber than I do with Dripper, so I don't want to evolve her too fast. I'll take the next egg and next shard if that's okay with you?"

"Thanks," smiled Aurin, happy with that deal.

Aurin walked forward to pick up the Solar Shard, but before he could reach it, he heard a click. He didn't even have time to register what had happened when, suddenly, two dozen Minakai appeared on the floor in a flash of light.

"A monster den trap!" yelled Aurin, realising he had just walked into one of the most notorious run-ending traps in the tower.

"What do we do?" asked Luna, as the Minakai all began to stir.

"We'll have to fight our way out," said Aurin as Shamtile began to wave his arms.

Chapter 7

Shamtile conjured his rocks, Innogon shot a jet of water and Dripper spat a barrage of high-speed bubbles. All three aimed in different directions, hoping to knock out the encroaching wild Minakai before they could attack Aurin and Luna. The pair of humans knew they were in danger and their Minakai were the only thing keeping them from harm.

"Let's use the Orb of Return," urged Luna, looking scared.

"Not yet, our Minakai can handle this," said Aurin, sounding more certain than he was. "You summoned Dripper for a reason, now she has a chance to prove herself."

Luna gripped Aurin's arm tightly, hiding behind him as the wild Minakai began attacking their three defenders.

Shamtile encased his arms in stone and blocked a charging Happynut. He began to beat down on the Happynut's head until it stopped moving and disappeared from the tower. Innogon was relentless in firing his water jet into a Pottemp. Each time the armless stone dinosaur tried to climb back up, Innogon knocked it down. Dripper's bubbles, rapid as they were, were no match for the swiftness of the Sproufloat—a monster resembling a large pea with a leaf atop its head, two leafy wings and bird-like talons—that was aiming for the tiny jelly.

"Sproufloat looks like a nature elemental, but it's an air elemental," warned Aurin, knowing air elementals were strong against water elementals.

"Be careful!" cried Luna.

Dripper slid out of the way of the charging Sproufloat, her slippery body giving her great speed of her own when on land. Dripper turned and fired a stream of bubbles while Sproufloat's back was turned. The air elemental was knocked to the ground, just in time for Shamtile to start pelting it with rocks.

The brawl continued with Aurin guarding Luna in the corner of the room while the Minakai continued to fight. Shamtile was throwing wild rocky punches, Innogon blasted water and Dripper slipped and slid across the room. With all of his might, Shamtile even conjured a large boulder and sent it rolling through a couple of Minakai, pinning them against the far wall.

"Now's our chance," said Aurin as he grabbed Luna's hand.

There was a small clearing in the chaos so Aurin dashed for the door dragging Luna behind him. Their Minakai covered their exit and then followed. The wild

Minakai gave chase as the group hurriedly searched for the elevator. More wild Minakai joined the stampede as the group hastily made their way through the floor, not even stopping for coins or items as they passed through the rooms.

"There!" called Luna, pulling Aurin down another corridor.

There it was. The elevator. Aurin and Luna ran as fast as their legs could carry them, throwing out their hands and then placing them on the blue sphere, which swiftly dragged them up to the next floor. The duo collapsed on the ground, panting, as they and their Minakai rematerialized in orbs of light.

"I think that's our closest call yet," said Aurin once he had his breath back.

"Why didn't we just use the orb?" laughed Luna.

"The Minakai kept us safe, didn't they?"

"That's true," said Luna as she looked at her Innogon and Dripper proudly.

Shamtile walked over to Aurin and he patted his lizard on the back, careful to avoid the spikes atop his head as he flailed around excitedly. It would not be the first time Aurin had accidentally pricked himself on his friend's sharp protrusions.

Luna started surveying the three exits from the room they landed in. She was deeply contemplating which way to go and finally settled on heading what she perceived to be north. As soon as she started to step down the corridor, she was interrupted.

"Okay, it's time to use the orb and get out of here," said Aurin.

"Are you serious?" asked Luna.

"Yes," said Aurin with a smile. "There's no point in me losing my egg and Solar Shard. It's good training if we keep going, sure, but we may as well enjoy the spoils of this tower run."

"I didn't even notice you picking that shard up. When did that happen?"

"You were too busy staring at the fight. I grabbed it near the start in case we had to quickly flee. A good idea if I say so myself."

Aurin laughed as Luna sighed. The young man withdrew his Orb of Return and focused on it. The duo and their Minakai disappeared in a burst of light, this time warping outside of the tower rather than a floor higher.

"A monster den trap, eh?" said Kyle. "Good job getting away from the horde. I've had my fair share of bad experiences with those. I'm about fifty-fifty on being able to successfully escape them."

Aurin and Luna had just finished telling Kyle their thrilling tale back at the ranch.

"Do you want to hatch the egg now?" asked Luna, sensing Aurin's excitement.

"I do," said Aurin with glee. He rushed into Kyle's house to grab the incubator and was back at lightning speed.

The young man placed his new egg into the incubator and pressed the button. The force field appeared and shortly after a large steely-grey light, bigger than that from any previous egg Aurin had seen, burst from within the shell.

The creature that emerged was his largest Minakai to date. It was shaped like a dolphin and was about as long as Aurin was tall. Dolphin-like as it was, you would not have wanted to see one of these coming towards you in the ocean. It was made of blue metal and had glowing top and tail fins along with rounded aquamarine eyes. It hovered about a foot off the ground, moving very little.

"Is that a Dolissile?" asked Aurin.

"It is," replied Kyle looking mildly impressed. "It's a rarer find, particularly on a lower floor. Metal elemental Minakai aren't very common in these parts. Train this one well and he'll be very useful to you."

"He's so beautiful," said Luna in awe.

"He looks like a deadly torpedo," said Aurin with a giant grin.

"That kind of takes the majesty out of it," sighed Luna.

Dolissile, unlike the more rambunctious Shamtile and stubborn Hornber, wasn't quick to show any real emotion. It swayed robotically as it hovered and tended to simply stare at whoever was speaking at the time. It made sense to Aurin, considering it was largely cybernetic, but Dolissile was an unsettling creature.

Aurin asked everybody to wait while he fetched Hornber. The small dinosaur looked to have recovered well after his tough tower battle. Aurin took out the Solar Shard from his pack and held it out to Hornber.

"Hornber," Aurin began, "we're trying to get stronger to conquer the tower and the tournament, right? I think this may help us. You know what it is, don't you?"

Hornber exhaled and grunted in agreement, appearing to almost nod. Never one to show much enthusiasm, Aurin was pleased to see that Hornber was receptive to the idea of evolution.

"Okay, let's use it now."

The young tamer placed the Solar Shard on Hornber's rough skin and the small dinosaur concentrated, activating the shard. The shard turned into a glowing golden light and entered Hornber, who glowed his usual red colour when touched by the magic.

Before Aurin's eyes, Hornber started to grow. His tail elongated and a new spike erupted from his head. The little dinosaur's legs grew and his body lengthened, becoming more muscular. The glow began to subside and Hornber was visible once more, but he was no longer Hornber.

"How do you feel, Hornferno?" asked Aurin, calling his Minakai by his new name.

The newly evolved Hornferno gave a proud roar and playfully head-butted Aurin's leg, albeit harder than he normally would have. Hornber had evolved, but he was still the same old Minakai inside. It was strange to Aurin, seeing this new form while trying to imprint in his mind that it was his Hornber. The tamer led Hornferno back to Luna, Kyle and the rest of the Minakai, who all stood at the edge of the pens. They turned to see Aurin walking with his now-waist-high Minakai.

"You evolved him?" asked Kyle in surprise.

"I wanted to see!" exclaimed Luna. "I didn't get the chance to say goodbye."

"He's still the same," laughed Aurin. "He just looks cooler now, right Hornferno?"

Hornferno snarled while Shamtile waved his arms in celebration of his friend's newfound strength increase. The masked reptile started pointing to his own spikes, then to Hornferno's spikes, then back to his own.

Aurin smiled. "I want to introduce you to the newest member of Team Aurin. Hornferno, this is Dolissile."

Dolissile simply stared at Hornferno, while Hornferno pushed his head against the metal dolphin, unsure of how to react. Dolissile suddenly whipped its tailfin at Hornferno, not wanting to be touched. The dinosaur roared in anger at this overreaction.

"Settle down, you two," ordered Aurin. "You're going to have to work together if we want to stand a chance at the tournament or in the tower. Got it?"

Hornferno scoffed while Dolissile let out a warbling screech. Aurin was pleased to see he wasn't entirely silent but knew he had a lot of work to do to ensure that the pair were on friendlier terms. Shamtile was intelligent enough to stay out of it and simply stood over near Kyle, bouncing up and down.

"It's not unusual for Minakai to bicker, they're all so different," said Kyle. "Just keep training and adventuring with both of them and they'll get over it."

"I'm glad we don't have that problem," said Luna, nudging Innogon with her knee.

The small blue dragon stared up at her with a big grin.

"We'll see about that," joked Aurin. "Who knows what'll happen when you evolve your Minakai? Maybe Innogon becoming a Guilgon will make him a grump?"

"Don't say that!" lamented Luna.

Aurin, Luna and Kyle sat down inside Kyle's house to eat a meal of steak and potatoes. Most of Kyle's dishes consisted of some form of these foods, but Aurin wasn't complaining. A hearty meal like this was the fuel he needed for his training regime.

"What's the plan for the rest of the tournament preparations?" asked Kyle. "There isn't much time left, you know."

"Eggs, shards and tower runs," said Aurin as he tore off a mouthful of steak.

"That's your big plan?" asked Kyle incredulously.

"What's wrong with it?" asked a puzzled Luna.

"There's more to training than getting more Minakai and fighting in the tower," said Kyle. "Don't get me wrong, those things are all important and useful, but...do you want my advice?"

"Of course," said Aurin.

"You need to get used to fighting more in environments outside of the tower. Ideally with an audience. It'll help with your confidence and the pressure of the spectators may throw you off your game, so you want that to become familiar to you. You'll make fewer mistakes in the long run doing that, trust me on this."

"I trust you on pretty much all matters, Kyle," chuckled Aurin.

"I know you do, but I want you to be able to think outside the box a bit more without my help," said Kyle. "If you go to another tower or leave Hazelton at all, I won't be able to help you much."

Aurin pondered this. "Well, that's true. I suppose I do need to be a bit more creative and not just in combat."

"Are you sure you won't enter the tournament,

Kyle?" asked Luna.

Kyle shook his head. "I'm busy enough here as it is and I'm out of practice. Besides, I make more money as a rancher than I do in the tower."

"How?" asked Aurin, realising the answer before Kyle had a chance to speak.

"Your Minakai stay here for free, but everybody else pays rent and care. I should start charging you, come to think of it. You're doing well enough in the tower to pay the bills."

Aurin wished he hadn't said anything, but Kyle started laughing.

"You know what, I think I should be paying," said Aurin. "You've been so helpful to me and I don't think the work I do here comes close to covering what I owe you."

"You don't owe me anything," said Kyle earnestly. "I consider you more of an apprentice than a freeloader so don't worry about it. When you win a national championship, just be sure to throw in an advertisement for the ranch into your victory speech."

Aurin, Luna and Kyle continued joking through the evening. Aurin had taken Kyle's words about battling outside of the tower to heart and he vowed to himself to do just that.

Chapter 8

Aurin and Luna walked through the Hazelton town square, fresh from their latest tower run. They had only climbed as high as the fifth floor, but that left them with plenty of time left in the day. Luna, in particular, wanted to spend some of the silver coins she had been saving up.

"Do you know what egg you want to get yet?" asked Aurin.

"No," admitted Luna. "I've decided to ask Cedric for his advice?"

"What about my advice?"

"You know that I always take your advice in the tower and for battling, but Cedric is an expert with years of experience. Don't take it personally."

"I know, I was just kidding," said Aurin.

The duo, along with Shamtile and Innogon, walked inside Taming Solutions, owned by Cedric. Aurin and Luna greeted him and Aurin immediately started to peruse the shelves to see if there were any new useful trinkets and items that he could get his hands on.

"Be careful, lad," warned Cedric. "I know the condition of each and every one of those. Don't drop anything."

Aurin scoffed and continued browsing.

"What can I do for you today, little Luna?" asked Cedric.

Luna hemmed and hawed, not quite sure how to ask. "I want a Minakai egg."

"An egg, you say? Have you anything in mind?"

"I was hoping that you would advise me?"

"Well, let's start with what I have in stock," said Cedric, opening up his log and surveying it. He ran his finger down the page and started to rattle through names. "Driftseed, Cryopillar, Peekan, Shamtile, Litehorn, Piggun, Feathrus, Spaqua, Plas—"

"What was that last one?" asked Luna.

"Spaqua? Yes, that's an interesting one. It's an ice elemental that can evolve twice. It doesn't start off the strongest, but if you train it and evolve it all the way into a Frocean then you would be hard-pressed to find a more useful ice Minakai."

"I'll take it," said Luna. "How much?"

"Two hundred ounces of silver normally, but one hundred and seventy-five for you," winked Cedric.

Luna handed over her heavy pouch of coins while Cedric opened up a display cabinet and removed the egg. He passed it carefully to Luna, who stared at it in awe. Aurin crept up and rubbed the egg, hoping to feel if it was cold like the ice Minakai it contained. Eggs always looked the same to him and he wanted to know how experts could tell the difference between species.

"Be careful with it," said Luna, swatting Aurin's hand away.

"Sorry," said Aurin, rubbing where Luna had slapped.

Aurin, Luna and their two Minakai said farewell to Cedric and began walking back to the town square.

"Does Dolissile evolve?" asked Luna.

"I don't think so," said Aurin. "I've never heard of an evolution for it at least."

"Cedric said that Spaqua can evolve twice."

"Does it have a branching evolutionary path?"

"I'm not sure. He said something about evolving into Frocean."

"Yes, it's a giant icy frog. I can't think of a better way to describe it, to be honest."

"What's going on up ahead?" asked Luna, pointing to the town square.

A large group of people had gathered around and were watching a Minakai battle. Aurin spotted a young man, around his own age, standing in the crowd. Aurin hurried over to stand beside him and nudged him in the arm.

"Hey there, Aurin," said Gardner, cheerfully. "Long time, no see."

"Hello, Gardner," said Luna, catching up.

"Luna!" exclaimed Gardner. "You're both keeping well?"

"Very well," said Aurin. "What's going on here?"

"People are having practice battles ahead of the tournament. Are you competing?"

"We both are," said Aurin.

"You should jump in there," urged Gardner. I've

already had a battle and I don't want to steal all the glory."

"Did you win your battle?" asked Luna.

"Well, no," answered Gardner awkwardly, rubbing his neck.

Aurin heard a loud crash and watched as a Volcarrow threw a Tormech to the ground. The large fiery bird had dive-bombed with the small tortoise in its talons and released the unwitting metal elemental reptile at full speed.

"Poor little thing," gasped Luna.

The crowd cheered for the victor, a tall man with wavy hair that was as black as night. He bore a couple of burn marks on his face and Aurin presumed they were caused by his own Minakai.

"Who's next to face me?" called the man.

The crowd looked apprehensively around, seeing if anybody would step forward.

"I'll do it," said Aurin, raising his hand.

"Somebody with an ounce of courage," said the man. "I hope you're no amateur."

Aurin walked through the crowd, who parted for him as he moved, into the large open space they were surrounding. The man stood at one end and Aurin stood at the other.

"My name is Devon," said the man. "You?"

"Aurin."

Devon's Volcarrow was flapping in the air in front of him. Its fiery body would illuminate any darkness with only its beak and talons visible through the flames. Aurin ordered Shamtile into the arena.

"Ready?" asked Devon.

"Let's go," said Aurin.

Volcarrow immediately flew into the air, keeping

well out of the melee range of Shamtile. It began to flap its wings hard, sending waves of fire at the lizard. Shamtile waved his arms and conjured rocks, hurling them at the flames to block the attack.

"Shamtile, stay on the defensive," ordered Aurin, hoping to find out what Volcarrow was capable of.

Devon's Volcarrow began to spin in the air, turning into a small fiery tornado. It charged at Shamtile, who scurried out of the way and narrowly avoided what would have been a knockout blow.

Shamtile tossed a rock at the Volcarrow as it steadied itself in the air, but it swerved just in time to dodge the attack. The Volcarrow was not impressed and it soared up into the air once more, keeping out of range to recover.

The flaming bird rose high and, once it had gathered itself, dove at Shamtile, who stomped a foot on the ground causing a stalagmite to burst up in front of him. The Volcarrow crashed straight into it and fell to the cobblestones limp.

The onlookers stood with their mouths ajar, Devon included. Shamtile's stalagmite retracted back into the ground as Shamtile used his magic to repair the cobblestones. Aurin cheered enthusiastically for his victorious Minakai, hearing Luna and Gardner doing the same somewhere nearby.

Devon started clapping and then let out a small laugh. "You caught me off guard, well done. I was overconfident."

"Your Volcarrow is impressive," said Aurin, approaching to shake Devon's hand. "That fiery spin would have taken us out if it had landed."

Devon shook Aurin's hand. "Thank you. Whoever faces you next should watch out. I hope to see you at the tournament."

"Who's next?" Aurin called to the crowd.

"I am," called a calm, deep voice.

A tall man with long brown hair approached. He was wearing a crimson hat and a pinstripe suit to match. Aurin thought the man would have fit in more at a business meeting than a Minakai battle.

"What's your name?" asked Aurin.

"Hunter," stated the man bluntly, but he did not look unfriendly. "I propose a three-round match. Let's push ourselves a little. What do you say?"

"Three rounds, three Minakai each," said Aurin.

"Alright," said Hunter as he raised his tamer glove.

Aurin raised his own glove and sent forth his Dolissile in a flash of light. One of Hunter's summoning stones glowed green and a large wolf emerged in the town square. It was a deep green with pink flower petals encircling its neck. Aurin recognised it as a Vinewolf, a fully evolved Petalcub.

"Strike fast," ordered Hunter.

"Charge!" yelled Aurin.

The Vinewolf's petals extended from its neck on vines at the charging Dolissile. Vinewolf hunkered down then whipped the vines downward, the petals striking Dolissile. The petals were as sharp as razor blades and Dolissile fell to the ground from that single attack.

Aurin stood there for a moment, stunned. He wasn't sure what had happened. The round was over before he could even make a move.

"Your next Minakai," said Hunter as he retracted his Vinewolf into the summoning stone, banishing it to wherever it was attuned.

Aurin cast his hand forward and summoned

Hornferno. Hunter conjured forth his next Minakai, a large silver snake with a spiked helmet of ice.

"Anacondice, encircle," commanded Hunter.

The snake slithered swiftly towards Hornferno, who darted out of the way. Anacondice began to move in wide circles, leaving a trail of ice on the ground below. Hornferno leapt over the ice, but as soon as he was above the ice it exploded. Shards burst upwards and knocked Hornferno to the ground, leaving Aurin standing there open-mouthed.

"I've won two of the three rounds," said Hunter as cool as ice. "I will not hold it against you if you bow out now."

"Shamtile, get in there," ordered Aurin as he withdrew Hornferno.

"Suit yourself," said Hunter as he banished Anacondice and sent forth an orb of red light.

The light dissipated and an orange behemoth of smooth metal appeared before Shamtile. It had a glowing blue eye inside its head and its body was shaped like a furnace. From the back of its head flickered a large flame, while from its behind, in place of a tail, was a much larger flame that streamed fiercely. Aurin had never seen this Minakai before.

"Flambot, take it easy on this one," said Hunter.

"No," demanded Aurin. "I don't want any sympathy points."

"If you insist," sighed Hunter.

Shamtile looked at Aurin and waved his arms in panic, not wanting to be burned to cinders. The Flambot clenched its fingers into fists and squatted down to brace itself. The grill on its stomach began to rattle. It started subtly, but seconds later it began shaking vigorously. Flambot thrust its stomach out and the grill burst open, unleashing a torrent of flame.

The fire flew like a horizontal pillar, streaming relentlessly across the battlefield. Shamtile was too stunned to move and let out a loud screech as he took the full intensity of the fire. He was knocked to the ground, his body and mask now blackened. As the reptile tried to sit back up, he flopped back down, unable to move.

"Shamtile!" cried Aurin, realising how foolishly prideful he had been. He raised his glove and immediately sent his companion back to the ranch through his summoning stone.

The crowd were shocked and tepidly applauded Hunter's victory as he approached Aurin; the tall suited man was still calm and collected.

"A few words of advice, Aurin," he began. "Know your limits. You were clearly outmatched and you continued the fight anyway. I watched your last battle and, while you and your Minakai are talented, you're still an amateur. I am not the strongest tamer competing in the tournament, so if you want to get anywhere close to the final then you'll likely be facing tougher opponents than me."

Aurin clenched his fists. "How do I get stronger?"

"Train hard, train always and put yourself in tough situations. You'll see what you're really made of and your Minakai will grow accordingly. I'm sorry this was a hard lesson for you, but I believe you'll come to appreciate it in time. Farewell."

Hunter patted Aurin on the shoulder once and departed. Aurin stood quietly in the square, humiliated, as the crowd continued to stare on in silence.

"Next match!" called Gardner, hoping to distract the crowd.

Aurin walked back into the crowd as the next pair of tamers took their positions.

"Are you alright?" asked Luna.

Aurin nodded. "I would expect myself to say no, but I think this is my tenth wake-up call since I arrived in Hazelton and I'm growing numb to them. I'm nowhere near the peak of this town, never mind ready for a national championship. My Minakai can rest today, but then it's back to the tower. How about you? Are you okay?"

"Me?" asked Luna.

"Yes. That guy is the calibre or tamer we'll face at the top end of the tournament."

"I didn't think about that," said Luna worriedly. "If you can't defeat a single one of his Minakai, how am I going to stand a chance?"

"Let's just hope we get lucky enough to draw an easy opponent first," said Gardner, scratching his chin.

"Wouldn't relying on luck make it something of a hollow victory?" asked Aurin.

"I suppose that's true," said Gardner. "At least we still have six weeks to train. I think a few evolutions are in order."

"How many Minakai do you have now, Gardner?" asked Luna.

"Four, but I would like to have a few more. Most of my Minakai are of the plant class or the nature element, so my coverage isn't great right now. Maybe I'll be okay if I have to fight metal elementals."

"Hmm, four is good. It means you don't have to use the exact same team every battle. That's my fear. That I'll be too predictable."

Aurin listened silently to the rest of the conversation between Luna and Gardner. They didn't seem half as concerned as he was. Perhaps it was Aurin's latest ego bruising, or perhaps it was his drive to be the best. Whatever it was, he knew there was still a lot of work to be done.

Chapter 9

Aurin and Luna had been in the tower for five hours and had reached their newest record of the ninth floor. Aurin was determined to push higher and higher, facing whatever tamers and wild Minakai the tower threw at him. It didn't hurt that he was earning plenty of silver on the way up.

This run, Aurin had defeated three tamers; in each match, he and his competitors had used a single Minakai, and Luna had defeated one tamer. All three of Aurin's Minakai had won a match with Dolissile winning his first. Shamtile clobbered a Techling, Hornferno scorched a Sproufloat and Dolissile torpedoed a Funglie. Innogon's resounding victory was against a tamer's Peekan, that he shot out of the air with an intense water jet.

All in all, it had been one of their most successful runs to date, however, despite collecting a few useful odds and ends, there were no eggs or shards to be seen today. It wasn't uncommon to get this far and not see one, as the magic of the tower loved to randomise and those items were among the rarest. It was no wonder that Cedric could charge such a high price for eggs.

Aurin had given a lot of thought to the events of the previous week. He was still embarrassed about how badly Hunter had defeated him, but he took Hunter's advice on board and had been training every morning. Luna had occasional classes to attend so he had even entered the tower twice by himself, reaching the sixth and seventh floor on each respective run. It was definitely tougher solo, particularly on his Minakai, but he was pleased to discover that he was capable of making it that far by himself.

"The elevator!" called Luna excitedly.

"You know what this means?" smirked Aurin.

"Double-digit floors?"

"Double-digit floors! We're finally there."

"Just a few more steps to go, Aurin," squealed Luna excitedly. "I wonder if the room will look much different?"

Aurin and Luna had often talked about reaching the tenth-floor milestone. Granted, the tower got progressively more difficult as they ascended, but it helped with their confidence to keep pushing forward. Kyle was adamant that the difficulty ramped up considerably on the double-digit floors, with a lot more already-evolved Minakai showing their faces.

If what Kyle said about the second half of the tower was true, floor twenty-five and higher had Minakai that a lot of people back home would never even have heard of. Minakai were a worldwide phenomenon, it was true, but not everybody's lives revolved around them in the same way most tamer's lives do.

Aurin and Luna led Shamtile and Innogon to the elevator. The two humans placed their hands on the familiar pedestalled blue stone and willed themselves to the next floor. Aurin had come to enjoy the initially stomach-churning whoosh of travelling between floors. It was a feeling he now associated with success.

"This is an unusually large room," said Aurin, admiring the white and blue tiles with silvery walls.

"All the better for an ambush, wouldn't you say?" called a voice from the corner.

Aurin and Luna jolted around to see a pair of Zodiac Squad members, both masked up, hurling orbs of light at them. One member cast a silvery light and a cream light, while the other cast two purple lights.

Shamtile and Innogon hurried forward while Aurin and Luna summoned Dolissile and Dripper, respectively, for backup. Shamtile headed for the Techwing—a robotic silver bird with a golden tail and crest that evolved from Techling—while Dolissile confronted a Peekan. Innogon charged at a Litehorn—a dark purple unicorn with glowing blue eyes—while Dripper hopped towards a Tuptup—a small blue beast with jagged teeth and a yellow, electrically charged tail.

The Zodiac members barked orders at their Minakai, hoping their ambush and rapid attack would give them an edge.

Aurin gave his own orders to his Minakai. "Shamtile, it's a metal elemental so you have no advantage. It's fast so make use of your defensive abilities. Dolissile, you outmatch Peekan in both speed and strength. Overwhelm it."

Shamtile encased its forearms in stone, forming a shield on one arm and a spear on the other. As the large metal bird charged forward, Shamtile tried to ward it off with the spear while keeping his guard up with his shield. Dolissile's fins glowed bright and the metal dolphin charged forth, homing in on the small bird. The Peekan panicked and flew back and forth speedily, looking to avoid Dolissile.

Meanwhile, Innogon was blasting water at the dark unicorn. Litehorn's eyes glowed blue and its horn shot electrical blasts towards the drake. The two were evenly matched, each blocking the other's attacks. Dripper on the other hand was being chased around the room by the small blue monster. The Tuptup whipped its pointed tail at Dripper and slapped the little jelly into the walls.

As the fight raged on, Shamtile was able to knock the Techwing to the ground. He dispelled his spear and shield, then sent a barrage of heavy rocks from the roof. The Techwing was brutally beaten by the falling rocks and it was ejected from the tower.

Dolissile's poor mid-air steering was made up for by his persistence and he too defeated his opponent. All it took was one well-placed strike and the Peekan vanished in a ball of white light. With both of his Minakai ejected, the Zodiac member yelled in anger before being booted from the tower himself.

"Litehorn, you'd better not let me down!" growled the other Zodiac member. "That goes for you too, Tuptup."

"Luna, do you need help?" asked Aurin.

"No, but wait on standby just in case," said Luna, determined to see the fight through by herself.

Litehorn's speed was giving it an edge against

Innogon and it slowly closed the distance gap as the two continued to throw lightning and water at each other. Luna ordered Innogon to change tactics and the dragon covered the area in mist while dropping to its stomach. He crawled in a zig-zagging motion towards the unicorn while the Litehorn blindly shot more zaps of lightning. Innogon reached his target and shot a heavy jet of water at point-blank range, ejecting Litehorn from the tower.

Dripper was taking a bad beating and Innogon joined the fight against the Tuptup just as Dripper was defeated. The dragon shot the Tuptup from behind, sending it out of the tower seconds after Dripper. The second Zodiac member let out another frustrated yell, mumbled something about the boss killing him, and he was gone seconds later.

Aurin, Luna, Shamtile and Innogon breathed easy, while Dolissile showed little reaction to anything that had just happened.

"They dropped an egg!" exclaimed Luna.

"Maybe that's why they were more irritable than usual when we defeated them?" pondered Aurin.

"It's your egg," said Luna, gesturing towards Aurin.

"Thanks, Luna."

Aurin walked over and picked it up, along with a nice collection of silver coins. The eggs were sturdy. Even after being dropped to the floor, it didn't have a scratch on it. Aurin stashed it carefully in his bag, just in case it wasn't as sturdy as he suspected.

"That was an intense match," sighed Aurin.

"I'm not ready for the tournament," muttered Luna, tearing up slightly. "I don't think I can do it."

"Why not? Innogon was great just now."

"He was great, but I don't think Dripper will stand much chance. She's not powerful enough and I'm not a good enough tamer to have her ready in time. I haven't even had the chance to use Spaqua in battle yet. We only have five weeks left. I can't do it."

"Ask Kyle to train you. I know he's busy, but he'll do it."

"I don't know..."

Aurin looked Luna in the eyes and placed his hands on her shoulders. "Trust me. It's worth it, even though he's a tough instructor."

Luna's face turned red. "Okay...I'll ask when we get back."

"Let's use the orb and get out of here. We've had enough excitement for one day."

"You still have three strong Minakai you can use. Are you sure you want to leave?"

"We got here once; we'll get here again. Don't worry about it. It's been a long trip this time."

"Thank you, Aurin," uttered Luna as Aurin retrieved his Orb of Return from his bag.

"I wonder if we'll have to spend the night in the tower when we reach the tenth floor?"

"Maybe..."

"Perhaps if we become tough enough we'll be able to get through the first dozen or two dozen floors with ease."

Aurin continued talking in a futile attempt to lighten Luna's mood. She had stopped listening after he began to take the orb from his bag. The young man meant well and Luna truly appreciated the early escape from the tower, but her thoughts of her own competence weighed heavily on her mind.

Luna sat quietly in her room, rubbing Innogon's head fin. When she previously spoke with her parents about the tournament, she would switch between excitement and anxiety. Today, she had confessed her recent fears to them. She didn't want to be embarrassed in front of thousands of people, nor did she want to let her Minakai down. Her mother had told her she could still choose not to participate, but her father agreed with Aurin's advice of asking Kyle to train her.

"What do you think we should do, Inno?" she asked Innogon.

Innogon let out a small roar and smiled.

"You're right, I did tell Aurin that I would ask Kyle already."

She knew that it wasn't what Innogon had said, but let herself believe it anyway.

There was still an hour or two of daylight left, so Luna departed from her home with Innogon. She had decided that running away from her fears wasn't the right answer. She was going to enter the tournament and she was going to give it her all.

Luna walked along the path out of town with Innogon casually strolling beside her. Every now and then, he would get distracted and watch the people pass or chase a bird along the side of the road. It was a pleasant evening for a walk and Luna could feel her mood lightening already.

Arriving at the ranch, Luna could see Kyle in the fields, dropping scraps of chicken into a trough for the Minakai to eat. It would be gone within ten minutes, easily.

Kyle waved when he spotted Luna. "If you're here to see your boyfriend, he's already fast asleep."

Luna blushed. "We're just friends."

"I'm just teasing you," chuckled Kyle, "but your face is awfully red for someone who claims there's no interest beyond friendship there."

Luna ignored Kyle. "What's he sleeping so early for?"

"He always falls asleep straight after dinner when he's been in the tower. That's normal for him these days. He'll be awake at the crack of dawn and go for a run with his Minakai to start the day. Well, he'll send Dolissile to swim up and down the river because it's where he's most comfortable."

"I didn't realise Aurin was as dedicated as that," admitted Luna.

"Yeah, he's pretty determined alright. I'd like to think it's because of my sage wisdom, but I think he'd have eventually come to see it as a good idea on his own. I just gave him a push that helped speed him along."

"That's actually what I'm here to see you about," said Luna timidly.

"What is?" asked Kyle, unsure of what she was getting at.

"You trained Aurin for a week. I want you to train me too. It's the only way I'll stand a chance at the tournament."

"Okay."

"Okay? You aren't too busy?"

"Nah, I just told Aurin I had a single week to spare so he felt the urgency to train without my constant help. Be here at six in the morning each day for the next week."

Luna jumped for joy. "Thank you, thank you, thank

you."

"You're welcome...now settle down."

"Alright, sorry."

"Make sure you wear something you can run in. Your usual skirt and boots won't cut it. There's going to be intense work for both you and your Minakai."

"Yes, Kyle," nodded Luna.

Luna bade farewell to Kyle and departed from the ranch. She skipped home with Innogon riding on her back; his favourite spot to be on a journey further than a few metres. For the first time in a while, she felt like she had a chance to perform well in the tournament.

.

Chapter 10

Aurin squatted beside the egg that sat in the incubator. The cracks started to appear before his eyes and then suddenly the shell shattered. A burst of creamy-white light appeared and, once it faded, Aurin's new Minakai was left behind. It was a small steel-blue lion cub with a tuft of dark grey hair atop its head.

"Cubtem," said Kyle. "This one is a good find. Personally, Leonite is one of my favourite neutral elemental Minakai."

"It evolves into a Leonite?" asked Aurin, thinking about his lost battle with Leo.

"Yes. Just give it an Astral Shard and it'll evolve."

"I have an Astral Shard that I bought to replace the one I lost when battling Leo."

Kyle shook his head. "I wouldn't evolve it so early if

I were you. You need to strengthen your bond with it and learn how to use the Minakai at each stage of its life to truly master handling it. I mean...I won't stop you, but I don't think it's a good idea. Walk before running, so to speak."

"It's alright," said Aurin. "I wasn't seriously considering it; the idea just came into my head. That's all."

"What's your plan tomorrow?"

"I'm going to go into the tower alone and see how I fare. I'd imagine Luna will be over shortly after dinner to ask you to train her, so pretend I didn't say anything."

"I won't, I promise," said Kyle.

"I'm going to sleep after we eat. I want to be up bright and early for the tower tomorrow. If I can make it to the eighth floor then I'll consider it a good run. I'll have broken my solo record."

"If I don't see you in the morning, good luck. Your orb has enough charges, right?"

"Two left before I need to find or buy a new one."

"Good. I'm just making sure you're prepared."

"I know, Kyle. I appreciate it, thanks. You can keep Shamtile here with Luna tomorrow for moral support. He could always use an extra workout."

Shamtile began waving his arms in protest while Aurin and Kyle laughed.

Luna knocked on Kyle's door with Innogon by her side. Even when the sun had barely risen, it was warm.

The summer had been very kind to central Bretonia this year. Today she had heeded Kyle's advice and wore a t-shirt, shorts and trainers.

Aurin answered the door. "Morning, Luna. Ready for your first day of Kyle's boot camp?"

"Morning, Aurin," smiled Luna. "I'm ready. Are you going to the tower today?"

"I am," said Aurin. "Today's mission is to reach the eighth floor with Hornferno, Dolissile and my new Cubtem."

"Oh no!" exclaimed Luna. "I forgot you were going to hatch the egg. I can't believe I missed it."

Aurin laughed. "It's fine. He'll be hanging around here until I summon him into the tower. Besides, you'll see him all the time when we're training."

"You aren't bringing Shamtile today?"

"Nah, he's okay here. He's had the most training so I need to start varying my roster so that everybody gets to battle. He can always do some exercise here with you. He's a veteran of the boot camp at this stage."

Aurin wished Luna luck and departed for the tower, leaving Luna to wait for Kyle. She walked into the fields with Innogon to find her Dripper and Spaqua, both of which were relaxing in a small pool with other Minakai that Kyle was taking care of on behalf of their tamers.

"Sorry to keep you waiting," called Kyle as he approached the field. "A Chopchop had cleaved through a fence during the night so I had to repair it before any Minakai broke out and got themselves into a fight with one of my Frogre guards."

"Are you ever *not* busy here?" asked Luna.

"No," lamented Kyle. "I love what I do, but I rarely have a moment to myself. It's why I have so many Frogre guarding the perimeter. It means if there's ever trouble whether that be external or from the Minakai, they'll sort it out."

"That sounds difficult to keep on top of."

"Nah," said Kyle, waving his hand dismissively. "Incidents aren't all that common, but I still need to maintain constant vigilance. Anyway, are you ready?"

"Yes," nodded Luna.

"Alright, head out to the fields and start doing laps. That goes for all of your Minakai too, including Innogon. He is not allowed to ride on your back or shoulders. As much as it would be good endurance training for you."

"What about Spaqua and Dripper? All they can do is bounce."

"They can bounce the laps. We'll let your Minakai do water-specific training another day, but for now, they need to be strong on dry land. That's where the majority of your battles will be."

Luna and her Minakai began to run. They were notably slower than Aurin when he first started. Luna wasn't in bad shape by any stretch, but she was far more used to walking than running. Innogon struggled, particularly with his stubby legs. Dripper looked shocked the whole way through and Spaqua bounced and rolled most of the way. Shamtile joined them halfway through the run, hoping his absence was unnoticed by Kyle. The laps continued for half an hour until Luna and her Minakai collapsed in front of Kyle's house one after the other.

"Done," said Luna breathlessly.

"Alright, take a one-minute breather and then we battle," said Kyle nonchalantly. "Shamtile, you do one more for trying to get out of training today."

Shamtile waved his arms in protest but relented and

started to run.

"Wait, it...isn't just...exercise today?" panted Luna.

"No, of course not. You and Aurin both had the same reaction to this. Why is it so surprising? Half of the training is whipping you all into shape and the other is to work on your battle skills. You need fitness and tactics, it's what will save you in the tournament. In fact, it will save you in the tower. I'm not sure you would reach the fifth floor alone without a lot of luck. I'm going to make sure you can reach it with ease using your skills."

"Is it going to be this tough every day?"

"Tougher, but you'll be stronger so it won't seem much worse. Well, maybe not for the first two days because you'll be very sore. I expect you to keep up similar training even after this week is over too."

Luna whined a little but then stood up.

"Let's battle," said Kyle as he walked over to the field in front of his house.

Shamtile finished his lap and waddled over to join Kyle while Luna slinked over to her side of the makeshift arena.

"Alright," called Kyle, "this will be a battle using all three of your Minakai against one of mine. You can choose to use them all at once or one after another. I want to see what you can do."

Kyle whistled loudly and the shadow of a large bird appeared in the sky in the direction of the ranch. As it approached, Luna could see that it was green and its wings were giant leaves. It was a Wingbloom, a fully evolved Driftseed.

"He looks so tough. How can I beat him?" asked Luna incredulously.

"This Wingbloom took me all the way to the thirty-seventh floor. He's my most experienced Minakai and is in full control of all of his abilities. There is no better sparring partner than him. I don't expect you to beat him, I expect you to show us what you're made of."

Luna knelt down beside her three Minakai and whispered. "Spaqua, you haven't seen a battle yet. Dripper, you are still new too. I think if we attack one by one then we might not land a hit. If all three of you go from different angles, then perhaps we can at least do...something."

Her Minakai looked at each other, uncertain, then back to Luna.

"Innogon, I want you to launch Spaqua into the sky. Spaqua, you can hurl a few icicles to distract Wingbloom while Innogon and Dripper go for a wing each. Got it?"

"You won't be able to do this during the tournament, so hurry it up," barked Kyle.

"Let's go, Team Luna!" Luna yelled enthusiastically.

Spaqua bounced forward and leapt into the air. Innogon ran underneath and fired a jet of water, propelling Spaqua thirty feet into the air. Spaqua was at eye-level with Wingbloom and it began to spit icicles from within its jelly. Wingbloom swatted them away with ease using the long feather atop its head.

While the plant-like air elemental was distracted, Innogon shot another jet of water. He aimed for the left wing while Dripper's stream of bubbles aimed for the right wing. Wingbloom was too quick for either of the water Minakai and ducked out of the way.

"Oh no!" exclaimed Luna. "Team Luna, everybody into the air. Shoot downwards."

Innogon blasted more water beneath Spaqua to keep it airborne before shooting downwards to raise himself higher. Dripper bounced high and aimed a high-powered bubble jet beneath herself. All three of Luna's Minakai were in the air.

"Mist, now!" ordered Luna. Innogon and Dripper unleashed a heavy fog on the battlefield to obscure Wingbloom's vision. "Spaqua, freeze the mist!"

Kyle raised an eyebrow as Spaqua slowly froze the mist. He was impressed with the inventiveness, but he knew that Spaqua was too fresh to be able to do it effectively. Wingbloom's flaps were slowed, but it was not enough to cause him to drop.

"Back to the first plan," called Luna.

Innogon and Dripper unleashed a flurry of bubbles and water streams at Kyle's Wingbloom who ducked out of the way once more, but not before taking a few hits to the tips of his wings. He lost balance for a few seconds but steadied himself.

"Alright, that's enough," said Kyle. "I've seen all I need for now."

"We just started!" cried Luna.

"I didn't even start, in case you didn't notice," said Kyle.

Luna and her Minakai all lined up in front of Kyle, Wingbloom and Shamtile.

"You never stood much of a chance against Wingbloom," Kyle began. "I wasn't really sure if I expected you to even land a hit. You're more creative in your methods than Aurin is, but you lack the power that he and his Minakai have worked hard to build up. If you had that, perhaps you could have done more damage, but considering your starting point today...you did a good job."

"Thank you," beamed Luna.

"With that said, you have a lot of work to do. There's

no denying that your Innogon is your strongest team member, so you need to work on your Dripper and Spaqua the most. If your Spaqua had been trained more, you could have been even more effective with the mist freezing. It would have been faster and more thorough."

Kyle continued to give Luna a full rundown of the things he noticed during the battle, both positive and negative, along with advice on how to do better in the next battle. Once he wrapped up, he told Luna to spend the rest of the training session doing laps.

The sun was high in the sky when Aurin wandered back onto the ranch, with his Dolissile by his side. Shamtile, who had been eagerly waiting near Kyle's front door, ran over to greet his master and fellow Minakai.

"How was your day?" asked Aurin, slapping Shamtile lightly on the shoulder.

Shamtile squealed and roared, waving his hands in various motions as though trying to mime a description of everything he had seen today.

"I think I'll have to just ask Kyle," chuckled Aurin as Shamtile slumped over in disappointment. Dolissile remained stoic throughout everything, floating eerily beside Aurin.

"Kyle?" called Aurin as he walked through the ranch.
"Over here," answered the rancher.
Aurin followed Kyle's voice and found him tossing a

few small fish into the river for a group of Dopefish to eat. As they started to munch on them, a large Doripper burst forth. Kyle tossed a large tuna into its mouth and it retreated back to the riverbed.

"I need to get one of those," said Aurin, marvelling at the monstrous Minakai. "Do you see those teeth? I bet it could tear even the toughest of metal elementals apart with those things."

"It's not even fully evolved, would you believe?" laughed Kyle. "How was the tower?"

"Floor seven again. It seems to be a sticking point for me."

"I noticed your Hornferno and Cubtem arrived back an hour or so ago. What took you so long?"

Aurin shook his head. "I thought it would be best to give Luna some space while she trained, so Dolissile and I hung back for a while and did some exercise in the forest."

"What happened that got you booted out then?"

"Well, I won against three tamers without losing a single Minakai. It was the wild ones that finished off Hornferno and Cubtem for the run. Cubtem did great for his first time. How was Luna?"

"She's more creative than you," jabbed Kyle.

"I know that," laughed Aurin. "She always gives good ideas when we're in the tower. She just needs to learn to think on her feet and...well, train more."

"That about sums it up."

"I actually brought her something from the tower today. It's a Lunar Shard for her Spaqua. I know what you said about not rushing evolution, but if she keeps up her training then it could be useful to evolve Spaqua before the tournament."

"That's a good idea," said Kyle. "Are you going to the

tower again tomorrow?"

"Not tomorrow. I'm going to help out with the training if that's okay with you?"

"Of course."

"Great!" exclaimed Aurin. "Now what's for lunch?"

"I'm not your maid," protested Kyle, digging Aurin in the arm.

Chapter 11

Aurin, Luna, Shamtile and Innogon walked towards the fountain in the Hazelton town square. Gardner waved to them as they came into view through the crowd. There were two weeks left until the tournament and it was the day of registration. All tamers participating in the tournament had to register themselves today and their Minakai are registered the day before the tournament.

"Hi, all. How are you both keeping?" asked Gardner.

"Exhausted," lamented Aurin.

"Yes," sighed Luna.

"I take it you've both been training hard then," chuckled Gardner.

Luna nodded. "I was training with Kyle for a week

and since then, we've been training both at his ranch, in the tower and organising battles with other tamers in town."

Aurin also nodded. "Once the tournament is over, we'll both sleep for a week."

"Where's the registration at?" asked Luna.

"They're doing the registration at the stadium," revealed Gardner. "The mayor is giving a short speech first and we won't want to miss that. Follow me."

"Wait, there's a stadium in town?" asked Aurin.

Luna stared at him in confusion. "Where did you think the tournament was going to be? Kyle's field?"

Gardner led the group five minutes through town to the stadium. There were tamers queued up, waiting to register. There must have been at least two hundred of them. Aurin, Luna and Gardner joined the back of the queue.

"How does the tournament work? Points or brackets?" asked Luna.

"Brackets," confirmed Gardner. "Only two hundred and fifty-six people will be allowed to enter and it's based on how high you've reached in one of the monster towers. It doesn't matter what type of tower it is, whether that's combat, puzzle, insanity; anything goes."

"If three hundred enter and everybody except us has hit floor fifteen then we're out?" asked Aurin nervously.

"Yup," said Gardner. "I don't think we have much to worry about. We've all reached floor ten and I think the average lowest entry in tournaments like this is usually about seven."

"What's to stop people from lying when they report their floor?" asked Luna.

"I...don't know," admitted Gardner.

The doors opened shortly afterwards and the tamers

all flocked into the stadium. Everybody spread themselves out over the grassy field, not too dissimilar from a football pitch, and waited for Mayor Boren to take to the makeshift stage in the middle of the arena floor.

Aurin looked around the crowd and noticed a couple of familiar faces, like Ilena, Devon and Hunter. Hunter briefly locked eyes with Aurin and gave him a courteous nod, which Aurin returned. He was dreading the prospect of facing him again, knowing how powerful he and his Minakai were.

Mayor Boren finally walked onto the stage and stopped at the central podium where a microphone was set up. "Welcome, tamers. I hope you're all excited for the beginning of the tournament. For the locals, I hope you like the new renovations to the stadium. For those travelling from afar, welcome to our humble town. It's going to be the biggest event in Hazelton in decades if not centuries.

"Minakai have always been a part of our lives. The big, the small, the fiery...the cosmic. It is with great care that we train our Minakai and it is with great pride that we battle them. I'm sure you are all tough and capable, with your Minakai both common and rare, but only one of you will become the first-ever official Hazelton Champion.

"I invite all of you to give it your very best and may everybody be invigorated by the battles that we watch. I look forward to shaking hands with the eventual victor and bequeathing him or her with this magnificent prized egg.

The mayor paused and gestured towards an egg that was being carried up by a tournament official. Everybody stared at it excitedly.

"I do not know what rare Minakai lies within, but I'm assured that it will be a valuable tool in your arsenal. As you know, the top four performing tamers in this tournament will advance to the national championships in Ludonia. I'm curious to see which of the faces before me makes it there. I wish you all an excellent tournament. Good luck."

The crowd applauded as Mayor Boren stepped down from the stage. Aurin, like most others, was more enamoured by the thought of winning the rare Minakai inside the egg than the mayor's speech.

Everybody dispersed and made their way inside and to the registration hall. There were eight different tables to sign up at, spreading the crowd out. Aurin, Luna and Gardner waited for their turn.

"Name?" asked the official at the desk when Aurin was finally at the front of the queue.

"Aurin," said the young man.

The official rolled her eyes. "Full name."

"Oh," said Aurin, apologising and giving his full name.

"Hold still please," said the woman, holding out a scanning device of some kind. She ran it up and down Aurin. "Tenth floor of a combat class tower."

"That's right," said Aurin. Luna's question from outside having now been answered.

Aurin continued answering whatever questions the woman asked of him. The woman even took his photograph and used the computer to print out a pass.

"Use this when signing your Minakai up for the tournament in thirteen days."

Aurin thought he might as well ask a question that had been bugging him. "Why are my Minakai signed up later?"

The woman sighed. "It's so that we have the most up-to-date record of your team before the tournament begins. You may obtain new Minakai or evolve your current ones in the run-up to the tournament. After the tournament begins, new Minakai cannot be entered. Old ones are allowed to evolve, but they must be reported at first notice to tournament staff."

Aurin could sense that she wouldn't take kindly to further questions so he stepped aside with Shamtile to wait for Luna and Gardner.

"She's a real grouch, right?"

Shamtile nodded his head furiously and made a scuttling noise with his mouth somewhere from behind his mask.

Once Luna and Gardner had received their passes, the group followed others outside. Everybody was walking back towards the town centre to grab lunch, having been standing around the last few hours to register.

"It looks like we've all reached high enough floors to make it," cheered Luna.

Gardner shook his head. "I asked the grumpy lady and she said that we'd find out tomorrow. Everybody who doesn't make it gets to keep their pass in case anybody drops out."

"Ouch!" yelped Luna. "Stop that man!"

Aurin spun around and watched as a man ran off with Luna's bag. He was wearing casual clothes, but a hat and mask that was worn only by somebody from...

"Zodiac!" called Aurin as he gave chase.

"There are a bunch of them!" shouted Gardner.

It was a Zodiac ambush. Members of the group were fleeing with tamers' bags, a few summoning stones and even a couple of Minakai were grabbed.

The one that robbed Luna grouped up with another two members, all of whom ran towards the bridge over the river. Aurin, Luna and Gardner gave chase while other tamers ran after their own targets.

When the thieves reached the houses, they all split off down different side streets.

"Split up," said Gardner, and he diverted off down another path.

Luna ran straight ahead while Aurin took a street to the left. He kept losing sight of the Zodiac member as he ran, but his training was paying off and he was making up ground. Aurin was nearly certain this was the one who took Luna's bag.

When they reached a clearing, the Zodiac member turned to face Aurin. He was wearing a lion mask.

"Leo," said Aurin.

"I'm glad you remember me," said Leo.

"You can't outrun me."

"Maybe not, but I can outbattle you with ease. I only want the shard she has inside. You can have the bag right now if you walk away."

"If I win, you return the bag with the shard."

"Fine," laughed Leo as he raised his glove high and sent out a green light. A Budescent appeared on the street.

Aurin raised his glove and summoned his Cubtem from Kyle's ranch.

Cubtem was small, but scrappy. He charged at Leo's Budescent as the young green wolf stomped its feet and summoned vines from the ground. Cubtem nimbly dodged and delivered a headbutt right to Budescent's jaw. The wolf was knocked back, but he retaliated by clamping down on Cubtem's neck.

The lion and wolf wrestled violently with each other

while their tamers refused to be distracted, even as people peered from their windows. Eventually, Cubtem was overpowered and fell down. Aurin used a stone to send him back to the ranch.

"Dolissile, get in there!" ordered Aurin and the dolphin burst forth from his silvery light and immediately charged at the Budescent.

Dolissile collided with the wolf and knocked it straight into a brick wall. The wolf collapsed, motionless. Leo removed him from the field and summoned his next Minakai, the same Leonite that Aurin faced in the tower.

Leonite used its intense speed to run circles around Dolissile. Dolissile's weakest point was his inability to turn quickly outside of the water, and he found himself overwhelmed.

"Dolissile, charge up your fins and wait for him to strike."

The metallic dolphin's tail and back fins begin to glow a bright blue. Leonite eventually stopped circling and charged at Dolissile, who flipped himself downwards and onto his back, slashing the Leonite across the face.

The lion began to bleed heavily, but it was in a rage. It roared loudly and sank its teeth deep into Dolissile, piercing his metal exoskeleton. Dolissile yelled in pain and Aurin withdrew him.

"It's up to you, Shamtile," said Aurin, sending forth his masked Minakai.

Shamtile encased his fists in stone and ran forward. He pummelled the Leonite in the torso while it was blinded by its own blood. It cleared its eyes and whipped its heavy tail into Shamtile, knocking him back.

Shamtile stomped on the ground and sent Leonite flying into the air with the stalagmite that erupted. Leonite recovered in mid-air and landed shockingly gracefully before immediately pouncing on Shamtile, pinning him down.

Leonite tried to clamp its jaw down on Shamtile, but the swift reptile encased his body in stone. Leonite broke through the stone, but Shamtile managed to avoid being badly hurt and threw Leonite off.

Shamtile used his magic to open a small chasm in the ground, which he dove into. The chasm closed instantly, as though never there. Leonite stopped and looked around for Shamtile, but it could not sense him at all.

Suddenly, the ground split open and Shamtile burst forth with his fists encased in spear-like stone. Leonite was struck and fell to the ground, unconscious.

"This ends here," said Leo as he tossed the bag on the floor and recalled Leonite. "I'm not so stupid as to leave myself without an escape method."

Leo summoned another Leonite and climbed upon its back. "We will see each other again, Aurin. I assure you." Leo departed as his second Leonite sprinted through the streets.

Aurin walked over to Luna's bag and picked it up. He looked inside to make sure the Lunar Shard that he gifted her was still there. Thankfully, Leo kept his word and returned the bag with the shard inside. Aurin wasn't sure why he did that when he could have easily fled with it.

Luna, Gardner and Innogon were already in the town square when Aurin and Shamtile arrived; they were spent from the chase and the battle.

"I got your bag back," said Aurin, handing it to Luna.

"Everything should still be there."

"You looked in my bag?" blushed Luna.

Aurin was embarrassed. "What? Oh, no...it was just to make sure he didn't get the Astral Shard. I didn't see anything else."

"It's fine," said Luna, nervously rubbing her arm. "Thanks for getting it back."

Gardner stood there awkwardly looking from side to side. Eventually, he broke the silence. "Those Zodiac ones, eh? What a bunch of crooks."

"We've met that one before," said Aurin, "his name is Leo. He beat me in the tower, but I managed to stop him this time. Granted, he only used two Minakai and I used three. Did you have any luck with the ones you were chasing?"

"Not me," admitted Luna. "She got away."

"So did mine," sighed Gardner, dragging his foot along the ground. "Just what is it that they were looking for?"

"Eggs, shards, Minakai," said Aurin, shrugging his shoulders. "Anything they can get their hands on to make themselves stronger. I really want to know what their ultimate goal is. Is it solely power for the sake of power?"

"It beats me," shrugged Gardner. "It could be anything, for all we know. Maybe they're looking for a specific Minakai?"

"Like what?" asked Luna.

Gardner stroked his chin. "There are countless Minakai out there. There are rare and powerful Minakai that are beyond our comprehension. It's like the mayor said, some are supposedly cosmic beings—not that I really know what that means—while others are near unique in their rarity and only appear once per century because the tower they dwell in is always locked."

Aurin knew all this was true, but he could never fully wrap his head around it. If Zodiac was seeking a specific powerful Minakai, what would it mean if they got their hands on it?

Chapter 12

Aurin and Luna had reached a new floor record in the tower. They stood on floor twelve for the first time, two floors higher than their previous record. The duo took it in for a moment.

It had not been the smoothest of runs. Shamtile had stepped on a poison trap on the sixth floor, but Luna treated him in time with one of her remedies. Aurin had triggered another monster den trap on floor nine, but everybody sprinted from the room before the wild Minakai knew what was happening.

However, it had not been all bad. It was also a run filled with fortune. Aurin had picked up bundles of silver coins, a new Orb of Return, a Solar Shard and an egg. He was feeling good about his haul so far and was particularly excited to hatch a new monster.

Luna meanwhile had picked up plenty of coins of her own, a few different herbs, an Orb of Tamers to identify whether other tamers were nearby, and an egg of her own. Much like Aurin, she was excited to hatch a new monster, but she spoke very fondly of the herbs. She told Aurin what they were for, but it went in one ear and out the other.

There were six days to go before the tournament and both Aurin and Luna had received confirmation that they had made the cut. The pair were excited, but also starting to feel nervous. Luna more so than Aurin, but he was anxious about being drawn against Hunter in the first match. He knew that would be a guaranteed loss for him and hoped to fight someone more on his level in his first match or two.

"Should we quit while we're ahead?" asked Luna, growing increasingly concerned about losing her herbs and eggs.

"Let's push a little more," urged Aurin. "There could be something good up ahead."

"We're down to one Minakai each, Spaqua and Dolissile. Are you sure?"

"No," admitted Aurin, "I'm not sure at all. But let's keep going anyway."

Aurin walked forward with Dolissile hovering above the ground beside him. Luna followed tepidly behind him while Spaqua rolled in its jelly ball, keeping close to her.

The young man walked into a nearby room and began to pick up the silver coins on the floor. Luna on the other hand spotted a rare berry in the corner and stashed it in her bag.

"Do you know what this berry can do?" asked Luna, excitedly.

"You know I don't."

"If a Minakai eats it in the tower, it can move twice as fast for a short while."

"Really? That sounds like a lot of fun. Can humans eat it?"

"I suppose so, but I don't think it'll have any magical effect. It wouldn't work on regular animals either."

Aurin wondered what would happen if Dolissile, already a very fast Minakai, ate the berry and charged at a wall. Could he break through the rooms in the tower and create shortcuts?

Suddenly, Aurin heard a loud crashing noise. Luna jolted from her own daydream as a giant tortoise barrelled into the room, straight at them. It was a Titanitoise, a fully evolved Tormech, adorned with large metal spikes on its green shell.

"Orb!" yelled Luna as Dolissile and Spaqua tried to ward off the Titanitoise.

The large tortoise took a full-speed charge from Dolissile and barely budged an inch. Spaqua cowered in fear, knowing it was severely outclassed.

"Orb," said Aurin, now in full agreement, as he hastily pulled it from his back and cast the spell within, a mere second before Dolissile was about to be dealt a run-ending blow by the behemoth.

"You two look shaken," said Kyle as Aurin and Luna dragged themselves into the ranch just before sunset. Dolissile and Spaqua followed close behind.

"Big Titanitoise on floor twelve," said Luna, her eyes still wide.

"Yes, they're brutal foes to face in the tower. They're not so common on floor twelve, so that's a bit of bad luck. Would you have lost anything good?"

"We would both have lost a lot," said Aurin, pulling out his egg and a shard.

"I found an egg and a Solee Berry, Kyle," chimed in Luna.

"Yeah, that berry is a good find alright," agreed Kyle, nodding wisely. "Great for tower combat, but sadly disallowed in tournaments. Can you think of what a great show it would provide? Two super-speed Minakai going head-to-head. I hope you've been on the lookout for spell crystals too. They're handy in a pinch."

"Incubator?" asked Aurin, ignoring Kyle and Luna's conversation.

"Go ahead," said Kyle, flicking his head towards the house.

Aurin jogged over to the house with a new burst of energy and returned moments later with the incubator. He passed it to Luna, letting her hatch her egg first.

"Thank you," smiled Luna, happily accepting.

"Are we taking bets on what it will hatch into?" asked Kyle.

"I bet it's another water Minakai," laughed Aurin. "You have two already plus one ice, which is sort of close to water."

"You do appear to have developed a theme," said Kyle.

Luna sat down on the ground and started the hatching process. As the glow from the incubator faded away, a small Minakai with reddish-brown skin, a light-brown face and a couple of leaves atop its head revealed itself.

"A Happynut?" said Aurin, surprised. "At least it mixes up your team a little bit."

Luna was very happy with her Minakai as it danced in place on its two tiny feet. Its smile echoed her own. "Your turn," she said to Aurin, handing him the incubator.

Aurin placed his own egg inside the incubator and watched excitedly as the light shone and then faded. A small Minakai with reddish-brown skin, a light-brown face and a couple of leaves atop its head revealed itself once more.

"Another Happynut?" said Aurin with an eyebrow raised.

"What are the odds?" asked Luna.

"It's a fairly common Minakai so it's not that unusual," chuckled Kyle as he watched the two looking in disbelief. "I don't know why you're both surprised by this."

"We haven't had any crossover members of our teams before," said Aurin. "We don't have very large collections yet so I thought it wouldn't happen for a while yet when there are so many Minakai in existence."

"Different towers have different species of Minakai and different floors have different rates of Minakai eggs appearing," said Kyle. "What you find in Ludonia will vary from Hazelton somewhat, and that's not even in another country. After a while, you'll start to exhaust the possibilities in one tower and move onto another."

Aurin hadn't thought of this before and stood silently, running through various scenarios in his head about what to do once he conquered Harmony Tower.

"I wouldn't worry about that for a while," said Kyle. "I don't think you'll reach the top for years."

"I know," said Aurin, "I just hadn't considered what my next move would be after reaching the top."

"There are always more towers, more tournaments and more Minakai to find. You could spend the rest of your life searching and you wouldn't be able to learn everything about Minakai. Don't stress about it. You've got far more pressing concerns."

"That's true," agreed Aurin, seeming brighter once again. "If I remember correctly, Happynut can evolve in different ways, right?"

"Oh yeah!" exclaimed Luna, throwing her Happynut in the air and catching it. The smile did not once leave the little seed's face. "I wonder if ours will evolve the same way?"

"I'm not sure," said Kyle. "If it evolves into Melansprout, it can evolve into either Desparee or Angree with a Lunar Shard. There are a variety of factors that determine which it will turn into."

"What are the factors?" asked Aurin.

"Well, um..." mumbled Kyle.

"You don't know?" smirked Luna.

"This is the first time you've been stumped by one of my questions," laughed Aurin.

"Shush, boy," barked Kyle. "You've still got lots of training to do if you want to stand a chance at the tournament." Kyle pulled out a couple of summoning stones. "How about a battle to see if you're even getting close?"

"Let's do it," said Aurin confidently, switching one of his summoning stones out for a Minakai that was ready to battle. Dolissile was still in good fighting condition, so he was staying put.

"It's going to be a battle of two rounds, seeing as two of your Minakai are resting and another is a newborn.

That leaves you with Dolissile and Hornferno left to fight with. I'll use two of my own just to keep things fair."

The three humans, Dolissile, Spaqua and the Happynuts walked over to the usual clearing where Kyle hosted battles at the ranch. Aurin and Kyle stood facing each other, while the spectators watched eagerly.

Kyle raised his hand and summoned a Frogre to the battlefield, while Aurin brought forth his Hornferno. The red dinosaur gave a hearty grunt and exhaled smoke from its nostrils while the snowy ogre punched his fists together.

"Go!" called Luna.

Frogre charged towards Hornferno who hunkered down and breathed deep. Frogre jumped into the air and threw its full weight behind its fist, aiming straight for the red dino. Hornferno breathed a jet of flame towards the brute, but Frogre barely noticed as its fist collided with Hornferno's jaw.

The ogre began to pummel the dinosaur, much to Aurin's shock. "Use your tail!" ordered Aurin.

Hornferno whipped its tail, smacking Frogre across the face. It was caught off guard and the dinosaur leapt backwards, ready to keep fighting against this tough opponent.

"If he can't find you, he can't hit you," called Aurin. Hornferno understood and exhaled a large cloud of smoke.

Kyle stood silently as his Minakai backed away from the cloud, waiting for his opponent to come out of hiding. His fists were raised, ready to jab at Hornferno if he came close.

"Jet manoeuvre!" ordered Aurin.

Suddenly, a jet of fire erupted from the smoke and

Frogre dodged. As it repositioned itself, a second jet appeared. It dodged once more, but it did not notice the dinosaur charging at him in time.

Hornferno's head spike pierced the Frogre's chest, leaving a big open wound. It looked agonisingly painful. Kyle beckoned two of his other Frogre guards over and they carried his Minakai off to treat his bad wound.

"Well played," said Kyle nonchalantly. "Let's see how you handle being one-upped."

The rancher summoned his next Minakai. It was a red dinosaur, not unlike Hornferno, but considerably larger. A bigger body, sharper teeth, longer spikes and a bulkier tail for whipping. It looked even more menacing.

"Is that an evolved Hornferno?" asked Aurin.

"Spikruption, finish him off," ordered Kyle.

The larger dinosaur charged forward and tucked itself into a large ball. It rolled across the battlefield like a bolder. Hornferno jumped out of the way, but the Spikruption circled around and began spitting flame while in its ball.

The grass was lit on fire as fireballs were flung across the ground. In the chaos, Hornferno was not able to avoid both the flames and Spikruption. He made the foolish mistake of dodging a fireball and leaping straight into his evolved form's path. Spikruption collided with him and Hornferno was knocked out cold.

"No!" yelled Aurin. "Dolissile, you're up!"

The blue metallic dolphin charged in from the sidelines, ready to avenge its fallen comrade. It bore its usual lifeless stare as it charged straight for Spikruption, who had uncurled itself.

"It won't be that easy," said Kyle, as his Minakai swept its tail and batted Dolissile out of the way.

The charging dolphin careened off to the side and almost out of the battlefield. He regained his composure just in time and spun around. For the first time, Aurin could see some semblance of expression on his robotic face. He had a faint look of anger written upon him, but it faded quickly, being replaced by stoicism.

"If he tries that trick again, shoot yourself into the sky!" ordered Aurin. Kyle looked confused at this command.

"He's up to something," Kyle warned his Spikruption. "Do not bat him away next time. Crush him into the dirt."

Dolissile darted at Spikruption, who rolled into a ball and retreated. The two hurried around the makeshift arena and Dolissile slowly started to gain on his opponent.

"Now!" ordered Kyle.

Spikruption unfurled himself and kept low. Dolissile collided with him. The force threw Spikruption back, but Dolissile fell to the ground, worse for the wear than his opponent. The dinosaur was far too heavy to break.

Dolissile recovered and retreated to the far side of the arena, where Aurin stood. His tamer whispered something to him while Kyle squinted, trying to work out what Aurin had said.

The dolphin suddenly charged forward once more and Spikruption remained down, ready to take the attack. Dolissile slowly started to tilt himself upwards, but Spikruption did not realise what was happening.

"Get out of the way!" ordered Kyle, but the dinosaur was too slow when he was unfurled.

Dolissile used Spikruption as a ramp and jetted into the sky, almost out of sight. The fading sunset made it even harder to see where he had disappeared.

Spikruption ran to the centre of the arena, staring at the sky while everybody watched, waiting for Dolissile to reappear.

At the speed of light, a giant torpedo burst from out of nowhere and collided with the dinosaur's back, forcing it to collapse onto the floor. Both Minakai lay on the ground, not moving.

Aurin watched while holding his breath. Kyle looked on patiently, hoping his Minakai would be the one to stand up first. Luna jittered back and forth anxiously, excited to see who had won.

After a few moments, Dolissile rolled over and floated back to its normal hovering position. Aurin and Luna cheered loudly, while Kyle clapped slowly.

"That was bold," said the rancher as he approached Aurin. "I knew you were going to try an aerial attack, but that could have just as easily been the end of you if you'd missed."

"It's a good thing I didn't miss," laughed Aurin. "Do you think we stand a chance at the tournament yet?"

Kyle looked uncomfortable and gave a begrudging answer. "Luna? I don't think there's even a slight chance you'll win." Luna looked sad to hear this, even though she believed it too. "You, Aurin? I don't think you'll be able to win either."

"After all this work?" Aurin asked.

"Don't get me wrong, you've both come a long way. It'll do wonders for your reputation as tamers if you can knock out a few opponents, but there are people entering that have been training ten or even twenty times longer than you. They have larger and more versatile teams too. Don't let it discourage you. Take each opponent as a new challenge, the same way each tower floor is a challenge."

"I'm looking forward to proving you wrong, Kyle. We're going to the finals."

Kyle laughed. "I truly hope so, you're both good kids and capable tamers. Evolving your teams more wouldn't hurt, I might add."

Aurin pulled out his Solar Shard and Luna pulled out her Astral Shard. They both stared at them, then at each other.

"Want to trade?" asked Aurin.

"I was going to ask you that," giggled Luna.

The pair swapped shards, then headed into the enclosures to seek out the Minakai they planned to evolve. They were both determined to do what Kyle said and make a name for themselves. With a good strategy, perhaps they could indeed make it to the finals and face off against each other.

The man with the bull mask sat with his hands clasped together. He stared at Leo as did his fellow Zodiac Squad members.

"You're sure you're ready for the tournament, Leo?" asked the man. "We need to make sure that you can get far enough so that most of the competitors are eliminated and you can get close to the egg. If you can't progress a few rounds, then you've wasted everybody's time."

"I assure you that I am ready, Master Taurus," insisted Leo. "I will not let the Zodiac Squad down."

"You had better not. I cannot risk blowing my cover

to obtain the egg, it comes with far too many benefits for us. Do it right or you will pay for your failure."

"I will take out anybody who stands in my way," said Leo defiantly. The other Zodiac members all stared at him confidently. They did not doubt him.

End of Arc 1
Welcome to Harmony Tower

Aurin's Team:

Luna's Team:

Chapter 13

Aurin awoke, ready for the day ahead. It was a big one, after all, for today was the opening ceremony for the Hazelton tournament. He was excited and leapt around Kyle's house, gathering everything he might need. Once he was cleaned up, dressed and ready for action, he gathered his Minakai in front of the house.

"The five of you have served me well so far," said Aurin, looking up and down his line of Minakai. "This is our first tournament so we have a lot to prove to not just the people of Hazelton, but to ourselves. You've all put in hard work, something I'm very proud of you for, and I believe it will pay off.

"Shamtile, you've really learned how to harness your magic. Hornferno, you're as tough as nails and will intimidate all of our foes. Dolissile, your coolness and lack of emotion keeps people guessing...myself included. Leonite, your recent evolution means you're a real force to be reckoned with.

"As for you, Happynut...we still have a lot of training to do. You haven't been in the group for long, but I'm still going to rely on you while your teammates are resting between matches. You show a lot of promise and I'll guide you as best as I can."

All of Aurin's Minakai nodded in agreement and gave various roars and squeaks. Well, all except Dolissile who remained silent. The young tamer had meant what he said, he was proud of how far they had all come in such a short time. Shamtile in particular had been with him through everything and faced each challenge head-on.

Luna must have been running late again because all of her Minakai except for Innogon were still at the ranch. They all looked nervous; her Happynut and her newly evolved Spritzard and Tadpool. He knew Luna would summon them if or when they were needed, but Aurin decided to bring them along with him and they'd hopefully cross paths on the way into Hazelton.

It was a clear and sunny morning which made the walk into town all the more pleasant. The birds were chirping merrily and the butterflies were fluttering amongst the flowers. Aurin breathed deeply, inhaling the beautiful spring morning and its sweet aroma.

He led the eight Minakai along the road and met many others who had just returned from nightlong tower adventures ahead of the tournament. They exchanged small talk along the way, but Aurin was careful not to give away his strengths and strategies just in case any of them was a future opponent.

He wandered through the town, curious as to where Luna had gotten to. Her Minakai looked especially confused, but Aurin reassured them that she would be here and was probably just running late. It would not have been the first time.

As the tamer and the Minakai approached the stadium, Luna caught up to them at last. She was out of breath and Innogon clung happily to her back, looking fully energised; a sight all too familiar at this point.

"Thank you," she said once she had caught her breath. "Kyle called my house and told me that you brought all of the Minakai with you."

"I thought it would be best," chuckled Aurin. "I knew you had probably slept in again."

Luna scoffed and walked inside, her Minakai now following her. Aurin continued to laugh and walked inside too. The registration hall was a mess of tamers and Minakai, all being guided along to various assessors and clerks.

Aurin walked up to the last free clerk and presented his registration pass. The man took it and examined it. "All seems to be in order, Master Aurin," smiled the clerk. "You're signing up five Minakai today? Very good. As I'm sure you're no doubt aware, you can evolve your Minakai between matches, but they must be reassessed by us before being allowed to compete. On a related note, while you are free to obtain new Minakai as you always are, they will not be eligible to compete in this tournament."

"I understand," said Aurin.

"Most excellent," smiled the man. He gestured to one of the assessors who began inspecting Aurin's Minakai. He took their height and weight, checked for any injuries and used odd devices that Aurin had never seen before to scan them. What they were doing, he couldn't even guess, but as long as the Minakai passed the assessment he didn't much care.

After a short while the assessor nodded to the clerk. "Perfect. Your Minakai are all fighting fit and ready for action. Best of luck young man. The first match-ups will be announced after the opening ceremony, so please return here to see when you're up and who you'll be competing against. It will be on constant display for the duration of the tournament, but better to make a note of it early."

Aurin thanked him and looked around the room for Luna. He recognised a few faces from around town and the tower, but he couldn't recall most of the names. He could see the wavy-haired Gardner and his team being registered. His Minakai team had noticeably grown, but he seemed to be sticking to plant types and nature elementals. Aurin noted that Dolissile would be in a tough spot should they fight as the nature element can overcome the metal element. He only wished he had an ice elemental to make those plants wither.

"It's quite the gathering, isn't it?" asked a voice from behind Aurin. He looked around and saw a tall man with slicked blonde hair and a black sleeveless leather jacket standing beside him.

"It is," said Aurin. "There are Minakai here that I haven't ever seen before. I sometimes forget that there are new ones still being discovered."

The man nodded. "New Minakai, new evolutions for old Minakai. It's all very fascinating, but sadly, there is nothing new for me today. I'm Frederick, by the way," said the man, extending his hand. "Is this your first tournament?"

"Aurin," replied the young tamer, shaking

Frederick's hand. "And yes, it's my first tournament. How about you?"

Frederick smiled confidently. "I was in the national championships last year but, like the rest of you, it's my first tournament in Hazelton. Surely that counts?" he asked with a laugh.

Aurin laughed back awkwardly, dreading the idea of battling somebody who had reached such a high level. "Did you reach the finals?" he asked the stranger.

"I'm sure you would have heard of me if I had," laughed Frederick again. "No, I'm afraid I did not make it very far. I barely scraped by in the qualifier, so perhaps you'll wipe the floor with me should we face off, eh?" He looked towards the door. "I'm going to go get a good seat for the opening ceremony. Best of luck to you, Aurin."

Aurin wished him luck back as he departed. There was something about Frederick that seemed familiar, but Aurin couldn't put his finger on it. He presumed that they had happened upon each other in the tower at one point and he had simply forgotten him; it wouldn't be the first time he hadn't recalled someone he had met in passing, far from it.

"Ready!" called Luna, skipping towards Aurin with her Minakai in tow. They all looked very happy, so Aurin could tell that they too had passed the assessment. "Shall we get a seat?" Luna asked eagerly.

"Let's wait for Gardner, then we'll head out," Aurin replied, glancing across the room. "He looks like he's almost finished."

Once Gardner had his Minakai assessed—and approved for the tournament—the three tamers and their Minakai walked out onto the field, where the tamers were filtered into a box along with one small

Minakai each. The rest of the Minakai stood outside, lining the edge of the stadium. Naturally, Shamtile and Innogon followed Aurin and Luna, while Gardner's Sproufloat accompanied him into the box.

The stadium must have been at full capacity. Everybody in town was here plus hundreds more from other parts of the world to mark the momentous occasion. It didn't hurt attendance that Minakai tournaments had eclipsed most other sporting events in popularity. The three waited while the last of the tamers took their seats.

Suddenly, music boomed in the distance and a marching band entered the stadium. They strode across the grass in perfect formation, including a Frogre with its hat askew on the bass drum. There was a lot of tape across the drum and Aurin was convinced the burly ogre had broken it at least once before.

The crowd went wild and cheered for the band as they played their upbeat song. A few minutes later, the band spread out, but they kept on playing, and the prized egg was marched in and displayed on a giant screen above the stadium for everybody to see. Aurin watched his fellow tamers and could see Frederick and Hunter eyeing it with great desire. Even Kyle, who had a surprisingly good seat, was staring at the egg intently. Aurin had a sneaking suspicion that he would love nothing more than to win it, but the rancher wouldn't admit to that.

As the band continued to play, a Pyrofly and Cryoth descended upon the stadium. Pyrofly had a pale orange segmented torso with a dull horn protruding from its head and two red feelers that sat on either side of the horn. From its rear, burst a flame that acted like a propulsion system to speed it along as it beat its wings.

Cryoth was sleeker with its smooth blue body and silvery feelers. It waved its four tiny limbs as it fluttered along.

The Cryoth shot large icicles into the air and the Pyrofly smashed them into hailstones. It then melted them into raindrops with a barrage of intense fireballs. The Cryoth used its icy powers to turn it into a cascade of snowflakes that fell upon the grass.

Once the two insects disappeared, a group of Techwing flew in formation around the stadium. They swooped and twirled. There were even a few close calls with audience members, but the Minakai were in full control. It was all part of the theatre.

Lastly, a large bipedal pig Minakai stepped out onto the field. Aurin knew it to be a Hogannon, but had never seen it before. He watched it raise its cannon arms as it walked into the centre of the field. The drummers began a drumroll and when it reached a peak, the Hogannon shot a burst of fireworks into the air.

The whole stadium burst into applause as the ceremony concluded. Mayor Boren stepped out and gave a very similar speech to the one from registration day, then told everybody that the first match would begin tomorrow. He thanked everyone for coming, seemingly amazed that even the opening ceremony had full attendance, and the stadium slowly began to empty.

Aurin, Luna and Gardner all rushed to see the brackets that were listed on a large screen in the registration hall. The crowd was thick and they had to push to the front to get close enough to make out their own names and faces.

"Miriam? Can't say I know her," said Gardner. "Where are you two?"

"I'm against a girl named Robyn," said Aurin,

locating himself somewhere near the top of the screen.

"Who is Sullivan?" asked Luna. "He must be from out of town, I know most of the people around here."

Aurin shook his head and grinned widely. "It doesn't matter who these people are. We're going to beat them and face each other before the end."

"At least we're not against Hunter right off the bat," laughed Gardner.

"Oh no," said Aurin, looking at the bracket.

"Oh no? What do you mean?" asked Luna, following Aurin's line of sight. "Oh no!" she exclaimed.

Gardner caught onto what the pair were so alarmed about. "It could be worse," he said. "You could be facing him straight away."

The three stared at the screen and looked just above Luna. If she and Hunter were both victorious, then her second match would be against the tough tamer with the Flambot.

Suddenly, all of Luna's hope and optimism faded away and she was left with only dread. Shamtile waved his arms in a way that he thought was comforting, while Innogon clung tightly to the back of her neck nervously. Even the small drake knew that he was not ready for this.

Chapter 14

"Just remember everything that you've worked for and how hard you've worked for it," said Kyle to Aurin. "I don't know anything about this Robyn girl, but that just means she's not very experienced."

"She's experienced enough to qualify for the tournament," said Aurin, starting to feel the pressure of his first match looming.

"You qualified too, right? Don't be such a whiner. You're going to have to fight against both less experienced and more experienced tamers. I have it on good authority that over a hundred tamers were rejected from entry. You'll be fine."

"I did defeat you, after all."

"Say that again when we go all out and I use my best Minakai," barked Kyle.

"Stop pretending that you were going easy on me!"

"My Wingbloom would wipe the floor with your entire team in a five-on-one match, and don't you forget it." Kyle gave Aurin a slap on the back. "I'm going to go take my seat. Good luck."

Aurin stood in the corridor leading into the arena with Shamtile, Dolissile and Leonite close by. He was as ready as he could be, but it wouldn't have mattered if he wasn't. He was due to go out in front of the crowd and face Robyn and her team.

The tournament staff member put his hand to his earpiece. "You're up in a few seconds, kid. A little piece of advice for you. When they call you, give a wave to the crowd to get them on your side. It works wonders."

"Thanks," said Aurin. He took a deep breath and closed his eyes. He listened for the voice of the announcer.

"For the seventh match of the first-ever Hazelton Minakai tournament, we have two more fine competitors. Give a big hand for Aurin!"

Aurin walked out of the tunnel and was very careful not to stumble. He waved to the crowd who cheered extra hard. He glanced back at the staff member at the edge of the tunnel who gave him a thumbs up. The young tamer took his spot at the edge of the battlefield and waited.

"And his competitor, a Hazelton local, Robyn!" The cheers were extra loud for Robyn, who emerged from the far side of the arena and took her spot. This was Aurin's first time seeing her in person. She had long, dark red hair and glasses, along with a black blouse and skirt.

"Tamers!" called the announcer. "Send forth your first Minakai!"

"Dolissile, you're up!" ordered Aurin and he took his place on the battlefield.

"Anacondice!" shouted Robyn and the large icy snake slithered over to face Dolissile. Aurin remembered the trouble Hunter's Anacondice had given him, but he had grown a lot tougher since then. This time he was ready.

Dolissile rocked slowly back and forth, waiting for Anacondice to make a move. Robyn ordered it forward and it charged, leaving an icy trail on the ground. That wouldn't do much to hold the hovering Dolissile back.

"Now!" called Aurin as Anacondice came close.

The metallic dolphin burst forward at an alarming speed and before the crowd knew what had happened, Anacondice was knocked so far back that it flew past its tamer and smashed into the stadium wall. It was twitching in pain, defeated by a single strike.

"Anacondice is done for!" called the announcer. "Aurin is a newcomer to the tournaments, but I think it's clear that he's not playing around, folks. What will Robyn do next?"

As if to answer the question, Robyn summoned her Pyrofly to the field. She was visibly outraged and the little orange insect's jet was burning intensely. It charged almost as quickly as Dolissile had done, aiming straight for the dolphin.

"Go!" Aurin ordered his Minakai and Dolissile charged forward too. In a head-on collision, Dolissile would win this.

At the last second, Pyrofly veered upwards and Dolissile braked hard and spun out of control. While Dolissile recovered, the Pyrofly burst downwards and flapped its wings, sending a wave of flame at the cybernetic dolphin. Aurin's Minakai took the hit hard and dropped to the ground.

"Hang in there!" he called.

Dolissile picked itself up and moved out of the way. Pyrofly flew high into the sky and began to conjure up a large fireball. Dolissile made a move towards it and Pyrofly waited. Something was wrong.

"Veer off!" ordered Aurin, but it was too late. The Pyrofly shot the fireball downwards at Dolissile, who burst through it, thinking he had hit the flying insect. Pyrofly had used the distraction and landed atop Dolissile, who tried to shake it off while charging back to the ground.

Pyrofly began charging up its flame jet and it began to burn Dolissile. The blue dolphin's armour heated up until it was red hot, and then he passed out from the intense pain. He was out of the fight.

"A fantastic distraction from Robyn, showing that even a smaller Minakai can defeat a bigger one with an effective strategy. What will Aurin's next Minakai be?"

Luna was poking Gardner in the ribs. "What's he going to do? What's he going to do?" she asked.

"Ouch, stop it!" replied Gardner. "If it were me, I think Shamtile would be a good bet. He's nimble and could squash the little bug with a few well-timed rocks."

Gardner was right and Aurin sent forth Shamtile. The little lizard ran goofily onto the field, waving its arms. The crowd all laughed and Shamtile looked towards them, unsure of whether or not it was him that they were laughing at.

"Ignore them!" shouted Aurin. "Show them what you're made of."

Shamtile hunkered down and encased his arms in stone gloves. The Pyrofly began to throw fireballs, but Shamtile beat them away with ease, the gloves protecting his hands.

"An impressive move," said the announcer.

Pyrofly began to glow an even brighter, more intense orange and then charged forward. It was hoping to burst through Shamtile's defences.

Shamtile stomped his feet and summoned a rock wall, but the Pyrofly broke through and narrowly missed the lizard. Luckily, the wall had slowed it down just enough to make it an easier target. Shamtile discarded his gloves and began to hurl rocks at the bug.

"Encapsulate!" ordered Aurin.

Shamtile conjured up dozens of rocks and surrounded his foe with them. He waved his hands and the rocks all closed in quickly around Pyrofly, trapping it within. Everybody from the tamers to the crowd watched intently as the rock ball shook with the Minakai trying to break free.

Shamtile held on tightly and then pulled the rocks tighter. He pulled until the ball stopped struggling, then released it. Pyrofly fell to the ground, defeated, as its tamer looked on in shock. Aurin grinned proudly at his Minakai.

The crowd were cheering wildly as the announcer tried to make himself heard. "What a move! Young Aurin still has two Minakai while Robyn is down to her final one. Which Minakai will it be and can it save her from a knockout in the first round of the tournament?"

"This one won't be so easy for you!" Robyn called to Aurin from across the battlefield. "Go Peekawe!"

A large turquoise bird, far larger than its earlier form, Peekan, descended from the sky and hung just above the grass. It looked serious and far more formidable than either of Robyn's previous team members.

"It's got the weight and speed advantage, Shamtile," said Aurin. "Don't let it get too close to you or you'll be in big trouble."

Shamtile gave a warbling grunt of agreement. The Peekawe began twisting and twirling around the battlefield as Shamtile hurled rocks, trying to knock it from the sky. The speedy bird effortlessly dodged the boulders that were being thrown its way and delivered a direct hit with its beak to Shamtile. The little lizard was knocked down and Aurin was left with only one monster.

"That looked painful," said the announcer. "It's down to the last Minakai for each of our competitors. Who will come out on top?"

Aurin gritted his teeth in frustration. "Leonite, it's down to you."

The steel blue lion nodded and jumped onto the field, eager to prove himself since his evolution from Cubtem. He was faster, stronger and more confident than his previous form. Now it was time to see how he fared against a tough and well-trained opponent.

Leonite watched and waited as the Peekawe resumed its previous tactic of zooming around the battlefield erratically. His eyes narrowed, keeping a careful eye on his opponent. Suddenly, the Peekawe made for Leonite and the lion leapt upwards.

The crowd were in shock as Peekawe took to the skies with Leonite clinging to its back, sinking his claws deep through the bird's feathers and into its flesh. The Peekawe cawed loudly in anguish as the sharp claws sank deeper and deeper.

"Shake it off! Fly higher and throw him to the ground," ordered Robyn. "You have the advantage, Peekawe!"

Her Minakai obeyed and began to climb higher and higher. If Leonite fell from this height, he was done for. Aurin braced himself for the worst but knew that his Minakai could get out of this. It wasn't over yet.

Peekawe spun around rapidly as it ascended, trying to throw Leonite to the ground, but the lion was clinging on tightly. It bravely lifted one of its claws out and dug it into the back of the Peekawe's head. It cried out even louder than before and began to slow.

The entire stadium was watching the sky as Peekawe began to drop to the ground. It sank slowly at first but then sped up. Both Minakai were in big trouble. Aurin and Robyn's mouths hung open as they waited to see what would happen.

Leonite jumped from the Peekawe a second before it hit the ground and rolled away. It was a hard hit, but Leonite climbed to his feet shakily. He had escaped the worst of the damage. Peekawe on the other hand lay motionless, having taken the full impact of its body colliding with the ground.

"It looks like we have our winner, folks!" cried the announcer. "Give it up for Aurin who will advance to the second round."

The crowd cheered wildly and Aurin looked over to Luna and Gardner who were on their feet, jumping for joy. He had done it. He had won his first match and had proved to himself that he was meant to be here. He could stand up against tough tamers and come out on top.

Robyn crossed the battlefield towards him and Aurin walked over to meet her. He outstretched his hand and she took it. "That was a good match," he said to her.

"Very good for you, but not so much for me," she

laughed. "I'll be back next year for a rematch. I know what to expect from you now."

"Why wait a year? Perhaps we'll meet in the tower."

The two parted ways and Aurin made his through the waiting room and took the roundabout route to the stands to join Luna. Gardner was missing, as his first match was about to begin once the battlefield was ready to go. A number of Petalcubs ran across the field, repairing the grass at surprising speed, leaving it pristine once again.

"You did really well," said Luna, looking proud. "I was getting nervous at the end, but it looks like evolving Cubtem was the right move. He couldn't have pulled that off if he was much smaller."

"Thanks," said Aurin, feeling slightly embarrassed. "I think you're right. It was the correct decision to evolve him."

"Oh look, they're starting!" Luna exclaimed as the announcer signalled for Gardner to make his way onto the field.

It was another exciting battle with Gardner coming out on top. His team carried him to an impressive victory, finishing with his Sproufloat using his wings to cut through a Pottemp. Aurin could see just how far his friend had come since their first encounter a couple of months ago.

Aurin cheered happily for him, while Luna clapped along a bit less enthusiastically. It was starting to dawn on her just how high the calibre of tamers who had entered the tournament was. The nerves were starting to build for her, and she would fight for the first time tomorrow.

Chapter 15

"You'll be fine, Luna," said Aurin, sounding like Kyle had sounded before Aurin's first match. "Just remember all of the training and trust in your Minakai. You can do this, okay?"

Luna's hands were trembling and her knees were shaking while she bit her lower lip. She did not look remotely confident, and her Minakai were trying to comfort her too. "I can't go out there. I'm going to look like a fool! What was I thinking, Aurin? Tell me!"

"You can go out there. You will go out there and you're going to win. Do you hear me?" pushed Aurin. Luna's Innogon, Tadpool and Spritzard all nodded in agreement. "Your Minakai believe in you, so it's time to believe in both yourself and them. Okay?"

"Okay," said Luna, still looking terrified.

"They're going to call you in the next minute or two, so I'm going to go to the stands and watch, alright? If you get nervous, just look to me."

"Can you wait here? Please?"

Aurin looked to the tournament official, who gave him a nod. "Yes," said Aurin, "of course I can. Your friends Emily and Hannah are probably supporting you from the stands already anyway. Shamtile and I can be down here cheering for you every step of the way, right buddy?"

Shamtile was fully recovered from the previous day's injuries and danced enthusiastically. He warbled and screeched, trying to boost Luna's confidence. He was certain that it was working, but Aurin knew it wasn't. Try as they all might, the only one who could push Luna through her fear was Luna herself.

The official put his hand to his earpiece, as he had done for Aurin. "You're up in a few seconds," he informed Luna.

Tears were starting to form in her eyes and her breathing grew quick and became shallow. She looked like she was on the verge of a panic attack.

"Good luck," said Aurin hurriedly.

"Welcome everyone to today's first match," said the announcer. "I hope you're all ready for a very exciting day, just as it was yesterday. First up, we have a tamer all the way from...well, right here! Please welcome Luna!"

Luna froze and Aurin had to give her a push out of the tunnel, as her Minakai waited at the edge of the battlefield to be summoned. Luna walked very slowly and took her spot, forgetting to wave at the crowd. They cheered for her anyway, no doubt sensing her anxiety even from a distance.

"Her competitor today is another Hazelton local. Please give it up for Sullivan!"

The crowd cheered for him even louder as he waved and bowed to them. He was working the crowd well and Aurin knew this wouldn't help Luna's confidence one bit. No matter, there was nothing he could do now other than watch. Luna had asked him to dress up in her clothes and a wig and fight on her behalf. He wasn't entirely certain that she was joking and refused immediately.

"Tamers!" called the announcer. "Let's see your first Minakai!"

"Go Flowl!" called Sullivan as the burning bird ran onto the battlefield and began hopping in place.

"I-I-Innogon," stammered Luna as her young drake ran forward, already knowing that he was up first. He wanted to make her proud and give her an early lead.

Flowl charged at Innogon who started shooting jets of water at it, but Flowl was surprisingly quick. Innogon had defeated many of these Minakai in the tower, but a trained one was another story. It moved effortlessly out of the way and leapt into the air as it got close.

It shot a burst of fireballs at Innogon, who was caught off guard and knocked out straight away. The crowd were in shock and Sullivan looked very smug. Luna's knees were shaking wildly at her favourite Minakai's easy defeat.

"Oh no, oh no," Aurin could hear her muttering.

"That was quick!" exclaimed the announcer. "Can Luna come back from this?"

"Tad...Tadpool," she ordered, as the bipedal frog ran out to take Innogon's place. "Make it...um...slippery?"

Tadpool blew an icy wind and covered the battlefield in a thick sheet of ice. Sullivan's Flowl began to emit embers that melted the ice almost immediately.

While it was distracted, Tadpool ran forward and headbutted the flaming bird, sending it flying through the air. Tadpool blew another icy wind and made a thick patch of ice right where Flowl was about to land. It hit the patch hard and was knocked out.

"Yes!" exclaimed Luna as Tadpool began dancing in celebration.

"A great comeback by Luna's Tadpool! What will her opponent do?" pondered the announcer as the crowd cheered.

Sullivan looked rattled. "Gorun!" he called as a rock bearing small yellow crystals emerged from his summoning stone. It sat motionless on the ground.

"Huh?" said Luna, looking confused. What could this rock do against something more mobile? Was it a joke? Aurin, however, knew Sullivan had a plan.

Tadpool shot an icicle from its back and it collided with the Gorun, who toppled over. It otherwise didn't seem fazed. It didn't even have a face to pick up a more clear reaction. The little rock was giving nothing away, while its tamer smirked.

Luna's Minakai ran towards it and pushed it forward with its foot, checking to see if it was even alive.

"Now!" called Sullivan, as the ground began to shake beneath Tadpool. The Gorun let itself fall, rolled over and shot a crystalline spike into Tadpool. It then did it again, and again. Tadpool was gravely injured by the sharp crystals, and Luna recalled him.

"That was a hard hit!" cried the announcer. "Luna is down to her last Minakai and Sullivan still has a spare in the tank. It's not looking good, folks. Can the young Hazelton local make a comeback after this? Let's see what she can do."

Luna was shaking again, but she clenched her fists and held back her tears. She raised her hand and pointed at the Gorun. "Spritzard! Blast that rock out of the stadium!" she ordered as her evolved Dripper joined the battle.

Spritzard flew towards Gorun with her arms outstretched and grabbed the rock. She tossed it into the air and shot jets of water from her fingerless hands, aiming straight for Gorun. The water jet was intense and relentless, and the rock was thrown high into the air.

When it came back down, it was falling fast. It hit the ground with a loud crack and everybody could see its crystals had broken. Sullivan dropped to his knees. "No!" he cried. "Thunding, get in there!" he ordered before the announcer had a chance to make any commentary.

A small grey humanoid wearing golden armour emerged from one of his summoning stones. It held a metallic spear which fizzled and crackled with lightning. Aurin and Luna had never seen this Minakai before, but it looked angry and ready for a fight.

"Supercharge it!" called Sullivan, and Thunding threw its spear at the jelly-like water Minakai. The spear narrowly missed and a wave of electricity spread from it upon impact with the grass. Thunding raised its hand and the spear returned to it.

"Don't let it hit you with that!" called Luna, the adrenaline flowing through her. "Surround it with water, so that it can't move as fast."

Spritzard shot a large wave of water at the Thunding and held it in place. Thunding tried to swim forward and out of the bubble, but Spritzard held strong and moved the bubble of water along with it.

Sullivan was getting visibly frustrated, having been convinced earlier that he would have an easy victory. "What are you doing? Throw your spears!" he demanded. Thunding tried to throw, but the water was slowing down too much. "Fine! Blast yourself upwards!"

Thunding shot a burst of lightning from its feet and flew into the air, wielding its spear high. Free from the trappings of the water bubble, it hurled its spear at Spritzard again, who split herself in two to avoid the oncoming attack. Mouths hung open in shock. The crowd were amazed by this ability as Spritzard's two halves recombined.

"You don't see that often, do you?" asked the announcer. "Luna is definitely not out of the game. Will she still be able to pull off a victory against the formidable Sullivan?"

"No more defence, Spritzard," said Luna. "Full force jet!"

Spritzard shot a weak jet of water from one hand that the Thunding dodged, but it wasn't prepared for Spritzard's other hand to shoot the strong jet that Luna had ordered. It took the blast hard and was thrown back against the wall of the stadium. Its head took a heavy hit that even its armour could not protect it from. It was done.

Luna was shocked that she had won, even as the crowd cheered loudly. Aurin clapped enthusiastically from the tunnel, proud that she had pulled it off. He knew that she could; the biggest obstacle was herself.

Her Spritzard flew over to her and she grabbed her jelly hands and began to spin her around in celebration. Sullivan meanwhile had dropped to his knees, devastated that he had lost. He took a moment to regain his composure and stood up, also clapping. He couldn't be seen as a sore loser, after all.

"And there you have it!" called the announcer. "Luna from Hazelton has won her first match in the first tournament in her hometown. It's quite poetic folks, isn't it? Let's see what she can do next."

Aurin and Luna headed to the stands to watch the next match as the Minakai cleaned up the wet and battered battlefield. They had both successfully won their first matches, but they knew the toughest opponents were yet to come. Aurin's next opponent was a tamer called Jimmy and Luna would have to face off against the fearsome Hunter.

As one of the tamers walked away from the stands to check his own next opponent, he was stopped by a figure in the shadows.

"You had better not lose," said the figure sternly. "Not that the competition can compare to you."

"I won't, boss," said the blonde tamer. "I've won my first match, if you recall. Or were you not in the stands for that?"

The figure let out a low laugh. "I have to be. It would be a bad look if I wasn't in attendance at the tournament every day. One must maintain appearances, after all. All other official business has been passed to the deputy for now."

"Are you not enjoying your holiday? It's been quite the show so far."

"Things are getting exciting," admitted the man in the shadows. "You would think that the hype would fade after the first matches, but people are getting more jubilant by the day. I suspect that once we hit the top sixty-four, then we'll be able to strike unnoticed. We have the metal elementals working on their magnetism as we speak."

"What of the secondary plan, Taurus? Do you think Libra is right?"

"I'm starting to suspect so. She doesn't quite have the sway that I have, but I'm sure that she can make a few of the disappearances go away. We need to make sure that it's subtle, of course. If we strike too often and take too many, we won't be able to suppress things the way we need to."

"Tell that to Sagittarius," said the tamer, looking away. "If anything will make it fail, it's him. He's too headstrong to be trusted with any sort of high-level decisions."

"And what of you?"

"I'm focusing on my training and the tournament, just like you asked."

"You're sure that the tournament isn't more important to you than Zodiac and our mission?"

"Nothing is more important than the mission. The prized egg will be ours and it will benefit our mission more than any other Minakai we possess. Its potential is endless, as you know. It's just a shame that you can't use that influence of yours to take it without fuss."

"I've told you that it's out of my hands. The tournament is not run by the town, it's all Department of Minakai business. The only thing we do is provide the venue."

"I know, it was just a joke," said the tamer as he walked away.

"Good luck, Frederick," said the man, putting on a more booming voice. "I hope you perform well."

Chapter 16

Aurin and Luna were on floor nine of Harmony Tower, taking a break from training at the ranch. It seemed funny to both of them that they were more relaxed here of all places, somewhere substantially more dangerous than the safety of the ranch. A tower run felt like a moment of respite when the tournament was all that was on anybody's mind.

In today's run, Aurin had been lucky enough to find a Lunar Shard that he planned to use to evolve his Happynut. It had received the least attention of all his Minakai on account of it being so young, but he was hurrying to make sure that it was tournament-ready.

"Are you not planning to use your Happynut?" Aurin asked Luna.

"I don't work as fast as you," she said. "I know my

Happynut won't be ready to fight at this level after such a short time."

"Minakai grow strong quickly, no?"

"Maybe, but I'm worried that you're pushing yours too hard because you want to win the tournament so badly."

Aurin considered this and thought that perhaps she was right. He had owned all of his previous Minakai a lot longer before evolving them. Kyle had said something similar previously about getting used to Minakai and their abilities before boosting them up to the next level.

"Okay," said Aurin. "I'm going to keep training Happynut, but I won't evolve him until he's had a victory in the tournament. That's how I'll know that we're both ready for him to become a Melansprout. What do you think?"

"I think that's a good idea," smiled Luna. She had expected him to ignore her advice, so she was a lot more pleased than she let on. "It's starting to get late. Should we go back and rest? We both have our second battles tomorrow."

Aurin agreed and used his Orb of Return, pulling both tamers from the tower and throwing them onto the grass. They staggered, but were able to maintain their footing, having now gotten much more used to the unpleasant sensation of teleportation.

Aurin walked Luna back to her house near the centre of Hazelton and said hello to her parents before returning to the ranch to speak to Kyle.

"Good run today?" asked the rancher upon seeing Aurin strolling up the path.

"I can't complain," said Aurin with a shrug. "Happynut is getting stronger, and I found a Lunar

Shard that I'm itching to use."

"Didn't we have this conversation before?" asked Kyle, raising an eyebrow.

"Don't worry, I'm not going to evolve him yet. I want him to have a chance to fight in the tournament first. If he's ready afterwards, that's fine."

"You've learned well! I'm glad you're listening to me."

"Luna actually put the idea in my head."

Kyle threw back his head in frustration. "I could tell you the sky is blue and you'd take little notice, but if Luna said it then you'd consider it a profound revelation."

"The sky is orange, Kyle. It's sunset," remarked Aurin. Kyle shot him a look of utter disdain and got back to work while Aurin laughed.

The announcer's voice boomed throughout the stadium as the crowd cheered wildly. "Aurin's Hornferno made quick work of Jimmy's Dopefish. What will the mighty red dinosaur do against his opponent's next Minakai?"

Jimmy wasn't deterred by losing his first Minakai and sent out his second; a Melansprout. It stumbled forward, looking depressed to even be there. It was not unusual for this Minakai to look downcast; it was the natural state of the sad creature. As Happynut's evolutionary tree progressed, its emotional state grew less and less stable.

Hornferno scoffed and puffed smoke from his nose as the Melansprout conjured up a storm of leaves. It sent the leaves towards Hornferno rapidly, hoping to slice up the dino with the sharp edges, but the dinosaur burned the leaves to ashes with a burst of flame from his mouth.

Having decimated Melansprout's attack, Hornferno charged forward and rammed his horns into Jimmy's Minakai who fell backwards and cried. Tears streamed down from its eyes and Hornferno's mouth curled into a rare smile, relishing the moment. He shot a fireball at his downed opponent, ending the fight before it had the chance to truly begin.

"That looked painful!" exclaimed the announcer as the crowd gasped. "Hornferno is not one to show mercy, but perhaps he was right? Maybe Melansprout was just faking those tears and it was gearing up for a sneak attack. We'll never know, folks."

Jimmy still did not look alarmed and sent out his final Minakai. It was a tiny golden alien-like creature with no arms. It had two fists resting beside its body, but no arms. The fists were only connected to its torso by a bluish vapour that encapsulated them and spread to the Minakai's torso.

"What is that thing?" muttered Aurin, having never seen this Minakai before.

"Jimmy has just sent out an Arium, folks!" called the announcer. "A sighting almost as rare as a real alien encounter! This little psychic creature packs a hefty punch."

Hornferno scoffed at the opponent standing before him. He ran towards the Arium, using the same tactic he had used to take out Jimmy's Melansprout. Suddenly, Hornferno was swept aside and thrown backwards.

Aurin was shocked. What had happened? He looked more closely and could see the Arium had moved its hands with its mind and redirected Hornferno. It had happened more quickly than a muscle could move. Aurin now saw the danger of the telekinetic fighter; it was a far more formidable foe than it looked.

"Don't get close!" Aurin ordered.

Hornferno stood up, but Arium's fists were immediately flung across the battlefield and began pummelling Hornferno into submission, all without moving its body once. Try as he might, Hornferno was unable to stand up or even drag himself out of the way. The dinosaur was out of this battle.

Jimmy looked very smug about his victory, but Aurin suspected that he was being carried in the tournament by one tough Minakai rather than his skill as a tamer. His other two Minakai had fallen almost instantly.

"Happynut!" called Aurin, sending Hornferno back to the ranch. The little nature elemental merrily bounced forward to take his comrade's place.

Aurin knew he had to get creative to overcome Arium's powers. He quickly cooked up a plan. "Make the grass grow around him," he called. Happynut spun around and did a little dance which caused the grass on the field to grow up, obscuring Arium from view.

Aurin quietly recalled Happynut and sent out Shamtile to fight instead. The little lizard ran into the fray and encased his own fists in stone. Arium's two fists shot out from the grass and Shamtile blocked both with his own. Arium was not expecting to be faced with such a solid defence.

Aurin switched his Minakai again, and Happynut

charged toward his opponent. "It's time to show him your roots," Aurin ordered his newest Minakai.

Happynut did another upbeat dance and, suddenly, tree roots sprang from the ground and wrapped themselves around Arium's fists. The roots were tough and Arium was struggling to pull free.

"Headfirst!" called Aurin as Happynut bounded forward and threw himself into the grass. There was a loud crack and the grass slowly retreated back into the ground and reverted to its regular length.

"Arium is done for!" cried the announcer to cheers from the audience. "Aurin has won his second match of the tournament and will proceed onto the third. Sadly, Jimmy won't go any further, but that Arium of his was mighty impressive. Give them both a big hand, folks!"

Aurin and Jimmy walked into the centre of the battlefield and shook each other's hands. "Where did you get that Arium?" asked Aurin.

"My dad brought me into the tower at the centre of Ludonia," said Jimmy with a big grin. "He took me and my Minakai all the way to the twentieth floor and it was a lucky find. It's pretty good, right?"

"It's great, I'd love to battle it again sometime," secretly marvelling at the idea of somebody making it to the twentieth floor of Ludonia Tower. Jimmy's father must have been quite the tamer.

"I'm sure we'll get the chance, Aurin. Good luck in the rest of the tournament."

The two parted ways amicably and Aurin headed into the stands to watch the final match of the day that was due to start soon.

"I didn't know you could switch Minakai in the middle of a battle," said Luna, looking puzzled at Aurin's tactic. "Isn't that cheating?"

"Did you not read the tournament rulebook before entering?" asked Aurin.

"No," admitted Luna, making Aurin laugh. "Although, I probably should read it. Changing Minakai would make it easier to gain the elemental advantage, wouldn't it?"

"That can help, but I wanted to catch the Arium off guard. Shamtile is a good offensive Minakai, but he's even better defensively, and that's what I needed to defeat Jimmy."

"Why did you switch back to Happynut?"

"I wanted to show the little guy that he could stand up against another tamer's Minakai and not just the tower monsters. I'm confident I could have won with Shamtile alone."

"So, it wasn't to justify evolving him before he's ready?"

"Not at all," said Aurin with a big grin. "He can stay as he is for a little while longer. He's shown that he can pack a punch now. Did you see his nature skills and the cannonball headbutt? If he's capable of that now, just think of what he can do when he finally does get to evolve."

"Okay, I believe you," laughed Luna. "Yes, he was very impressive. Who are you up against next?"

Aurin looked over at Gardner who was sitting a few seats to the left. "That depends on how Gardner's next match goes," he said.

"He's gotten a lot stronger than when you first battled. Both of you have."

Aurin nodded. "It'll be a good match. I'm certain that Gardner will win, and we'll get to battle very soon. I just have a feeling about it."

"Where did Jimmy go?" Luna asked, scanning the

small crowd in the tamer box.

"He must have gone home. I wouldn't want to watch the next fight if I had just lost. I'm sure he'll be back tomorrow once he's ready."

Jimmy walked out of the stadium, upset from his loss, but glad he made it to the second round of the tournament. He strolled along the square as the sun began to set, then walked through the quiet streets of the town, unaware of the shadowy figures that were following him.

Chapter 17

Luna was at the ranch giving her Minakai a pep talk. Her match with Hunter was in an hour and she'd spent the morning watching Aurin defeat Jimmy. Aurin would have understood if she hadn't attended, considering she had little time to prepare, but she wouldn't let him down.

"Okay, you three," she said to Spritzard, Tadpool and Innogon. "We won our last battle by the skin of our teeth, but this time we're going to win by a mile. We are going to grind our foes into the dirt, so badly that they won't be able to walk afterwards...but not so badly that they're permanently maimed. That wouldn't be good. Alright?"

Spritzard twirled around, Tadpool nodded in agreement and Innogon jumped and yapped. After her victory, Luna was feeling optimistic. Even an opponent like Hunter couldn't bring her down much right now.

"Kyle, what do you know about Hunter?" asked Luna.

"What makes you so sure I know anything about him?" he asked.

"Because you know everything about everything. That's what Aurin says, at least. He isn't being sarcastic about it either."

"I'm touched," chortled Kyle. "Are you sure that you want to know?"

"Yes," replied Luna with certainty.

"Hunter was in the national championships last year and he did pretty well for himself. I can't remember his ranking, but his Flambot was a monster. It tore through his opponents in his qualifying tournament and then a few more in Ludonia. He's a real force to be reckoned with, as I'm sure you noticed when he battled Aurin."

Luna gulped nervously. "He's a regional champion?"

"Yes. Regional champion and national contender. I'm sure you won't, but please don't underestimate him. His battle style isn't cruel, but it is very direct. If he sees an opening, you can bet that he'll take it."

"Please, Kyle," Luna begged. "Have you got any last-minute advice on how to defeat him?"

"Your best bet is to strike hard and fast. Give him no chance to size you up. If you can take out his first Minakai, that gives you the number advantage. You could get lucky and use three Minakai to tire out his two remaining Minakai."

"That's a lot easier said than done."

"It won't be easy at all," admitted Kyle, "but it's the best chance you've got."

Luna thanked him, now feeling nervous again, and

brought Innogon with her into the town. She decided that she would summon Spritzard and Tadpool into the battle rather than let them wait by the sidelines. Most tamers tended to do that to have the element of surprise on their side.

Aurin was waiting in the stands with Shamtile, who was waving his arms in anticipation. Luna and Hunter would take to the battlefield any moment and the atmosphere was thick with anticipation.

"Stop it," snapped Aurin. "I'm already anxious for her and you aren't helping."

Shamtile slapped him on the back of the head and squealed at him. He resumed his dance immediately.

"You're right, I'm sorry," said Aurin, rubbing the back of his head. "I shouldn't take it out on you, buddy. What do you think will happen today?"

Shamtile yelped and screeched various garbled sounds, making no sense to anybody in the vicinity, but Aurin was pretty sure he got the gist of it.

"I agree, it's going to be a tough battle. Spritzard is her best bet if Innogon gets taken out early. Maybe she'll lead with Spritzard this time? She hasn't told me. How are the Minakai feeling?"

Shamtile growled.

"Keeping it together? That's good. It'll stop Luna from panicking too much."

Feedback from the microphone brought the chattering crowds to silence as the announcer readied himself. "Everybody, it's time for our next match! It's the final one of the day and it's going to be a good one. Please give it up for a national contender from last year's Ludonia tournament, Hunter!"

The crowd whooped and cheered. Aurin did not know Hunter before recently, but it was clear that a lot of the audience did. He clapped politely, having a great deal of respect for Hunter's abilities, but he didn't overdo it in case he looked unsupportive to Luna.

"His opponent today, fresh from her first-ever ranked win...Hazelton's own Luna!"

The crowd cheered almost as much for Luna as they did for Hunter. It was noticeably louder than during her last match. Her victory must have won her a few fans.

The match began and Luna sent out her Spritzard against Hunter's Vinewolf. The very same one that Aurin had faced not so long ago.

"Spritzard," said Luna, "be careful because the petals around its neck are razor sharp. Make use of your body structure against him."

Vinewolf sent its petals shooting forward on the green vines and it whipped at Spritzard. Her body split in two as the petals cut through her, then she recombined once they retracted towards the green wolf's neck.

Hunter smiled, knowing what he needed to do. As Spritzard shot a blast of water, his Minakai dodged with ease and whipped its vines once more, this time repeatedly. Spritzard was cut up into a dozen pieces, then she recombined again.

"Keep it up," said Hunter, as his Minakai whipped again. Each time Spritzard recombined, she was cut up. With each cut, her healing slowed down. When Hunter's Vinewolf finally relented, Spritzard merged back into one and then collapsed, all her energy now spent.

"No!" cried Luna, as her strongest Minakai fell. She sent Spritzard back to the ranch and ordered Tadpool into battle.

The icy frog landed on the field and breathed a jet of cold air onto the ground in front, turning the grass into a frosty sheet. "This has to work," Luna muttered to herself as she forced Vinewolf to remain at a distance.

As Hunter's Vinewolf hurled its petals once more, Tadpool breathed his ice onto them, weighing them down as they froze. Vinewolf struggled to lift the petals and reeled in its vines, dragging them slowly backwards.

"Now!" Luna called as Tadpool ran towards his foe, propelling himself along the ice and then sprinting along the grass.

Vinewolf tried to dodge, but its own weighted vines slowed it down as the petals remained encapsulated in the ice. Tadpool sprung into the air and hurled a barrage of icicles at his foe, who managed to dodge most of them, but a few lucky strikes landed in its side and shoulder. It fell to the ground, unable to battle any further.

"An unbelievable comeback!" shouted the announcer, unable to contain his own excitement. "That was something I don't think anybody expected. What a tactic from Luna. It goes to show that a good plan can make up for being outmatched in size and strength."

The crowd were shocked, almost as much as Luna was. Hunter slowly nodded and let out a faint smile. "Well done," he called over to the comparative amateur. "I won't underestimate you any further, it's time for the big guns. Flambot!"

The large furnace-like Minakai spawned onto the field, standing tall on its thick legs, with its two flames blazing from the back of its head and its lower back, as though it were a tail. It stomped forwards, its large blue eye focused on Tadpool.

Tadpool kept its distance and threw icicles at the blazing behemoth, but Flambot tossed fire that melted the icicles instantly and it merely ended up watering the grass. The frog looked unnerved. He couldn't attack easily from a distance, so he would either need a distraction or to get closer.

"Tadpool, make it hail!" called Luna. The crowd murmured in confusion about what Luna was doing, but she had a plan.

Tadpool conjured up a hailstorm straight above Flambot. The ice pellets were flung down, much faster than hail you would find on a cold day. This storm was designed to hit hard. Flambot blasted fire at the hail, causing it all to melt. It started raining heavily as the ice melted and it dampened Flambot's blazing flames. They were slowly diminishing, its weakness revealed.

"Turn up the heat!" ordered Hunter.

Flambot's stomach began to rumble and its flames erupted with new strength. The rain evaporated before it could even touch the Minakai and rendered Tadpool's attack useless.

"End it," said Hunter.

His Minakai opened up its stomach furnace and sent a jet of flame out that burned up the field before engulfing Luna's Tadpool. His icicles melted and then he collapsed to the ground, with Luna hurriedly sending him back to the ranch.

"That was intense!" roared the announcer. "Luna's Tadpool had an impressive performance against two

Minakai, but it couldn't keep up with Hunter's Flambot."

"Inno!" called Luna as the small dragon rushed onto the field. "That attack took up a lot of energy, so hit him fast. Surf along the field!"

Her Innogon summoned a wave of water and he rode it towards the Flambot. Once he was close, Flambot shot another fire blast, aiming straight for the drake, but he shot his water jet downwards, sending himself high into the sky.

"Full strength!" cried Luna, and Innogon unleashed a powerful water beam from its mouth. It hit Flambot straight in the stomach, seeping through its furnace grill and dousing its fuel. The robot was knocked back into the wall and lay on the ground, unable to battle.

"Yes!" cheered Luna, but Hunter began shaking his head with another small smile on his face. "No, it can't still be going," said Luna as Flambot began to stir.

Its flame was a small, glowing ember that began growing and expanding into an inferno once more. Innogon landed on the ground, softening the descent with a controlled jet. He looked unsettled as Flambot stood up, back to full strength once more.

"I'll give you the chance to bow out," said Hunter as Flambot waited patiently. "You know how this will end."

"No," replied Luna. "We'll keep fighting. Innogon, finish it this time."

Innogon shot a much weaker jet than before at Flambot, who sent its own burst of fire towards the draconic Minakai. The attacks collided, but the fire broke through the water, turning it to steam. It hit Innogon, who couldn't take the heat. He was out of the fight and Luna was out of the tournament.

"That had to hurt!" called the announcer. "And with

that impressive comeback, Hunter is one step closer to reaching the National Championship. Luna had a strong performance, but it just wasn't enough. I don't know about you folks, but this tournament is really starting to heat up. I can't wait to see what's in store next."

Everybody applauded for the two tamers. Aurin was sad for his friend, knowing that she would take the loss hard. Much to his surprise, she was smiling and clapped for Hunter too.

He approached and the two shook hands. "You pack quite the punch," he said to her. "If you keep training, I know you can reach much further next year. All you need is to build up experience and have a few more strategies like the one you and your Tadpool had cooked up."

"Thanks, Hunter," said Luna, wiping the tears from her eyes, keeping her smile wide. "If you think I'm good, wait until you fight Aurin again. He's been training specifically to defeat you."

Hunter laughed. "I look forward to that. Perhaps we'll be paired up soon. Best of luck with your training."

The two left the battlefield and Luna walked outside, saddened by her defeat but pleased with her performance. She didn't truly expect to be able to defeat Hunter, but taking out one of his Minakai was a great achievement in her eyes. It was time to double down on her goal of becoming a great medic, knowing that her Minakai would carry her far in the tower.

Little did Luna know that a figure watched her from the shadows. He wore a lion mask and had his summoning stones at the ready. As he emerged, he spotted three figures joining Luna.

"You did great, Luna," said Aurin proudly as

Gardner nodded along. "Hunter's very tough and his Vinewolf wasn't an easy customer to deal with. Tadpool and Innogon really shone today. You should be very happy.

"See what you can do when you work hard and put the effort in?" asked Kyle. "You even surprised me and I haven't been surprised in a while," he added with a chuckle.

The figure in the shadows retreated, stowing his summoning stones. He didn't want to risk getting caught and being removed from the tournament. Taurus could do his own dirty work if he wanted to grab the tamers' summoning stones. This greed would threaten all the effort they put into the infiltration. No, Leo would bide his time and go for the egg when the time was right.

Chapter 18

The tournament had taken a break on the Sunday to allow challengers to rest up and prepare for their next matches. It was most welcome as Aurin and Luna were already starting to feel burned out; Luna in particular after her defeat by Hunter's Flambot.

"Why are you so tired when you get to relax now?" asked Aurin. He realised afterwards how callous he sounded.

"I'm tired on your behalf," said Luna, as the pair wandered the seventh floor of the tower. "You're working so hard that it's spilling over onto me. I can't believe you're using your rest day to train more."

"You can bet that Gardner's training."

"Probably," admitted Luna, "but that doesn't mean it's the right strategy. What if your Minakai are too tired tomorrow?"

"You've seen how fast they recover. Tadpool had his icicles melted off and they regrew after some good food and rest."

Everybody still standing in the tournament had made it to the top sixty-four, with only a quarter of the qualifying tamers remaining. It felt like Aurin had come a long way, but there were six matches standing between him and being the tournament champion. So close, yet so far; there was no way that he could rest.

"Watch out for the Shroomlie!" exclaimed Aurin, grabbing Luna and pulling her out of the way of its spores. They both moved back to a safe distance. "Shammy, get him!" ordered Aurin.

Shamtile charged in, waving his arms. He erupted a stalagmite from the ground and it slammed the Shroomlie into the wall, taking it out with ease. A technique like that had been well outside of Shamtile's abilities a few months ago.

"Good job, mate," said Aurin as Shamtile danced around enthusiastically. Innogon danced too but wasn't quite as rhythmically blessed as his fellow reptilian Minakai.

The quartet roamed the floor, adding coins to their ever-expanding pile. Kyle had yet to earnestly ask for any rent, but Aurin had been slipping some of the spoils from his tower runs into Kyle's wallet when he wasn't looking. He didn't like that he had been a bit of a leech after the rancher had done so much for him. Luna suspected that Kyle knew that Aurin had been doing this, but hadn't said anything, silently appreciating the gesture.

"Straight ahead," said Aurin as a Lunar Shard came into view in a room at the end of the corridor. The magical tower was always full of surprises, both pleasant and unpleasant.

"It's all yours," said Luna as they hurried forwards.

Inside the room was a large, sleeping Frogre. The icy ogre snored loudly, and the group stopped moving, not wanting to wake it. Aurin tiptoed forwards and lifted the Lunar Shard, quietly stashing it in his bag.

A sudden whoosh broke out and a small grey-feathered sprite materialised out of thin air in a whirling vortex. It was a Feathrus. It had two large eyes and a short curved body along with two tiny wings that emerged from its back.

"Gurgh!" grunted the Frogre as it awoke. The two wild Minakai attacked Aurin, but Shamtile conjured a stone wall to protect his master. The masked lizard made for the Frogre while Innogon charged at the Feathrus.

Shamtile covered his fists in stone and brawled with the Frogre. He was easily outmatched in size and strength, but each block caused the Frogre's blood to start seeping through its gloves. Once it was unable to punch without immense pain, Shamtile sent a barrage of rocks at the beast, burying it within the tower.

Meanwhile, Innogon spat water jets at the flying sprite which were all cast aside by the intense gusts of wind the Feathrus summoned forth.

"If you can't hit it directly, hit it from all angles," ordered Luna.

Innogon nodded and summoned two waves of water, one on the Feathrus's left and one on its right. He pulled them together and they collided, submerging the Minakai. The two tamers stood back, to avoid getting soaked.

The Feathrus spun around and burst free from the

flood, but it was met with another water jet to the face and it was ejected from the tower, back to wherever it came from.

"Do you want to quit while we're ahead?" asked Luna, as she swung Innogon around in celebration.

Aurin and Shamtile looked at each other. "No," said Aurin as Shamtile warbled.

"Okay," said Luna cheerily, content to continue onwards.

"Are you two alright?" asked Kyle as Aurin and Luna slumped slowly towards the ranch. Both shook their heads in response, clearly exhausted from whatever had hit them in the tower. "Ejected?" asked Kyle, wide-eyed.

"Narrowly...avoided," panted Aurin.

"Swarmed by Electrout on a water-laden floor," said Luna.

"You'd think that a water-based floor would be your bread and butter," chuckled Kyle, enjoying the two's misery. "You don't come across floors like that often, but at least you didn't get a floor with lava patches. Those are usually higher up."

Aurin and Luna looked at each other, unsure if he was joking. They both suspected not but didn't say anything.

"Any good spoils?" asked Kyle.

"Just the usual," said Aurin. "Coins, herbs and so on, plus a Lunar Shard."

"That's always a nice find," said Kyle.

Aurin's eyes lit up suddenly and he rushed off towards the enclosures, looking for one of his Minakai. He hurried back a few moments later holding his Happynut in his arms. He set it down and it waddled in place merrily.

"You're evolving him?" asked Luna.

"He's proven himself enough now," said Aurin. "He handled himself well in the tournament and his training and tower battles have been getting better and better. I think he's ready."

"Fair enough," shrugged Kyle, letting Aurin make his own decision.

Aurin held the Lunar Shard against the nature Minakai causing him to glow before changing forms in a burst of green light. The Happynut grew taller and bulkier as his shell-like skin became smooth, green and fibrous while sprouting a tail from his rear. His happy smile slowly morphed into a downcast frown, no longer his youthful and vibrant self. Happynut had evolved into a Melansprout, as melancholic as his name suggested.

"Let's put some work in tonight before the tournament tomorrow, Melansprout," said Aurin enthusiastically, at which Melansprout wept. He suddenly had doubts about evolving his Happynut less than twenty-four hours before he was due to battle.

"I think you jumped the gun," said Luna.

"I'm sure it will be fine," replied Aurin, trying to convince himself as much as her. "Melansprout are always depressed, it's in their nature."

"That's true," admitted Kyle, shaking his head wearily. "It's a typically depressed adolescent."

"We're not depressed," said Luna.

Kyle laughed. "Ah, you're from a generation where

everybody is happy and satisfied with life. How I envy you youngsters."

Two figures emerged along the path through the forest, heading straight towards the three. As they came closer, Aurin could see that it was the two detectives, Knot and Scarlett. They looked very serious, so Aurin thought it best to hold back any comments on their ineffectiveness against Zodiac.

"What are they doing here?" asked Luna.

"I actually called them," said Kyle. "I think you'll both be interested to hear this too. Frankly, you likely had a narrow escape, Luna."

Luna looked startled, not sure about what he was referring to.

"Kyle," said Knot in greeting as the detectives finally reached them. "Aurin. Luna. Good to see you both."

"I didn't think the pair of you would be here," said Scarlett.

"I live here," said Aurin.

"It wasn't meant to be a slight against you. I just didn't expect it, that was all," she said and then held a hand to her chin. "You know, it's actually good that you *are* here because tournament competitors would be good to speak to if you don't mind?"

"Speak about what?" asked Luna.

"You haven't told them yet, Kyle?" asked Knot.

Kyle shook his head. "I'll leave that to you two, detectives. You know more about the situation than I do."

"Very well," began Knot. "It started during the first round of the tournament after the first couple of matches had gone off without a hitch. Tamers reported losing their summoning stones, some seemed to have misplaced them and others were adamant that they were mugged.

"The information started trickling in at first, but we think it's pretty clear now that Zodiac is behind it. They've been using the cover of the excitement of the tournament as a distraction. As soon as somebody loses a match, they're jumped and at least one of their stones is taken.

"Even at your last battle, Aurin. Remember Jimmy? His Arium's stone was taken. I suspect that you yourself were a target, Luna, but Kyle said that you all left the stadium together so you wouldn't have been easy pickings. Certainly not with strong tamers by your side who have a full team of able Minakai at the ready. We're going to be making an effort to increase security at the arena considering everything that's been going on."

"What has this got to do with you, Kyle?" asked Aurin.

Kyle looked dismayed. "A number of those tamers keep their Minakai here, linking them to their stones, right? What would happen if somebody else got their hands on the stone?"

"The Minakai are summoned away and kidnapped?" gasped Luna.

"Precisely," said Scarlett. "Zodiac has obtained a lot of Minakai, some of them rather rare. I don't know if it's for power or if it's for the black market, but it's a serious crime either way. We hoped you would be able to tell us anything suspicious you may have noticed after your last battle. Did either of you two notice anything?"

"No," said both Aurin and Luna instantly. Nothing unusual had occurred, so Knot must have been right about Luna being lucky having had Aurin, Kyle and Gardner nearby.

"I'll show you around the ranch, detectives," said

Kyle, as he walked towards the enclosures. His Frogre guards continued to keep a careful watch.

Aurin hung back and grabbed Luna by the wrist, stopping her from following.

"What's wrong?" she asked. "Aside from this whole situation, of course."

Aurin had a plan in mind, but it would involve putting himself and others in harm's way. He knew it would be risky, but if the authorities were useless, then there was only one other way to deal with the string of Zodiac thefts.

"I'm up against Gardner tomorrow, right?" he asked rhetorically. "One of us is going to lose. I'm going to talk to him before the match. The loser will leave the stadium alone and we'll make sure either he or I are followed at a close distance."

Luna looked uneasy. "Do you want to tell Detective Knot and Detective Scarlett about this plan?"

"No. They'll only tell us it's a bad idea."

"Isn't it a bad idea?"

"Only if it fails," said Aurin. "We're going to catch the Zodiac members and put a stop to these thefts, even if we have to do it vigilante style."

Chapter 19

"I don't like it," said Gardner, sipping a chocolate milkshake. "Do you know how dangerous this is? If we're outnumbered and outmatched, with one of us without our best Minakai, it could get ugly."

"Two of us will have lost our best Minakai after we beat each other black and blue," said Aurin nonchalantly as he drank his strawberry shake, "but we still need to put a stop to it. The police here have been less than useless for the last few months, right?"

"That's true," admitted Gardner, "but I still have nightmares about the time I got attacked. It's fortunate that I haven't been jumped in the tower again since."

"Yet you keep going back. You're more than capable of defending yourself if you lose our match, as am I. I shouldn't need to remind you that the summoning rule only applies to the tower. I have two Minakai that I won't be using in the fight that can be called upon if needed. How about you?"

"I have one spare," said Gardner. "I'm not telling you which though," he added slyly.

Aurin laughed. "I wasn't expecting you to. Notice I didn't tell you which of mine will be in the battle. I did have to have one reassessed, however. A special surprise for you."

"An evolution, eh?" smirked Gardner, glancing at Shamtile who was scratching his stomach while sitting on the next chair over. "Well, it wasn't Shamtile. I don't think Dolissile can evolve, can it? Unless I'm not aware of its evolutions. It's either Hornferno or Happynut, and I know you wouldn't use a nature elemental against me."

"You'll have to keep guessing all the way up until the match," said Aurin. "Speaking of which, we're due to start in an hour. Can I count you in on the plan?"

Gardner sighed. "Alright, I'll do it. I'll follow you at a distance when you lose."

"Glad to have you on board. It's like I said, it's on us to do something about the Zodiac Squad if nobody else is going to."

"You're right, but I'm not going to pretend to be enthusiastic about it."

The two competitors stood at opposite ends of the fields, the crowd watching them with great enthusiasm.

It was the second match of the day and they were all fired up, the announcer egging them on. Luna sat in the crowd, holding her breath while watching her two friends intently. She wanted Aurin to win, and he knew that, but she wouldn't say it out loud.

"Time to show them what you're made of Melansprout!" called Aurin.

"Budescent, let's start strong," commanded Gardner. The two Minakai were summoned to the field, ready to follow their masters' orders. "

"An interesting start!" said the announcer. "Is that Melansprout one and the same as the Happynut that Aurin used in his last battle? Official sources are telling me that it is. Let's see if that evolution will give him the edge he needs against another tough competitor."

Melansprout stood firm, albeit looking miserable, while Budescent charged in. It was small in comparison to Hunter's Vinewolf, but the green lupine Minakai was speedy. It dove, teeth first, at Aurin's Minakai and sank its teeth into his leg.

"Now!" called Aurin, having guessed who Gardner would lead with and what his tactic would be.

Melansprout tore the wolf from his leg and held it in a tight bear hug. Budescent struggled, but Melansprout whipped its head and the sharp leaves atop it sliced through the wolf's fur and cut its skin. Melansprout squeezed tighter until his foe stopped moving. It was already out of the battle.

"What a start!" cried the announcer. "Less than thirty seconds and Aurin already has a lead. Let's hope his Melansprout didn't take too hard of a bite to its leg or it may not last long."

Gardner looked frustrated while Aurin remained cool. "I was hoping to save you for later, but let's switch it up," he said as he summoned his next Minakai.

It looked similar to Melansprout, but longer and with an orange-brown bark-like flesh. It was a powerful nature Minakai called Desparee, a possible evolution of Aurin's Minakai. It didn't look depressed like Melansprout did, but it did look to be in anguish; another level of despair altogether.

"It's got more power than you," warned Aurin, "but let it be overconfident so that we can hit it by surprise."

The Desparee closed in on Melansprout

Desparee ran towards Melansprout on its long legs and Melansprout planted roots in the ground to keep itself stable. The hefty tree collided with the chunky sapling and the two wrestled, each trying to throw the other to the floor.

"His leg is weak!" called Gardner.

The nature tamer's Desparee kicked the spot where Budescent had bitten a chunk out of Melansprout's leg and he dropped to his knees, even with his roots holding him in place. Desparee clobbered its foe in the face as he collapsed and the poor Melansprout was done.

"Get out here, Leonite!" ordered Aurin, recalling Melansprout, and his cobalt lion burst onto the field, charging full pelt at Desparee.

The lion Minakai leapt at the tree and dug his claws deep into its bark body. Leonite bit down and tore strips of the bark flesh away, knowing that he would be able to best this foe with ease.

"Drain him," ordered Gardner.

Desparee held Leonite tightly, who could not pull his claws out fast enough. He squeezed and vines wrapped around his trapped opponent. They started to glow a bright green and pulsate. Leonite was looking weak while Desparee was healing before the audience's eyes.

They were all cheering at the effective counter.

"It looks like Aurin's Leonite won't be able to hang on much longer," said the announcer. "Aurin went from having the numbers advantage to having a single Minakai against Gardner's two, all while Desparee is looking fit and healthy after that absorption technique."

Once Leonite had passed out, Aurin sent him back to the ranch. One of his Minakai had been completely wasted by rushing in. Would Gardner suspect the same tactic twice? What if he hit Desparee twice as hard?

"Torpedo!" cried Aurin, which caught Gardner by surprise.

Dolissile burst forward in a silvery grey light and charged directly at Desparee. Before the tree could even react, the cybernetic dolphin had collided with its chest and broken its bark. The tree-like Minakai was thrown back twenty feet and writhed in pain, unable to fight on.

"Unbelievable!" cried the announcer as the crowd gasped. "What a powerful strike from Aurin's Dolissile. He's still in the game now that Gardner is down to his last Minakai. My gosh, folks, this is an exciting one."

Gardner looked fired up and punched his fist forward, summoning Sproufloat to the field. Aurin expected him to use an aerial Minakai, which was why he had saved his own Dolissile for last. It wouldn't be easy as Sproufloat was much more nimble, but if he could hit it then the match was over.

"Knock him off course," said Gardner, growing frustrated. Sproufloat spun around and conjured up a gust of wind. The deceptively plant-like Minakai was not Gardner's typical nature elemental, rather it was a wind elemental and Aurin wouldn't fall for the trick.

"Outpace the wind," ordered Aurin.

Dolissile zoomed around the field, the blasts of wind

that Sproufloat had spawned were unable to keep up. Dolissile was too reactive and speedy to be caught, leaving Gardner looking panicked.

Dolissile turned and aimed straight for the Sproufloat which dodged with ease. The two continued to do this back and forth, neither willing to concede and neither gaining any advantage over the other. They were at a stalemate.

The crowd were watching, hoping that one of the Minakai would slip. "It's gridlock, folks," said the announcer. "It may come down to who tires first and makes a wrong move."

Gardner suddenly cried out after Sproufloat dodged one more attack. "Blast him away!"

Sproufloat breathed in and shot a directed and heavy beam at Dolissile who had his back turned. If this hit, Aurin was done for.

"Hit the ground and counter," he ordered, and Dolissile skidded into the dirt. He rotated hurriedly and charged at Sproufloat who was drawing its breath back in, ready for another strike.

"Now!" cried Gardner before Sproufloat was ready.

The powerful blast was much weaker this time and Dolissile charged through, wobbling, but still aiming true. He collided with Sproufloat who fell out of the air and crashed into the ground. It was over. Sproufloat had lost and Gardner was out of the tournament, Aurin having bested him in battle once again.

"And there you have it folks," said the announcer. "A good attempt to counter by Gardner, but he was out-countered by Aurin. What an exciting match that was, right?"

The crowd all cheered while Aurin and Gardner applauded each other. The two walked forward and shook hands with no hard feelings between them. They always knew one of them would walk away victorious, but both were glad it was a close match.

"You almost beat me," laughed Aurin.

"I just wanted to lower your guard a bit for our next match," chuckled Gardner. "You'll think you can beat me three times in a row, but that's when I'll hit you hardest. I'm playing the long game, my friend. The long game."

"My long game is to just keep winning."

"Well," said Gardner, raising an eyebrow, "if it really is that simple then it's a good plan."

Aurin laughed before his face turned serious. "You ready for the next part?"

"I'm ready," confirmed Gardner, knowing that he would be leaving the stadium moments later and what likely awaited him.

Suddenly, tamers started brawling in the stands. Aurin and Gardner both looked over and could see that a number of the people fighting were wearing masks; masks patterned with stars. They weren't just tamers; they were Zodiac members.

"Wasn't it meant to be outside of the stadium?" asked Gardner.

"This isn't right," said Aurin, unnerved.

He summoned Shamtile and Hornferno, immediately sending them over to the stands along with Dolissile. Tamers and Zodiac members summoned their own Minakai and the entire stadium erupted into a fight as the civilians without Minakai fled to escape the chaos.

"The egg!" cried the announcer over the speakers.

Aurin looked over and spotted a man riding a Leonite removing the prized egg from the glass cabinet atop the stage near the competitor's box. It was guard-free, as they had rushed off to quell the fight.

"Leo!" shouted Aurin, using his summoning stones to immediately bring his three remaining Minakai back to his side. He hopped on Dolissile's back and held on tightly as Leo sped off down the stairs and out of sight with the egg in his hands.

Chapter 20

Aurin, Shamtile and Hornferno clung to Dolissile and flew into the stands then down the staircase Leo had fled. There was no way that he was getting away with the tournament prize if Aurin had anything to say about it.

As they zoomed through the corridors, trying to track their target, Luna appeared beside him riding on Spritzard's back with Innogon holding tightly onto her shoulders.

"Where did he go?" asked Luna in a panic.

"He must be making for one of the exits," said Aurin.

"Let's split up and see if we can find him. There's only one easy path out of here once he's out in the courtyard."

"Good idea."

The two split up and looked for an exit each. Luna headed eastwards and Aurin headed westwards. Aurin had never realised how big the stadium was until this moment. He ordered Dolissile to go faster, but the Minakai was trying hard to avoid colliding with the walls already.

"There!" the tamer called as he spotted a tail whip around a corner. Dolissile sped ahead and used all of his might to turn the corner sharply, Aurin, Shamtile and Hornferno hanging on tightly to avoid being thrown off and down the corridor.

The two tamers raced outside and Leo finally came to a halt. He dismounted and summoned two additional Leonite to his side. "You're quite the pest, has anybody ever told you that?" he asked.

"I prefer to think of myself as persistent," said Aurin as he ordered his Minakai into battle against Leo and his three lions.

Shamtile wasted no time and threw a stone spear straight into the centre of the three, who all scattered. The spear whizzed past Leo's ear as he leaned away, narrowly avoiding getting hit by the lizard's attack.

"You'll pay for an attack like that!" roared Leo, not caring that Shamtile was aiming for the Minakai and not him. "No mercy," he ordered his three cobalt lions.

Each of Aurin's Minakai faced off against a separate Leonite, while Aurin and Leo eyed each other from across the square. The prized egg was held tightly in Leo's hands, and he was almost daring Aurin to come and take it from him.

Dolissile was having a hard time against his opponent, already exhausted from the battle against Gardner's team. The Leonite sunk its teeth deep into the dolphin's metal armour, breaking through to the flesh below. Dolissile let out an echoed screech of pain, alarming Aurin; he was not used to reactions from him. The tamer banished him back to the ranch, seeing that Leo would kill Aurin's Minakai without a care if it meant he could escape with the egg.

"Are you insane?" asked Aurin angrily.

"No mercy," Leo said again and the Leonite who had defeated Dolissile attacked Hornferno, who had been faring well against his first opponent.

The two lions flanked the red dinosaur as he hurled fireballs wildly, hoping to strike lucky, but the unfocused attacks gave the two beasts the chance to get close and sink their fangs into him. They bit deeply, and without metal armour to protect him, Hornferno was in agony.

As they clamped down, he summoned all of his might and bit one of the Leonite in the eye. The Leonite roared furiously as its vision filled with blood, and Leo yelled for it to retreat. It ran back to its master's side, having been Leo's steed during the egg theft. Perhaps this was his favourite of his Minakai, and Aurin eyed it up carefully.

The young tamer banished Hornferno back to the ranch as he collapsed, leaving Shamtile to fight alone against two Leonite while another watched from the sidelines, ready to join the fight should it be necessary. The masked lizard was outnumbered badly.

Suddenly, two jets of water blasted Shamtile's opponents to the ground as Luna came running. Ahead of her were Innogon and Spritzard, charging straight for Leo's team.

"Good timing," sighed Aurin in relief.

"But not good enough," said Leo, as he climbed atop his Leonite once more. "Until next time," he said, as he sped off.

Spritzard began to chase the Zodiac member, but the two remaining Leonite had already climbed back to their feet and blocked the way. They were more than capable of fighting without their master present to give orders.

Shamtile hurled rocks, Innogon spat powerful jets while Spritzard conjured up waves, but the Leonite were nimble and avoided each attack. They leapt over the water and side-stepped each rock, but made no attempts to attack.

"They're stalling!" called Aurin.

Luna summoned Tadpool and Happynut to her side and the two Minakai continued the assault against the Leonite, but it was starting to seem fruitless. Leo was well outside of their reach now. Seconds later, his Minakai vanished, having been called back to him, wherever he was now.

Aurin threw his head back in exasperation. "He played this smart," he said. "I wonder if the police and the stadium guards have rounded up the Zodiac members who caused the fights?"

"I hope so," said a worried Luna. "A few of them had already made their way into the corridors by the time I made my way out here. They're bound to have a proper getaway plan, right? It would be a suicide mission to jump all of the most powerful tamers in town."

"What do you mean that it wasn't recorded?" yelled

Aurin as Detective Knot, who had been questioning the young tamer about his pursuit of Leo.

The detective sighed. "They've tampered with the equipment somehow, probably using a Minakai. Each tamer we ask is giving a different account of who was wearing a mask, and all of the masks were conveniently burned to cinders by all of the fire elementals that the Zodiac members had used."

"So there's nothing you can do?" asked Luna, growing tired of saying something similar to Knot so often.

"Do you think we're not angry?" barked Detective Scarlett. "Do you think we're not sick of being held back time and time again? I could tell you at least two tamers who I know were wearing Zodiac masks, but there are another dozen who will insist that they weren't and had been fighting alongside them against Zodiac."

"And there isn't a single working camera anywhere? Not a single recording?" asked Kyle, also getting very angry.

"Check your own phone," said Knot.

"I don't have one," said Kyle, as Luna pulled out hers.

"You're right," she said, furiously trying to turn it on. "It's destroyed. How did they do that?"

"All it takes is a strong metal elemental Minakai to send out the right electromagnetic pulse," admitted Kyle, "and it can fry whatever it wants. It can hit everything, or if it's really in control, it can target certain ranges or devices. There's a reason we haven't had a major war in a long time. Minakai are all deadly weapons."

Aurin still couldn't believe what he was hearing. "Do you two not know how to do your jobs?" he snapped.

"You saw who these people were, drag them in for questioning."

Scarlett poked him in the chest. "If we do that and they have more alibis than you can count on your hand, then we're right back to square one. The legitimate tamers and audience members? Every statement we've taken is a mess because of the confusion. You missed it when you dashed out of the stadium, but there was haze and smoke summoned that blocked everybody's vision. It was absolute chaos."

"Let's just go," said Luna, worrying that Aurin was getting close to really flying off the handle. "We need to cool down somewhere else."

"Yes," agreed Kyle as he began to steer Aurin away from the two detectives. He was equally as frustrated but knew that there was no point arguing with them.

The three were quiet as they headed back to the ranch, barely even looking at each other on the walk out of town. The sun was close to setting at this point and the entire town was abuzz from the day's events, but the three tamers didn't have the energy to talk to anybody else about what had happened.

When they reached the ranch, Aurin dropped onto the grass and stared at the sky. "They're hiding something," he said.

"Who? Knot and Scarlett?" asked Luna.

"Yes. I wouldn't be surprised if they were Zodiac members considering how they're conveniently never in a position to do anything. Too many alibis? What absolute rubbish."

"I agree," said Kyle, alarming Luna. "I think they're either getting pressure put on them from above or from somewhere else. They're right about the pulse that certain Minakai can use, but I don't buy for a second that every single camera was fried."

"You're right not to buy it," said a voice, as a figure in a trench coat walked up the ranch path. "However, I would suggest keeping your voices down as you never know who may be nearby."

"Detective Knot?" asked Luna.

"You're not the only ones who are angry," said the detective as he drew closer. "If it were up to me, we'd have tossed dozens of the known Zodiac members in the cells and thrown away the key, but our hands are being tied behind our backs and then we're being kicked into the mud."

Aurin had never heard him talk this way; he had always seemed so professional, but it was a welcome shift. "What do you mean?"

"I can't say too much right now, but I didn't want to let it lie," said a disgruntled Knot. "I don't know who's giving the orders, but we're being told not to investigate certain leads, key evidence is going missing, and other evidence is being ignored. It's angering me more than it's angering any of you, I assure you."

"Is there anything we can do to help?" asked Aurin, climbing to his feet. "I'm serious. I want Zodiac out of the way so that things are finally normal around here. Not that I've ever seen them normal," he admitted, "but surely it must be a lot better than this before Zodiac showed up."

Knot let a grim laugh escape. "I have good reason to believe that there are a few tournament competitors who are Zodiac members. Most of them have been knocked out, but I think their star player is still in the game. He's probably arrogant enough to think that nobody has caught onto him yet, but I'm a lot more observant than most of you realise."

"Who is it?" asked Aurin. "What can we do?"

"Funnily enough," said Knot with a small smile, "you're up against him in your next battle. I have a plan if you're truly interested in putting a stop to them. If we're lucky, the egg won't have been hatched, and we may be able to recover it."

The three tamers leaned in close, listening intently to everything that Knot had to say.

Chapter 21

Aurin, Luna and Kyle stood in the tunnel that led to the battlefield moments before Aurin was due to fight in his next match. They had spent all evening listening to Knot and hashing out their plan to recover the egg from Zodiac. All three were feeling nervous about it, but it was the best chance they had if they were to have any hope of recovering the tournament prize.

"Do not forget how incredibly dangerous this is," warned Kyle. "It should be me going in instead of both of you," he added.

"What are you talking about?" asked Aurin incredulously. "It's your job to make sure that we get out alive if things start to go badly. Your job is just as important."

"It's true, Kyle," said Luna.

"True or not, I would be able to handle myself a lot better."

"But you're also a much more recognisable face around town. Almost everyone knows you, whereas we're small fries."

"She's right," said Aurin. "Who am I? Nobody knows outside of a couple of tournament matches. Half the town uses your ranch to keep their Minakai safe."

"We'll be fine, Kyle, now let's go take our seats before Aurin gets brought out."

"I'm still not happy about this," said Kyle, shaking his head, "but good luck with your match, Aurin."

"Beat him badly," said Luna, giving him a quick hug, before she and Kyle ran down the tunnel, leaving Aurin alone with only the arena-side staff member. Maybe he was a Zodiac Squad member too? Aurin considered it for a second before shaking it off. He was starting to get paranoid.

"You ready for this, kid?" asked the official. "Top thirty-two is the big leagues in these kinds of qualifiers. You've got the whole town talking, you know? Granted, they're a bit distracted after the whole business from yesterday, but there are a lot of folks in your corner."

"I'm ready," said Aurin confidently. "Truth be told, I had my doubts that I would make it this far, but now I'm more determined than ever to keep going."

"That's the spirit," said the staff member. "You're up in a few seconds," he added quickly after listening to whatever had just come through on his earpiece.

"Welcome everyone to the first match of the top thirty-two of the first Hazelton Tournament!" called the announcer. "Now, I would just like to assure everybody that we've doubled up on our security so there should be no more unexpected events like yesterday. We will also have a new prized egg with us in a matter of days."

The crowd cheered, as though they had forgotten the previous debacle and were lost in the moment once more. Kyle and Luna had just taken their seats and were eager for Aurin's match to begin.

"Introducing our first competitor!" cried the announcer. "You've seen him win three times already, and it's only his first tournament. Can he make it four? Give it up for Aurin!"

Applause and chanting broke out as Aurin walked into the stadium, ready for the fight of his life. He waited patiently for the announcer to call his opponent.

"Fresh from last year's national tournament in Ludonia and steamrolling the competition here in Hazelton...it's Frederick!"

The tall tamer walked from the tunnel and waved to the crowd. He was clearly very popular, but Aurin looked at him with disdain. How did he not see it before? Frederick was Leo this entire time. He had approached Aurin on purpose at the assessment. Was it to taunt him?

"Let the match begin!" called the announcer, as both tamers summoned their first Minakai to the field.

"Melansprout," ordered Aurin, calling forth the depressed nature Minakai.

He appeared in a burst of green light and slumped forward, looking defeated before the match had even begun. But it was his melancholia that, ironically, gave him the drive to fight. He would do anything to relieve that feeling and it just so happened that a victory was the momentary relief he sought.

"Make it quick," said Frederick, summoning a Gorungra. This fully-evolved form of Gorun was a large quadruped golem with golden-yellow crystals erupting from its body. Its glowing eyes stared at Melansprout menacingly.

Melansprout slammed a fist into the ground, causing roots to erupt from underneath the soil in a direct line for Gorungra. The golem behemoth swiped one of its sharp, crystalline claws at the thick roots and cut it neatly in two.

It charged forward, making the ground quake with each bound. For such a large and heavy beast, it was shockingly fast. Far faster than a normal Gorungra. Speed seemed to be Frederick's trick, certainly with his army of Leonite.

Melansprout focused and, as the golem closed in, a large flower burst from the ground and the Minakai was flung into the sky. He landed roughly on Gorungra's back, avoiding the protruding crystals. He began to summon vines from his hands, which wrapped around the neck of the beast.

Frederick's Gorungra bucked and spun, trying to shake Melansprout off its back. The nature Minakai hung on tightly and started beating the back of Gorungra's head, trying desperately to do damage, but the titan seemed impenetrable.

"Flip," ordered Frederick plainly.

Gorungra stood up on its hind legs and threw itself onto its back. Melansprout was crushed beneath the golem and Aurin sent it back to the ranch.

"Oh, that must have hurt!" exclaimed the announcer. "The first point goes to Frederick. Can Aurin take down Gorungra or is his entire team going to be wiped out by the powerful Minakai?"

Aurin summoned Hornferno to the field and the red dinosaur snorted before blowing bursts of flame from its nose. He was ready to go, already recovered from the previous day's injury. It was always remarkable to Aurin how Minakai could recover at alarming speeds.

"Turn that stone into magma," ordered Aurin as Hornferno broke into a sprint. He breathed in deeply and spat out a wave of flame that blocked him from Gorungra's view.

The golem ducked down to shield its face from the intense heat of the blast, but Hornferno had another plan in mind. He used the wave as a distraction and stood directly in front of his foe's face, and as soon as Gorungra looked up, he exhaled an intense flame.

Gorungra stood up and stumbled backwards, its crystalline eyes flashing, unable to see clearly. It started to stomp wildly and with each stomp, a mighty stalagmite burst from the ground.

Hornferno leapt from side to side trying to avoid each of the attacks, but it was too unpredictable. The chaotic stalagmites finally caught the dinosaur and tossed him into the sky. He landed in a heap, but the stalagmites kept coming.

"Stop!" called Aurin as Hornferno was tossed around like a rag doll, taking beating after beating by the sharp stones.

"Gorungra, that's enough," ordered Frederick as the crowd gasped.

They were murmuring about bad sportsmanship, and it seemed to irk Frederick, but he had clearly wanted revenge for what Hornferno had done to his favourite Leonite yesterday. Only Aurin, Luna and Kyle knew that, of course.

"That was hard to watch," called the announcer. "Hornferno is out of there. Can anything stop this insane Gorungra? You had better think of something fast, Aurin."

"Last chance," muttered Aurin, losing hope in a victory. "Leonite!" he ordered, as his Minakai appeared in a burst of off-white light.

The cobalt lion stood tall and proud, letting out a low purr. He was truly a majestic beast, but the ferocity in his eyes was shining strong. He slowly began to pace toward the Gorungra, not showing even the slightest hint of fear.

Gorungra slammed its fist into the ground and a large pillar of stone rose up, carrying Leonite ten metres above the battlefield. It would not be easy to land a jump from here unhurt. Gorungra began to shoot yellow crystals from its back, forcing Leonite to duck and dive to avoid them.

"More," said Frederick, and the Gorungra began throwing more crystal spears at an even more rapid pace.

"Down!" called Aurin, letting the Gorungra tire itself out.

Leonite leapt from the pillar and dove onto the grass as the crowd all held their breaths in suspense. The lion smoothly rolled onto his feet and leapt onto Gorungra's face, sinking three of his claws in deep.

Aurin's Minakai used his free hand to scratch at Gorungra's eyes, and the golem tried to shake off the wild predator. Leonite, however, was wedged in firmly and would not let himself be tossed aside. He continued to attack the much larger opponent and, finally, it dropped to the ground with a heavy thud.

When Leonite disengaged, the whole stadium could see that Gorungra's face was destroyed. Large chunks of stone missing, his crystal eyes chipped. If there was any question as to whether a creature like that could feel pain, Leonite had given them the answer.

"Aurin is not out of the game yet! What a savage attack," said the announcer. The crowd cheered for him, still not over Frederick's overly harsh treatment of Hornferno.

"You think you can come back from this?" Frederick asked Aurin. "How about we fight fire with fire? Leonite!"

One of Frederick's own lions appeared on the field. Aurin recognised it immediately. It was the same one that he had ridden out of the stadium with the egg. It was the same one that Hornferno had injured, and it was ready for a fight.

Frederick's Leonite roared a fierce roar and ran straight for Aurin's Leonite. The two lions swiped and clawed at each other, neither conceding an inch. As Frederick's went for the throat, Aurin's dodged. As Aurin's bit Frederick's on the neck, it was met with a bite right back.

The two Minakai fought and with each hit landed, the crowd gasped and cheered. It was an intense fight, with each of the two being whittled down and tired out little by little.

"Tail!" called Aurin, seeing an opening.

Aurin's Leonite grabbed hold of Frederick's Leonite's tail and bit it so hard that everyone was worried the tail would come off. Frederick's Leonite howled in pain, then Aurin's followed up with a few more bites and swipes to the torso.

Suddenly, both Minakai whipped their claws and drew deep cuts with their nails across each other's faces and the two fell to the ground, exhausted. They breathed heavily, but neither was able to stand up as they were utterly spent.

"And there you have it, folks!" called the announcer.

"Both of these Leonite are evenly matched and have taken each other out. Commiserations to Aurin who put on a great showing at his first tournament, and congratulations to Frederick who will move onto the top sixteen."

Luna turned to Kyle. "Don't try and go rogue on the plan, okay?"

"I promise I won't," he sighed back.

Aurin walked to the centre where Frederick stood and forced a smile onto his face as he reached out his hand. "Great match, Frederick. That's a powerful team you've got there, I can't imagine what your third Minakai would have been."

"It was a good fight," said Frederick, surprising Aurin with how earnest he sounded. "Perhaps we will face each other a second time?"

"I hope so," said Aurin with a grin.

The two parted ways and Aurin wiped the stupid smile off his face. He wanted to punch Frederick then and there, but he could not give the game away. He had to remain calm until Frederick left the arena.

He was upset about his loss, but as soon as he found out that Leo was Frederick, he knew that he wasn't going to win. Still, he had hoped. Perhaps this made the plan that Knot had cooked up that much easier to execute. Frederick would be on a high from his victory and be that little bit less alert.

Aurin met Luna and Innogon at the exit of the stadium. "Ready?" she asked.

"Ready," he replied as the two ran towards the river that flowed through town and right past the stadium.

Shamtile appeared in an orange light, having been summoned from the ranch. "Rock cage, quickly," Aurin ordered and the lizard did a little dance, surrounding the two tamers and their Minakai.

They watched the south exit and waited. A few people came and went, but it wasn't long before Frederick appeared. He walked away from the stadium, unaware that he was being watched. As soon as he was a safe distance away, Shamtile dissipated the cage and the group followed the Zodiac member.

Chapter 22

Frederick walked into a warehouse by the river without a hint of Zodiac about him. He could have owned the place, maybe even worked here. Nobody would question a man walking into a building that they wouldn't even have realised existed.

"So, their base is right here in Hazelton?" asked Luna, peering over from around the corner. "I always thought it would be closer to the tower. In the forest or something."

"I always figured they were regular folks who changed and masked up before they entered the tower," said Aurin.

"You're only saying that because that's what Knot told you."

"Not true. I thought of it before he said it."

Shamtile started poking Aurin in the leg and quietly warbling. Three people had walked out of the warehouse, two men and a woman. The perfect targets. If Knot and Aurin's theory was right, this would make things much easier for the next phase of the plan.

"You're both up," said Luna to both Shamtile and Innogon. The two Minakai reacted with glee, eager to have some peace brought back to the town so they could explore the tower without dangerous tamers sabotaging them.

The two reptiles walked casually forward, pretending to not even notice the humans. Once they were close enough, Innogon blasted their bags off of their backs with powerful water jets while Shamtile trapped them inside a rocky cage.

Their screams for help were stifled by their prison as Shamtile rolled them away and into a back alley. They were none the wiser as to who had ordered the attack and they wouldn't be escaping anytime soon.

Innogon brought the packs back to the two tamers, who started rifling through them.

"Yes!" exclaimed Luna, thrilled to find a white Zodiac uniform, complete with mask, in the woman's pack. It would fit her perfectly. She looked over at Aurin who had already thrown on the white leather jacket and the boots that one of the men carried.

"Look away," said Luna before getting changed.

"Ah, right," muttered Aurin, looking to Shamtile. "Mate, conjure up a wall to hide Luna for a minute."

Once they were ready, they donned the masks and hats, praying that they would not meet Frederick or any of the other members who may recognise them. The notoriety they had gained from the tournament probably wouldn't aid their stealthy approach, but they had to try anyway.

"Inno, wait with Shamtile," ordered Luna. "We'll summon you if things take a turn for the worse. Kyle will be watching from the skies and should be close by already, so call out to Wingbloom if we call upon one of you. Understood?"

Innogon yapped in agreement and Luna hoped that her Minakai had indeed grasped what she was saying, but there was no more time to waste. The longer the two tamers took, the better chance there was of them being rumbled.

They walked up to the warehouse door and tried to open it, but it was locked. "Password?" came a man's voice.

Aurin and Luna looked at each other. "It's us," said Aurin. "Hurry up and let us in, that bloody Detective Knot was tailing us earlier."

"Knot? Ah, hurry up and get in here. Are you sure he's not still tailing you?" The door opened and the man let them inside.

Aurin nodded. "We managed to ditch him, but we've got to report it to the boss quickly. Has Leo returned yet?"

"Yeah, only a few minutes ago," said the man, looking worried. "He seemed to be in a good mood for a change, so I would go speak to him now before he's back to normal."

"Thanks," said Aura and he left with Luna.

The warehouse from the outside had looked like a typically large shed of metal and wood, but inside it was far grander. Zodiac had gone all out on designing this place to resemble the various floors of the tower, from the walls to the ceiling and even to using torchlight.

"Where should we go?" asked Luna.

"Wherever we think the egg might be," replied Aurin, without the faintest idea.

The two wandered the halls somewhat aimlessly looking to find some sort of lead while avoiding eye contact with the other Zodiac members. It was made slightly easier by the masks, but they still received a few funny looks.

"You there," called a voice from inside a room. It was a man sitting at a table with a few other Zodiac Squad members.

"Me?" asked Aurin, trying not to let his trembling affect his voice.

"Yeah, you," said the man. "We've got a game of cards going. A lot of silver to be won, if you're good. Just had a tower run so we're stacked to the rafters. No sign of Ethruki, but the spoils were fantastic either way."

Ethruki? That name didn't ring bells to either Aurin or Luna. Was it a person or a Minakai? The man spoke as though they should know, so they didn't question it further.

"I wish I could," said Aurin, "but I got booted out. I'm not feeling the luck today. Maybe next time."

"Suit yourself," shrugged the man and he returned to the game with the rest of his teammates, all eager to make themselves richer.

"What's an Ethruki?" asked Luna, hoping that Aurin knew more than she did. He merely shrugged with a confused look on his face.

The two continued to wander, stopping just outside of a large set of doors that led into what was presumably the main floor of the warehouse. Aurin placed his ear against it, not sure what he was expecting to find.

He shook his head at Luna, then tried to open it. Much to his surprise, it did open, but even more surprising was what he found inside. There were Minakai trapped in cages, most of them muzzled and bound to stop them from breaking free. These must be the ones stolen from the tamers after the fights, meaning the Zodiac Squad would have had their summoning stones that they could use to recall any escapees. As Aurin thought about this, it made the cages and bindings seem that much crueller to him.

"Look," he said as quietly as he could while pointing to a golden alien-like Minakai, "I think that's Jimmy's Arium."

"If they've got the summoning stones, they can bind the Minakai to the cages," gasped Luna. "Even if they break free, the Zodiacs can just force them back in with the magic of the stones. They're so cruel." She looked as though she was tearing up, even behind the mask.

"We'll keep looking around for the stones. I think this is even more important than the egg, but perhaps if we can find one, we'll find the other. This place is only so big, so there couldn't be that many places to hide things."

Luna nodded silently in agreement and the two continued to roam the corridors. They were even more cautious than before, knowing exactly what Zodiac was capable of.

"I don't like this one bit," came Leo's angry voice, from a room further into the base. Aurin and Luna ran up to the door to listen.

"It doesn't matter if you like it, Leo," said a woman's voice. "If Taurus says that's what we're doing, then that's what we're doing."

"Maybe you're not cut out for this anymore," said a snide man.

"Don't dare question my loyalty to Zodiac,

Sagittarius," barked Leo. "Have I not proven myself time and time again? It's thanks to me that we have the egg. It could have cost me the tournament, and we know now that it isn't even a cosmic egg."

"Do you care more about the tournament than finding Ethruki?" asked the woman.

"Libra, perhaps when you actually do something useful you can question my intentions," scoffed Leo.

Sagittarius laughed while Libra fumed. "You're a real piece of work sometimes, Leo. You know perfectly well what I've done for our organisation. How many times have I thrown the authorities off of our scent?"

"Taurus is far more effective at that than you are, and you know it. You're just a backup that barely contributes. How you were promoted to an elite still evades me to this day."

"Why you loathsome little..."

The two continued to bicker while Aurin dared to glance into the room, praying the Zodiac members were distracted enough to not notice him. His eyes widened upon seeing what lay inside. The three villainous tamers were surrounded by summoning stones. Dozens and dozens of summoning stones sat on the shelves, along with another curious item; the stolen tournament egg. It was gathering dust, having been left unhatched.

"Children, please," laughed Sagittarius, enjoying the bickering between his two comrades. "Once the tournament is over and we have Minakai for the black market, we can evolve more of our teams, buy more eggs of our own, then get back to finding Ethruki."

"We've already made a killing in the tower," argued Leo. "Why are we doing even more underhanded business? We aren't common criminals, we have a purpose. A damn important purpose and you both know that full well. Besides, we have a lot more tower hunting to do. Capturing an Ethruki and finding its eggs is only the start. How many more cosmics are there still to track down?"

Luna tugged on Aurin's sleeve. She indicated to him that somebody was coming down the corridor, so they hurried off so their eavesdropping would not be obvious. Everything was happening so quickly that Aurin didn't have time to process what he had just heard.

What was this Ethruki that the Zodiac Squad wanted so much? Aurin knew of cosmic elemental Minakai existing, but he didn't know what they were. All he knew was that they were exceptionally rare. He needed to talk to Kyle and Knot about this as soon as he could but to just leave like this was not acceptable to him.

"I'm going to go back there and grab the egg," he said, stopping in the middle of the hallway.

"Are you sure?" asked Luna, worried that Aurin was being reckless again.

He nodded. "I'm sure. I want you to start opening the cages and causing as much confusion as possible. Bring this place into a state of utter chaos, alright?"

"This seems risky. This isn't a tower run where a loss would get us booted out. Who knows what these Zodiac members would do to us if we get found out?"

"It is risky," agreed Aurin, "but let's disrupt them as much as humanly possible," he added with a smile.

Luna sighed. "Fine," she said, not wanting to spend more time here than necessary. "Summon Shamtile into their room, trap the Zodiac members, then grab as many stones as you can. I'll summon Inno into the cage room and he can break the locks open."

"My thoughts exactly," said Aurin.

"I'm not just a pretty face," winked Luna.

"Well, you're as smart as you are pretty then," said Aurin without thinking. Luna blushed and before Aurin could say anything else, he ran off.

He made his way back to the room but could see Leo and three others heading in the opposite direction. The Zodiac member who had wandered into the corridor while Aurin and Luna had been listening in on the conversation must have retrieved them for another matter. This was exactly what Aurin needed.

He slinked into the room and began stuffing as many summoning stones as he could into his bag, but there were too many. Dozens didn't even cover it, there must have been at least two hundred of them. He called upon Shamtile who appeared in a flash of orangey-brown light.

"Can you make a bowl, mate?" Aurin asked him.

Shamtile waved his arms and summoned a boulder. He cleaved it in half and hollowed it out with his magic. Simple as it may have been, it would do the job. The masked lizard happily placed the summoning stones into the bowl that he was so very proud of.

Finally, Aurin picked up the egg and cradled it carefully. The tamer and his Minakai ran from the room as people began to shout. The Zodiac members were in a panic and called their Minakai to aid them as other Minakai of all shapes, sizes and elements barrelled down the corridor, attacking their captors.

Luna and Innogon ran towards Aurin. "Can we leave now?" she asked. Aurin laughed, seeing how good of a job she had done, and the pair bolted through a hole in the wall that a Metortoise had made and back onto the streets.

Chapter 23

"This was not the plan," said Detective Knot, wiping his forehead with a handkerchief. "How could you all be so foolish?"

Aurin, Luna and Kyle met with him at the ranch that evening, having been carried away from the warehouse by Kyle's Wingbloom. They were safe and sound and Aurin did not see what the big deal was.

"We did the original plan...mostly," he said, muttering that last word. "We just added a little bit extra into the end. We have the egg, we recovered the summoning stones and we also now know why the Zodiac Squad exists in the first place."

"You hadn't told me that part yet," said Kyle, looking very curious.

"We didn't have the chance to," said Aurin. "They're

hunting for cosmic Minakai and using their silver from the tower and whatever black-market money they can bring in to have an army of strong Minakai. As far as we understand it, they're looking for something called Ethruki."

"I'm not familiar with that Minakai," admitted Knot.

Kyle stared off towards Harmony Tower, which loomed over the land from the forest nearby. "I know of it," he said pensively. "It's a cosmic elemental Minakai that resembles a bull. There are many cosmic elementals, but they're exceptionally rare to encounter. I've seen maybe a dozen in my entire time as a tamer, but I've never found one of their eggs. There aren't many who have and the ones that do, well, they have a difficult time controlling the cosmic element."

"What about here at the ranch? Are there any?" asked Aurin, his interest piqued by the idea of such rare Minakai.

"I haven't had this ranch open long enough to attract a Minakai like that," said Kyle. "Keep in mind how recently Harmony Tower unsealed itself and the keys were made available. Tamers who own cosmic Minakai tend not to have them for very long, either because they can't train such powerful Minakai or because they want to get a lot of gold for selling them."

"Gold?" asked Luna. "They're so valuable you measure them in gold and not silver?"

"Absolutely," confirmed Kyle. "A single cosmic Minakai egg could go for hundreds of gold if not thousands."

"Be that as it may," said Knot, "now that Zodiac's base has been disrupted and there have been a few token arrests, I would expect a few sacrificial lambs thrown under the bus while the big players set up shop elsewhere."

Aurin knew all this already. He wanted to give Zodiac a bloody nose and bring temporary peace to Hazelton more than anything. It would take a lot more to put tamers like them, particularly their most powerful ones, in their place and shut them down for good.

"Maybe we'll get lucky and they'll leave Hazelton and Harmony Tower alone?" suggested Luna. "After all, there are dozens of other towers in the country."

"Even more if they leave Bretonia and just leave us alone," said Aurin. "Them being here makes me want to stay less."

Luna looked a little upset by the comment, but Aurin thought about what he had said for a moment and realised he didn't mean it. He would rather they stay here where he can continue to ruin Zodiac's plans.

"I suspect we'll have a quiet period, followed by another storm," lamented Knot.

It was clear that the man was very weary and had been dealing with a lot more than it had seemed on the surface. Aurin and Luna had newfound respect for him, no longer believing him to just be incompetent. No, he was an ally worth having, even if he didn't approve of their disruptive tactics.

"So, what do we do next?" Aurin asked.

"Nothing," said Knot.

"Nothing?"

Nothing," the detective affirmed, looking Aurin square in the eyes. "You have painted a target on your back because it will only be a matter of time before word reaches the strongest Zodiac Squad members that you were behind what happened at their base. In fact, I'm sure it already has."

"I didn't think of that," admitted Aurin.

"No, you didn't. But what's done is done and you should make sure you use the quiet time to strengthen your monsters." With that, the detective departed, bidding the three farewell.

Night had fallen and although the warehouse now lay abandoned, Aurin was pleased about what he did. The lingering thought of making himself a target now sat at the back of his mind, but he tried to block it out.

"Are we all going to watch the tournament matches tomorrow?" asked Luna, sounding excited once again.

"You bet," said Aurin, giving a thumbs up. "I want to see Frederick, or Leo, get beaten by somebody. Maybe our good friend Hunter can do it?"

"I'll pass, thanks," said Kyle. "I don't like leaving the Frogre in charge here. They're a bit reckless when it comes to dishing out the food when I'm not here to supervise. The two competitors I wanted to see are sadly not competing anymore."

"We're always glad to have you in our corner, Kyle," said Aurin.

"Who said I was talking about you two?" laughed Kyle flippantly. Everyone had a good chuckle and Aurin walked Luna home before heading back to the ranch to rest for the night; a rest that was sorely needed.

The next few days of tournament matches were some of the most exciting yet, and Aurin was enjoying being a spectator only slightly less than competing. He was thrilled to have made it to the top thirty-two, but the top sixteen were another league, and the top eight was even more insane.

Large, powerful Minakai sent shockwaves across the entire stadium, testing the structure of the whole building. Watching small, rapid strikers make quick work of their opponents, who were tough enough themselves, was just as exciting as being in the thick of it. It was a tournament that he would not forget and it only made him more eager to enter again the following year.

A few days after destroying the Zodiac base, the tournament was down to the final four. Still competing were Hunter and Frederick along with two other tamers called Bentley and Esmond. Bentley specialised in metal elementals and used a Titanitoise as his ace, while Esmond had used a Shamasaur, leaving Shamtile to watch keenly at what he may one day evolve into.

"After coming all the way to the semi-finals, Frederick has been defeated by Hunter," said the announcer as Flambot roasted Frederick's favourite Leonite. "A real disappointment, I'm sure, but all four semi-finalists will still be moving onto the national championships in Ludonia. Perhaps there's a rematch in store for these two and, if Frederick plays his cards right, he may come out on top."

Hunter and Frederick shook hands, and the second of the semi-finals unfolded shortly after with Bentley defeating Esmond. Aurin and Shamtile were dismayed, having been rooting for Esmond because of his fantastic taste in earth elemental Minakai.

"Anybody who has trained a Shamtile must be a good guy," said Aurin while Shamtile warbled and nodded in agreement. Luna rolled her eyes at Innogon as the little drake bounced up and down happily.

The next day was the final match of the tournament and the stadium was almost at breaking point. Aurin was certain that people had snuck in without tickets seeing that people were sitting on the staircases to watch because they didn't have seats.

"The first point of the finals goes to Hunter," called the announcer as Hunter's Anacondice defeated Bentley's Chopchop, a large bipedal ant-like Minakai who had large blades where its hands should have been.

The match continued and Bentley's Dolissile defeated Hunter's Anacondice, but then Hunter brought out the big guns. He summoned his Flambot which defeated the Dolissile in a matter of seconds, paving the way for Bentley to bring out his own champion Minakai, Titanitoise.

Titanitoise tried to flatten Flambot, but the robotic furnace heated up the metal tortoise's shell, turning it red hot. It wasn't long before the Titanitoise couldn't take it any longer and collapsed, giving Hunter a surprisingly easy victory for the finals. It was clear to all just how insanely powerful and well-trained his Flambot was.

And with that, the first Hazelton Regional Tournament was over. Hunter had won a resounding victory and would be one of the four competitors going to Ludonia for the national championships the following month.

"On behalf of the Bretonian Tournament League, and the great town of Hazelton, I present you with this beautiful trophy," said Mayor Boren in front of a captive audience. Hunter held it up and waved to the crowd, cool as a cucumber in front of the thousands of eyes staring directly at him.

"I also present you with what may be an even greater prize," said the mayor. Aurin could have sworn he winced upon saying it. "This prized egg is now yours, Hunter. Be sure to tell the good people what it hatches into."

Hunter graciously accepted the egg and gave a small bow before holding it up for the crowd to see. Everybody cheered and, not long after, the stadium was empty. It had been quite the tournament and a fantastic final match.

"At least I was knocked out by the eventual winner," said Luna with a big smile. "You got knocked out by a quarter-finalist," she teased.

"Hush," scolded Aurin in a joking way, not taking her seriously. "I've got to get back into the tower tomorrow and start building up my team again. I love my five, but that's too low of a number. Outside of Hunter, most of the best competitors had large pools of Minakai they could use to their advantage in their different matches. Hunter largely relied on the same three throughout."

"But Hunter won, so maybe a focused approach is better?" posed Luna.

"Maybe so, but I can still have a lot of Minakai and then focus later if it proves to be better. If I don't build up a team now and that was the more effective strategy, then it'll be harder to get a bunch of eggs."

"You're going to find them in the tower rather than buy them? Don't you have a lot of silver to spare?"

"If I find them in the tower, I get to train along the way," said Aurin, itching to start exploring the mysterious, magical tower once more. "I'm going to save my silver for when I really need it, and if I have a larger team then I'll use my savings to pay the ranch fees. Kyle was talking about putting them up now that the tournament has brought more people to Hazelton and I don't want to be a freeloader."

The two arrived at the ranch, still talking endlessly about their plans. Luna had a list of herbs and berries she was looking for in the tower, but she wanted to expand her own team a little too. Aurin kept asking her what each of the items did as she listed them off, but Luna knew that he would have forgotten if she asked him an hour from now.

"You two have a visitor," said Kyle, gesturing towards a tall figure in a red suit who walked towards the pair.

"Hello Aurin and Luna," said Hunter, holding the prized egg he had received less than an hour before. "We have something important to discuss."

Chapter 24

Aurin and Luna were shocked to see Hunter waiting for them at the ranch. He had just finished winning the Hazelton tournament and had come to meet both of them? It seemed strange to the pair, but they wanted to hear what it was that he wanted to discuss.

"I believe I owe both of you a big favour," he said, holding the egg up. "If what I've heard is correct, you were the ones who retrieved the egg from the Zodiac Squad and returned it to the league officials, is that right?"

"That's right," said Aurin, but Luna nudged him in the ribs.

"I was there too," she said, "but it was Aurin who got the egg back and handed it over."

Hunter laughed. "How modest of you," he said. "I

thank you too, Luna, perhaps I can repay you another way? Aurin, I have a proposal for you, if you're interested?"

"Let me hear it," said Aurin as Shamtile waved his arms excitedly and gargled incoherently at his tamer's side.

Hunter nodded as he spoke. "I don't think it's right that you should do so well at the tournament, recover the egg from those vile thieves, and then have me walk away with the prize. I want to challenge you to a Minakai battle, and the winner will get to keep the egg."

Aurin, Luna and Kyle's mouths all hit the floor. "I can't possibly defeat you," said Aurin in shock. Shamtile hid behind him, terrified at the thought of fighting Hunter's Flambot.

"That is true," said Hunter with a smile, "but you have come a long way since our last battle. What I'm suggesting, to make it a more level playing field, is that any three of your Minakai face my Flambot, who is already tired from his last battle, and if you can take him down, then I'll consider that a victory for you."

"Why are you being so generous?" asked Kyle, unable to hide his suspicion.

Hunter laughed, brushing off any hidden accusations that Kyle may have had tucked away. "Can't I just be grateful that somebody did the right thing when so many others would not?"

Kyle let it go, and Aurin's face broke into a wide smile. "I'm in," he said. "We'll head over here to the field and battle right away. I don't want your Flambot getting any more rest in case he's back to full strength soon."

Hunter held out his arm, letting Aurin lead the way. The two tamers stood facing each other at opposite sides of Kyle's makeshift arena. All five of Aurin's

Minakai stood on the sidelines, watching to see what would happen. None of them knew who would be called to fight. Shamtile was prodding Hornferno, who headbutted his fellow reptile in the shoulder, pushing him away.

Luna brought out all of her own Minakai to watch, while Kyle's Wingbloom perched atop his roof, wanting to see how things would unfold. Wingbloom thought that he would be able to defeat Hunter's Flambot, eager to have a tough battle after so much time spent at the ranch.

"Are both of you ready?" shouted Luna to the two tamers.

"Ready," they said in unison.

"Fight!" she called.

Both tamers summoned their first Minakai, Flambot appearing from out of nowhere, and Leonite teleporting in from the sidelines to begin the assault against the mighty fire elemental.

"Leonite, blitz him with your speed!" ordered Aurin. He had seen Hunter fight with Flambot enough times now that he knew this was the Minakai's weakness. He was big, bulky and powerful, but it made him cumbersome.

Leonite burst forward and leapt at Flambot, who unleashed a flamethrower attack from his palms. Leonite took the hit but pushed through and sank a claw into the robot's arm. The cobalt blue lion never failed to pierce anything material with its claws and Flambot's metallic body was no different.

The lion bit and scratched, tearing up the Minakai's arm, but Flambot was far from done. He grabbed Leonite's head and engulfed the lion's dark mane in a roaring fire. Leonite released the arm and rolled around in the grass to try and put himself out. After the flames were gone, he lay still on the grass; he was already spent.

"Good effort," said Aurin, who banished his first Minakai into the pens. "Dolissile!" he called, warping his second contender in from the sidelines. It was time to torpedo the furnace.

"Don't let this one get any momentum or you're in trouble," warned Hunter. He had clearly been watching Aurin's previous Minakai to see how he battled, and he had used Dolissile a lot recently.

The cyborg dolphin circled the battlefield as Flambot hurled waves of flame around, trying to rid himself of the aquatic pest. Dolissile suddenly turned to face him and charged forward. Flambot swerved out of the way, trying to grab his opponent as he passed, but Dolissile was too sleek.

Aurin's Minakai slowed and turned, before continuing to circle the battlefield. This time he moved more quickly. "Easy," said Aurin as Dolissile passed him, "throw a few more weak ones before blasting off.

"Change tactic," ordered Hunter, and Flambot planted himself on the ground and focused, building up an intense flame inside his stomach. "You know what to do when he gets close."

"Forget what I said, Dolissile," said Aurin. "Explode!"

Dolissile burst forward and accelerated towards Flambot, who exploded in a ring of intense fire. Dolissile was almost thrown off course, but he broke through the intense heat and collided straight with Flambot's grill, bending it inwards.

"What?" exclaimed Hunter, who seemed shocked for the first time. Luna and the Minakai cheered from the sidelines but halted as Kyle held up a hand.

Dolissile careened off to the side and collided with the dirt, unable to fight anymore. Flambot, injured as he was, was still standing.

Aurin smiled, having chipped away at his enemy and called Shamtile onto the field. "He's at the weakest we've ever seen him. You know where his weak point is, hit it as hard as you can."

Shamtile ran forward, yelling and waving his arms. An avalanche of rocks spawned from the sky and pummelled the Flambot, doing almost nothing to him. While he was distracted by the raining stones, Shamtile conjured up a rock cage, entrapping his opponent.

"It's going to take more than that," said Hunter.

"We know," said Aurin confidently.

As Flambot forced his way out of the trap, Shamtile covered his entire body in stone armour and squatted down. He waved his hands once more and the ground rose up faster than the spectators could blink and flung the magic lizard straight towards Flambot.

Shamtile flew through the air and straightened himself into a stone spear. Flambot turned to look at his suddenly-aerial foe, just in time for Shamtile to smash into his large blue eye that rested within the black screen in his head. The pair fell to the ground, both knocked out.

Hunter was taken aback as he watched his strongest Minakai fall to the ground. After a few moments of recovering from the shock, he began clapping. He then started to laugh as Aurin cheered from the other side of the field.

"A double knockout?" asked Luna, uncertain as to whether she should be congratulating or commiserating.

Kyle chuckled at Aurin's strategy. "The terms of the battle were that Aurin had to defeat Flambot. There was nothing to say that any of his Minakai had to remain standing, and Hunter knows that."

"Well done," said Hunter, walking towards Aurin and past the two defeated Minakai. He banished Flambot back to wherever he was kept and Aurin banished Shamtile to the pens. "It's been a while since anybody knocked out Flambot. There have been a few close calls, but he's only taken that bad of a beating in high tower floors."

"It was a fun challenge," said Aurin. "It made me realise why I enjoy battling so much. There's always a way to overcome a superior opponent," he added as he began rubbing his neck. "Granted, that opponent was tired, and it took my three strongest Minakai to do it."

Hornferno snorted in the background as everyone laughed. The red dinosaur considered himself the strongest of Aurin's Minakai.

"Here you go then," said Hunter, handing over the egg. "Make sure to use it well and perhaps we'll battle again next year. If I don't come back to Hazelton, maybe it'll be in the national championships?"

"You should come back," said Aurin with a stupid grin on his face. "I'll give you the battle of a lifetime after another year of training. You'll want to see for yourself before we fight in the nationals."

"I'll think about it," said Hunter, starting to walk away. "I've got a train to catch. Sadly, I can't teleport like my Minakai, but it's a chance to take in our beautiful countryside, right?"

"Right," said Aurin, also appreciating how beautiful this place was compared to the big city.

"Thank you again, Luna," said Hunter. "Kyle, I hope

you'll consider what I said like I plan to consider what Aurin said."

"I will," said Kyle, leaving Aurin and Luna confused about what they were talking about. "Take care."

Hunter departed from the ranch and made his way to the train station, the same place where Aurin began his adventures in Hazelton. It didn't feel as though he had been here for many months, but it also felt like another life ago that he was last back home in Buckstone. Perhaps he ought to visit his parents soon?

"What was Hunter talking about, Kyle?" asked Luna, wagging her finger.

"Hmm?" said the rancher, pretending not to know what she was talking about.

"Don't play dumb. What does he want you to consider?"

"First of all, don't wag your finger at me," said Kyle, brushing her aside. "Secondly, mind your own business."

"I'll battle for you the answer," suggested Aurin. "My Minakai against your Wingbloom. Then will you tell us?"

Kyle laughed heartily. "You have two Minakai still in fighting shape, while another is huffing because you told him he's either fourth or fifth in your power rankings."

"Huh?" said Aurin as Hornferno wrestled with Melansprout in the background, eager to get back to serious training and claim top-ranked status in the team.

"What's in the egg?" asked Kyle, diverting attention away from himself.

Aurin had almost forgotten even though the egg was resting in his arms. Luna bent down and stared at it closely. She squinted, trying to work out what lay inside, but sighed and gave up. She walked off to fetch the incubator for Aurin, returning a minute later.

"Let's hatch it," said Aurin eagerly as Luna placed it on the ground.

The tamers and Innogon gathered around, standing before the egg that Aurin set carefully upon the incubator's base. Shortly after he pressed the button, the grey egg began glowing with a cream light. Everyone was waiting in anticipation as the small form of the Minakai was revealed.

The light started to fade and before them stood a silvery Minakai made of metal. It was a little over a foot tall and had a cord for a tail that ended in a two-pronged plug. Sat inside its rotated square body was a black glass screen, with one glowing blue eye that darted around erratically.

End of Arc 2
The First Hazelton Tournament

Aurin's Team:

Luna's Team:

Chapter 25

It had been months since Aurin had arrived at Hazelton and began his wild adventures in the mysterious, yet wondrous, Harmony Tower. Summer had truly fallen upon the picturesque countryside town and the evening was warm at Kyle's ranch on the outskirts of town, where hundreds of Minakai were kept.

"What is it?" asked Luna, squatting down beside the small robotic Minakai that Aurin had just hatched from the prized egg that Hunter had gifted him.

"I...don't know," muttered Aurin.

"Microbot," said Kyle, knowing all there was to know about Minakai as per usual.

Aurin poked its metallic body, and it flinched. "That eye looks awfully familiar," said the young tamer as he suddenly realised something. "Will it evolve into

Flambot, just like Hunter's one?"

The large furnace-like Minakai had stormed its way through the first Hazelton tournament and Aurin would love to add a force like that to his team. He couldn't help but bounce up and down with excitement, before pulling himself together.

"Worked it out, have you?" asked Kyle. "Microbot is a rare Minakai. You know how some Minakai can evolve into different elementals or change their type?"

Aurin and Luna nodded. "My Melansprout can do that, right?" asked Aurin.

"Right, but it changes type rather than element. Similar to that, Microbot can evolve into each of the elements. Flambot is his fire elemental evolution, Steambot is his water elemental evolution, and so on," Kyle stared into space thoughtfully for a moment. "Now that I think about it, it's no wonder Zodiac was so eager to steal this egg..."

"It can evolve into a cosmic elemental too?" asked Luna, now knowing exactly what the Zodiac Squad sought after the daring warehouse infiltration a few days prior. She didn't know why they wanted cosmic elementals, but Leo, Sagittarius and Libra's conversation had made it clear that they wanted them, starting with Ethruki.

Kyle nodded. "It must be able to, but I'm not sure what its cosmic evolution is. I'll have to look into it and see if there's anything in my folders inside. There are too many Minakai to keep track of in my head."

"So what element is Microbot?" asked Luna. "He looks like a metal elemental to me."

"He doesn't have one," said Kyle, at which both Aurin and Luna were taken aback. "He's like your Leonite, he's a neutral elemental. No affinity one way or another. He's a little blank slate that can be inscribed in ten different ways."

"He's made of metal, but he isn't a metal elemental?"

"Correct," said Kyle.

"Alright," said Aurin, eager to test out the abilities of the little robotic Minakai. "I'm going to hit up the tower solo tomorrow to give Microbot a first run. I want to see what he's made of."

Luna looked relieved and she caught Aurin's eye. "I'm sorry, I just need a day off after everything that's happened lately."

"We've been watching the tournament for the last few days."

"I know, and that's been tiring too. I want to go shopping with Emily and Hannah tomorrow."

"Don't worry," laughed Aurin, picking up Microbot and examining him. He was always curious about how robotic Minakai worked. "You go spend your hard-earned silver and I'll get this guy whipped into shape by the next time you see him."

"Shopping for new Minakai?" asked Kyle.

"Nope," said a happy Luna. "I'm shopping for a new bag!"

The Harmony Tower doors opened in front of Aurin, pulling him forward. It had been a little over a week since his last visit, yet it felt like an eternity. Was it an addiction to the riches the tower had in store or was it the thrill of the challenge of reaching a new floor and fighting a new foe?

Between his travels in the tower and the battles in the tournament, Aurin had laid eyes upon many Minakai, yet his team consisted of five...well, six now that Microbot had been hatched. It was time to double down on his tower escapades. He would strengthen his team both in power and number and be ready for whatever came his way, be that Zodiac or another tournament.

"Are you ready?" he asked Shamtile. The masked lizard gave a warbled grunt of agreement. "How about you?" he asked Microbot. The little robot's eye looked towards him and his spindly metal legs trembled at the prospect of going towards the swirling vortex that called to them.

Aurin walked a couple of paces towards the door and his Minakai were pulled into the tower along with him. They landed on the all-too-familiar tiles but, as ever, the layout had randomly shifted.

The tamer and his two Minakai walked down the corridor, looking for a fight. Two of them did, at least. Microbot stayed very close to Aurin's legs and his eye darted around at the flickering of the lights and even at Shamtile's occasional grumbling.

As they ventured into the first room they spied, a small rabbit-like Minakai appeared before them. It purred gently and it appeared to be waving, but suddenly it shifted into battle mode and showed off its fangs. The wild Rabbacat bounded forward and attacked.

"Microbot, you're up," said Aurin. The little robot refused to move as the wild Minakai encroached at a rapid pace.

Shamtile pushed him forwards, and the Rabbacat

clawed at him. If it weren't for his tough casing and the rodent's general weakness, things would have gotten ugly. Microbot ran around like a headless chicken, trying to avoid the Rabbacat. Aurin and Shamtile looked at each other, both terribly embarrassed. They were glad nobody else was here to watch.

"Just finish it for him," sighed Aurin. Shamtile hurled one heavy rock at the Rabbacat, and it was knocked out instantly, banished from the tower and back to wherever it came from.

"Microbot," called Aurin as the little Minakai waddled over. "I know you've never fought before, but next time I'd like you to try. We're going to be partners for a long time, right? Let's start strong."

Microbot looked at his tamer in confusion, then did a small hop. The three then continued into the tower, Aurin loading up on silver as he passed through the various rooms, skipping over a few of the lesser items that littered the floor, but he did pick up one common healing herb for Luna.

"You zer," said a heavily accented voice from the shadowy corner of a room.

"You looking to battle?" asked Aurin, having had this conversation dozens of times already.

"Precisely! Zey call me Vlad," said the man, emerging from his poor hiding spot. He wore a purple suit and a black cape, looking more like a cartoon villain than a tamer. "And you?"

"Name's Aurin. Have you been waiting here to ambush somebody on the first floor? You're not another Zodiac joker, are you?"

"Zodiac? Me?" asked Vlad. "No no, my friend. You have got zis all wrong. I come seeking adventure and challenge."

Aurin was suspicious about this character. Was he trying to resemble a vampire lord on purpose? "Alright, Vlad. Let's battle!"

"Zis should be easy," chortled Vlad. He threw his cape over his shoulder and thrust his hand forward, summoning a Skrow from a yellow summoning stone embedded in his glove. The evolved Chull was a large bird with a skull covering most of its head along with a white skull and crossbones pattern on its black chest feathers.

Microbot tepidly walked forwards upon Aurin's command, certainly not ready to fight. Shamtile fidgeted nervously by Aurin's side as though he was watching a little brother compete in his first karate match.

"Skrow, get zat leetle robot!" ordered the eccentric tamer.

"Microbot, roll aside, then follow up with a tail whip," commanded Aurin.

The neutral elemental robot froze in place, unable to muster up the courage to move its tiny legs. Skrow collided with it, beak-first, and Microbot was ejected from the tower immediately.

Aurin rubbed his forehead with his thumb and forefinger. He would need to severely rethink his training strategy this time. He ordered Shamtile into battle, who ran in with his usual flailing arms.

"Zis one vill also be no problem," laughed Vlad, with a goofy smile.

Shamtile didn't need Aurin's orders to handle this opponent. When Vlad's Skrow soared in for an attack, Shamtile raised a stone wall and the bird smashed skull first into it. It was ejected from the tower immediately after.

"No!" called Vlad, before being banished from the tower himself.

"I don't want to waste an orb usage here," said Aurin, frustrated at the events of the day so far. "Let's keep going for a few more floors before we call it quits."

Shamtile grunted and warbled.

"Yes, I know that the Skrow was too tough for Microbot, but the Rabbacat definitely wasn't. We'll come up with a new plan at the ranch so let's focus on hitting floor ten."

The two wandered the floor, dealing with the occasional wild Minakai. It wasn't long before they found the mystical elevator and warped up to the second floor.

"Microbot training went badly?" asked Kyle, at which Aurin raised an eyebrow. "I noticed him returning before you did."

"Ah," said Aurin as Dolissile hovered alongside him. Shamtile had an unfortunate encounter with a poison trap on the seventh floor and was defeated upsettingly early. "I think we'll take the old approach of training him against my current Minakai. Perhaps that will be less scary for him?"

"It's worth a shot," said Kyle. "I wouldn't be too worried about him though. You'll break through his fear eventually."

"I hope so. If he has even half the potential that Hunter's Flambot did, then he's going to be a great addition to the team."

"He doesn't have to be a Flambot, you know."

"That's true," said Aurin as he headed towards the house.

"Chores!" scolded Kyle as Aurin slumped off to the fields to clean up Minakai waste.

Chapter 26

Aurin meant business today. "Alright, listen up. We're going to train Microbot one way or another. I've talked you all through your different approaches and I expect that each of you will follow those instructions. If there are any complaints, tell me now."

Shamtile warbled incoherently, Hornferno grunted and snorted, Dolissile floated in place, Leonite bowed his head and Melansprout hung his head in sadness. As far as their tamer could tell, they were all in agreement.

"Shamtile, you're up first."

Luna stood at the far side of Kyle's field and Shamtile rushed over to join her. She would be playing the role of Aurin's opponent while using Aurin's pre-instructed team. If Microbot is too scared to fight, then Aurin would have to try every trick in the book, including tricking the cowardly robot.

"Microbot," said Aurin, squatting beside his newest team member, "you'll be fighting against friends, alright? None of them will do anything to hurt you. All they'll be doing is helping you. Do you understand?"

The robot beeped and booped, his blue eye whizzing around his monitor. Aurin took that to mean he understood, but he wasn't filled with confidence. No matter, it was only the beginning.

"Ready, Luna?" he called.

"Ready!" she replied.

"Microbot, go show Shamtile what you're made of," ordered Aurin, pointing at his magical masked lizard.

Microbot calmly walked forwards, but as soon as Shamtile ran forward, Microbot turned around and stumbled. Aurin massaged his temples, trying to remain calm.

"You can do it, Microbot," he said. "Shamtile isn't all that tough. Just walk right up to him and hit him with your plug...erm, tail."

The robot hopped back onto his feet and tepidly approached Shamtile, who stood still, enjoying the breeze. When he was within a foot of his target, he whipped his cord and the metal plug slapped Shamtile in the leg.

Shamtile exaggeratedly clutched his leg and then threw his arms in the air before falling over. He was very much defeated. Microbot looked confused, then turned to stare at his tamer. Did the human take him to be some kind of fool? Microbot began to bleep angrily.

"Alright, I'm sorry," said Aurin, not realising how clued in Microbot was. "Okay, we'll try a different opponent. No more nonsense, eh?" he lied.

"Dolissile, you're up!" called Luna. "Hit him hard!"

Dolissile obliged and sped forward, seemingly not realising he shouldn't be listening to Luna. He collided with his comrade and the little robot was thrown into the air, before slamming into the ground. He booped in pain and Aurin shooed Dolissile away, scolding him for listening to Luna and not following the plan.

"I thought Hornferno was the loose cannon," he muttered to himself as the second of Microbot's five opponents failed in their attempts at boosting Microbot's confidence.

"Melansprout," said Luna as Microbot shakily stood up, still reeling from Dolissile's attack.

The depressed tree wandered onto the battlefield and examined the injured robot. He wept immediately, feeling horrible for the pain that his newfound friend had just endured. The nature elemental didn't have the heart to even pretend to attack him.

"Are you serious?" shouted Aurin, his anger starting to get the better of him. "Next opponent."

Luna was trying to hold back laughter at this utter spectacle from an otherwise competent tamer. "Leonite," she giggled, "give him your best."

The lion ran forward and Microbot ran away immediately, too scared to face the scarred lion. This entire training session had shaped into a disaster Aurin was on the verge of giving up entirely, but he figured he might as well finish the job.

"Hornferno," he ordered, not giving Luna the chance to call any more shots.

The red dinosaur strolled forward confidently and Microbot started to run away once more. The last couple of days, his only interactions with his fiery teammate were Hornferno snorting ash at him, leaving Aurin to wipe Microbot's screen clean time and time again.

"I give up," lamented Aurin. "We'll try again tomorrow with your team, Luna."

"Wait," she said, no longer giggling.

Hornferno was chasing Microbot and he tackled him to the ground. The dinosaur roared mightily, standing on top of the robot, until Microbot whipped his tail, smacking Hornferno in the eye.

Everybody held their breaths, expecting Hornferno to lose his temper and retaliate tenfold, but he remained calm. He took a deep breath, pretending to store up energy for a fire attack, then was smacked in the face once more.

The dinosaur backed away a little, giving Microbot the chance to stand up. The robot plodded forwards and jammed his tail into Hornferno's leg, sending pulses through it and shocking Hornferno. For a moment, Aurin was convinced that Hornferno's roar of pain was genuine. Surely not?

Hornferno leaned down and growled, but Microbot leapt on top of him and kicked him with his baton-like leg. Hornferno fell over but managed to not be as over the top about it as Shamtile.

"You did it!" cheered Aurin as Microbot looked around, confused. His tamer and Luna rushed to him, then threw him into the air and congratulated him. The other Minakai walked up to him and made their various grunts, roars and echoes as they celebrated Microbot's victory.

Aurin took his Hornferno aside. "Good job, Hornferno. This was just what he needed. A little more of this and it's tower time again. I'm surprised you held back your temper."

Hornferno snarled and playfully bit Aurin's leg.

"You didn't want to have Microbot embarrass you, right? Having a scared teammate isn't a good look for a Minakai as tough as you."

The look in Hornferno's eye told Aurin that he assumed correctly, but the dinosaur made no sound of confirmation or denial. He patted his fiery monster on the back and the two walked back over to the others to celebrate.

"It looks like the strategy worked," said Kyle, emerging from the enclosures.

"I'm a master tamer already," joked Aurin.

"Steady on now," laughed Kyle. "I'll concede that you're a master tamer the moment you clear your first tower."

"I'm going to hold you to that, Kyle. Even if it takes me a few decades, I'll get to the top of Harmony Tower."

"Let's hope that it hasn't closed its doors by then. That's always a risk."

Aurin hadn't considered that. "Which tower was it that you reached the thirty-seventh floor on?" he asked the rancher.

"Ludonia," he said. "All the way in the capital."

Aurin was amazed, as Ludonia was a notoriously difficult tower to ascend in. There were hundreds of tamers inside at all times, and even if they were separated by different dimensions of the tower, you would run into people constantly. Each and every one of them was keen to battle, looking to prove that they were the better tamer.

Following Hornferno's lead, the rest of the Minakai gave a much better performance the second time around. The third round didn't require anywhere near as much fakery, and in the fourth round they went more on the offensive. They spent the rest of the day training and, by the evening, Microbot wasn't even recognisable as the same Minakai.

"Impale with your tail," rhymed Aurin, unintentionally, as Microbot fought against Rodney's Spaqua on the third floor of the tower. Aurin was hoping to make this his Minakai's eighth victory of the day, and not a single one had been against one of his other monsters.

Microbot jammed his tail into the Spaqua's bubble and pulsed, causing the little tadpole to spasm within its rippling bubble shield for a moment before losing consciousness. It was banished from the tower, but Rodney remained, having at least one Minakai in reserve.

"Alright, you win," he said. "I knew I didn't stand a chance against you when I first spotted you."

"How come?" asked Aurin.

"I recognised both you and Luna from the tournament, you were both great," at which Luna beamed brightly.

"Thanks, Rodney. Were you competing?"

"Me? Nah, I didn't qualify. I hadn't made it high enough on the tower and I only had two Minakai back then anyway."

"Maybe we'll see you around town or at the tournament next year?" posed Luna.

"I hope so," the tamer replied as he searched his bag for an Orb of Return. "Going to cut my losses and get out of here for now. Good luck with the rest of the run, both of you. Take it easy," he said with a wink as he warped away.

Aurin and Luna proceeded happily along, both proud that Microbot had come so far in a matter of days. Aurin was personally confident that the shiny little robot would be a great addition to his team and he had been thinking all day about what Microbot would evolve into.

He was curious about what its cosmic elemental evolution was, but he had no idea how to find out and Kyle didn't have any information in his numerous files, both physical and digital. No, Aurin would happily take another element. The only problem was that he could only choose between the three evolution shards.

An Astral Shard would doubtless give him the neutral evolution, but the Solar and Lunar Shard was where the true choice lay. A Solar Shard would evolve Microbot into one of his fire, water, air or water evolutions, whereas the Lunar Shard would result in a nature, lightning, ice or metal form.

He was going to wait and see what else he would find in the tower and what other Minakai he would add to his team before making the final decision. So far, he had Shamtile to cover the earth element, Dolissile for metal, Hornferno for fire, Leonite for neutral and Melansprout for nature. He still needed water, air, lightning, ice and the ever-elusive cosmic element for full coverage.

The young tamer knew that he hadn't been using elements and types to their full advantage, but that was going to change. He was going to be far more strategic going forward to ensure that he was prepared for whatever battles lay ahead, tournament or otherwise.

The two tamers ascended to the fourth floor,

determined to challenge Microbot. If he could carry them all the way to the end of the fifth floor by himself, then he had proven himself beyond a shadow of a doubt that he was ready.

Chapter 27

"There's the elevator," said Aurin excitedly. He and Luna were accompanied by Shamtile and Innogon, their first respective Minakai of the day. Zero knockouts before the tenth floor was their agreed goal, and it was going well.

"Let's not waste any more time then," said Luna, placing her hands upon the orb.

Aurin joined her and the two were pulled through space and transported to the ninth floor. They expected to be standing in a typical room, but something was very amiss.

"Just what...what is this?" asked Aurin.

"How would I know?" asked Luna. "I'm a little scared...what should we do?"

The rooms were normally connected by typical

corridors and the rooms themselves were not especially big, but this time was different. The entire floor appeared as a room so gigantic that all they could see was the walls. Even the wall torches were so far away from them that they would have to walk through a dark abyss to reach them.

"Let's get out of here," said Luna, the faint outline of her face bore a terrified look.

"No way," said Aurin. "This is something I've never seen before. There must be good treasure here. A shard or an egg? Maybe even some of those rare herbs, fruits and berries that you always talk about."

"Fine, but if things start to go badly, use your Orb of Return and get us out of here."

"Agreed," said Aurin, happy to have his way. He had occasionally spotted anomalies in the tower, mostly insignificant ones, but this was a mystery far greater.

The two cautiously walked forwards in the direction of one of the walls, but there was suddenly a burst of flame as a Dogember spawned, and barked a fireball from its mouth straight at Shamtile. It hit him square in the mask and he batted the flames out before encasing his hand in stone and punching the fiery dog right in the snout.

An unexpected whoosh and a Techling zoomed past Innogon, its metal wing cutting deep into the miniature drake's arm. It whirled around again, going straight for the throat, but a jet of water knocked it off course.

Snip snip, came a sound as a scuttling insect walked forwards. The armoured, purple Snippet used its scissor hands to take a chunk out of Shamtile's arm before the reptile summoned an avalanche to crush the bug. Luna rushed to his aid and applied an ointment before bandaging up the arm.

More and more Minakai were spawning in the darkness, far more numerous than even a den trap. Even with the strength of their Minakai, the numbers were not in Aurin and Luna's favour.

"Orb!" urged Luna, desperately.

Aurin rummaged in his pack and brought out the magical crystal ball. He cast the spell it held within and...nothing happened.

"It's empty," said Aurin.

"Empty?" cried Luna, panic well and truly having set in.

"Get to the walls as fast as you can. At least we'll have more light there. We can worry about the elevator later."

The two ran through the ever-growing horde of Minakai and by the time they reached the walls, both of their Minakai had been lost in the crowd. Their summoning stones glowed momentarily as they were banished from the tower and sent into stasis.

"Inno!" called Luna in despair, as she summoned Spritzard.

Aurin meanwhile called upon Hornferno, who began to blast the enemy Minakai with waves of fire. Spritzard wasn't kind enough to douse the flames, and instead shot each foe that broke through the fire wall, sending them straight back into the crowd.

"Let's keep moving," urged Aurin as momentary peace set in. "We need to find the elevator if we want to keep going up."

"Can't we just leave?" asked Luna, not thinking straight.

"I'm not going to sacrifice my Minakai for a quick exit, and I know you don't want that either. We keep going and we pray we find another orb. If we don't, then we'll go down swinging."

"You're right...you're right."

The two edged along the wall for a short while, seeing nothing helpful along the way. They then decided they must run into the darkness while things were sufficiently quiet. Hornferno continually lit the way with fireballs and Spritzard floated alongside the tamers, using her water barrier to keep them from harm.

Aurin suddenly tripped on something and fell to his knees. He saw what he had caught his foot on and stashed it in his bag.

"There!" exclaimed Luna, pointing towards a glint of blue and gold, illuminated by a flickering fireball that whizzed past it.

A sudden burst of green light and a Funglie blocked their way. It began to spit poison spores but was banished by a combination of thick flames and a torrent of water from Hornferno and Spritzard.

The two tamers placed their hands on the blue elevator orb and focused, letting the magic pull them upstairs and away from the danger, but not before they saw Spritzard get body slammed by a hefty Metortoise, sending the water demon into the pocket dimension, awaiting return to the ranch.

Aurin, Luna and Hornferno landed on the ground with a thud, too tired to brace themselves. They all took a second to catch their breath, very pleased to be in a normal room on a normal floor of the tower. The tenth floor, in fact.

"I'm glad that's over," sighed Aurin. "Great job, Hornferno."

The red dinosaur roared mightily, proud of the ferocity of his own attacks. Aurin felt as though he hadn't given him enough chances to test his might and Hornferno would have agreed, but a single floor more than made up for it.

"Spritzard..." lamented Luna, tearing up a little. "I didn't even see the Metortoise coming. I was too focused on escaping."

"She'll be fine," said Aurin, doing his best to console her. "Here, I found this downstairs when we were trying to escape."

"Is that what you almost broke your neck on?" Luna asked as Aurin passed her a Lunar Shard.

"I hoped you didn't see that part," he laughed.

Luna called upon her Happynut, the last of her remaining three Minakai that she could use in this run. The little plant danced cheerfully, glad to be seeing some action outside of training at the ranch.

"Thanks," said Luna, accepting it with a smile. "Come here," she said to her Happynut, and she pressed the Lunar Shard against it.

Aurin was taken aback as her Minakai evolved into a Melansprout on the spot. "Just like that?" he asked as the green glow dissipated.

"He's trained plenty," said Luna, "and besides, I want him to have a chance of surviving the run without being knocked out. Using the shard also means that we can't lose it should we be forcefully kicked out of the tower."

Aurin decided it best not to bring up the hard time she gave him for wanting to evolve his own Happynut only a month ago.

The two tamers and their Minakai departed from the empty room and walked the corridors of the tenth floor, seeking whatever rooms they could find in the hopes that the treasure it held included at least one Orb of

Return.

"Floor fourteen," said Aurin out of the blue.

"I'm sorry?"

Aurin was smiling. "I think we'll find one on floor fourteen and then leave. All things considered, it isn't that bad if we lose before that. We know one new danger to be on the lookout for, we got plenty of training in, and you evolved your Happynut. Worst case scenario is pretty good!"

"We haven't been that high before. Usually, I'm the optimistic one," giggled Luna. "Why the sudden change in your attitude?"

"I've got a clearer goal now. Before, I wanted to reach the top of the tower and train for the tournament. That's fine, but one is a long-term goal and the other is very general. Now, I know that I want to find a few eggs, evolve a few team members and train to beat a few very specific tamers."

"I'm glad you've got a more focused approach. You've seemed much more positive since the battle with Hunter, even with the frustration of training Microbot. I'm surprised he's not here with you."

"He will be," said Aurin, holding up his glove and showing off his third summoning stone. "I'm saving him for last."

Hornferno glowered at him, offended that Aurin didn't think he could carry him until they found a way out.

"I meant to say, I'm saving him for if I need him," laughed Aurin. "I have every faith in you, Horn. You'll squash any enemy like a fly, right?"

The dinosaur roared and the tamers laughed, their spirits much brighter than when they first landed on the tenth floor. Luna had decided that Aurin was right, it wasn't so bad now that they were out of the danger of the open floor.

They explored the floor for a while, lifting whatever treasures they could carry. Silver coins, unusually coloured berries, a few crystals which Aurin ignored—obviously less valuable than silver—as well as herbs of various shapes and sizes. Aurin asked what each of them was for and took in very little of Luna's response.

"Here's a question for you," he said, finally thinking of something to further the conversation. "What's the rarest berry you can think of and what does it do?"

"Hmm," said Luna, pondering intently. "That would have to be a Roche Berry," she said. She deliberately paused, letting Aurin stare at her in expectation of an answer.

"Well?" he asked.

"I'm just relishing the fact that you're taking an interest and that you're going to want to compete with me for berries in the future once I tell you what it does."

"Come on," he urged, starting to not care so much.

"It can turn a Minakai into an egg."

Aurin's mouth hit the floor. "It can what?" he exclaimed, proving Luna correct.

"Yup."

"Where can I find one? How do I get it? Are they on sale in the shop? Would Cedric know?" he asked, his mind and mouth both running a thousand miles per second.

"Relax," said Luna, holding up her hands. "They're so rare that they go for hundreds of gold ounces. Tamers save them for cosmic elementals as well as epic Minakai they come across in the towers."

"I bet they do," said Aurin, who had immediately decided he wanted to do that very thing.

"If you really want one, I believe they start appearing after the thirtieth floor. It's super rare though, most reports are that it's slightly...*slightly* more common around floor forty-five."

Aurin was reinvigorated, and now considerably more interested in berries. He strolled along at a brisk pace as Luna struggled to keep up with him. They roamed from room to room through the vast and winding corridors, but suddenly...

"Well, well," came a voice from the room that the duo stepped into.

Standing before the tamers, was a man and a woman wearing white jackets and trousers complete with black undershirts and boots. Their hair was covered by white hats and, adorning their faces, were masks with a star pattern.

"Zodiac," muttered Aurin, as the two tamers raised their hands to summon their Minakai.

Chapter 28

"Didn't we teach you enough of a lesson?" asked Aurin, as Hornferno growled, raring to go. There had been no word from the Zodiac Squad since the chaos that Aurin and Luna had caused in their warehouse base.

The male member smirked. "You don't remember us, do you?" he asked.

"You all look the same to me," replied Aurin. "I'll admit the outfits are cool, but the masks make you all look like clowns. Especially Leo's mask. What sort of man wears a lion on his face?"

"Shut up," snapped the woman. "Do you have any idea of the destruction you caused?"

"That *was* the idea," said Aurin.

"Do you think there'll be no repercussions for what you did? Boy, you don't know the level of power that the

Zodiac Squad holds, Minakai or otherwise. You'll rue the day you crossed us."

Aurin shook his head slowly. "I don't think you realise what *you're* up against. You think that I did damage to your little group already? Well, I'm going to do some serious damage here too, if you're looking for a fight."

Luna was less confident than Aurin, but she knew she didn't have a choice. Aurin's Minakai were tried and tested, but her Melansprout had just evolved and it was the last one left in her party. A loss here meant banishment from the tower.

"You bet," said the man, readying a summoning stone.

Aurin and Luna sent forward Hornferno and Melansprout, while the Zodiac duo summoned an Anacondice and a Gittup, the evolved form of Tuptup and a powerful lightning elemental.

"Melt that Anacondice, Hornferno!" ordered Aurin, fired up.

Hornferno charged in, his nostrils flaring and emitting smoke. He took a deep breath and unleashed a flamethrower from his mouth, but the slippery snake escaped the flames, quickly coiling itself around Melansprout.

"You can break free, Melansprout," said Luna, but the plant was struggling, the ice elemental Anacondice having an advantage over his nature affinity didn't make things easy for the newly evolved Minakai.

Hornferno leapt to his teammate's defence and sank his teeth deep into the snake, as the Gittup zapped the dinosaur with lightning from his glowing golden tail. Hornferno kept it together and breathed fire into the wound he had made on the Anacondice and it recoiled, releasing Melansprout.

Luna's Minakai tugged on Gittup's tail, getting shocked in the process, but distracting the beast for long enough for Hornferno to ram his horn into their foe. Melansprout then straightened his tail and whipped the sharp leaf across Gittup's side, taking it down. It was banished from the tower, sending the Zodiac woman out of the tower with it moments later.

"You're going to pay for that," said the Zodiac man angrily. "You're going to pay for everything, mark my words."

"I don't think so," said Aurin. "Finish him off!" he called to his Hornferno.

As Anacondice writhed on the ground, the dinosaur pounced on his nearly-defeated enemy, and with another deep bite, it was ejected from the tower.

"We will come for you," warned the Zodiac member. "We will be back stronger tha—"

Aurin and Luna looked at each other and laughed as he was cut off mid-sentence, banished from Harmony Tower, but reality set in very quickly afterwards as the two thought about the implications of Zodiac rebounding so quickly.

"Did you need to start taunting them and threatening them further?" asked an exasperated Luna. "As if we don't have enough trouble with them."

"I'm hoping they don't call my bluff," shrugged Aurin. "If they think I'm tougher than I am, maybe they'll leave us alone."

"Maybe he's bluffing too?" asked Luna.

"He seemed pretty serious, they both did," said Aurin, but he considered it was possible. "Granted, we haven't had much adventuring in the tower since the tournament, but this is the first we've heard about

Zodiac since."

Luna looked deep in thought, but she didn't say anything. She was clearly troubled, even more so than Aurin was.

"They recognised us immediately, we've met them before?" asked Aurin, breaking the silence.

"You don't remember?"

"No, should I?"

"They were the two that we met the same day we met Gardner," said Luna as it slowly clicked into place for Aurin.

"Ah! They had the Petalcub and Heatpup. That was them, right?"

"That was them, yeah," confirmed Luna.

"They certainly know how to hold a grudge. That said, we probably do deserve to be on the receiving end of their ire considering everything that's happened."

"I'm just glad we didn't run into any Zodiac elites like Leo," sighed Luna. "I suspect he wouldn't be attacking the Minakai, he would be attacking us directly."

Aurin agreed. "I suppose there's nothing else for it now, we'll just have to keep moving. If there are any more lurkers, we'll take them as they come."

The pair roamed the tenth floor until they found the elevator, picking up various odds and ends as they explored the rooms. They encountered little trouble outside of a few stray Minakai that were lurking in the corridors.

"Blast it right out of the tower," ordered Aurin, as Hornferno handily dealt with a measly Peekan.

"You've got the advantage," said Luna to Melansprout as he faced off against a tougher foe; a wild Cybuzz. The evolved form of Metaworm buzzed around on wings of metal with two sharp spears on its arms, seeking whatever target it could find.

Floor eleven was more of a challenge, with dozens of Minakai around every corner, but they persisted thanks to Luna's various healing herbs and berries. She had used them before but didn't want to drain her supply too quickly. Today it felt much more necessary and Aurin was glad that she was so resourceful.

The twelfth floor was tougher still, as a Hogannon blasted Hornferno and Melansprout with fireballs from its cannon arms. The pair narrowly avoided defeat with a lucky grapple from Melansprout, leaving the Hogannon open for Hornferno to strike at.

A confusion trap almost ended the run as Hornferno was suddenly unable to control where he was going and recognise who was a friend and who was a foe, but the tamers were able to outrun him until he snapped back to reality.

"Floor thirteen," said Aurin, growing as tired as his Minakai. It was clear to him now why so many tamers quit doing tower runs and instead bought and traded Minakai and shards.

"This is our new record," beamed Luna, managing to remain upbeat after the exhausting run.

"Just another twenty-five and we'll have beaten Kyle."

"I have a newfound respect for how high he reached. It sounded like an impressive number, but we're only around a third of where he got to."

"And when you think about it, it'll only get harder with each successive floor."

"That's true. Stack the increasing difficulty, your Minakai being whittled down, the fatigue of spending days on end here, unable to sleep because of monsters spawning, and it sounds nightmarish."

"I wonder if people go crazy here? Maybe there are feral humans living near the top, trapped in limbo," said Aurin, his eyes growing wide.

Luna laughed, but he kept a straight face for just long enough that she thought there was a chance he was serious. "Let's get going, shall we?" she asked.

Aurin agreed and led the way down the torchlit corridor. The jade green tiles glistened as they walked, reflecting the light onto the golden-brown walls. It was a pleasant floor to be on, but the pair were too focused on escaping the tower with their loot. Aurin in particular had amassed enough silver that he could pay Kyle's rent charge for a full month and still have change leftover.

As the pair reached a fork in the road, they heard a sudden loud stomping growing closer from behind. They turned to see what was approaching and spotted a Gorungol, a quadrupedal evolution of the limbless Gorun, charging at them. The in-between evolution connecting Gorun and Gorungra was about to crush the pair and their Minakai.

Aurin pushed Luna to the left and quickly dove down the right path, but Hornferno was slammed against the wall by the stone construct. Aurin's summoning stone glowed an orangey-red briefly as his Minakai was ejected.

"Run!" he called to Luna, as the Gorungol turned towards him. "I'll lose it and meet you by the elevator."

"No!" cried Luna.

"I'll be fine," said Aurin, summoning Microbot, his final Minakai of the tower run.

Aurin turned and sprinted in the opposite direction, Microbot clinging to his back with the cable of its tail and its two spindly legs. The small Minakai had its plug ready to shock the Gorungol should it get too close, but it wasn't much of a threat when the robot was clearly outmatched by a far stronger enemy.

The two weaved in and out of rooms, throughout the narrow corridors, but the Gorungol refused to back down. It barrelled through other wild Minakai without a second thought.

"Of all times," said Aurin as he ran through a room where an egg sat. He found a way to loop around, then snatched the egg from the ground, hurriedly stashing it in his satchel.

"I've got an idea," he said to Microbot, explaining the plan to his Minakai. The robot beeped and booped in agreement, but his old fear was starting to creep in once more. This time, however, the fear wasn't for himself.

They reached a corridor that led to another fork. Microbot hopped aside as Aurin stood against the wall, waiting for the Gorungol to crush him. The golem was inches from him when he rolled aside, and it crashed into the tower wall.

It was Microbot's chance. He climbed atop the dazed Minakai and jammed its plug into the Gorungol's eye socket. He sent a pulse through it, cracking the golden topaz-like crystal. As the Gorungol recoiled, he did the same to the other eye, blinding his target.

"Let's get moving," ordered Aurin, as the wild Minakai began thrashing erratically, trying to kill whatever had blinded it.

Aurin and Microbot made a hasty retreat, Aurin evermore glad that Kyle had made him train alongside his Minakai. Kyle always had a reason for the things he did, but it wasn't always clear at first. When it was clear, Aurin felt silly for ever having questioned him.

He wandered the floor at a more relaxed pace, but still careful to check around each corner. Although Microbot had come far, the thirteenth floor was too advanced for his current level. He avoided other Minakai like the plague, finally coming across the elevator, but Luna was nowhere to be seen.

Chapter 29

"I'll be fine," said Aurin, as Luna saw Microbot appear in a flash of light at the other side of the Gorungol.

She grabbed Melansprout by his stumpy hand and the pair ran in the opposite direction. She wanted to defend Aurin, but she knew that he could always get himself out of tight spots. She would find the elevator first and call out to him when she did.

"This is really testing your new form, right Happynut?" she said, still used to calling her Minakai by his old species name.

Melansprout began to weep uncontrollably, as depressed as Aurin's usually was.

"You'll be okay," said his tamer, patting him on his back. "I'm sure that when you evolve again, you'll be a lot happier. I'll try and make sure that it isn't too far away, okay?"

The Melansprout cried louder, knowing it would end up in complete and utter despair or feel a never-ending rage. A cruel fate, but the tragic nature of his evolutionary line.

"Please stop crying," begged Luna, afraid that wild Minakai would be drawn to her position.

Once Melansprout was under control, they began moving from room to room, in search of the familiar blue crystal within the golden pedestal. Luna was especially careful checking for traps hidden within the floor tiles. They were hard to spot, but not impossible.

Her bag was at capacity, stuffed to the brim with various healing herbs, so she ignored most items that she found on her travels. The herbs were more important. She could treat light wounds, cure toxins, soothe burns and even restore feeling to numb limbs.

"Oh!" she exclaimed upon seeing a Solar Shard. "Aurin could use this."

She picked it up and carried it in one hand, planning to give it to her friend as a gift. Admittedly, it was his fault for not checking the uses remaining in his orb, but it was also thanks to him that they hadn't been forcefully booted from the tower.

Luna had been quietly wondering if it was worth fighting against a foe they knew they couldn't defeat solely to lose and be sent home, but she knew Aurin would refuse to take a deliberate loss. She also knew that it was unfair to their Minakai to let them suffer just so the tamers could escape.

"Where to go?" she pondered, feeling vulnerable at a crossroads of corridors. She threw a silver coin into the air and it landed closest to the path to her right, so she followed it. Luck may or may not have been on her side today, but she trusted the coin to guide her true.

Luna walked for some time, but she felt no closer to finding the elevator than she did when she started. In fact, she was certain that she'd passed most of these corridors before. The rooms? Yes, she remembered leaving these items behind the first time around. She was definitely going in circles.

Suddenly, a loud crashing sound, as a heavy stone Minakai with golden yellow crystals stomped around wildly. She recognised it immediately, having seen it mere minutes ago.

"Oh no," she sighed, watching the Gorungol approach. She turned to run, worried that Aurin had been ejected from the tower alongside his Microbot, but something was wrong.

Observing the Gorungol for a moment, she could see that it wasn't making a beeline for her. It wasn't going in a straight line at all. It bumped into the walls, it scraped its shoulders on corners, and its two eye crystals were heavily damaged.

"We can take him, Melansprout," she said, her voice wavering. Melansprout wept, but was it a confident weep? It didn't matter, anything to get rid of this menace once and for all.

Melansprout flung its head back and then thrust it forward, dislodging two of the leaves from atop his head. They spun so fast that they were as sharp as steel. Whizzing through the air, they sought Gorungol's crystals on its back. As the leaves collided with their target, the crystals shattered and sent shards of yellow through the air. The beast they belonged to toppled soon after, its strength waning.

The depressed tree Minakai leapt on top of the weakened Minakai, who flailed blindly. It bucked and bashed, trying to shake off Melansprout, but he pounded his fists upon the beast, slowly wearing it down. It wasn't long before the golem collapsed, and vanished from the tower.

"We did it!" cheered Luna, jumping for joy. Melansprout, in a rare moment of happiness, gave a boisterous leap of his own before slumping over once more. Luna rushed over and hugged her Minakai tightly.

They wandered further, still careful to avoid Minakai who weren't blinded, and they finally saw it. The elevator. Standing beside it was Aurin, waiting patiently with his Microbot.

"I was starting to wonder if you ran ahead without me," he said.

"I would never leave you behind," she smiled. "You didn't think I was halfway back to the ranch after a miserable defeat?"

"Nope, I knew there was no way you'd let anybody take you out today."

Luna suddenly realised something. "Did you blind that Gorungol?" she asked.

"You saw it?" Aurin said with a small laugh. "Yeah, Microbot and I hatched a little plan."

"Melansprout finished the job."

"Well done, Melansprout. Evolving him was definitely the right choice. He's been great today."

"Shall we?" asked Luna, gesturing towards the elevator.

Aurin nodded and the two placed their hands atop the blue crystal and vanished from the thirteenth floor, pulled through space and onto the fourteenth floor. They had broken their record on the very same run they had broken their last record.

"I don't believe it," said Aurin, laughing.

"What?" asked Luna.

He pointed to the room ahead of them, where an orb lay in waiting. They rushed over to it excitedly, hoping it was an Orb of Return and not one of the other magical orbs on the tower.

Aurin picked it up and examined it. "It's an Orb of Return alright," he said confidently.

"How can you tell?"

"I have a strong feeling about it."

Luna furrowed her brow. "What nonsense."

"Watch," said the young man, harnessing the magic from the orb.

The two were pulled from the fourteenth floor as fast as they had arrived and found themselves standing outside the tower as the sun was setting. Aurin knelt on the dirt path and cradled the loose pebbles in his hand, before letting them fall through his fingers.

"At last," he said. "I thought we'd be stuck there until tomorrow."

"Let's get back to the ranch before I need to get home," said Luna.

The two walked along the path, admiring the beauty of the grass, the trees and the hills in the distance. It was a pleasant summer evening and they couldn't have felt better after such a trial.

When they arrived at the ranch, Kyle was walking out of the pens. "There you are," he said. "Successful run?"

Aurin and Luna looked at each other.

"That bad, huh?" he said but noticed they each had a Minakai with them. "You made it out in one peace, at least."

"We broke our previous record," said Luna.

"Floor thirteen?"

"All the way to floor fourteen.

"Hey, that's not bad, you know?" said Kyle, mildly impressed. "Any good spoils today?"

Aurin reached into his bag and pulled out the egg he had found. "For you," he said to Luna, handing it over to her. "It's my fault we were stuck there for so long, so this is my apology."

"You didn't need to apologise," said Luna, refusing to take the egg.

"I insist," said Aurin.

"I actually have something for you," she said, retrieving the Solar Shard. "I'll take the egg if you take this. Deal?"

"Deal," said Aurin as they exchanged their gifts. He already knew exactly what to do with this and rushed off the pens as Luna retrieved the incubator from Kyle's house.

"I need to start charging you two for using that," he said when she returned.

"Yeah, yeah," scoffed Luna. "You've made that joke before."

"Joke?"

Before Luna could retort, Aurin returned seconds later with a somewhat recovered Hornferno. The red dinosaur was still bloody and bruised, but he seemed otherwise okay.

Aurin cleared his throat. "As a reward for your hard work today, Hornferno, Luna has kindly given me the means to take your power to the next level. You will no longer be a mere Hornferno, powerful as you may be. Instead, you will be..."

He held the Solar Shard to Hornferno's skin, and it began to glow as the dinosaur shone redder than ever, and changed shape. Hornferno grew notably larger and his neck lengthened, becoming as thick as a tree and almost as long. It extended to almost the length of the rest of his body while his legs bulked up to accommodate. After a few seconds, the red glow faded and revealed Hornferno's new form.

"Spikruption," finished Aurin, as the large dinosaur stood even before him, now much taller than his tamer. "Do you feel powerful?"

The newly evolved Minakai roared loudly, shaking the fence posts and alerting Kyle's Frogre guards. The rancher told them to back down, and they did so.

"Now we both have one," remarked Kyle, reminding Aurin of when the young tamer fought his before the tournament.

"You two can reminisce later," said Luna as she clumsily placed the egg on the incubator, excited to see what Minakai lay inside, waiting to be born.

She pressed the button and the egg glowed blue. "Water again?" remarked Aurin. "That would have been good for my team," he said as Luna shushed him.

When the glow faded, Kyle laughed heartily at the Minakai Luna was presented with. She frowned, then glanced at Aurin. "Are you sure you still don't want it?" she asked.

A greyish-blue bloated fish sat on the grass, its mouth open as wide as its vacant eyes. It goofily waved its tail fin and bounced around, making a sloshing sound as it slowly moved towards its tamer.

"Dopefish?" said Aurin.

"Dopefish," she sighed as her Minakai rubbed itself against her leg. It was both smooth and slimy, making her skin crawl.

"Don't count him out," said Kyle, still laughing. "He's

a force to be reckoned with when he evolves, right Aurin?"

"I suppose so," said Aurin, thinking about the times he had to deal with a tamer's ferocious Doripper that lived at the ranch, "but what can Luna do to train him in the meantime?"

"Precious little," said Kyle as Luna stood there looking upset. "While it isn't completely useless, it's a bit...well...alright, it's pretty useless."

Aurin suddenly remembered something. "Zodiac!"

Luna immediately snapped out of her funk. "Oh!" she exclaimed. "That's right. How could we forget?"

Kyle raised an eyebrow at the seemingly random yelling. Aurin and Luna then told him about their encounter with the Zodiac duo in the tower. He nodded along as he listened, not entirely surprised by the reemergence of the villainous tamers.

"We knew they'd be back eventually," he said. "While it could be an isolated incident and these two jokers are acting alone, but I would say that it's worth taking them at their word. Presume that the Zodiac Squad are quietly gathering strength again, readying themselves for their comeback. Maybe they're building a new hideout, maybe they're bolstering their Minakai army, or maybe they're up to something else entirely while concealed in the shadows. Take the threat seriously."

"We plan to," said Aurin as Luna agreed.

"Good," said Kyle. "Then there's not much else to do about it. I'll let Knot know tomorrow, rather than you two going down to the station or the mayor's office and causing hysteria."

Aurin and Kyle walked Luna home. Most of the conversation was Aurin poking fun at Luna's Dopefish while she tried not to listen. She huffed about it for the rest of the evening, but there was no chance that she would be mentioning that to Aurin the next day.

Chapter 30

Hazelton was bustling today, not quite as much as when the tournament was underway, but the sunny August weather had everybody in town outside and enjoying themselves. This included Aurin and Luna who were waiting for Gardner at a small cafe along with Shamtile and Innogon.

"Are you sure you want to tell him about the Zodiac attack?" asked Luna with trepidation. She was considering what Kyle had said about causing hysteria by saying too much.

Aurin wouldn't change his mind. "Gardner's been on the receiving end of one of their attacks, and he was going to help us out when we thought they would jump one of us after our battle. If anybody deserves to know outside of ourselves, it's him. I think that's only fair."

"I understand," said Luna, relenting. She couldn't deny Aurin made a good point.

As they waited, Shamtile and Innogon were excitedly sharing a banana milkshake. It wasn't long before they started bickering as Innogon was hogging most of it.

"Well, that's your fault for having to sneak some under your mask, Shammy," scolded Aurin. "I know you won't take it off, but that's not Innogon's fault."

"Come to think of it," came Gardner's voice as he approached where they sat in the sun. "I've never seen a Shamtile without a mask. What does he look like?"

"Hi Gardner," said Aurin and Luna in unison.

"I couldn't tell you," replied Aurin. "I've never seen him take off his mask either. If you want to lose a battle against him, try it. He'll crush your hand, human *or* Minakai."

The three spent a few minutes catching up on what they'd been up to since the tournament. Gardner had been travelling to other towns and cities across Bretonia, seeing what other monster towers had to offer.

"There are only about thirty towers open across the country," he said, "so it would take forever to really try and explore all of them. I've been to five of them and the trip cost me half of my earnings from my tower runs here. Worth it though!"

"Did you see any new Minakai that you've never seen before?" asked an excited Aurin.

"I found a couple of them that are rare here, but more common on those towers. I think I would need to explore higher floors to really see the crazier creatures."

"How about the eggs?" asked Aurin.

"Slow down," said Luna, nudging him.

Gardner laughed. "It's fine, honestly. I'd be doing the

same if it were the other way around. Yeah, I found two eggs, so it paid off nicely. Got myself a Cryopillar and another Happynut, if you can believe it. Hopefully, this one evolves into Angree, so I've got an adaptable pair between it and my Desparee."

The three continued to talk for a while before Aurin finally broached the topic of Zodiac.

"Our favourite group of thieving tamers is still around," said Aurin, rather bluntly. Luna gave him an awkward side-eye.

"I figured it would happen eventually," sighed Gardner. "What's the story there?"

Aurin and Luna explained what had happened in their tower run a couple of weeks ago, and Gardner listened intently. Indeed, it didn't seem that surprising to him, he was more concerned about how quickly they had re-emerged.

"I suspect they'll limit their activities to the tower or suspected members may start getting jumped in the streets. Word about their antics has spread to a few other towns. I wouldn't call it a big topic, but it made the news. It didn't hurt that I spread the story on my travels."

"The more recognition they have, the better," said Aurin. "People need to be aware if they come to Hazelton, never mind wanting to challenge Harmony Tower."

"Agreed," said Gardner. "We're not living in safe times, but I suppose it's nothing compared to what things were like when people let Minakai run around unrestricted."

"That's true," said Luna. "We don't have it too bad. At least we have our own Minakai to protect us." She glanced at Innogon who was trying to take the last of the milkshake back from Shamtile who was hiding under the table to conceal his mouth as he drank.

"Have you heard much about Hunter?" asked Aurin.

"You didn't watch the National Championships?" Gardner asked incredulously.

"I forgot it was over the last couple of weeks," said an embarrassed Aurin. "I was so caught up with training that I've barely left the ranch or the tower. It only occurred to me this morning."

"Top sixteen this year," said Gardner. "The others from the Hazelton qualifiers didn't even crack the top sixty-four. And on top of that, it's another year of Tobias reigning supreme at the top of the league. No World Championship this year though, so he's going to need to keep defending the national title if he wants another shot at that title too."

Tobias was known throughout Bretonia. He had been ranked number one throughout the country for five years now and was notorious for turning down most of the sponsorship deals he was offered. Previous national champions would have had their faces plastered over every other advertisement, but he was an outlier.

"A five-year streak is an impressive run," said Aurin. "I think it's fair to say that he didn't just get lucky once if he can defend the title for so long."

"If he can make it to ten, then I'll be impressed," joked Luna.

The three tamers finished up their drinks and then Aurin and Luna bid Gardner farewell. They promised to meet up again soon now that he was back home for the time being. Gardner even suggested they all do a tower run together, bringing them to the three-person limit before they get split into different instances.

As the day was still young, Aurin, Luna, Shamtile and Innogon took a walk through the forest on the way back to the ranch. They were feeling burned out from the tower so it was the perfect day for relaxing. Shamtile and Innogon ran ahead playfully, neither giving each other a break after their milkshake squabbles.

"I wonder what it was like when Minakai could roam freely without their tamers?" asked Aurin.

"I've heard that there are still places where they can," replied Luna. "Private islands, special regions of different countries. I can't say I know much about it."

"Me neither, but I'm definitely curious to see what they get up to."

"Haven't you seen enough wild Minakai in the tower to know that they'll just attack you?"

"Maybe it's different outside of the tower?" suggested Aurin.

"I can't say I know either," came a husky voice, "and I'm a rancher, so you can take that for what it's worth."

A young man emerged from the trees. He had floppy blonde hair and wore a white shirt with a red waistcoat. He looked serious, and the two tamers immediately held their gloves out, presuming him to be part of the Zodiac Squad.

"Easy now!" exclaimed the man, holding his hands up. He was wearing a glove of his own but made no sudden moves. "Why are you so jumpy? I'm just heading to the tower."

Aurin and Luna looked at each other uneasily. "It's been a rough couple of months," said Aurin. "There's been a lot of trouble here lately with a group called the Zodiac Squad. Sorry for jumping the gun."

The man nodded understandingly. "I've heard all about that, believe me, but I'm not from around here.

That said, there are a few troublemakers in my town too. Name's Evan."

"I'm Aurin and this is Luna," said Aurin as Luna gave a bright wave, happy to take the stranger at his word. "These two are Shamtile and Innogon. No nicknames, at least not ones we use often."

"Pleased to meet you. Forgive me for being forward, but would one of you be up for a battle? I'm looking for a warmup and to test my strength before entering the tower."

"I'll do it!" exclaimed Aurin. "Unless you want to?" he asked Luna.

"Be my guest," she said, stepping aside.

"Perfect," said Evan. "How does a two versus two match work for you? First to lose both their Minakai loses the match; switching is allowed too."

"Let's not allow switching," said Aurin. "It'll be more challenging that way."

"Suit yourself," said Evan.

Aurin threw his hand upwards and summoned Dolissile to the field. Evan, however, was not using the stones embedded in his glove. He held his stones in his hand and tossed one into the air, catching it and then summoning his Minakai.

"Splashard," he said. "Let's show this Harmony fella how Maple Tower Minakai fight."

Splashard, the final evolution of Dripper materialised. It looked similar to Luna's Spritzard, but the Splashard had a larger body and a notably longer antenna.

Aurin didn't hesitate. "Dolissile, full charge."

Dolissile burst forwards, but the Splashard split itself in two just in time, then recombined once it had avoided the attack. Dolissile skidded to a halt in mid-air, then rotated.

"If that's all you've got, it won't be enough," warned Evan.

His Splashard threw its head forward and whipped its antenna at Dolissile, grabbing the dolphin tightly. It began to slap him around like a punching bag with its fingerless hands.

"Pulse!" shouted Aurin.

Dolissile emitted a massive shockwave that shook the grass and leaves, but more importantly, rippled intensely throughout Splashard's body. It released Dolissile and floated around, completely disoriented.

"Finish it off," said Aurin as Dolissile backed up. The dolphin charged forward and punched straight through the confused Splashard, defeating it cleanly.

Evan used his stone to send it away and summoned his next contender, a Volcarrow. The flaming bird soared into the air and cawed, raining fire onto the field. Dolissile took a couple of hits, but it wasn't enough to take him out.

Volcarrow swooped in, breathing like a flamethrower and scorching the dolphin, but it wouldn't give up. He emitted a pulse as the bird passed, sending it off course. He charged at it, but it swerved out of the way and Dolissile collided with a tree.

"Now!" ordered Evan, and the Volcarrow struck at Dolissile's back. The cyborg fell to the ground, finally out of steam.

"So, it's down to a one-on-one match?" remarked Aurin. "Spikruption!"

The huge red dinosaur appeared in the forest, ready for his first tamer battle. Aurin had trained him at the ranch and in the tower, but this was his first real test as a fully evolved Minakai. Spikruption's roar shook the trees and the sparks of flame lingering on the forest floor merely tickled his feet.

"I'm glad you're not some rank amateur," said Evan, "but you still won't win this."

Aurin wasn't going to take that. "Spikruption, you heard him. Prove him wrong."

Spikruption charged at the Volcarrow, faster than the bird had expected, and grabbed its torso with his teeth. He clamped down hard and began slamming it into the ground, then whipping it into the trees. He tossed it aside and then whipped his tail down on it; it lay limp.

Evan's mouth hung open in shock. He wasn't sure what to do, but eventually dismissed his Volcarrow. "I...didn't expect that," he said. "You're good, Aurin."

"Thanks, Evan," smiled Aurin. "You're not bad yourself, but you caught me on a rest day after a long week of training. My Minakai were itching to fight and show off what they learned."

"Bad timing for me, I suppose," Evan muttered. "No matter," he added, more positively, "it's what I get for underestimating an opponent. There are a few folks back home who wouldn't let me forget it."

"You said your Minakai come from Maple Tower," said Luna. "Does that mean you're from Maplewood?"

"Yep," Evan replied. "My sister Elodie and I run a small ranch down there. Outside of Ludonia Tower, I don't think there's another tower open longer than Maple Tower. We're a bit out of the way for most folks, not a lot of tower tourists, but we do alright."

"We'll have to pay you a visit sometime," said Aurin. "I live at the ranch just southeast of here. Maybe I'll try your tower too one day."

"Sounds like a plan," nodded Evan. "I'd better get

moving if I want to be out of Harmony by nightfall. Lots of hunting to do."

The tamers parted ways while Aurin and Luna spent the rest of the day roaming the forest and fields. It was a much-needed day off for the pair and their Minakai, except perhaps for Dolissile, and they were recharged for their next run at the tower.

Chapter 31

"To what do I owe the pleasure?" asked Cedric as Aurin and Luna entered his shop; he was asking Luna more so than Aurin.

"We're buying shards today, Cedric," said Luna merrily, jingling her bag and letting the silver clink together.

Cedric's eyes lit up. "Both of you in the market, eh?"

"Both of us," grinned Aurin. "How's business been since the tournament?"

"During or after?" scowled Cedric, clearly irked by something. Aurin thought that it was maybe because the shopkeeper didn't like him.

"Either?" asked a curious Luna.

"Well," began Cedric, as Aurin braced himself for a rant, "things started off well. The tournament brought lots of business. Tamers looking to buy a few eggs, shards were selling out completely, then there was an even bigger boom when that brawl at the stadium broke out and people were looking to defend themselves better.

"Now, however, sales have trickled to a crawl. The tourists that show up here are mostly here for the spectacle of what happened at the tournament, rather than tamers themselves. Sure, there are a few, but a lot of the ones that used to show up have left for other towns with towers."

Aurin raised an eyebrow, but Luna looked thoughtful. "I suppose it makes sense. Why come here when there's the risk that somebody will try and abduct your Minakai?"

"Exactly that," sighed Cedric. "Other businesses are doing well, but shops like mine are just scraping by."

"I'm guessing you won't cut us a deal then?" asked Aurin, but the shopkeeper simply glared at him.

"What do you want?" he said, turning to Luna.

"Two Lunar Shards, please," she beamed.

"Evolving a couple of Minakai, eh? Not a problem."

Aurin and Luna paid for the shards—full price for Aurin and a slight discount for Luna—then they walked through the streets of Hazelton, making their way to Kyle's ranch once again. They always enjoyed the walk down the path out of town and through the small section of forest that the ranch lay on the other side of.

"I was wondering when you'd pass by here," said Detective Knot, emerging from behind a tree.

"Are we that predictable?" asked Luna.

"Yes. It's why I knew I would find you easily. Perhaps you should mix up your route every now and then in case somebody is following you."

Aurin didn't see the problem. "Are we being followed?" he asked. The detective was clearly growing paranoid.

"Not that I'm aware of," admitted Knot, "but I wouldn't rule out the possibility. You made a lot of enemies recently and, as I'm sure you know, they're all well aware that it was the pair of you behind it."

"How *did* they find out?" asked Luna.

"I have a few theories," said Knot.

"Care to share them?"

"No."

Aurin was growing tired of the evasiveness and wanted him to get to the point. "Why were you looking for us anyway? Can't you talk to us in town?"

"I wanted to make sure that we could talk privately," he said. "Kyle obviously has spoken to me about your tower run-in, but I've done a bit of digging in the meantime. It's been hushed up, but there have been a few other reports of Zodiac activity."

"Who's hushing it?" asked Aurin.

"That's something I also have a few theories on."

"And you won't share that either?"

"I'm not going to start throwing accusations out without more evidence," said Knot. "What's important, however, is that all of this has been activity located solely in Harmony Tower. At least a dozen incidents of them jumping tamers and stealing eggs. No stolen Minakai directly this time, but they seem to be back to their pre-tournament modus operandi."

"Why do you think they changed it up for the tournament?" asked Luna.

"My best theory, which I *will* share," Knot said with a knowing smile, "is that they got greedy. The summoning stones weren't theirs, so they didn't truly own the Minakai they stole, it isn't how the magic works, but perhaps they have a way of forcing tamers to relinquish ownership if they found the monster they were looking for?"

Aurin and Luna glanced at each other. They knew that they were thinking the same thing. "Roche Berry," said Luna.

"Come again?" asked Knot.

"It's a special type of berry, exceptionally rare, that can revert a Minakai into an egg. Maybe if it's then hatched again, it severs the magic of a Minakai bonding with a tamer?"

Knot looked thoughtful. "That sounds plausible. I'll look into that. Roche, you say? Spell that out," he said, taking a notepad from his coat pocket, and noting down what Luna said.

He looked pleased. It must have been the only thing he could investigate that didn't leave him getting his hands tied again. It was obvious to Aurin and Luna that his meeting them secretly meant that he was still under orders to leave Zodiac alone.

"Excellent," said Knot. "I'll leave you two to go about your day."

The tamers bid him farewell and discussed the odd meeting the rest of the way back to the ranch. Kyle was busy trying to fish Luna's Dopefish out of the river after it had jumped in and made it past the barriers he had built. This was not the first time the goofy fish had given him trouble, and he knew it wouldn't be the last.

"Got the shards?" he asked excitedly as he pulled Dopefish up by the tail.

"Got 'em," said Luna, holding hers up as Aurin ran into the pens to grab both Melansprout.

When he returned, the two tamers, Kyle, Shamtile

and Innogon gathered around. In truth, Aurin had wanted to evolve Microbot but decided on Melansprout because he wanted to see which of its branches it would evolve into at the same time as Luna discovered hers.

"Ready?" he asked her, at which she nodded.

The two placed their Lunar Shards on their depressed Minakai, dooming them to either anger or despair. They both glowed green as they absorbed the energy of the shards, morphing into their new forms within the light.

"They're different," said Kyle, as their shapes shifted and the light began to fade.

Before the small audience, stood a Desparee, similar in appearance to Gardner's, along with an Angree. True to his name, he looked furious. He looked much closer to a large wooden puppet than a tree and had three leaves sweeping back from his forehead. He wore a skirt of leaves and flexed his carved arms menacingly.

"Feel good, you two?" asked Aurin, while Luna and Kyle scoffed. "I mean, do you two feel more powerful?"

Desparee hung his head and clutched his face. He felt even more down than he did as a Melansprout.

"Which one is which?" asked Kyle.

"Desparee is mine," said Aurin.

"I'd rather my Minakai be angry than sad all the time," remarked Luna.

"You would?" asked Kyle.

Luna paused for a moment. "Now that I think about it, they're both bad. Hopefully, a few good battle wins will cheer them up."

"How about now?" asked Aurin, itching to test the strength of his once-jovial and now fully-evolved Happynut.

"Let's do it," said Luna excitedly.

The two ran over to Kyle's field arena and their newly evolved Minakai followed. Shamtile and Innogon stood on the sidelines while Kyle got back to work. He had seen enough of their silly battles to know how this one would go.

"Go!" called both tamers as they pointed towards the other's Minakai.

Aurin's Desparee ran forwards, putting aside its exposed emotions to fight his friend. Luna's Angree, however, charged in with its emotions fuelling it. It angrily started beating on Desparee as the tree-like Minakai blocked as fast as it could, but the fury of the enraged Minakai was too much to keep up with.

"Stop trying to block and go on the offensive," said Aurin. "Rapid fire!"

Desparee inhaled and began to spit out nuts like they were bullets. They didn't do any damage to Angree, but they did irritate him enough to force him to retreat.

"You're more skilled at magic than he is," said Aurin.

Desparee seized the opportunity and planted his feet firmly on the ground. He absorbed more energy from the soil and conjured a ball of raw elemental power in his hands.

"Now!" ordered Aurin.

Aurin's Minakai unleashed the nature energy blast from his hands as Angree charged head-on, thinking that he could take the attack, but he could not. Luna's Minakai fell to the ground, unable to fight any longer.

"That was fast," remarked Luna, as she walked over to her Angree to make sure he was alright.

"I've been doing my research," said Aurin. "I know what both Desparee and Angree can do well and what they can't."

"You spend too much time around Kyle."

Aurin laughed. "I'm not going to apologise for preparedness. Kyle's stronger than me, so I'm going to do what he does until I reach his level."

Luna smiled at him. "You don't need to apologise," she said. "I'm happy that you won for a good reason and didn't stumble your way to victory. I think you'll really go far at the next tournament. If you keep all of this up, you'll definitely make it to Ludonia."

"You think so?" Aurin wouldn't say it out loud but hearing that from Luna meant a lot to him. He knew she would be in his corner, but she was always honest with him too. If he was struggling or making a mistake, she would tell him.

"Yep," she smiled, as her Angree started to stir. "Oh, you're still awake?"

Angree stood up and beat his chest wildly like a gorilla. He ran straight over to Kyle's house and began punching through the walls in a rage, looking for something to destroy. He would never hurt the humans, but Kyle's house was fair game to him.

The Frogre guards ran over to try and stop Angree as Luna stood open-mouthed, shocked at just how bad her Minakai's temper had become.

"At least he isn't depressed anymore," said Aurin. Shamtile nodded fervently, not daring to approach, while Innogon was busy rolling around in the grass and enjoying the sun.

"My house!" cried Kyle, hurrying over from the pens with a bag of feed pouring out a trail behind him.

Luna sighed and reached into her bag, pulling out her purse. She began counting her silvers to pay Kyle for the repairs. The entire front wall of his house had already been decimated.

Chapter 32

It had been an eventful trek through the endlessly changing Harmony Tower and Aurin and Luna were on a lucky streak. The two young Minakai tamers still had an active team of three monsters each and had just ascended to the fifteenth floor for the first time.

They had taken this run very seriously, bringing most of their strongest team members and plenty of healing herbs and berries to keep them rejuvenated at each step of the way. The tower limited what you could bring with you before it refused you entry, and they had finally run out of what they had carried in with them.

"Think you can use some of what we found along the way to keep us strong?" Aurin asked Luna.

"Some of the berries will be useful, but these particular herbs need to be refined into ointments," said

Luna, inspecting what she had in her bag. "I'm sure we'll be just fine," she added with a smile.

Space was rather limited as both tamers had found eggs, Aurin on floor seven and Luna on floor twelve. They were both itching to leave and hatch them, but the lure of higher floors was too great. A new record meant new Minakai appearing and new items ahead. It was too good to pass up when they had barely broken onto the double-digit floors on their last few runs.

"Do you ever plan to return home?" Luna asked Aurin out of the blue.

Summer was finally starting to come to an end and Aurin had spent a good half a year in Hazelton to date. He knew that he had learned an unfathomable amount about himself and Minakai, but the road was still long. He was grateful to have even gotten this far.

"Someday, yes," he said, truthfully. "My parents will be coming here in a couple of weeks to visit. They've finally hit breaking point with phone calls alone."

Luna was taken aback. "You didn't tell me that!"

"Was I supposed to?"

"Yes. I need to get them a gift."

"Why?"

"Because they're your parents."

"So?"

Luna rubbed her temples in frustration. "It's just a thing that's nice to do. Do you need to nitpick at something like this?"

"I suppose not," said Aurin, still not sure why she was annoyed at him.

"What sort of things do they like?"

"My mum is easy, just get her a plant or something. My dad? He isn't a tamer in the typical sense, but he does have a Heatpup that he treats like a regular dog. If you find a spare Solar Shard, he could evolve it. I wouldn't buy one though, that's quite pricey for you."

"Leave it to me," smiled Luna. "Your parents are going to love the presents."

Suddenly, galloping erupted as a dark unicorn charged towards the pair and their Minakai. It had purplish grey hair and a dark silvery mane, along with a glowing blue horn and eyes. It was a Thundarun, an evolved Litehorn.

"Shamtile!" called Aurin and the reptile burst into action. He conjured up a rock wall for the unicorn to charge into, but it bounded over the wall effortlessly.

Aurin, Luna, Shamtile and Innogon dived out of the way to avoid being trampled on by the charging beast. Innogon got back to his feet first and shot a jet of water at the Thundarun as it spun around to attack again, but it avoided the attack.

It reared up and let out a hearty neigh as it shot a lightning bolt from its horn, striking Innogon in the chest. The water drake was knocked backwards and then ejected from the tower. Luna hurriedly summoned Spritzard to take his place.

Shamtile began hurling rocks at his opponent while Spritzard conjured up a wave that filled the corridor, pushing Thundarun back as it tried to make a run for Shamtile.

"Cover the horn," ordered Aurin, and Shamtile encapsulated the lightning unicorn's horn in stone.

The Thundarun wasn't to be deterred and blasted the small stone cage apart from within. Its feet then began to glow with lightning, and it ran forward at super speed, ramming into Shamtile and knocking him out cold. The magic lizard was sent into stasis, and Aurin summoned Leonite to replace him.

The unicorn conjured more lightning, which Spritzard blocked. Leonite used the opening to pounce on the wild beast and take a bite out of it. He sank his claws in for good measure as the equine Minakai cried out in agony. Spritzard joined in with some blunt pummelling and, between them, she and Leonite defeated the tough opponent.

"That didn't go so well," sighed Aurin, turning to Luna. He was upset that such a successful run was so heavily disrupted and they were each left without one of their team members.

"We've hit a new record and have two Minakai each," said Luna, still remaining optimistic. "Two of our strongest, I might add. We'll be just fine."

"That's true. It *has* been a good run."

"Just don't forget that we have the eggs, alright?"

"I won't," said Aurin, patting the Orb of Return in his jacket pocket. He wasn't going to suffer the embarrassment of forgetting the number of charges a second time. He had bought a spare from Cedric that he kept in his pack just in case.

"What's that sound?" asked Luna, as they continued through the corridors.

Aurin listened quietly, expecting to hear more hooves on the tiles, but it was more of a rumbling. It rose and fell every few seconds, followed by a brief period of silence, before rising once more. "Is that snoring?" he wondered aloud.

"I...I think it is," said Luna.

The two followed the sound with Leonite and Spritzard sticking close to their tamers' sides. Leonite was particularly eager to keep the tower run going for as long as possible. He had plenty of training at the ranch but had only entered the tower a handful of times since the tournament and was itching for a good fight. The Thundarun battle had reawakened the lion's bloodlust.

The source of the snoring finally became apparent. Lying flat on its back in an isolated room at the far side of the floor was a large rabbit. So large that it had clearly enjoyed plenty of meals in its time. It was an evolved Rabbacat, known as a Rabbafat.

"Let's get out of here and not wake it," whispered Aurin.

"Why?"

"They're deceptively powerful," warned Aurin. "They have a rock-solid defence and they're more than happy to take a bite out of you. While they're not great at running, their fists and legs can punch and kick as fast as that Thundarun can gallop."

Luna nodded with wide eyes, then slowly backed out of the room. Leonite looked disappointed while Spritzard had no expression whatsoever. No, it was best to stay away from an opponent like this if it could be helped, Aurin was certain.

The tamers continued to wander the floor, fighting whatever Minakai spawned. Leonite took little pleasure in defeating a Cubtem, Spritzard washed away a yappy Hornferno, and the pair of them teamed up to defeat a Peekawe that was notably nimble despite being forced to fight in the confines of the corridor.

This had been the longest time Aurin and Luna had spent on a floor this entire run. They were certain that they'd explored every nook and cranny of the place, but there was no sign of the elevator. The items they had left behind were still missing, which marked each room for them. It wasn't making sense.

"I don't get it," said Aurin as they walked past the

same room for the third time. "Where's the elevator?"

"We must have missed a room somewhere," Luna said, trying to map out the floor in her mind. "Let's loop around again."

It suddenly clicked for Aurin. It was obvious now, to the point where he felt silly. "The Rabbafat room," he said. "He's sleeping in front of the elevator, isn't he?"

"Oh!" exclaimed Luna, as they hurried back to the room.

They crept in, a feat which was much easier for the floating Spritzard and the pad-footed Leonite than it was for their boot-wearing tamers. As they edged around the wall, it wasn't long before they spotted the familiar blue and gold. It was indeed behind the sleeping Minakai.

"Fight or make a break for the elevator?" whispered Luna.

"Leonite, attack!" ordered Aurin, and his Minakai sprung to action excitedly. Luna, peeved at Aurin's lack of notice, ordered Spritzard to do the same.

The lion swiped at the sleeping Rabbafat, but its belly just wobbled as it stirred. It wasn't hurt in the slightest by the savage attack and climbed to its feet slowly. Leonite continued the assault as Spritzard joined in from a distance.

Not one of the attacks fazed the rotund rabbit, and it merely frowned in annoyance at being disturbed from its sleep. Leonite leapt at it, aiming for the head, but Rabbafat jabbed him rapidly in the nose. The lion hopped back, dazed from the sudden fast and hard strikes.

Rabbafat bounded towards Spritzard with heavy thuds as the water elemental continued to soak the wild Minakai. The Rabbafat jumped up and belly-flopped on top of the water demon. She was squashed so thoroughly that her jelly oozed out from underneath the rabbit, but she vanished seconds later and was ejected from the tower.

"Oh no," said Luna as she summoned Tadpool to join the fight.

Leonite meanwhile was attacking his foe once more, angry at being punched in the nose. He sank his claws deep, but the Rabbafat smiled and gave him a tight bear hug, nearly breaking his back. He too was ejected from the tower, leaving Aurin and Luna with one Minakai each.

"Desparee," said Aurin, summoning his final team member to attack.

"No," said Luna while Tadpool threw icicles at Rabbafat. "Let's get out of here now while we still can."

"We can beat it," said Aurin as Desparee conjured vines to hold the Rabbafat in place.

Almost immediately, Rabbafat ripped the vines from the ground and swung them around, whipping Tadpool and Desparee, the vines cutting into their skin. They weren't looking too good and Rabbafat had still yet to even take any serious damage.

"Can we please go?" pleaded Luna.

Aurin looked at the two Minakai taking a beating. "Okay, we'll leave," he relented, reaching for the Orb of Return. He unleashed the spell inside and the two tamers and their Minakai were pulled from the tower, returning to the doors outside.

Luna let out a sigh of relief. "You were right the first time; it *is* tough. Why did you attack it?"

Aurin shook his head in shame. "I thought we could take it out before it came to. It was stupid of me, I'm sorry."

"It's fine," said Luna, checking on Tadpool. "At least we got out of there in time."

Despite getting out safely with a new record and two eggs to their name, Aurin was displeased. He didn't like getting bested by wild Minakai at the best of times, but the Rabbafat bothered him more than usual. Its defences seemed impenetrable. He knew he would never encounter that specific Minakai again, but he was going to ensure that he could find a way to defeat other members of its species.

Aurin and Luna walked back to the ranch to retrieve the incubator and hatch their new team members from their eggs. It would be a happy ending to the day even if the tower run finale had been disappointing.

Chapter 33

The train slowly chugged to a halt on the pleasant Autumn morning. There was a light breeze in the air and most folks at the station were there for their morning commute, but today, Aurin and Shamtile were waiting for somebody to disembark. In fact, they were waiting for two people.

As the carriage doors all slid open, Aurin glanced up and down, trying to see where his parents would emerge from. He was both excited and nervous, yet he wasn't sure why. He spoke to them at least once a week and had even called them yesterday to double check that he had the right time for their arrival.

"My little boy!" exclaimed his mother, Alice, as she ran towards him with her arms outstretched. She was tall and slender, with green eyes that she passed on to her son, and dark brown hair.

She hugged him tightly as his father, Edwin, pulled their luggage along with them. It was a surprisingly large case considering they were only staying until Sunday evening before taking the train back to their hometown of Buckstone.

"You're getting taller, Aurin," chuckled Aurin's father who still towered over his sixteen-year-old son. He looked like an older version of Aurin, with the same dark blonde hair and pleasant demeanour; the only difference was his blue eyes. "Happy birthday," he said and handed him a box as his mother finally released him.

"Thanks, Dad," said Aurin, red in the face after being squeezed so tightly. "I'll open it when we get to the ranch later. How was the journey?"

"Never mind that," said Alice. "Where's this Luna that you're always talking about? You said she was going to meet us here, right?"

Aurin sighed. "She's late as usual. She should have been here fifteen minutes ago. We'll get moving and she can catch up with us later."

Shamtile screeched a warbly screech and waved his arms furiously, not content to stand there and be ignored. Everybody laughed and Edwin kneeled down beside the Minakai.

"Of course, we haven't forgotten about you, Shammy," he said. "How have you been?"

Shamtile conjured rocks around his body, forming a stone armour, then erected a pillar on the ground, boosting him up so that he towered over everybody else. He posed mightily, as though he were an ancient statue.

"You've learned a few new tricks, I see," said Edwin, as Shamtile sank the pillar back into the ground and repaired the brickwork he had just destroyed. "Best money we've ever spent, I'd say," Edwin said to Aurin with a chuckle.

"I'd say so too," said Aurin with a smile. It only just hit him how much he missed both of his parents. Hearing their voices over the phone or speaking to them on a video call didn't compare to seeing them in the flesh.

"Are you going to show us around Hazelton first?" asked Alice, looking around the open-air platform.

"Of course," said Aurin, leading them through the gate and onto the streets.

Aurin and Shamtile walked them through the town, with their first major stop being the stadium. It was mostly being used for football games, musical concerts and the occasional Minakai exhibition match, but he had heard rumours that the tournament organisers were already putting together their plans for the next tournament which lay just over six months away.

"So this is where all the magic happens, eh?" asked Edwin. "Funny this, it looks familiar." Alice shushed him.

"What?" asked Aurin suspiciously.

Alice sighed. "Your dad can't resist dropping hints, can he?"

"We were here for two of your matches," said Edwin with a sly smile. "We didn't want to say anything and increase the pressure any further."

"I thought you said you had work?" asked Aurin incredulously. "I spoke to you on the days *of* a few of my matches."

"We agreed to keep it a secret," said his mother. "There was no way that my little boy was going to be having his first professional Minakai battles and we wouldn't be there to see at least a few of them. We supported you from the audience, hidden in the crowds. Your brother even showed up for one of them, but he couldn't stay long."

"Why didn't you stop by after and say hello?" asked Aurin, a bit miffed by this revelation.

"It wasn't fair to not give you notice," said his father. "Now that you've got your first tournament out of the way, however, we'll let you know when we show up to the next one. Deal?"

"Deal," said Aurin, still in a state of shock. Shamtile looked from person to person, not quite sure what the problem was.

Aurin didn't bother showing them the inside of the stadium as he had originally planned, so he took his parents for a walk along the river and showed them the cordoned-off warehouse that was once the Zodiac Squad headquarters.

Alice expressed disbelief that her son would be foolish enough to get involved in such matters and make himself an enemy of a criminal gang. "We should have dragged you home the moment you told us that," she said, but Edwin quietly congratulated his son on a job well done.

"Thanks, Dad," whispered Aurin back, convinced that the Zodiac disruption had been the right call. His dad was one of the smartest people he knew, and if he was happy about it, it was the right move.

Next, Aurin took them through the town centre, showing them the various cafes and restaurants he frequented. He showed them the outside of Taming Solutions but dared not go inside. Aurin and Cedric did not get along all that well and he only used that shop when Luna was there. He used another vendor when she was elsewhere, which granted, wasn't very often.

The last stop before Kyle's ranch was Harmony Tower. Aurin's parents were in awe of the grand structure. It had been a while since Aurin himself had stopped to appreciate what a magnificent building it was. The finely carved brick that carried the tower halfway to the clouds, the intricate carvings along the pillars and supports, the beauty of the heavy wooden doors that separated you from other dimensions. It truly was a sight to behold.

He had long stopped thinking about the origins of the towers and how or why they worked the way that they did. He had personally chalked it up to ancient wizards using long-lost magic. There were those who didn't believe in magic, even to this day, but Aurin's answer to that was to show them a summoning stone and it shut them up very quickly.

"How have your earnings been?" asked Edwin, who worked as an accountant.

"More than an entry desk job, that's for sure," laughed Aurin. "You're still richer than me though, but I'll make sure that doesn't last long. I'll buy you both a nice countryside manor one of these days and then you can retire."

"I like being productive," chuckled Edwin, "but I appreciate the gesture, Aurin. Keep whatever money you make for your future."

"And make sure you're safe when you're in there," said Alice sternly. "Shamtile, if he gets hurt, it's your fault."

Shamtile waved his arms and spun in circles, as though he was doing a tribal dance. He then shouted furiously, startling Aurin's mother. "What's he saying?" she asked him.

"He says that he's not always in the tower with me. It's not his fault if I get torn to pieces when he's at the ranch."

"Oh!" exclaimed Alice. "I forgot all about your other Minakai. The ranch is nearby, right?"

"Right," confirmed Aurin, moving along once more.

The three humans and Shamtile continued through the forest path and finally reached Kyle's fabled ranch, bringing the tour of Hazelton to an end. Kyle had just finished feeding the Minakai and was washing his hands at the tap outside.

"Hello there," called Edwin, waving as he walked up the path.

Kyle turned and waved back, quickly drying his hands before rushing over to meet Aurin and his family. He held out his hand and shook Edwin's, then Alice's.

"It's nice to finally meet both of you in person," said Kyle, having spoken to them briefly on the phone a couple of times previously.

"Likewise," said Aurin's parents.

"I'm glad he has somebody here looking out for him," said Alice.

"And particularly a tamer like yourself," said Edwin. "I still remember watching one of your matches at the National Championships not long before Aurin was born. That Wingbloom of yours was quite the powerhouse."

It only just occurred to Aurin that Kyle was around the same age as Aurin's parents. He had always thought of him as an older brother rather than a guardian, but he had effectively been just that since Aurin started living with him.

"Wingbloom is still a contender," said Kyle, whistling loudly with his fingers in his mouth.

Kyle's favourite Minakai flew from the forest and landed on the grass beside him. He patted the plant-bird's wing gently.

"Marvellous," said Edwin.

"I actually have something for you, Kyle," said Alice, reaching into her bag. "It's a small token of appreciation for taking good care of our son."

"Thank you," said Kyle graciously accepting a small wrapped box. "It's not only out of the goodness of my heart. He pays rent secretly and thinks I don't notice when my wallet gets heavier."

"So you did know the whole time," said Aurin, confirming his suspicion.

Everybody had a good laugh about this, then Aurin ran off to fetch the rest of his Minakai. He lined them up and presented them one by one: Spikruption, Dolissile, Leonite, Desparee, Microbot, and Chull; Aurin's newest member.

"I don't remember hearing about this one," said Alice, examining the black bird with the white bone mask around its eyes.

Aurin nodded. "I only hatched him a short while ago. Luna and I both found eggs in the tower. Chull was in mine and Luna's contained a Rabbacat. It's a funny story," he said before launching into the tale of the Rabbafat they were bested by and how shocked they were when Luna hatched its pre-evolved form minutes later.

Just as Aurin finished explaining, Luna ran up the path. Her red hair was messy and her hairband sat askew. She was out of breath and looked an equal mix of embarrassed and apologetic. Innogon hopped off her back and bounced around playfully, oblivious to her distress.

"I'm...so sorry," she panted. "I slept through...my alarm.

"A tale as old as time," said Aurin, but he stayed quiet after Luna shot him a terrifying look.

"Luna, is it?" asked Aurin's mother, pulling her into a hug. Luna's eyes bulged out of her head, but it was more from the shock rather than the tightness of the hug.

"I can't apologise enough for not showing up on time," said Luna.

"It's quite alright, dear," said Alice genuinely. "These things happen."

"Gifts!" exclaimed Luna, clumsily. She reached into her bag and handed over two wrapped presents, one for Aurin's mother and one for his father.

"You didn't need to do that," said the pair, but then thanked her anyway.

"Where's mine?" asked Aurin.

Luna frowned at him. "Your parents are visiting here for the first time," she said. "You'll get something on your birthday."

Aurin's parents looked at him, realising that he hadn't told her it was today. He shook his head, not wanting them to say anything. It wasn't a big secret; he just didn't want anybody to feel obligated to throw any sort of party for him.

"Open them, please," said Luna, back to her usual bright and cheery self.

"Alright," said Edwin, as he unwrapped his Solar Shard. "Ah, I can finally evolve my Heatpup. You know, I've been meaning to do that for years, but never got around to it."

Alice opened hers and found an egg inside. Aurin and Kyle were shocked.

"What's this?" asked Aurin.

"It's a Minakai egg," said Luna.

"I know that, but what's in it?"

Kyle fetched the incubator and everybody gathered around as Alice hatched her first-ever Minakai. When the green glow faded away, a small seed with a face stared up at his new tamer. It flapped a small leaf atop its head and hopped around a little.

"A Driftseed?" asked Kyle. "Where did you get that from?"

"Cedric sold it to me," said Luna. "Aurin said you liked plants, but they don't always last very long. I thought that this plant would be evergreen for you. It's a low-maintenance species. Light, water and a few pellets every now and again should keep it happy."

"That's very thoughtful, Luna," said Alice, captivated by the Driftseed.

"Shall we go inside?" asked Kyle. "I've grabbed a few of the finest steaks in town for Aurin's birthday lunch."

Luna dropped her bag. "His what?"

Everybody walked inside while Luna scolded Aurin. They all had a great meal together, courtesy of the master chef, Kyle. It was one of the best birthdays Aurin had ever had and he was pleased to be able to celebrate it with his family, friends and team.

Chapter 34

Chull swooped in, aiming for Rabbacat's throat, but the speedy little bunny hopped out of the way. The two had been training together for weeks and they finally had their chance for an all-out battle. Aurin and Luna watched, trying their best to resist giving commands. That was their respective Minakai's chance to shine.

"Rabbacat's looking strong," whispered Aurin, seeing his nimble little bird's attack be avoided so easily.

"She's only strong if she can actually land a hit," replied Luna.

Rabbacat knew she had to keep moving and build up some momentum if she wanted to actually win. She bounded around the grassy field, expecting that it wouldn't be long before Chull would turn around and swoop in for another attack.

True enough, Chull flew in a sideways arc, then aimed for the little rabbit once more. The undead bird suddenly sped up, riding the wind it conjured with his air elemental powers.

Rabbacat bounced up and delivered a heavy kick to Chull's little beak. The bird Minakai rose up higher into the air and then smacked down onto the grass. Rabbacat had won the fight and Luna ran over to her Minakai, picking her up and tossing her around gleefully.

Aurin sent Chull back into the pen before approaching Luna. "Congratulations," he said to her and her Minakai. "He's not listening to me well. I've told him time and time again to try and outmanoeuvre opponents rather than charge in each time. Charging in is Dolissile's speciality and he has the power to back it up. Chull does not."

"He's fine when you're commanding him directly," said Luna, setting her Rabbacat back onto the grass where she lay down for a rest.

"The rest of my Minakai know what to do without commands most of the time. We're in good sync, but Chull hasn't gotten to that point yet. He needs more training."

Luna agreed but was still on a high from her win. "Maybe it's just a bad day for him?"

"He's like this all the time, even when I put him up against my other Minakai. I think I got lucky that Happynut was whipped into shape before the last tournament and found a rhythm with me so quickly. If it had been Chull, it would have been a disaster and could have cost me dearly."

Aurin and Luna headed inside Kyle's house to grab a drink. Aurin had stocked up on plenty of cans of root beer, a rarity in small towns like Hazelton. Luna politely declined when he offered her one and she poured herself a glass of water before walking over to Kyle's kitchen table and sitting down.

"How do you think your team are doing?" Aurin asked after taking a swig of his root beer.

"In what way?" she asked.

"Combat abilities."

Luna paused and thought about it for a short while. "Innogon is Innogon," she said with a laugh. "He's smart enough to handle himself, but also happy to trust me with whatever plans or tactics we adopt. I don't have any fear when we're fighting together, especially in the tower.

"Spritzard and Tadpool are more or less the same as Innogon, but they have more raw power. Both of them listen well and adapt well. Angree, however, is more of a nuisance than anything. He listens for a while and then his temper gets the better of him. If he could get it under enough control, he could be my strongest fighter. Rabbacat speaks for herself, I suppose."

"What about your other Minakai?" Aurin asked, but Luna looked confused. "Dopefish," he said pointedly.

"Ugh," said Luna, dismissing the goofy-looking fish.

"He's not that bad," laughed Aurin. "Train him up and evolve him into a Doripper and he'll be a force of nature."

Luna took no notice of what he said. "What about your team? Aside from Chull, of course."

"Everybody is pulling their weight," said Aurin. "Spikruption is better than ever, Dolissile is increasing his capabilities, Leonite is improving his speed, Desparee is my strong magic striker and Microbot...well, he's still the weakest link of that bunch, but it's nothing an evolution won't fix."

"When are you evolving him?" asked Luna.

"When I think he's ready."

"How do you know when that is?"

"Just a feeling, I suppose. How do you know when your Minakai are ready?"

Luna thought about it. "Just a feeling," she said with a smile. "There's something else I wanted to talk to you about."

"Go for it," said Aurin.

Luna hesitated, not sure how to put it into words. "I've been thinking," she finally said, "that I'm not going to enter the tournament next year. Tournament battles aren't for me. I love my Minakai, I love training them and going to the tower, but I don't want to take part in the competition side of things."

"How come?" asked Aurin, shocked by this sudden news.

"I don't like the pressure of being in front of a big crowd. I hated that feeling."

"If that's what you want, then I'll respect it," said Aurin, but he was a little disappointed. He knew Luna was a tougher battler than she gave herself credit for, but it also was not where her passion was. Herbology and healing were what interested her the most.

"On that note," said Luna, "how do we get you at your best for the tournament? Keep doing what we're doing?"

"I'm going to ask Kyle to train me again. It's been a while since he and I have fought, and I don't think he's ever used one of his strongest Minakai against me."

The two tamers finished their drinks and headed back outside to train for another hour before Luna had to be home.

Aurin and Kyle had finished cleaning out the Minakai pens for the day, just as night set in over Hazelton. It had been a hard day of work for the pair of them and Aurin was thinking how to best approach Kyle about training. He figured the direct way was the best way.

"Kyle, will you train me again for the next tournament?" he asked.

"Why?" replied Kyle.

Aurin didn't expect that question. "Because I need somebody leagues ahead of me to teach me and help me improve."

"You don't need that at all."

"I think I do."

"Here's a lesson for you, Aurin. You can do it without me just fine. I'm just the one that gives you that little extra nudge along the way."

"Alright," said Aurin, quickly thinking of a compromise, "how about instead of training me, you just battle me once a fortnight to see if I'm getting any better."

Kyle put his hand on his chin, thinking for a moment. "I'm going to change that plan up a bit," he said. "I'll battle you at the end of each month until the tournament, but first I want to arrange a special match for you. It'll let you see how far you've really come, far more than battling me regularly."

"Alright, sounds good to me. Who's the special

match against?" asked Aurin.

"That would be telling. I've got this person's number written down somewhere, so I'll call them later."

Aurin had a big grin on his face. "Thanks, Kyle."

"Don't mention it," he said. "But if I catch you spoiling the surprise and checking my phone records then I'm kicking you off the ranch. You'll still have to work here, but you can find somewhere else to live. Got it?"

"Got it," said Aurin, suddenly having the idea of checking Kyle's phone records tomorrow once the rancher's guard was down. No, he decided it was best not to do that.

Kyle started walking into the pens once again. "Seeing as the work is done, there're a few things around here I want to show you."

Aurin followed him, unsure of what he would see here that he hadn't seen before.

"Many years ago, I was a national-level tamer," Kyle began, "but I wasn't good enough to win the championships. There were times when I did very well, that's for sure, yet it always managed to fall just outside of my grasp. I met many great tamers, from my old friend Vai to the former Bretonian Champion, Aldwin.

"The most important relationships that I built, however, were with my Minakai. They had to trust that I could lead them into battle and I had to trust that they could carry out my orders without question, knowing that I had an ultimate plan. That's where I think you're doing best, Aurin; you're building trust with your team. They aren't nameless soldiers fighting an unknown war, they're *your* troops and you share a mutual respect.

"I've got a few dozen Minakai of my own, but there are five in particular that carried me to my best tournament performance and to my highest tower run. One of them, you already know well."

"Your Wingbloom," said Aurin.

"My Wingbloom," confirmed Kyle. He had let Aurin into a pen where nearly two dozen Minakai were resting. Kyle whistled and Wingbloom appeared from the sky moments later, from where he had come, only Kyle knew. "Over here, team," he said.

Two other Minakai ran over to him and stood in line with Wingbloom. It almost seemed like a drill sergeant was inspecting his soldiers' uniforms. Kyle walked Aurin over to the first of the monsters, a Hogannon.

"This Hogannon is one of the mightiest in all of Bretonia. He was on my best-ever tower run and in my final professional battle along with Wingbloom."

The Hogannon stood proudly and held his cannon arms up. Aurin thought it must be uncomfortable to have weapons attached to your arms in place of your hands, but he thought that now was not the time to speak this thought aloud.

"This is the third member of my core team, Snowlem," he said, indicating the snowman-like Minakai who bore an eerie smile made of coal and wore a red scarf around his neck. "He may look unusual, but he's the stuff of nightmares if you get him on a bad day."

Aurin had seen this Minakai lazing around the pen before, but never up close, and certainly not in the tower. "Pleased to meet you all properly," he said to Kyle's team. "I hope we'll get to battle soon."

The Minakai looked excited at the prospect, but Kyle raised his hands, and they calmed down quickly. "You'll all get to battle soon enough," he said, "but let's not get ahead of ourselves just yet. There's still a lot of work to be done."

"I'm working my backside off training," sighed Aurin.

"Not for you," said Kyle. "It's been a while since these gentlemen have been truly tested. I'll need to make sure they're all fighting fit. The last thing I want is my lack of preparedness to mean that I lose to a newbie like you."

Aurin frowned and Kyle laughed heartily. Aurin joined in the laughter, very much used to Kyle's teasing at this point. He was harsher with his words than Luna, but he picked on Aurin because he knew he wouldn't take it the wrong way.

"Who would you currently consider your core team?" Kyle asked Aurin.

For a while, Aurin said nothing. "Shamtile is a given," he said. The young man was struggling to answer this question as he liked all of his Minakai, particularly his most tried and tested ones. "I would say that maybe Spikruption and Dolissile round out my main three, but at the same time, I like using my Leonite and Desparee a lot. They've proven themselves many times already, both in their current forms and their prior."

Kyle shook his head. "I didn't say your core team had to only be three. You can always rotate them in the tournament matches to suit your opponent, much like how you did during the summer."

"I would say those five then," said Aurin.

"Exactly," said Kyle. "You've built the strongest bond with them and you've given them strength beyond what mere training will do. Similarly, you're a better and stronger person for having trained along with them and taken care of them. It's a symbiotic relationship as you've all put in the work."

Aurin thought about this quietly while Kyle was

speaking to his Minakai. It was starting to get chilly in the late Autumn night, so they decided to head inside for the evening. It had been an enlightening day for Aurin in many ways.

He had even spotted the spark reignite in Kyle's eyes when he talked about his Minakai. He clearly missed being a full-time tamer, but perhaps he would be willing to give it another try if Aurin could defeat him. After all, what would give him more drive than losing to a newbie?

Chapter 35

"I see him coming now," said Luna, looking down the busy Hazelton street. She and Aurin were sitting outside their favourite café on this chilly October morning. They were waiting for a friend who had called Aurin up out of the blue and said he was visiting Hazelton for a couple of days.

"That's him alright," said Aurin as Hunter walked down the street, dressed in a blue pinstripe suit. He always dressed to impress, never allowing himself to be caught wearing anything too casual.

"Aurin. Luna," he said, giving them a curt nod. "How have you both been keeping?"

"Well," said Luna with a big smile. She had always liked Hunter, even though he was the one who had knocked her out of the tournament.

"Always excited to see a celebrity like yourself," joked Aurin. "I heard you got quite far at the championship this year."

"I did alright," said Hunter, modestly. "I was shooting for first place and wanted to hit the top thirty-two at a minimum, so the top sixteen was a welcome result."

The three tamers exchanged casual chitchat for a short while, before moving onto a more serious topic. Aurin knew that Hunter was going to ask about it eventually.

"Has there been any further Zodiac activity since the summer?"

"Little bits here and there," said Aurin. "They've mostly kept to themselves and fought in the tower rather than jumping people in the streets."

Hunter didn't seem all that surprised. "I suspect the big boss decided it was too risky. He wouldn't want his whole operation to be rumbled by getting careless again. At least he had the sense to pull back when things were getting messy. If he were a common criminal, he probably would have kept things going rather than curtail it."

"I don't think they'll stop until they get their hands on an Ethruki and whatever other cosmic elemental Minakai they can," said Luna.

"I expect so," agreed Hunter. "There are more powerful Minakai than cosmic elementals, however, so it's a wonder that they aren't chasing those instead. Granted, the Minakai of myth and legend would be notably harder to get your hands on than cosmics."

"What's so special about that element anyway?" asked Luna. She had wondered this for a while but didn't want to seem stupid by asking.

"The cosmic element doesn't have any elements that it is weak to and the Minakai of that persuasion tend to be naturally stronger than other Minakai," said Hunter. "Their powers are varied, almost temporal in how they work. You wouldn't want to fight one unprepared because, even when you are prepared, they're a real challenge."

"It makes sense now why Zodiac would want them," said Aurin. "They're powerful, but not rare beyond obtainability."

Hunter nodded. "That could indeed be why," he said. "They'll struggle to find an eclectic range of cosmic Minakai in Bretonia, however. Ethruki is one of only three that I'm aware of that can be found in towers in this country. I wonder if once they have a trio of cosmic elementals, will they move along?"

"I don't want them to move along," said Aurin. "I want their organisation crushed and their members imprisoned."

Hunter let out a rare laugh. "That would be nice," he said. "How is your Microbot doing? Have you evolved him yet?"

"Not yet," admitted Aurin. "I don't know what it is that's holding me back from doing it."

Hunter looked at him understandingly. "Think about what you need for your team. If you lack a strong neutral elemental, you would want to use an Astral Shard. If you lack one of the four core elements, then a Solar Shard is what you would want to take a chance on. Similarly, if you lack a mixed element, then a Lunar Shard. The good thing about the different shards is that it doesn't leave you stuck with one in ten odds of getting what you want. It's one in four or a dead certainty."

"What would you suggest?" asked Aurin.

"It's like I said, just examine your team and see where the elemental gaps are. You want to be versatile so that you can adapt to whoever you're faced with."

"Kyle said something similar recently," said Aurin. "I think you're both right."

"How's this for a plan," began Hunter. "We both currently have a Microbot of our own. We'll head over to the ranch and battle them in Kyle's field to test how well we've tamed them. At the end of the battle, if there isn't too wide of a strength gap, we'll each evolve ours."

"I don't have any shards right now," said Aurin.

"I have plenty," replied Hunter, waving off Aurin's concern. "You can have one of mine. What do you say?"

"Alright, let's do it."

Aurin paid for Luna and Hunter's drinks, despite Hunter insisting that it was on him, and then they headed for the ranch. When they arrived, Kyle was nowhere to be seen; presumably working somewhere nearby.

The two tamers stood at opposite ends of the battlefield, just as they stood when Shamtile and Flambot knocked each other out. It gave Aurin a sense of déjà vu that he didn't have when he fought Luna, presumably because battling with her was almost routine.

"Are both of you ready?" asked Luna as Shamtile and Innogon stood by, waving and bouncing in support of Aurin.

"Ready," said the two tamers.

"Fight!" called Luna.

Aurin and Hunter summoned their Microbot simultaneously, Hunter's travelling a far greater distance through space to reach the ranch. The little robots spawned on the field and stood facing each other.

"Pull him in, Microbot," ordered Aurin.

Aurin's Microbot activated a magnetic field and Hunter's Microbot was dragged across the grass by a powerful unseen force. It countered by swinging its tail forward, using it as a spear and jabbing Aurin's Minakai.

"Push him back," said Hunter.

His Microbot reversed the attack and sent the opposing Microbot on a trip across the battlefield. He was flung by a magnetic pulse and landed awkwardly on the ground. Microbot stood up, a little disoriented, but otherwise alright.

The two Microbot charged at each other, focused on not letting the other push or pull it in the other direction. They used their tails like cattle prods and jabbed pointedly, each of them trying to short-circuit the other. Hunter's Minakai got the better of Aurin's and then switched up his magnetic field to force himself backwards and away.

"Charge up," Hunter ordered as his Microbot's eye began to glow brightly. Aurin's Minakai stood up just in time for Hunter's to unleash a powerful blue laser from its eye.

"Redirect and counter," ordered Aurin.

His Microbot materialised a forcefield in front of himself, redirecting the attack, and then shot his own laser beam at Hunter's. Not expecting the reversal, Hunter's Microbot took the attack to his casing and was knocked over onto the grass.

"Go and surge," said Hunter, realising how prepared Aurin was for a battle like this. The young tamer had trained his robot well.

Hunter's Microbot pulled himself towards Aurin's before he had the chance to activate his own magnetism. As the two Minakai collided, Hunter's Microbot sent out a powerful shockwave that shook the grass and tossed Aurin's into the sky. He landed hard and stayed down.

"Hunter is the winner!" called Luna once she was certain that Aurin's Microbot wouldn't get up. Shamtile groaned loudly and lay on the ground. He was taking the loss far harder than his tamer.

Aurin picked up his Minakai to make sure he was alright. His blue light was flickering on and off but he would be fine. It was a tough battle, demonstrating to Aurin that Hunter had more knowledge and skill in using a Microbot. After all, he had trained a previous one and evolved it into a Flambot.

"Excellent job," said Hunter, approaching Aurin. "I didn't think it would be so close."

"I've been training him hard," said Aurin, setting his Minakai on the floor now that his eye had stopped flickering. He stood up and stumbled around, trying to regain his balance.

"I can see that. Nice usage of his metal properties. I'm glad you didn't let his lack of specialisation in metal elemental techniques stop you from using what he can do. Crossover is a powerful utility, even if it isn't the strongest attack."

"I made a commitment to learn and understand each of the elements better," said Aurin. "I think that's key to me performing well in combat."

"I believe you're correct," said Hunter. He rummaged in his bag for a moment and pulled out a few shards. "What will it be?" he asked.

Aurin looked at the Lunar Shard, considering what a nature, lightning, ice or metal Microbot evolution would be capable of. The Astral Shard didn't interest him much as he had Leonite to serve as a neutral elemental. The Solar Shard caught his eye and he thought about the raw power of fire, air, water and earth Minakai.

"Solar Shard," he said, reaching out for one.

"Very good," said Hunter. "I'll take a Lunar Shard. Let's see what we get, shall we?"

Luna, Shamtile and Innogon gathered round excitedly. It was always exhilarating watching Minakai evolve, but even more so when there was no guarantee of what one would evolve into.

Aurin and Hunter held the shards against their two Microbot and the two robots were enveloped in a cream light. Aurin's light changed to a deep blue while Hunter's turned green. The hard-to-see shape of the Minakai changed before the small crowd.

As the light faded, standing before Aurin was a Steambot. He was almost seven feet tall, stood on two legs, and bore armour of blue metal plates that glistened in the sun. Within his torso was a hole, where the familiar blue eye rested in a void of black. On Steambot's back were two small exhausts that puffed out hot steam. This new form reminded Aurin of a cross between a deep-sea diver and a steamboat.

Hunter's Minakai, however, was a quadruped. The Treebot had rough brown plates that covered it like an armoured vehicle. At the front was its eye and on top of its back was a thick layer of leaves that grew from within its armour.

"Two powerful Minakai," said Kyle, appearing from nowhere.

"Where were you?" asked Luna.

"I was watching from inside," he said. "I didn't want to be a distraction."

Shamtile walked up to Steambot and began poking him. The water titan puffed even more steam clouds from its pipes and jovially threw Shamtile into the air. The little reptile curled into a ball, enjoying being tossed around.

It suddenly clicked with Aurin. "Kyle, was this the special match you wanted to organise?"

Kyle and Hunter looked at each other and laughed. "Yes," confirmed Kyle. "Thank you again for accommodating, Hunter."

"I'm happy to help," he said with a smile. "I consider you a friend, Aurin, and I help my friends."

"Thanks to both of you," said Aurin, having enjoyed the battle and glad he had finally evolved Microbot. He turned to Hunter. "So that means you now have two Microbot evolutions that I need to defeat."

Hunter waved his hand through the air, illuminating two summoning stones that sat in his glove. From a red light, came his Flambot, and from a blue light, a Steambot of his own. "Not quite," he said, as his three robotic Minakai gathered around.

"Alright, you show off," joked Aurin.

"No wonder you're so good with your Microbot," said Luna. "You've trained up three of them."

"Repetition breeds skill," he replied. "I'm building a team of all the Microbot evolutions. I have three and there are seven to go. It'll be a long journey, but it will pay off well before I'm too old to battle."

"Versatility," said Aurin. "You'll have every element covered so you can't be caught by surprise...unless you're in the tower with only three of them, of course."

"Exactly," said Hunter. "On that note, shall we head back into Hazelton for lunch? Kyle's buying for dragging me all the way here, and he won't take no for an answer."

Everyone laughed and they walked into town, while all of the Minakai except for Shamtile and Innogon stayed behind. Aurin felt good about his growing team. He was itching for another tower run and was determined to break his record with the power of his Steambot.

Chapter 36

Tensions were running high on floor twelve of Harmony Tower. Aurin was irked by a comment Luna had made about how he couldn't get to this floor height without her help. It annoyed him mostly because he believed it to be true and wanted a chance to prove his abilities here alone.

"Then go by yourself," Luna said, wishing she hadn't made the throwaway comment that sparked the fight. "Each new floor, we'll head our separate ways and meet back at the elevator."

"Are you sure you can get to the elevator alone?" snapped Aurin, immediately regretting the unpleasant remark.

Luna looked furious and stormed off in a huff with Innogon. Both tamers had a full team of three Minakai remaining and were at full strength thanks to Luna's herbs.

"I didn't mean it that way, Inno," said Luna to her drake as he scurried after her. "I meant that it's good we're both able to help each other in here."

Innogon looked at her curiously. As smart as he was, he did not understand the senseless bickering of humans. He was happy to settle things with a water blast to his face. That usually ended his fights more quickly.

Luna's mood suddenly picked up. "Do you see that egg?" she asked, as Innogon let out a cheerful screech.

She ran towards the much-desired tower treasure and picked it up, unaware of the shadowy figure that was already in the room.

"Well, well," muttered the voice, walking towards her. Luna's eyes widened and Innogon rushed to attack the figure's roaring Minakai.

Shamtile tugged at Aurin's sleeve. "I know, I know," said Aurin as he watched Innogon run around the corner after Luna. "I'll apologise when we see her at the elevator."

The magical lizard was very fond of Luna and hated when the two tamers bickered, which admittedly was a rare occurrence. He warbled and groaned as Aurin walked onward, seeking the elevator and whatever treasures this floor held.

The first room he reached was the resting spot of a

pair of sleeping Minakai, a Techwing and a Pottemp. Shamtile crept up, looking to catch them both unawares. He pounced upon them with ease, burying them under a pile of falling rocks.

"We can do this ourselves, no problem," said Aurin as Shamtile waved his arms, celebrating the easy victory over the defenceless, sleeping Minakai.

Aurin and Shamtile wandered the corridors, travelling from room to room. They defeated many Minakai, most of which were awake, but things took a wobbly turn when Shamtile stepped on a rather ironic avalanche trap.

The magical lizard cast the rocks aside with his magic, injured, but able to continue. Aurin checked him over to make sure the wounds weren't going to hold them back too much, then they continued forward, but Aurin took a precautionary measure first.

He brought out one of the orbs he had been saving, an Orb of Traps, that revealed every trap hidden on a floor, making them very easy to avoid. Aurin had saved up a few of these useful tools but always prioritised bringing on other items. The tower restricted your carrying capacity greatly, refusing to allow you entry if you were too well prepared.

The rest of the floor was relatively easy, but Shamtile was almost defeated by a particularly feisty Hornferno. Fighting the beast reminded Aurin a lot of his own Spikruption, reminding him of how he had trained his Minakai with Luna's help.

"There it is," said Aurin, walking into a room and looking around. The elevator sat in the far corner, but there was more in the room. Glowing brightly, identified by the orb, was a trap waiting to be triggered. "I wonder where Luna is?" Aurin pondered aloud as he and Shamtile crossed the tiles.

"It's not wise to turn your back on a doorway in the tower," came a familiar voice.

"Leo," muttered Aurin, turning around.

The Zodiac member stood near the doorway with his favourite Leonite beside him. "I've heard rumours that you've been very busy in Harmony Tower," he said. "It would be a shame if your run came to an end early."

"Yours will end before mine," warned Aurin.

Leo looked around exaggeratedly. "You're alone? I don't see your girlfriend around here. Did you two go your separate ways?"

"What did you do?" asked Aurin. "If you hurt her, you're not going to make it out of the tower."

Leo's lip curled downwards. "What do you take me for exactly, Aurin? You think I am a murderer? You think I take delight in hurting teenage girls? I, along with my Zodiac brethren, have a single mission. We may be harsh and we may even be thieves, but the Zodiac Squad was not formed by sadistic killers."

"Where is she?" Aurin asked.

"She's probably waiting for you outside, somewhere," said Leo, revealing an egg from behind his back. He twirled it in his hands. "She gave me this as a parting gift."

"Hand it over," demanded Aurin. "It's not an Ethruki egg and you know it."

"Ah, so you're aware of Ethruki and what we seek in this tower? I'm surprised, but perhaps I shouldn't be. You were resourceful enough to find our old base and infiltrate it. You would have made a good team member."

"I would never join Zodiac."

"Nor do we want you to. We do not forgive and forget

easily. Master Taurus would deal with us severely for even daring to suggest such a thing."

"You're a talented tamer, Frederick," said Aurin. "What went wrong that led you to this?"

"There is nothing wrong," said Leo. "I have chosen this path of my own volition. My reasons are my own and you would do best not to ask that question again."

Aurin could see he had touched a nerve. "So, are we fighting or what?"

"Leonite!" barked Leo, and his Minakai sprang into action. It didn't look in too great shape after its time in the tower.

"Stone armour!" ordered Aurin, and Shamtile conjured armour in mid-air that clung to his body. If he was going to defeat Leo, he needed to be strategic.

Leonite swiped at Shamtile's armour, but the spellcasting lizard conjured another piece to replace what Leo's Minakai broke. He waved his arms wildly, and rocks pelted the Leonite, making him flinch and try to bat them away, but they just kept coming. The cobalt lion leapt out of the way, creating a distance between him and his enemy.

"The one closest to you," ordered Aurin, surprising Leo with the bizarre command.

Shamtile moved into position and summoned a large boulder that he held overhead. He was daring Leonite to approach. Taking the bait, the lion charged at him and stepped on the trap that only Aurin and Shamtile could see.

Leonite fell to the ground, completely limp. "No!" cried Leo, as Shamtile slammed the boulder onto his Minakai. The Zodiac member's best Minakai was ejected from the tower, and Leo summoned his next monster; a second Leonite.

"Shouldn't you mix it up?" asked Aurin.

"Why would I do that when your Minakai is clearly injured already?" asked Leo. "You can't pull that same trick twice. The trap is dead."

Aurin stayed silent. This Leonite was in good shape and bounded forwards, charging straight for Shamtile. The lizard was too slow to react and it swiped at him, knocking him back and shaking off the armour around his shoulders. Leonite bit him deeply and swung him around in his mouth, flinging Aurin's Minakai at the wall. He hit it hard before smacking into the ground.

As Shamtile was sent to stasis, Aurin had two Minakai left to use. "Steambot!" he called, summoning the Minakai he had evolved only a few days ago.

"Is that the Minakai you stole from our base?" asked Leo.

"I returned this Minakai to the tournament winner," said Aurin. "He was kind enough to let me earn it from him. We're not all immoral scumbags like your group."

Leo was getting angrier by the second. He ordered his Leonite to attack and it dashed towards Steambot, who fired a blast of water. The Leonite dodged the attack effortlessly and hopped on top of the water automaton, sinking both his claws and teeth into his metal.

"Release the pressure," said Aurin with a smile, seeing Leo play into his hands.

Steambot grabbed Leonite and tore him away, throwing him over his back and draping him upon his pipes. He sent a burst of scalding, pressurised steam at the lion and it roared in agony as its flesh was cooked by the intense heat.

"No!" barked Leo, looking furious.

Aurin's Minakai threw the Leonite into the air and

smashed a hefty fist into it, sending it flying towards the roof. It hit it with a heavy thud before plummeting to the ground. Steambot drew back its leg and delivered a powerful kick to the lion, sending it whizzing through the air and back at its tamer. It smacked the ground and rolled to Leo, but it was out cold and vanished from the tower before reaching him.

"We'll meet again soon, Aurin," said Leo, moments before he too was forced outside by the magic of the tower.

"Huh," said a surprised Aurin to Steambot. "I figured he would have a third Minakai."

He thought about it for a moment and realised that Leo had entered alone, whereas he and Luna had teamed up. Shamtile and Innogon were there to have each other's backs in difficult situations, and going it alone made for a much tougher road in a deadly place like Harmony Tower. Perhaps Leo *did* have a third Minakai and it was defeated earlier in the run. Aurin had to remind himself that even tough tamers like Leo were only human and even wild Minakai could give them a run for their money.

Aurin walked over to the spot where Leo had stood and picked up the egg that he dropped. He wanted to return the egg to its rightful owner and turned to Steambot.

"Let's leave too," said Aurin, pulling out his Orb of Return and turning his back on the elevator.

In a flash, he landed on the ground at the front of the tower with Steambot by his side. It was early afternoon and there was still plenty of time in the day. Leo had made himself scarce quickly and another couple of girls were walking towards the tower.

"Did you get thrown out?" asked one of them, while

the other stared in awe at Steambot.

"No," said Aurin to the tamer while Steambot flexed and puffed steam to impress the tamer admiring him. "My friend was banished before me and I don't much feel like going it alone today. Have a good run, girls. Best of luck."

Aurin walked back to Kyle's ranch with Steambot, who was admiring the forest along the way. His tamer was inclined to believe that he would have preferred to have evolved into a Treebot like Hunter's, but he was grateful for Steambot's power. All of the training as a Microbot had paid off, preparing him for this stronger form.

As Aurin walked up the path towards the ranch, he could see Luna leaning on a fence with her Tadpool by her side. He gave her a small wave and she waved back, with an apologetic look on her face.

"I'm sorry," they said together when Aurin drew close.

"I shouldn't have taken it so personally," said Aurin. "The truth is the tower wouldn't be half as fun without you there and I really wouldn't have made it this far alone."

"You would get there eventually," said Luna. "I didn't mean it the way it sounded."

Aurin handed the egg to her, and she looked surprised. "Is this my egg?" she asked and then glanced at Steambot. "If he's with you, that means you left voluntarily. You beat Leo?"

"I thought you would appreciate a little bit of vengeance," smiled Aurin.

Luna smiled back. "Shall we go hatch this egg?" she asked.

"Maybe it's another Dopefish?" joked Aurin.

"We've just made up, don't start something else," said Luna with a frown, but then she stuck her tongue out and laughed.

The two headed into Kyle's house together to retrieve the incubator. It had been a tough couple of months of training and tower runs, but both tamers could see the results. Their teams were growing both in number and in strength, and they felt ready for whatever the Zodiac Squad would throw at them next.

End of Arc 3
Building a Team

Aurin's Team:

Luna's Team:

Chapter 37

Dolissile's fins glowed a brighter blue than ever and cut through Eclare's Metortoise's hard green shell. The Minakai was thoroughly defeated by the speedy cybernetic dolphin, and it was resoundingly ejected from the tower.

"Let's call the battle here," said Eclare, not wanting to be ejected from the tower herself. The pretty blonde girl swept her hair back with a smile. "You've got me beaten," she said. "That Dolissile is a lot more powerful than he was at the tournament."

"Sounds good," said Aurin, pleased with his victory and another opportunity to test his Minakai's strength. "Were you competing at the tournament?" he asked.

"Knocked out in round two," she said as she summoned a Pyrofly to continue guiding her through the tower. "I have to at least double that next time if I don't want to be the shame of Hazelton," she joked.

"Maybe we'll get a chance to fight again at the next tournament?"

"I hope it isn't in the first three rounds then. See you later," said Eclare with a laugh. She blew Aurin a kiss, which made Luna frown, and then continued onwards to the tenth floor, leaving the two younger tamers behind.

Luna inspected Dolissile to make sure he had no injuries that she needed to treat, but he looked to be in perfect shape. It had been a strong start to the run for the duo with their teams of three Minakai each still standing strong, something that was a rarity by the later parts of the ninth floor.

"This is a far better day than yesterday," said Luna, thinking back to their horrendous performance the day before.

"We said we wouldn't talk about it," scolded Aurin. The pair had lost all of their Minakai on the seventh floor and, along with them, they let an egg slip through their fingers. "Kyle can never know that we were bested by two Frogre. He'll never let us hear the end of it."

"Come on now, would it really be that bad to tell him? Maybe he'll sympathise. He's bound to have had plenty of bad luck in his time in the towers."

"Every time we walk past one of the Frogre guards at the ranch, he'll make a snide comment, 'Aurin, be careful,' or something like that."

"Okay, yes. That does sound exactly like him," admitted Luna.

The two tamers placed their hands on the blue orb and were magicked away from the ninth floor and onto the tenth floor. They landed with their Minakai by their side while determination and optimism flowed through them; they were ready to smash through their previous record before the day was over.

Landing on the particularly shiny tiles, the tamers felt good at hitting the double-digit floors. They walked along with Dolissile and Innogon floating and walking alongside them, respectively. Innogon in particular was bouncing along merrily.

"I'm wondering..." said Aurin.

"What?" asked Luna.

"Are you ever planning to evolve Innogon?"

"Haven't you asked me something similar before?"

"I have," said Aurin, thinking back, "but now that he's stronger and more capable, do you think he's nearly ready?"

"I could ask you the same about Shamtile," said Luna, feeling uneasy about the question. As much as she loved each of her Minakai, there was no denying that Innogon was her favourite, and they had a special bond.

"Shamtile could evolve any time," said Aurin, "but he's powerful enough for what I need him to do as is. If he evolves, he'll be physically stronger at the cost of his speed, which is something that's come in handy for him before. Shamasaur is on the bulkier side and the element of surprise that a little trickster like Shamtile can give has helped us before."

Luna thought about it and she agreed. "Yes, that's a fair answer. I suppose I like that Innogon is a good battler, but still cute and cuddly at the same time," she said as she watched her little Minakai bobbing along. "I would miss carrying him around on my back too," she added.

"He could carry you around on his back," said Aurin. "You wouldn't have to worry about back pain after half an hour.

"I suppose so," laughed Luna. She was unable to imagine Innogon as a Guilgon. In her mind, when he evolved he would look the same, but be scaled up in size. "I like to think that I have a strong back after all of the carrying."

"I'm not trying to put any pressure on you to evolve him, I was just curious about your current thoughts on the matter. You could be seventy and still have Innogon as he is now, and I wouldn't make an issue of it."

"I know," said Luna. "You don't need to explain yourself; it was just a simple question. To tell you the truth, it's something I have thought about before. The inclination was strongest during the tournament when I was feeling most competitive, but I don't see the need anymore."

A sudden click in the room that they had just entered. "Oh no," muttered Aurin as something began raining down from the ceiling.

The two tamers covered their heads, but Innogon jumped for joy trying to catch the falling objects. They were a nuisance, but they did not hurt. In fact, they clinked soothingly as they hit the floor and shone in the dim light.

"Is that...silver?" asked Aurin.

"Not just silver," said Luna, uncovering her head. Her eyes nearly burst from her skull. "Orbs, berries, and look at this one," she said, rushing over to pick up a magnifying glass. "I'm pretty sure this is an Identifying Glass."

"What does that do?" asked Aurin. He was certain he had seen one before on a solo tower run but didn't pay it any notice.

"If you hold it in front of an egg, you can know what

Minakai is inside it," said Luna, twirling it in her hand. "It's most often used when you run out of carrying space to see if it's worth keeping an egg or your other treasure."

"Or for deciding between your eggs," said Aurin, seeing how it could be useful.

"That's right," said Luna, throwing the enchanted magnifying glass to Aurin, who stashed it in his pack. "Do you see these crystals too?"

"The ones I usually ignore?"

"Yes," said Luna, remembering how Aurin had scoffed at a crystal on one of the duo's earliest tower runs. "Kyle told me what they do. You use them and they cast a spell, similar to orbs, but it's a direct attack."

"Hang on," said Aurin, surprised nobody had told him about this before. "I can help my Minakai more directly if I use these?"

"Yes, Kyle told me about them one time when you were running off to find the incubator."

"And you didn't think to mention it before this?" asked Aurin, irked that Luna had withheld such useful information. "How many of these have we skipped over?"

"I was waiting for you to ask, but you never did."

"My mum told me she would rather I stay in school and get a good job in an office," laughed Aurin, throwing silver into the air playfully. "It took my dad months to convince her to allow me to become a full-time tamer."

"It was the other way around for me. My dad wanted me to become a doctor for people, but my mother was the one who let me follow my passion. Dad changed his tune right around the time you arrived and I showed him the first silver I earned in the tower."

The two scoured the room, picking up as much silver

as they could hold. Aurin grabbed a few of the orbs, including a brand-new Orb of Return, whereas Luna picked up herbs and berries enthusiastically. It was unusual for a trap to bring any sort of benefit, but it was a rare treat that left them feeling upbeat and motivated rather than downcast and defeated.

The group continued onwards, conquering the challenges that lay ahead before ascending to floor eleven. Dolissile smashed a Pottemp to pieces, while Innogon dampened out a Flowl. "It's far too weak to be at a floor as high as this," scoffed Luna, banishing the creature from the tower.

Floor eleven was also a success. There was little in the way of treasure, but Dolissile and Innogon teamed up to defeat a group of three miserable Melansprout that tried to violently share their misery with the group. Innogon impressed the tamers by beating a swift Peekawe solo in less than thirty seconds.

On floor twelve, things started to get a little more difficult. A wild Shamtile attacked and sent a barrage of rocks at the tamers and their Minakai. Aurin took offence to this, usually, the one ordering his own Shamtile to do the same to others, and made sure that it wouldn't bother anybody else for quite some time.

Dolissile also struggled in his fight against a rampaging Thunding, who wildly hurled his spears at the cyborg dolphin. Normally, it wouldn't have been a problem, but the particularly tight corridor meant that Dolissile struggled to turn around and left himself open for head-on attacks. In the end, he overcame the difficult battlefield and sent the lightning warrior back to its home.

As luck would have it, floor thirteen was much more straightforward. Most of the Minakai they found were fast asleep and they took them out quickly or avoided them altogether. Aurin was secretly hoping he would find another sleeping Rabbafat to exact his revenge on after the last one that had given them trouble, but he did not see one.

"Almost matching our previous record," sighed Luna as the group landed on the fourteenth floor.

"We're going to make it to floor sixteen today and break that record," said Aurin optimistically. "I can feel it in my soul."

"In your soul?"

"Yes."

"Lead the way then," said Luna.

Aurin walked around the corner and immediately turned back, running in the opposite direction. He grabbed Luna's hand and sprinted, their Minakai following them close behind.

"What is it?" she asked, starting to panic too.

"Three angry Windjinn," he said.

The evolved form of Feathrus, Windjinn was a sky serpent with wings and a lot of feathers. The three soared along the corridor, handling corners and curves with ease, while the tamers dashed from room to room, trying to give them the slip.

"Why don't we fight them?" asked Luna.

"Not until we find a bigger room for Dolissile," said Aurin, trying to think strategically. They were so close to their record and each of them had a full team remaining. "There's one, just up ahead!" he said, relieved at the much bigger battlefield he could make use of.

Click.

As suddenly as silver had rained previously, monsters spawned all across the floor. Creatures of almost every element were surrounding them, a Sproufloat, a Hornferno, a Funglie, two Cubtem and three Gittup. Not the worst monster den trap that they could have sprung, but when they were being chased by three other powerful foes, things did not look good.

"We don't have a choice now," said Luna as the Windjinn followed them into the room.

"Attack!" cried Aurin.

Chapter 38

Dolissile torpedoed into one of the attacking Windjinn, breaking a few bones and knocking it into the wall. It was zapped from the tower right as Innogon took a hard hit from the charging Hornferno.

"Dolissile, give Innogon a hand," said Aurin, trying to keep an eye on all of the wild Minakai at once.

"Focus on the Windjinn," said Luna confidently. "Innogon will be okay. Take out the strongest ones first."

Dolissile's fins glowed bright blue and Aurin ordered him to burst forward. The cybernetic dolphin slashed at the side of one of the Windjinn and banished it, but he was then hit from behind by a strong wind from the last Windjinn that redirected him into the ceiling.

The wild Hornferno spat a storm of fireballs at

Dolissile, who lay helpless and unable to dodge. He disappeared in a burst of grey light and was sent to stasis.

"No!" exclaimed Aurin, furiously. He summoned Spikruption into the tower. "Your fire has the advantage against the air elemental. Burn him to cinders."

Spikruption charged in ready and eager to do some damage. He grabbed the Windjinn with his teeth and swung it around while breathing fire and igniting the serpent. He slammed it into the ground and it writhed in pain before disappearing. The Windjinn were all gone, now it was time to finish the job.

Innogon had made good work of the other monsters, defeating the two Cubtem and one of the Gittup, but the Sproufloat's barrage of razor-sharp leaves was too much for him to take and he collapsed, unable to fight any longer.

Luna was riled up. "Heatpup!" she called, summoning her most recently hatched Minakai. The enthusiastic fiery dog jumped up and sank its teeth into Sproufloat's leg, giving Spikruption the chance to gore it with his horns.

The Funglie unleashed a cloud of spores, taking out its fellow wild Minakai, Hornferno, who breathed in more spores than oxygen. Spikruption returned the attack with his own breath weapon, his flamethrower. He sprayed a fire so intense that the Funglie began rolling on the ground before it too was done for.

The remaining two Gittup zapped Aurin and Luna's Minakai with lightning bolts from their tails, but Spikruption crushed one under its feet and Heatpup hurled a fireball straight into the beast's hairy face, which caught fire. It was done for, and the tamers were free to breathe easy at last.

"I'm surprised we got off so lightly," said Luna, sitting on the floor to rest.

"So am I," admitted Aurin. "Why Heatpup?"

"I panicked," said Luna, "but he did need a chance to fight in the tower rather than train at the ranch. Trial by fire, so to speak."

"I'll say," chortled Aurin. "Two Minakai left for each of us. We're still doing well enough that we should break our record."

"Give me a minute to enjoy the peace and quiet before we keep moving."

"That's fair," said Aurin, sitting down to also take a short rest. Between the heat and the dissipating spores, it was hard to feel truly relaxed, but they faded before long.

Once the duo was ready, they led Spikruption and Heatpup further through the floor. It wasn't long before they stumbled across the familiar elevator. They touched the blue orb and ascended to floor fifteen, matching their previous floor record. The two tamers were eager to break that record today.

They roamed floor fifteen, where Spikruption did most of the fighting. Many of the Minakai on this floor were too tough for Heatpup, but Luna resolved to give him a chance anyway. Aurin was rather uncertain about this decision, but he held his tongue.

The two tamers ignored most of the treasure on the floor, having come close to the point of being overburdened by their previous findings from this tower run. It was unusual for them to ignore the piles of silver coins, but they were forced to overlook the enticing treasure.

"We did it," said Luna excitedly, spotting the elevator at the far side of the room they entered.

"Quick, before we trigger another disastrous trap," said Aurin, skipping over as many tiles as he could on his way to the orb.

Luna walked more casually to join him and the duo placed their hands on the orb once more, breaking their record. Landing on the sixteenth floor, the purple walls and black floor tiles made it seem darker than a lot of the other floors they were familiar with.

"This one is kind of spooky, no?" asked Luna.

"It's hard to see," agreed Aurin. "Even the orb lanterns are darker than normal."

"I hope this isn't the same the whole way to the top. I don't like it."

"One way to find out," said Aurin, marching on ahead with Spikruption stomping along behind him.

The two walked from room to room, defeating whatever Minakai they happened upon. Heatpup had a few close calls that would have been the end of the underpowered dog had the giant dinosaur not been there to hurl his opponent against the wall or crush it beneath his massive feet.

The darkness of this floor did not make things any easier, with wild Minakai finding it much easier to attack from the shadows. Even Spikruption had trouble when a small, oozing Minakai attacked him. The brown sludge-like Plasmun pierced the dino's ankle with its sharp horn, making it much harder for him to move around. Luckily, Heatpup used the opportunity to pay back Aurin's Minakai and boiled the ooze.

"We're doing well today, so don't you ruin it," said a grumpy voice from the room to the left.

"Stop bickering, you idiots," snapped a familiar voice.

Aurin and Luna stopped dead in their tracks. "Hide,"

whispered Aurin, dragging Luna away from the doorway. Luckily, they had yet to be spotted.

"Sagittarius?" mouthed Luna soundlessly. Aurin nodded.

It was unmistakably one of the elite Zodiac Squad members they had encountered in their old warehouse headquarters. Aurin and Luna had only heard him speak once before, but his drawl was distinct. He had been discussing Ethruki with Leo and Libra, but it sounded like he was with subordinates this time.

"All I'm saying is that there's no way we'll find him at a floor this low," said a third man.

"That may be true," said Sagittarius, "but it's not so easy to reach the floors where we're more likely to find him. Hell, we could get to floor thirty and still just have a bad run of luck. Point is, try and stay positive or I'll slap you silly. I don't want my mood ruined on a good day."

"Sorry, boss," said the Zodiac member.

Aurin and Luna could hear their footsteps approaching. Luna started to back away slowly, but Aurin silently ordered Spikruption to walk past the doorway.

"Quick," said Sagittarius in a low voice," before it sees us. The footsteps retreated, and they were gone.

"I don't like this at all," said Luna. "How are we supposed to keep going if there are three of them and only two of us?"

"Thankfully, there can't be more than three of them in the same group or the tower would forcefully split them across different dimensions."

"That's true, but there are still three of them. How are we supposed to avoid them? Two of the minions are enough trouble, but elites like Sagittarius could give us real problems if Leo's team is anything to go by."

"Thank you, treasure trap," said Aurin, pulling out an orb.

"I didn't say I wanted to leave," said Luna, surprised that Aurin would give up without a fight.

"Watch and see," said Aurin, activating the magic of the Orb of Tamers. Suddenly, he could see the glowing outline of the three Zodiac members through the walls. They shone red, standing out particularly well on this dark floor.

"It...it didn't do anything," said a rather underwhelmed Luna.

"The orb means that my Minakai and I can see them across the entire floor. It's given me a limited x-ray vision, so I'll know where they are at all times and what we should do to not cross their path."

"We should use these more often."

"Yes," said Aurin. "Yes, we really should."

The two tamers continued to roam the corridors, hoping to find the elevator before the Zodiac members so they could create some distance between them, but that was easier said than done.

Aurin kept an eye on his enemies the whole time while Spikruption handled battles without his tamer's orders. Luna and Heatpup were there to give him a helping hand whenever he needed it.

"Something's happening," said Aurin, watching the red silhouettes in the distance.

"Tell me, tell me," urged Luna.

"One of them just got slapped and he's being directed to go elsewhere."

"He must have been being too negative again."

A smile stretched across Aurin's face as he turned to look at Luna. "Now's our chance to even the odds," he said, sounding very sinister.

Luna smiled back. "Let's get him."

Aurin led them around the tower floor, being sure to stay clear of Sagittarius and the other Zodiac peon. Spikruption kept the path clear as they snuck up on the isolated Zodiac member from behind. He wouldn't know what hit him.

Aurin peered round the corner and could see that the man was walking alongside his own Minakai, a Vambra. The bizarre creature was made up of a giant eyeball with a pair of drooping arms and two long, but thin, wings that it flapped around on. The undead Minakai did not look all that tough.

Spikruption ran forwards, his footsteps rumbling the floor with each heavy thud. He hurled a fireball ahead of himself at the flying eye. It batted it aside with one of its wings, then swerved out of the way of the dinosaur's lowered, spiked head.

"It's you!" cried the Zodiac member. "I knew this day was going too well," he lamented before ordering his Vambra to attack.

The demon swayed slowly back and forth as its eye began to spiral. Spikruption could not look away and was trapped in a daze. Even Aurin was starting to feel drawn in by the hypnotic attack. The Vambra's eye started to glow purple as it charged up a swirling beam of energy that it was seeking to unleash.

Luna's Heatpup sank its teeth into the Vambra's arm as it fired, throwing it off balance and making the beam strike the wall. Spikruption came too, no longer under the trance. He rammed his head straight into his opponent's eyeball, sending it crashing to the ground before it vanished from the tower.

"No!" cried the Zodiac member. "I'm in so much

trouble now." He was ejected, leaving Aurin and Luna standing in the corridor with their Minakai.

"I'm glad you're here," said Aurin.

"I am too," said Luna with a smile. She felt good being able to save Aurin for a change. She stroked her Heatpup, but his fur was so toasty that she had to blow on her hand to cool it down afterwards.

"They're coming this way," Aurin said, looking at the two remaining red figures approaching.

"We should avoid them for as long as we can," said Luna.

Aurin agreed and they ran in the opposite direction. They were no longer outnumbered, but they were fearful of what would happen should they be caught by Sagittarius. Something in his gut told Aurin that the man happy to attack and dismiss his own allies wouldn't play as nice as Leo.

Chapter 39

"It's out of charge," said Aurin as he and Luna arrived on the eighteenth floor. The young man shook the Orb of Tamers, hoping that it would somehow work better, but he knew it was pointless. "It was good while it lasted."

"Should we get out of here?" asked Luna, concerned that Sagittarius and his fellow Zodiac goon would appear around the corner.

"No," said Aurin. "We know he's lurking around this floor somewhere and I don't see the point in running from him now that we're evenly matched. As nasty as the guy seems to be, I still want to teach him a lesson."

"You love poking the bear, don't you?"

"Yes."

Luna frowned. "If this turns out to be a bad idea,

don't say that I didn't warn you."

"Zodiac are bad guys, sure, but they're not murderers," said Aurin, remembering his most recent encounter with Leo.

"You don't know that," said Luna. "They're a bad bunch and you have no idea what could happen if you push them too far. I'm sure we're treading on thin ice as it is."

Spikruption and Heatpup had both fallen on the seventeenth floor, so Aurin had called upon Desparee while Luna called upon Angree. The newly selected Minakai had a couple of minor battles on the previous floor but were no worse for the wear.

Sensing that it would be useful, Aurin used an Orb of Traps to reveal the hidden hazards on the current level. If he could align things right, perhaps they could be used on the enemy just as he did in his last battle against Leo.

"Five tiles ahead and one to the left," warned Aurin, as Luna was getting close to a trap in one of the rooms.

"Thank you," she said merrily as she skipped past the trap and towards a pile of silver coins. She picked up only a small handful, already heavily burdened. Aurin gathered the rest, discarding the drained Orb of Tamers that weighed him down.

The eighteenth floor was surprisingly kind to them with few wild Minakai lurking around. Aurin chalked it up to Sagittarius and his minion wandering somewhere ahead of them and dealing with the bulk of the opposition that he and Luna would have otherwise faced.

There was some trouble with a Totempo, an evolved and equally broken Pottemp, that Angree charged in and attacked before Desparee could let off a stealthier ranged attack, but once the two started working together effectively they overcame the Totempo and knocked it out stone-cold.

Aurin held up his hand and listened carefully, certain that he had heard a voice. Yes, there was somebody close by.

"Who is it?" mouthed Luna, not emitting a sound.

"It's them," Aurin mouthed back at her, identifying Sagittarius's voice.

She pulled him around a corner, not wanting to risk fighting against the Zodiac duo. "We shouldn't do this," she said. "It was fine when we had more Minakai, but we're down to our last each."

"I don't think we have a choice," said Aurin. "There's a target on our back already after what we did at the warehouse. We need to find out if we can defeat them before they eventually ambush us."

"What makes you so certain they'll come for us?"

"It's in their nature. They're not the sort of people who will let something lie. Zodiac may be biding their time now, focusing on their task, but they'll come for us eventually. Please, trust me."

"I do," said Luna. She knew that he was right, no matter how much she would try and deny it, even to herself.

The two tamers took a deep breath and wandered towards the voices. They were skulking about a room with a Thundarun and Minakai that looked like a large icicle with an eyeball; a Pillaberg. The two humans were picking up silver and an unknown orb. Aurin stepped into the room with Desparee, followed by Luna and Angree.

"Are you still looking for Ethruki, Zodiac?" asked Aurin.

The minion jumped out of his skin, but Sagittarius looked around, cool as a cucumber. "Look who it is," he said. "So nice of you to join us somewhere so isolated, Aurin. I see you've brought your friend with you."

"I'm glad that you recognise me," said Aurin with a smile. "It will make it that much easier to run when you see me coming from now on."

Sagittarius let out a wild cackle. "You've got a pair, boy. You really are as bold as Leo says, but that isn't a surprise considering you were smarmy enough to sneak into our warehouse and cause the mess that you did. I should thank you for that, by the way."

"Thank me?"

"We've redoubled our efforts to find Ethruki for the time being. Clearly, you know that's what we're seeking in Harmony Tower. It's nice to have a focused goal rather than spread ourselves too thin. It may have irked some of our other members, but it works very nicely for me."

"Let's smoke him, boss," said the minion.

"Speak when you're spoken to," barked Sagittarius before turning back towards Aurin. "Forgive him, he's awfully rude. Is it a battle you're looking for, youngsters? I'm more than happy to oblige."

"I hope you're ready," said Aurin, standing firm.

"Thundarun, charge!" called Sagittarius, pointing directly at Aurin.

Sagittarius's lightning-imbued unicorn dashed straight for the tamer, ignoring his Desparee. It was inches from Aurin when Luna's Angree delivered a heavy punch, knocking it aside.

Luna looked at Aurin with a terrified look on her face. "He wants to kill us."

"This is the game you want to play?" asked Aurin.

Sagittarius merely smiled as his Thundarun fired lightning at Angree, while Pillaberg conjured icicles and hurled them at Desparee. Aurin knew he would have to watch out because either of the Zodiac Minakai could turn towards him at any point.

Desparee summoned vines to smack the icicles out of the air, then charged a nature beam in his hands, firing it at the Pillaberg. The enemy Minakai pulled an ice wall from the ground and blocked the attack, countering with a snowstorm.

Angree took lightning bolt after lightning bolt but remained standing. He pummelled the side of the shadowy unicorn, but it too refused to buckle. It reared up and delivered a brutal kick to the wooden puppet warrior, cracking his body.

Desparee was struggling to aim through the snowstorm, but Pillaberg had no such problem. It froze Desparee's arms and legs in blocks of ice, rendering most of his attacks unusable. It slid along the floor towards its target and stabbed the tree Minakai with one of its pointed arms.

"Easy," said Sagittarius to his goon. "We're going to knock them out of the tower. Let's try something else."

Thundarun directed a powerful bolt to Angree, flinging him against the wall. As he tried to climb up, Pillaberg froze him in place. Aurin and Luna's Minakai were not yet defeated, but they were completely incapacitated.

Luna looked terrified as Aurin reached into his bag for the Orb of Return, desperate to leave. They had lost and had to escape the tower quickly.

"Not so fast," said Sagittarius as his Thundarun charged at Aurin, knocking the orb from his hands before he could cast the spell.

"No...no..." muttered Luna, afraid that she was going to die.

"I'll make it quick," smirked Sagittarius, before laughing. "That's a lie. It will be slow and painful. Your last thoughts will be how you should never have messed with us."

He pulled a knife from his waistband and approached the tamers. Luna turned to run, but Pillaberg slid across the floor and blocked the door she was making for.

Aurin dove at Sagittarius, knocking him to the ground, but he didn't let go of his knife. Aurin grabbed his wrist and tried to wrestle it from him as the other Zodiac member rushed over to grab Luna. Sagittarius was much stronger than Aurin and was overpowering him easily.

"I suppose it will be quick," he said, bringing the knife within an inch of Aurin's throat.

Suddenly, a phantom-like creature burst into the room. The burly creature had glowing blue hair, deep orange eyes and a yellow segmented stomach. It charged straight for Pillaberg, and through the other side of the room, disappearing from sight as fast as it had appeared.

"Ethruki!" cried Sagittarius, climbing to his feet and running after the Minakai.

Unbeknownst to the Zodiac elite, Pillaberg and its tamer were both banished from the tower after the cosmic beast shattered the icy Minakai. He was left alone to defend himself against the now-freed Minakai of the tamers he had tried to murder.

Desparee charged up a nature energy beam, unleashing it at the charging Thundarun, while Angree followed up with a flurry of blows to its head. The unicorn was devastated by their power and ejected from the tower.

Sagittarius turned towards the two tamers, realising what had just happened. "I'll see you both soon," he warned sinisterly before disappearing in a burst of light. It was clear he intended to make good on that threat.

Aurin and Luna turned to look at each other, both wide-eyed and lost for words. They had been inches from death and saved by the wild Ethruki. Neither knew for certain whether the beast saved them on purpose, or if it was the most fortunate of coincidences, but they breathed a sigh of relief.

The tamers thanked their Minakai for finishing off their attacker and Aurin whisked them away from the tower with his orb. Both were relieved to see that Sagittarius was nowhere to be found outside the tower, and they ran back to the ranch, keeping close to their Minakai the whole journey.

Neither Aurin nor Luna said a word to each other, but they immediately dragged Kyle out from the pens to explain everything. Even at the warehouse, it had felt like they were never in any real danger, but now everything seemed much more serious.

Chapter 40

"So, once again, you're going to do nothing about this?" asked Aurin, standing in Mayor Boren's office with Luna, Kyle, Knot and Scarlett.

"And do you have any proof that this happened?" asked Mayor Boren. "I believe you that it did, but my belief isn't going to allow the two detectives here to simply arrest this Sagittarius fellow."

"You're the mayor," said Aurin, more frustrated than ever before, "you must have some sway."

Boren stared at the young man intently. "Do you have any idea what his real name is? What he looks like? Anything that can be followed up on in any way? If you do, I would love to hear about it."

Everyone stood in silence as all eyes were on Aurin. In truth, he had nothing outside of his and Luna's story of the events in the tower. There was no way they could even find Sagittarius without knowing where the new Zodiac headquarters was located.

"I have nothing," said Aurin, breaking the silence.

Mayor Boren sighed. "I understand your frustration, young man. I mean that sincerely. Between all of us in this room, if I could drown that man in a river, I would," the mayor stood up and gestured towards the door. "If you find anything else, please report it directly to the detectives. Knot, can you show them out?"

"Certainly, mayor," said Knot, walking everyone but Boren and Scarlett outside.

Knot looked around to make sure that nobody was listening in. "I'll meet you at the ranch later," he whispered.

"When?" asked Luna.

"When I can," he said, heading back inside.

Aurin, Luna and Kyle walked down the street, leaving the town hall behind. It was the second time that Aurin and Luna had left it in disappointment, and it was for very similar reasons last time. The major difference this time was that the other Zodiac Squad members hadn't tried to kill them.

"Just what are we supposed to do?" asked Aurin.

"Kill Sagittarius before he kills you," said Kyle with a sullen expression.

"Do you mean that, Kyle?" asked Luna incredulously.

"Oh, I mean it alright, but I don't think I have the nerve to go through with it."

"I agree that it would be the simplest solution," said Aurin, "but I don't think I could do something so...final either. There's no going back after killing another human."

"Can we stop talking about killing him?" asked Luna. "It's making me uncomfortable."

"This whole situation is uncomfortable," said Aurin. "When he said he was going to see us soon, you know that he meant it. This guy is a whole lot worse than Leo ever was."

Aurin and Kyle returned to the ranch after leaving Luna home. Her parents had been understandably concerned after she told them what happened and wanted to keep a much closer eye on her. If Kyle hadn't been accompanying them to the mayor's office, she wouldn't have been allowed to leave the house at all. Aurin felt like they blamed him for it, but Luna was too nice to say it. He would have been lying if he said that he didn't feel responsible for deliberately aggravating Zodiac time and time again.

The young tamer sat on the grass with Shamtile, looking towards the mountains in the distance. "We could always hide up there, Shammy," he said to his favourite Minakai.

The masked lizard waved his arms and screeched loudly, alerting most of the monsters at the ranch.

"Easy for you to say," said his tamer, sensing what his Minakai meant, "you can defend yourself much more easily with your magic. The best I can do is throw a few punches or run for my life."

Shamtile flapped around and emitted a warbled, guttural growl.

Aurin nodded. "That's true. We're not bound by the rules of the tower if we don't go into the tower. I can summon all seven of you at once if I need to."

Shamtile danced happily. He wasn't so much excited by his good point, but more that his tamer understood him near-perfectly every time now. Last spring, half of

Aurin's guesses at deciphering the reptilian Minakai's grunts, grumbles and screeches were so far off the mark that he would interpret them as the opposite of what Shamtile had meant.

Just then, Detective Knot appeared from the trees. He was walking briskly with his collar up, but it was obvious to anyone who had been in town for more than a month that the man in the trench coat was usually the detective.

Shamtile ran off to get Kyle, while Aurin brought the detective inside. If he was so concerned about being spotted, then being indoors would put his mind at ease. Aurin made him a cup of tea, serving it just as Shamtile returned with Kyle.

"Is young Luna going to be joining us?" asked Knot.

"I don't think it's likely," said Kyle. "Her parents are angry about the entire situation, and I can't say I blame them."

Knot nodded understandingly. "It's quite the mess. As far as intel goes, there have been no reports of Zodiac members ever killing, or even trying to kill. I suspect this Sagittarius fellow is going somewhat rogue and throwing caution to the wind."

"You would think after they left themselves so open at the tournament, they wouldn't want anything raising the alert," said Kyle.

Aurin couldn't help but think about what happened the last time he met Leo in the tower. "I think your intel is correct, detective. Leo ejected Luna from the tower when we were separated recently. He didn't try and hurt her and when I found him, I insinuated that he may have and he seemed almost...offended?"

"I don't blame him," said Kyle. "If he's a true Zodiac Squad loyalist then having your entire group going from being perceived as thieves to killers would be aggravating. Now that one of them seems to be trying to do just that, I'm sure he would be even more angry at Sagittarius than he is at you."

Something else was bothering Aurin. "Why won't Mayor Boren pull a few strings and give you more resources to push back against criminals who are destroying his town?"

Knot was sipping his tea and abruptly stopped. "I'm certain that he's been paid off to obstruct the matter," he said, stone-faced.

"Yes, it seemed that way to me," said Kyle.

"I believed him when he said that he would see Sagittarius drowned," said Aurin.

"Oh, so do I," said Detective Knot. "It's a real nuisance for him to have to deal with all of this nonsense, but if he's already taken a bribe then he's obligated to keep doing so or whoever had bribed him could sink his entire career."

"What do you suggest we do?" asked Aurin.

"You should train like you've never trained before," said Knot. "Not just your Minakai, but you as well. If you don't know hand-to-hand combat, you should learn. If you can't sprint fast, then start running until you can."

"And the police force won't be able to help at all?" asked Kyle.

"Have we been able to so far?" replied Knot with a pointed stare.

"That's a good point," admitted Kyle, also at a loss.

"What good will it do?" asked an irritable Aurin. "We're completely outnumbered if all of Zodiac decides to follow Sagittarius's methods. We don't have the number of tamers around us that we did during the tournament."

"While we're here at the ranch, we have numbers," said Kyle. "You have Minakai, I have Minakai and there are many other Minakai belonging to those very same tamers from the tournament."

"But we can't use them," said Aurin.

"No, we can't," said Kyle, "but that doesn't mean they won't choose to help us if Zodiac comes for us at the ranch. If you stay away from the tower, then you leave yourself far less vulnerable."

Aurin thought about it. He knew that he would have to abandon any desire to venture into the tower again until he was certain that the threat had been dealt with. He couldn't allow himself to put Luna in any danger and, alone in the tower, he was vulnerable.

Aurin met with Luna at their favourite café in Hazelton on a cold winter morning. Shamtile and Innogon immediately started bickering over who got the chocolate milkshake and who got the banana one. When Shamtile tried to take both from Innogon, he was met with a blast of water to the face.

Luna giggled at the pair before her expression turned more solemn.

"I'm guessing you have some bad news to share," said Aurin.

"Yes," sighed Luna, her eyes glistening with tears. "My parents are taking me away to my aunt's house over Christmas. We'll be away for a month, but in the meantime, I'm forbidden from entering the tower or going to the ranch. They say that if I want to see my Minakai, I can summon them and banish them as I please."

"Is this because of everything?" asked Aurin.

"Why else?"

Aurin nodded. "To be honest, I entirely understand. I've managed to get us into a lot of danger. Even my dad asked me if it was best to just come home and get away from Zodiac."

"It's not your fault," said Luna. "They started everything, and you were right when you said in the tower that they would come for us eventually. We really did paint a target on our backs by destroying their warehouse and recovering all the tamers' Minakai."

"I shouldn't have tried to face off against Sagittarius. I should have listened to you and left him be."

"I am always right after all," said Luna, smiling once again.

Aurin laughed. "You're right a lot more than me, it seems."

The two continued talking, avoiding the topic of Zodiac for the rest of their time at the café. It was nice to ignore the heavy weight they were carrying, even for a short while.

Aurin paid for their drinks and walked Luna back home. Shamtile and Innogon were still fighting, neither willing to concede who deserved which flavour of shake earlier.

"I suppose this is goodbye for a while," Aurin said.

Luna hugged him tightly. "Be safe," she said as she released him. "Have a good Christmas and I'll see you when I get back."

"Take care," said a red-faced Aurin.

Shamtile and Innogon had finally stopped fighting

and were patting each other on the back, sad that they would be apart for a while. They had grown as close as their tamers even though they had a very different way of expressing it.

Luna and Innogon headed inside while Aurin and Shamtile returned to Kyle's ranch. Aurin had decided that Knot was right. He wouldn't wallow in fear or self-pity. He would train both himself and his Minakai to prepare for whatever storm was coming.

Chapter 41

"Stop slacking," pestered Kyle, catching Aurin in yet another daydream.

"I'm not slacking," insisted Aurin. "I'm catching my breath."

"I know how hard you can work when you're focused, so I know that's just an excuse. You have plenty left in the tank, so get back to shovelling."

Aurin had been tasked with his least favourite task in all of the ranch, shovelling the Minakai dung into the composter. It wasn't so bad when dealing with Minakai that barely had a body, like Dripper, or purely robotic Minakai like his own Steambot, but when it came to the big animal-like Minakai like Spikruption, it was a miserable experience.

Kyle was right, however, in that Aurin had been lost

in a daydream. He was staring over the treetops at Harmony Tower, wishing that he and Luna had the chance to explore it freely once more. She had only been out of town for a couple of days, but that was the longest stretch in a row that he hadn't seen her since he arrived in Hazelton.

Her Dopefish bounced along the grass in front of him, making its way towards the river. Knowing that Minakai, it was going to be the only fish that ever drowned on Kyle's ranch. He chuckled at the goofy blob, before picking him up by the tail and tossing him back into his shallow pond.

The morning dragged on, and Aurin was far from giving his best work. Kyle marched over to him at lunchtime, looking more sympathetic than he had ever looked. "I'll get the Frogre to finish off, alright? Let's get out of here."

"Where are we going?" asked Aurin. It was a rarity for Kyle to leave the ranch so casually.

"Grab all of your Minakai," said Kyle, suddenly smiling and pointing over at the mountains. "We're going for a hike to clear your mind. It'll do you good to get out of here for a while and, obviously, the tower is off-limits."

Aurin wasn't so sure it was going to help, but he appreciated Kyle trying. The young tamer fetched his whole team; Shamtile, Spikruption, Dolissile, Leonite, Desparee, Steambot and Chull. Once he had cleaned the filth from his boots, the group set off.

It only just occurred to Aurin that in the eight months he'd been at the ranch, he had never gone past the western boundary of Kyle's land. He had been so focused on Minakai that he was either in town, in the tower or at the ranch. He had planned on going home for Christmas, but his heart wasn't in it this year so he opted to stay here and work.

"You know it isn't the end of the world, right?" said Kyle as they walked through the forest.

Aurin sighed. "I know, but it's not a nice feeling to be targeted. The worst part is that I don't have a good way of tracking down Sagittarius and dealing with the problem head-on. I feel like I'm sitting around, waiting for somebody to come along and shoot me."

"It's serious, sure, but you don't need to be so dramatic about it. What happens if he shows up here at the ranch?"

"The Minakai step in."

"The Minakai step in," said Kyle. "You forget just how powerful each of them is. Your Dolissile is a reusable, living missile. Your Leonite is a mighty lion that is forever loyal to you. Even Chull can be strong one day," said Kyle, nodding towards the undead bird that flapped its way alongside them. It squawked at the rancher, getting the gist of what he had said.

"Don't mind him, Chull," said Aurin. "You haven't had much opportunity in the tower yet, but once this is all over, you'll get your chance."

"There you go," said Kyle positively. "You're already thinking past this whole ordeal. That's a step in the right direction, isn't it?"

The rancher had a point. "Alright," said Aurin, "for the rest of the trip, we aren't going to discuss Zodiac. We're going to talk about how you're going to help me prepare more for the tournament. Remember what you said before you enlisted Hunter for that battle?"

"Haven't I done enough?" barked Kyle, but Aurin knew he wasn't serious.

"Nobody has been more helpful, not even Luna.

Which is why I'm perfectly content to take advantage of your generosity."

"You're a little rat, you know that?" said Kyle as the pair chuckled.

The Minakai paid little attention to the humans. Spikruption's horns kept getting caught in tree branches and he was too frustrated to listen to their nonsense, while the others simply didn't understand the need for humans to fight constantly, even when they weren't really fighting.

Aurin poked Shamtile in the back. "I've seen how you and Innogon fight over milkshakes," the tamer said.

The walk through the forest was pleasant, but as they reached the mountain, things got considerably steeper. He was used to running, still training alongside his Minakai most mornings, but Aurin found the incline much more challenging.

"Lazy," called Kyle, pulling ahead with the Minakai.

"Easy for you to say," said Aurin. "You're a foot taller than me."

"That's not why it's easier for me. It's because I work harder than you."

Leonite pushed his nose into Aurin's back, offering to let his tamer ride on his back the rest of the way.

"Thanks, Leonite, but...I can do it," panted Aurin.

The chilly December air made things much tougher, but Aurin kept going and, eventually, Kyle stopped at a small outcropping that overlooked the entirety of Hazelton and its surrounding area.

It was beautiful. The sun was already setting in the mid-afternoon and all of the houses had their lights on, illuminating each of them with a faint orange glow. Aurin could see the monster tower in the distance, stretching still higher than where they stood on the mountainside.

"What's the tower roof like?" asked Aurin.

"Come to think of it...I'm not sure," admitted Kyle.

"Couldn't you fly up to it on Wingbloom?"

"I suppose I could, but I don't see any reason to. Why don't you fly up when you have a flying Minakai?"

Chull squawked at Kyle again.

"One that can carry his weight," said Kyle, trying to cover up forgetting about Aurin's most recently acquired monster.

"What do you think my chances are at the next tournament?"

"Not this again," sighed Kyle. "It's months away, so you still have so much time to improve."

"Aren't there diminishing returns on that? What if I don't get much better."

"My gosh, you can be a real simpleton sometimes."

"I'm nearly forty and I'm still learning more about Minakai. Has your progression through the tower not shown you that you can keep pushing to new heights? I don't see why there has to be a cap on your abilities, particularly as your monsters get stronger and more varied. You'll always learn new strategies and you'll always find something you can improve on."

"Just how many Minakai are native to Bretonian towers?"

"To my knowledge? There are currently one hundred and twenty-one, but I couldn't name them all. I get them mixed up with foreign Minakai sometimes."

"Currently?"

"There are species who have disappeared entirely. I'm not sure if they go extinct in whatever dimension they come from or if they're lost because the tower they appear in seals itself, but it's something that happens."

"There are thousands worldwide, right?"

"With some crossover between those found in other nations, yes," said Kyle. "There are even Minakai found here that can evolve into Minakai only found in other towers."

"What do you mean?" asked Aurin.

"Your Microbot can evolve in ten different ways, right? Well, only Microbot, Flambot, Steambot and Treebot will appear in towers in Bretonia, whereas the other forms appear elsewhere while Flambot may not."

"I really do have a lot to learn," said Aurin, embarrassed about what he had said moments before.

Kyle furrowed his brow. "When you first arrived here, I'm pretty sure you said something about having studied Minakai and towers for years."

"Not all day, every day!"

Kyle laughed, satisfied at having gotten under Aurin's skin enough for one day. "Shall we get back before we lose all light? I don't want to have to use your Spikruption as a torch."

"We're not that far from the top."

"Much like the tower, my young friend, let's save the top for another day."

"This is your floor thirty-seven all over again," said Aurin, pointedly.

"Shut up. It's getting dark and I don't fancy breaking my neck trekking down a mountain today."

Aurin laughed but quickly went silent after seeing the look on Kyle's face. He had clearly touched a nerve, bringing up his tower record.

Kyle summoned Wingbloom and hopped atop his back, while Aurin climbed on Leonite. The journey back was considerably faster and they were at the forest in no time.

Leonite suddenly started sniffing the air furiously. "What is it?" asked Aurin.

A few seconds later, the two tamers could smell it too. "Smoke," said Kyle.

As they reached the edge of the forest, they could see a burning red glow from the direction of the ranch. The source of the smoke suddenly became very clear as they watched Kyle's house burning along with the fences of the ranch. All the while, a group of shadowy figures stood by, admiring their work.

Chapter 42

Aurin, Kyle and their Minakai approached the ranch as it burned in the night. Standing in front of a horde of unconscious Minakai, including all of Kyle's Frogre guards, was a large gang of Zodiac members and their own monsters.

Sagittarius and Libra stepped forward, both looking very proud of themselves. "You're finally back," said Sagittarius. "I had hoped that you would have been here for our arrival, but I think it works out better this way, don't you? The look on both of your faces was worth the wait."

"What is the meaning of this?" demanded Kyle, hopping off his Wingbloom's back.

"Revenge for that one's constant interference," said Libra. "Sorry, Kyle, but you're collateral damage in this."

"No, you're not," said Sagittarius. "You're every bit as involved as he is. We know your Wingbloom was in the skies the day our warehouse was raided."

"You're monsters," said Aurin. "How could you hurt all these innocent Minakai? I'm the one you want revenge against."

"You think you're going to get away from this unscathed, boy?" asked Libra. "You'll rue the day that you ever crossed us. It was one thing to destroy our warehouse, but I heard from Sagittarius that because of you, Ethruki escaped."

"What does it matter?" asked Aurin. "It was a wild Minakai, not an egg."

Libra didn't answer him, but she glared at him intently from behind her mask. Whatever she wanted to say, she held back.

"It's not about an egg," said Sagittarius. "It's about learning about our target, and you wasted a golden opportunity for the Zodiac Squad. The boss wasn't best pleased, so we've been sent to teach you a lesson."

Aurin was seething with rage. He wasn't afraid any longer; he was angry and wanted revenge for what they did to Kyle.

"Dolissile, pulse!" he called, sending a shockwave through the air and disorienting the Zodiac members. "Shamtile, give them a quake!" he ordered, knocking the whole group off their feet.

"Attack!" shouted Kyle, summoning his already-tired Hogannon and Snowlem to join his Wingbloom in charging the masked tamers and their monsters. Tired as they may have been from defending the ranch against Zodiac, they were ready to do some damage to the villainous group.

"You heard him," said Aurin, and his group of seven Minakai followed in to face the horde of Zodiac Minakai that stood before them.

It was carnage. Aurin watched as the Minakai clashed, illuminated by the flames of Kyle's burning ranch in the background. He could see the water elementals who had attempted to put the flames strewn across the ground nearby, having suffered for their attempted heroism.

"Steambot, douse the flames!" called Aurin, and his robotic Minakai leapt into action. He unleashed a pressure cannon technique into the air, where it spread apart and rained throughout the entire ranch.

A Flaround, a larger and fully evolved form of Heatpup, used his flame breath to try and superheat Steambot's metallic body, but a pressure cannon to the face put a quick end to the attack and any other attacks the fiery hound would have dared attempt.

Shamtile had his hands full trying to counter a wave of flying Minakai that were taking swipes at him. Even his rock armour and rock wall were not enough to shield him from the barrage of attacks.

Kyle's Hogannon rushed to the masked reptile's aid, using his cannon arm to blast the fliers out of the sky. One of the flying Minakai, a Sproufloat, caught fire and rushed back to its tamer who just so happened to be Libra. It collided with her arm, burning her.

Thanks to Hogannon quelling a number of his attackers, Shamtile was no longer so severely outnumbered and made a glorious comeback. He hurled a huge boulder at three of his enemies, crushing them beneath the weight of the heavy rock.

Leonite and Spikruption were taking turns to swipe, bite and tackle the opposing forces. They were laying waste to everything that came in their way and most of the other Zodiac Minakai tried to avoid them, going for the weaker targets instead.

Dolissile was brawling with a Gorungra, chipping away at its rocky body with each impact, while Kyle's Snowlem was tactically seeking out every nature elemental Zodiac Minakai it could find, playing into his ice elemental advantage.

Desparee was not faring as well with the lack of light to help supercharge him, so he was forced to fight against weaker Minakai, backed up by Chull. As Desparee entangled their foes, Chull blasted them with a sharp wind and followed up with a high-speed strike with his beak.

Kyle's Wingbloom was in a one-on-one fight against Sagittarius's Thundarun. The dark unicorn shot glowing bolts of lightning through the air, trying to take out the plant bird, but it became clear why Wingbloom was Kyle's favourite. He rolled through the air, avoiding each strike, whizzing towards the Thundarun and cutting it deeper each time he passed.

Sagittarius's anger had grown so much that he was shaking with rage at what was happening to his own favourite. "Electroburst!" he called, and all the humans dropped to the ground immediately.

Thundarun let out a highly charged explosion of electrical energy, that targeted everything in sight, making no distinction between friend or foe. Most of the Minakai were knocked down or out, but Wingbloom had veered upwards, soaring high enough to avoid the attack.

The Thundarun was weakened by unleashing such a sudden, powerful attack. Wingbloom dived down in an arc and grabbed the beast in its talons, carrying it fifty feet in the air before dropping it. Sagittarius's Minakai fell to the ground, landing hard with a gruesome crack as a few of its bones snapped on impact. It was done and it would take more than a short rest for it to recover from such injuries.

The Zodiac elite ran forward, but Libra grabbed his arm and shook her head at him. The pair surveyed the battlefield and could see that they weren't going to come back from this. If they waited much longer, the police were bound to come and find them all at the scene.

"This isn't over," roared Sagittarius. "You're just lucky that most of our forces were already taken out by your ranch guests."

"Expect to see us again, whether that's here or in the tower," warned Libra. "If you don't regret your interference now, there's a lot worse coming your way that will ensure you do."

The Zodiac members retreated, hopping onto their remaining Minakai, and dashing into the forest out of sight. The battle was over, but the damage they had left in their wake was immense.

Steambot finished putting out the last of the flames, exhausting himself. "Go recharge in the river," said Aurin, giving his Minakai a much-needed break.

"They're going to pay for this," said Kyle in a hushed voice. He seemed surprisingly calm for somebody who had their livelihood destroyed, while Aurin was still shaking from adrenaline.

"I'm sorry, Kyle," said the young tamer. "It's all my fault that this happened."

"Stop," said Kyle. "Stop feeling so much pity for yourself. It was their actions and theirs alone. You are not the bad guy here so snap out of it and get it together. I need you focused because we're going to get them back for this. We're going to tear their whole little group apart, do you hear me?"

Aurin had never seen him like this, so angry and fired up yet still so controlled. "I hear you," he said. "Just tell me what we need to do."

"First, we're going to speak to Knot," he said. "Then we're going to get both of us in fighting fit shape to make sure that if they come back again, we're ready for them."

Snow began to fall on the cold December evening as the men and the Minakai did what they could to repair what was left of the ranch and Kyle's house. They worked through the night, exhausted, but thanks to the Minakai's abilities, they were able to repair most of the fencing by dawn. The house on the other hand was not such an easy fix.

"I found my old tent and a couple of sleeping bags that we can use," said Kyle, emerging from the wreckage.

Aurin stopped feeding the recovering Minakai for a moment. "Shouldn't we get hotel rooms or something?"

"We're not leaving this place unattended unless we absolutely must," said Kyle. "I don't think they're going to come back straight away, but I also didn't think that they would try something like this in the first place."

"The idea of there being any order or rules to their actions seems to have gone out the window," admitted Aurin, finally disregarding what Leo had said about his organisation. Whatever his own principles were, they were clearly not that of the rest of his elites or the Zodiac goons.

"I'm going to send word to Knot," said Kyle, "but I don't think he'll be able to meet us straight away."

"Why didn't any officers show up here?" asked Aurin as it finally clicked with him just how lawless things were in Hazelton when it came to Zodiac.

"If I were to be naive, I would say that they didn't see the fire because Steambot doused it quickly enough."

"And if you're being honest?"

"They were told not to come until later."

Aurin held his face, exhausted physically and mentally. "It's about time Knot quit and got a job here at the ranch. It would be much more useful than whatever he's doing now."

"You can tell him that when you see him," said Kyle. He watched as Aurin yawned, his eyes looking heavy. "You should get some sleep and I can take over feeding this lot."

Aurin reluctantly agreed. He wanted to keep helping and felt like sleeping was useless, but at the same time, he knew that if Zodiac returned then he would be too tired to command his Minakai effectively. He and Kyle assembled the tent and, the moment Aurin lay down, he fell straight to sleep.

Chapter 43

Aurin awoke at midday, cold from the dreadfully low temperature. The snow had lain thick on the ground and would have been beautiful to sit and admire had it made the job of rebuilding the ranch considerably more difficult.

Kyle approached him, seeing that he was finally awake. "Rise and shine, lazy bones," he said, prodding Aurin with his boot. "It's been almost six hours and that's plenty of sleep for a youngster like you."

"I hope you haven't been walking through Minakai dung," joked Aurin. "How's the cleanup going?"

"Slowly," said a weary Kyle. "I don't think we'll be done before Christmas. At the very least, we can get your Shamtile to make us a makeshift hut out of stone and Hogannon is an expert at making fire pits. We should be able to dry out enough wood to keep a fire going throughout the night so we don't die from hypothermia in our sleep."

"Speaking of sleep, do you want me to keep an eye on things while you take a nap? You look like you need it."

"Thanks, but I'll last. Knot should be here any minute, but it's official business so he'll probably have Scarlett with him. I don't know how much she knows about his involvement with us, but I suspect it's very little. Keep your mouth shut about our partnership unless he indicates it's otherwise okay."

"I know," said Aurin. "I handled it fine in Mayor Boren's office, right?"

"That's true. I don't think my head is screwed on right now. It's been a long twenty-four hours."

It wasn't long before the two detectives, wrapped in many layers, walked up the path towards the remaining half of Kyle's house. Knot gave him a curt nod while Scarlett held her coat tightly.

"This doesn't look good," said Knot bluntly, looking around the remains of the ranch.

"It was worse last night," said Kyle. "We've gotten most of the fence repaired, but my house isn't going to be fixed so easily."

"Tell us everything," said Scarlett, bringing out her notebook.

Kyle relayed the tale to the detectives in excruciating detail. He and Aurin even brought out their Minakai, who made various yelps, screeches and grumbles at different parts of the story to prompt more detail and some praise from the two tamers.

It was obvious to everyone how devastated he was, but when he spoke of his Minakai fighting against the attackers his pride escaped from him. It was the most upbeat he has sounded since the mountain trek. His Minakai all looked very pleased with themselves.

"This is a well-known spot and you have visitors most days, mostly people coming to see their own Minakai, correct?" asked Scarlett, brushing off Leonite who sniffed her. "Get away from me," she said.

"I don't know about most days; people usually summon and banish their Minakai once they've dropped them off here the first time. There's a large swelling of people that show up on the last day of the month to pay their rent in silver."

"My point is that you're a well-known figure in Hazelton and this ranch is highly regarded. Why do you think they targeted you here?"

"I thought that would be obvious after what we said in the mayor's office?" asked Aurin, not intending to sound as rude as he did.

"I'm aware that you're the target," said Scarlett, "but why here?"

Knot had been unusually quiet up until now. "I have a thought about that," he said. "I suspect they were looking to kill Aurin's Minakai. That way, he wouldn't be able to interfere again. You would probably leave town at that point, right?"

"Probably," said Aurin, dreading to think what may have happened had his team been left at the ranch while he and Kyle were away.

"You think the Minakai were the target rather than Aurin himself?" asked Kyle.

"It's just a thought," said Knot. "It would be a way to get rid of you rather than have a murder investigation to deal with. It would still be a crime if your Minakai were killed, but it wouldn't carry half the weight that a human death would."

Scarlett didn't look convinced. She was about to say something but refrained at the last second. Instead, she put her notebook away in her jacket. Her sleeve caught on one of her buttons, pulling it up and revealing a bandage on her arm. It went unnoticed by everyone but Aurin, whose brain started running a thousand miles a minute.

The detectives wrapped up and said their goodbyes before heading back to the station as the snow began to fall heavier. Aurin commanded Shamtile to create a stone shelter around the tent, while Kyle's Hogannon blasted a fiery hole in the ground. A few of the other Minakai ran to fetch some firewood while the men sat down on newly erected dirt chairs.

"Scarlett is Libra," Aurin blurted out.

"You...what?" asked a very confused Kyle.

"Her arm," said Aurin. "Remember when your Hogannon was helping Shamtile deal with the aerial attacks? One of Libra's Minakai was set alight and it collided with her. She burned her arm."

"And how does this tie into Scarlett?"

"She had the same arm wrapped in a bandage. There's no way that's a coincidence."

"You're sure it was a bandage? It wasn't a jumper or shirt?"

"It was a bandage," insisted Aurin. "Trust me on this, okay? I know a bandage when I see one."

Leonite approached and roared loudly.

"What is it, Leonite?" asked Aurin.

He pawed at the smoke coming from the fire, trying to communicate what he meant.

"Smoke?" asked Aurin.

"He was sniffing Scarlett," muttered Kyle.

"Is that it? She smelled like smoke?"

Leonite bowed his head in response, while Aurin stroked his mane. Kyle was staring at the fire, deep in thought. He was trying to put the pieces together but was held back from not wanting to believe what Aurin had told him. Yet, he knew Aurin was honest and wouldn't state it with such certainty if he wasn't sure. If it wasn't true, why would Leonite try and convince him too?

"Alright," said Kyle.

"Alright what?" asked Aurin.

"Alright, I believe you. Was that not clear?"

"What should we do now?"

"First things first, I'm going to sleep. Secondly, we're going to keep fixing what we can and get straight back to training. Thirdly, we're going to the tower. Together."

Aurin was caught off guard. Kyle hadn't expressed much interest in ever going into a monster tower again. "Both...both of us?" he asked.

"Yes," said Kyle. "I clearly don't have enough Minakai of my own to be able to defend this place so we're going to hunt for some eggs. Maybe you'll even learn a thing or two along the way."

"I'm in," said Aurin, excited at the prospect.

"You're not afraid of going into the tower again?"

"With both of us there, we'll be just fine. Although if I'm down to my last Minakai, I may just leave. I don't want to end up cornered again."

"Cast off your armour," ordered Aurin as Shamtile trained against Desparee.

The magical lizard shattered his rock armour which burst into shards of sharp stone that hurtled through the air in all directions like daggers. Desparee held up his arms to block, while Chull nimbly dove to the ground to avoid the attack.

"You're getting there," Aurin said to Shamtile. "It's important that you can pick up speed and force with this attack. It'll mean that if you're ever surrounded, you don't need to rely on throwing stones, you've got a full rack of spears you can throw at any time."

Shamtile shook his arms while warbling and grunting.

"Remember when Kyle told me that he's learning something new about Minakai all the time?" asked Aurin. "Well, I'm trying to learn more about you too, Shamtile. If we can improvise a few new techniques on the back of your old ones, it'll make us much more versatile."

Kyle wandered over from tending to the Minakai. "Did you call your parents to wish them a merry Christmas yet?" he asked.

"An hour ago, yes," replied Aurin. "I gave them your best too. They're just glad that we've gotten this place back into good shape again."

"I would say it's better than before," said Kyle, admiring the newly reinforced fences. It had taken a lot of work from the pair of them, but the ranch looked better than ever. All that was left to fix was the house.

"Are you ready to go?" Aurin asked him.

Kyle held up his glove, with three summoning stones embedded into it. "Ready as ever. Let's get moving so we don't leave this place deserted for too long."

"Alright," said Aurin, dismissing Desparee and Chull.

"You're not bringing these three?" asked Kyle. "Who's coming with you today then?"

"Shamtile, Dolissile and Steambot," replied Aurin as the lizard hopped enthusiastically by his tamer's side. "How about you?"

"If you can guess, I'll let you keep the first egg that we find."

"Wingbloom, Hogannon and Snowlem?" guessed Aurin, presuming Kyle would take his favourite trio.

"Close, but no cigar," he said. "Two out of three isn't bad, so I'll let you take the second egg if we're lucky enough to find one."

"Who's the third?" asked Aurin.

Kyle responded with a laugh and walked down the path out of the ranch and into the forest while Aurin and Shamtile followed, pestering him to tell them who his third Minakai was for the tower run. He waved them away and brushed off each question, enjoying tormenting his young friend.

Chapter 44

Kyle had brought a rather useful orb into the tower with him, one that Aurin had overlooked many times in favour of other items; an Orb of Ascension. It allowed the rancher to see the location of the elevator through the walls, letting the pair breeze through the first six floors with ease before it ran out of charges.

"How did you not know about this?" Kyle had asked, shocked that Aurin had never used one before.

"I'm certain I read about it before, but forgot about it," Aurin had replied. "Come to think of it, I think I've only ever used the Orb of Return, Tamers and Traps."

Kyle went on to explain to the young tamer about half a dozen orbs and their various purposes, including one that he called the Orb of Recollection.

"It restores an unconscious Minakai?" asked a

flabbergasted Aurin.

"And you can summon it back to the tower again, yes. It's a real run saver, but it's rare for it to have more than a single charge before becoming just a heavy crystal ball."

With each new floor, Kyle found new items to show Aurin. He explained to him in detail what each of them was used for, including a few spell crystals that Luna had once mentioned.

"Watch what this Neutral Crystal can do," said Kyle as a Peekan approached. He focused on a colourless crystal he had picked up, which then emitted a powerful concussive blast that knocked the turquoise bird from the sky. The crystal shattered instantly and Wingbloom finished off the Peekan with ease.

"That's fantastic!" exclaimed Aurin.

"I'm amazed that you two managed to brute force your way to the eighteenth floor without making use of all of the items in the tower," said Kyle, dumbfounded at Aurin's lack of competence in using the tower and its spoils to his advantage.

"If I used these, I could have beaten your record already," said Aurin.

"Steady on," laughed Kyle. "These will only get you so far, particularly as the Minakai get progressively stronger and the traps more deadly and frequent. You could probably use them to buy yourself another couple of floors."

The two continued to explore. Kyle kept a close eye on Aurin, seeing how he operated without stepping in. Likewise, Aurin watched Kyle's every move intently, trying to learn as much as he could from this rare opportunity.

It wasn't long before the two were on the tenth floor

and Kyle had picked up his first egg.

"I wonder what's inside it?" asked Aurin.

"There's an item for that," said Kyle.

"That, I do know," replied Aurin. "An Identifying Glass, right?"

"At least that's one thing you can use."

Aurin neglected to mention that he had only recently learned about the mystical magnifying glass when he and Luna had triggered the treasure trap on their previous run.

On floor twelve, the duo landed on a bizarre type of floor that Aurin had yet to see. It was filled with water up to his waist, soaking the entirety of his lower half. Shamtile was so short that he had to swim, which angered the small lizard greatly.

"This is unusual," said Aurin, looking at Kyle. "One time I had water up to my ankles, but this is something else. Ever seen a floor like this before?"

"Maybe a half dozen times?" said Kyle, also rather unhappy at having to wade through water on one of the few occasions he wasn't wearing working clothes. "It's more common than the completely open floor you experienced once, but there are a few other types of anomaly floors that you'll probably see before you've progressed as far as floor twenty-five."

It had struck Aurin how little he knew, even today. His hubris had gotten the better of him recently, thinking that he had already hit the point of diminishing returns in what he could learn, experience, and achieve. He now knew just how wrong he was.

"Just wait until you see one of the floors that swaps the tiles out for ice," said Kyle with a hearty chuckle. "That will really test your patience. Even a fire Minakai won't be able to melt it."

A leaping brown log with green leaves skipped through the water towards the pair. When it was close, Aurin could see that it was a Seawub, an aquatic Minakai that looked like a wooden fish with seaweed fins.

"Careful," warned Kyle. "It's not very powerful, but you're in its territory today."

Shamtile tried to focus on casting his earth magic but was unable to do so as he treaded water. The Seawub jumped high, landing with a thump on Shamtile's head before diving back under the water.

As the lizard tried not to sink, the Seawub summoned a mighty root from the floor that wrapped around Shamtile's feet, pulled him underneath and held him tightly. It wasn't long before bubbles emerged as Shamtile started to drown.

Aurin wasn't sure what to do other than switch his Minakai, but as he raised his hand to use his summoning stones, Kyle grabbed his hand. "Check your bag," he said.

"Right," said Aurin, knowing how to help his best friend. He pulled out an icy blue crystal and took aim at the Seawub that was biting Shamtile's legs under the water. As the water turned red, Aurin unleashed an icicle from the crystal that pierced the nature elemental's side, breaking its concentration and dissipating the root.

Shamtile rose to the surface and gasped for air. He scrambled away from the fish while it was disoriented and breathed in the sweet, sweet oxygen deeply. He then conjured a small pillar on the floor that protruded from the water.

"He's going to leap any second," said Aurin. "Be ready."

Moments later, the Seawub burst from the water and began to fire razor-sharp leaves at Shamtile, who countered with a rock wall. The leaves collided with the hard surface, as did the Seawub. It fell back into the water and out of sight once again.

"Conjure your armour and don't let your guard down," ordered Aurin.

Shamtile complied and covered himself in his stone coating. The Seawub attacked with vines from beneath the surface, but Shamtile dropped low and held steady. The vines were not strong enough to pull his weight. He grabbed onto the vines and pulled hard, throwing the Seawub into the air.

"Finish him!" called Aurin.

The masked lizard summoned a rock and fired it at the wild Minakai, crushing it against the wall. As it fell down, it vanished in a green burst of light as it was banished from the tower.

"Great work, Shamtile," said Aurin, as Shamtile did a victory dance atop his pillar.

"If you want to really challenge yourself, you should enter some tournaments where they use themed fields," suggested Kyle.

"I suppose I could," said Aurin, failing to hide his reluctance.

"You'll have to eventually if you're planning to become the national champion. You'll be obliged to do various exhibition matches so you wouldn't want to look silly, would you?"

"Point taken," said Aurin, remembering watching one of Tobias's matches on television a couple of years ago. The famous Bretonian tamer had battled on a field surrounded by lava against an opponent who exclusively used the fire element. Somehow, the champion overcame the field and defeated his opponent.

Aurin and Kyle waded through the water while Wingbloom sat atop the water and swam along like a giant duck. Shamtile had accepted the leafy bird's offer to ride on his back, which the reptilian Minakai used as a chance to kick back and relax.

"There's my egg!" called Aurin, spotting an egg underneath the water in one of the rooms.

"Go for it," said Kyle, remembering his agreement with Aurin about who would get a second egg if there was one to be found.

Aurin was fully waterlogged after retrieving the egg and Kyle couldn't stop laughing at him. "It always works out for me," said the rancher.

"I wouldn't say always," said Aurin, thinking about the current state of Kyle's house.

Kyle glared daggers at him.

"Okay, that was uncalled for," said Aurin. "Sorry."

"Let's keep moving before I drown you."

Wanting to survive the tower run, the two pushed ahead and escaped from the water-covered floor, ascending to the thirteenth floor. Kyle's usage of various orbs, items and crystals guided them through to the eighteenth floor with only a few battles giving them trouble.

Wingbloom was still going strong, but Shamtile was starting to look exhausted. "We're going to break our record, Shamtile," said Aurin, trying to keep his Minakai's spirits up.

Kyle was surveying the various corridors and their offshoots. "I was hoping we'd find another egg before we left, but three eggs in a run is wishful thinking even if we were to climb another half dozen floors."

"Can't you use one of your treasure orbs or something?" asked Aurin.

"I'm tapped out already. I've mostly been picking up silver to help cover the cost of the repairs, so I've got little space left for items. You'd think my insurance company would accept arson by a criminal gang, but they weren't so obliging."

"Let's go this way," said Aurin, pointing to the left.

"How come?"

"I have a gut feeling about it."

"You do?"

"I've gotten this high up without you before, right?"

"With Luna, but I take your point."

The rancher followed Aurin's directions and the duo happened upon a particularly large room where a third egg awaited them. Guarding the egg, however, was a Frocean. The large, pale blue frog bore a grumpy expression and was covered in frozen boils, while three large icicles protruded from its back. It stared at the tamers and their Minakai menacingly.

"You're up," said Aurin.

"Alright," said Kyle. "I'll show you how we handle tough opponents. You know what to do, Wing."

Wingbloom beat his leaf-like wings hard, sending a powerful gust at his opponent. The Frocean sat there, unmoving. It blinked a few times, hoping his attackers would turn around and leave him be. When Wingbloom charged at him, he relented and reluctantly stood up.

The ice frog inhaled deeply and blew an icy wind through the air. Wingbloom's flapping slowed, but the air elemental plant pushed through and rammed his beak into the Frocean. It took the hit hard, but it remained standing.

As Wingbloom turned around, he was hit with a

sharp icicle to the wingtip, sending him crashing to the ground. The Frocean leapt into the air and slammed itself down on Kyle's Minakai, sending him right out of the tower.

Kyle's mouth hung open in surprise. "Gittup!" he said, summoning the lightning elemental. "Use your advantage," he ordered.

The blue beast zapped lightning from its golden tail, smashing apart each of Frocean's frozen boils one by one. The relentless assault left the giant frog open and Gittup charged in, glowing from his electrical energy. He collided with the Frocean, shocking it brutally. The wild Minakai shook violently before being banished from the tower.

Aurin didn't say a word, waiting for Kyle to react. The rancher sighed. "Alright, I'm definitely out of practice. Wingbloom should have been strong enough to overcome an opponent like that. We need to start training more intensely to get back to full power."

"I think this calls for a weekly tower run," said Aurin.

"Maybe monthly," said Kyle, picking up the egg. "I'm too busy to give up a day each week. Maybe if you ever get a proper job, you'll understand."

"This is going to be my job," said Aurin.

"We'll see."

"Just admit that you had a lot of fun coming back into the tower. You still remember how it works inside-out and you retired how many years ago?"

"I don't remember," replied Kyle nonchalantly as he retrieved an Orb of Return from his bag.

Aurin was alarmed. "What are you doing?" he asked.

"I'm not carrying you higher than this on my back. When you break your record again, it'll be because you've earned it. Take what you've learned today and apply it."

Aurin wasn't going to argue with him, he considered it a fair enough reason to leave. He was leaving with plenty of additional knowledge and a new egg, while Kyle had gained two eggs. It was an incredibly fruitful trip, far more than he had expected.

The two warped out of the tower and made their way back to the ranch. For once, it was Kyle enthusiastically retrieving the incubator while Aurin waited by the gate to the pens. The pair agreed to hatch their eggs in the same order they had found them.

Kyle was up first and placed an egg into the incubator, pressing the button to activate it. As the incubator worked its magic, the forcefield glowed a light blue and a small, winged Minakai flapped within the glow. When the light faded, it was revealed to be a Coldbat. The icy blue bat landed on Kyle's shoulder, already comfortable with her master.

"My turn," said Aurin, paying little attention to Kyle's newest team member.

The incubator glowed a deep orange while Aurin was hatching his Minakai, and a Gorun was born from the egg. "How am I supposed to train this?" asked the young man, looking at the brown limbless rock that sat still while a topaz crystal stuck out from the top of it and another sat in its centre as though it was an eye.

"Figure it out," said Kyle, placing his second egg on the incubator. Seconds later, it was revealed to be a Techling. Kyle was more than happy to add the silver and gold metallic bird to his aerial arsenal.

The two spent the rest of the chilly Christmas day getting to know their new monsters; a task that was much easier for Kyle than it was for Aurin and his new pet rock. The other Minakai on Aurin's team weren't sure how to react to Gorun either. All in all, it had been a good day and Aurin was reminded of just how rewarding exploring the tower was. Once Zodiac had been dealt with, he would continue his ascension until he reached the top.

Chapter 45

"What happened here?" exclaimed Luna as she ran down the path to Kyle's ranch with Innogon on her back. Aurin and Kyle had spoken to her on the phone while she was away but had neglected to tell her about the ranch burning down so that she could enjoy the rest of her time out of town.

"It's a funny story..." began Aurin.

"No, it's not," said Kyle incredulously. "It's not funny at all."

"I meant figuratively," Aurin clarified.

"It's not funny literally or figuratively. We've spent weeks putting everything back together as best as we can, and my house is still a wreck."

"Will you two quit the bickering and explain?" said Luna, already exhausted from being home. "I'm not allowed to be here for very long so stop wasting time."

Aurin and Kyle told her everything, stopping every now and then to let her rant about keeping this from her for weeks. Shamtile and Innogon sat on the grass, their eyes darting between the three humans as they all said their piece. They would rather deal with Zodiac by burying them under rocks or blasting them into the sky with a water jet, but sadly it was not so simple.

"If we had told you about it, you would be thinking about it the entire time you were away. Besides, almost all your Minakai were here during it and helped defend this place. You were here in spirit."

"That's not the point!" exclaimed Luna. "This is so much more serious than anything that has happened before, even more serious than the two of us being attacked in the tower. They're getting far bolder in their attempts to get vengeance."

"She has a point," said Kyle. "They are indeed getting more brazen, so who's to say they wouldn't have tried to track you down while you were away from us and your team."

"Exactly," said Luna. "We're not safe anywhere now, not even in our homes. We need to put a stop to this and quickly. When my parents get wind of this, and they will, there's no way they'll ever let me come back here."

"How?" asked Aurin.

Luna stood there in silence for half a minute, staring at him. "I don't know."

"Do you think it's time we go to Knot about your theory?" Kyle asked Aurin.

"What theory?" asked Luna.

Aurin explained to her about Libra's burn and Detective Scarlett's mysterious bandage the next day when she showed up to investigate.

"Isn't that a bit far-fetched?"

"No," said Aurin. "I'm telling you that Scarlett is Libra. She's one of the Zodiac elites. You believe me, right Kyle?"

"I do," said Kyle. "I also say that we should speak to Knot. He's been forthright with us about everything and he's clearly no friend of Zodiac."

"I can't stay long, so can we go speak to him about it now? It's a Saturday so he may be at home."

The three agreed. Kyle was reluctant to leave the ranch for too long, so they hurried along with each of them bringing a Minakai with them. There was never a moment in the last few weeks where Aurin and Kyle had travelled without Shamtile and Wingbloom, respectively. It was particularly awkward for Kyle considering the size of the large bird-like plant but needs must.

When they grew close, Kyle insisted that they leave the Minakai nearby and summon them if needed rather than drawing too much attention. They hurried up the small garden path to the detective's front door and Aurin rapped his knuckles on it.

"What are you doing here?" asked Knot upon answering "Hurry up and get inside, you fools."

"Are you being watched?" asked Aurin.

"I can't rule that possibility out," said the detective. "It was a bad idea to come here."

"With all due respect, Detective Know, we're probably being watched too," said Kyle. "I'll remind you who Zodiac is targeting and whose ranch got burned down a couple of weeks ago."

Knot sighed. "Yes, you make a good point, Kyle. What is it that you all want anyway?

"You may want to sit down," said Luna.

"This is my house, I'll sit down if I like," said Knot grumpily. He looked exhausted, as though he hadn't slept properly in months.

"I'll cut right to it then," said Aurin. "Your partner, Scarlett, is Libra. She's an elite member of the Zodiac Squad."

Knot sighed and did indeed sit down. He held his face in his hands, looking up after a moment. "What leads you to that conclusion?" he asked.

"Libra was burned during the ranch attack and when Scarlett showed up with you the next day, her arm was bandaged up. After you both left, my Leonite told us that she smelled like smoke. It's a bit too coincidental for my liking."

"Yes," said Knot, avoiding eye contact with everyone. "I'm sorry to say that the evidence is stacked up against her at this point."

"You knew?" exclaimed Aurin.

Knot shook his head. "It's only started to become clear to me recently. There were a few odd signs over the last couple of years, where she would disappear for a while. I initially presumed she was at Harmony Tower and out of contact due to its magic, but then I started to notice the timings.

"She would disappear at particularly inconvenient moments, notably around the time of the tournament when Zodiac activity was at its highest. Whenever you infiltrated the warehouse, I couldn't find her anywhere, but who was in there with you?"

"Libra," said Luna.

"Yes. There have been a number of other examples too, but I think you've heard enough. I'm certain that there are other Zodiac members in the force too so reporting her will only lead to a squashed investigation before it even begins."

"I have an idea," said Aurin. "I've had plenty of time to think about this."

"What's that?" asked Kyle.

"We break into her house and find more evidence. Perhaps she's been sloppy enough to leave something there? Maybe even her Zodiac jacket or mask."

Luna's jaw dropped. "You're not serious, are you?"

"I like it," said Kyle. "There's no way we'll be able to get into their new headquarters. Security is probably tenfold and they'd likely recognise you coming a mile off. Targeting one of their homes is the best way forward if we want this dealt with quickly."

"There's nothing else for it at this point," said Knot. "We need to be certain to begin with. What's the next step of your master plan?"

Aurin smiled, excited to see that the older men were listening to him and not seeing him as a gung-ho teenager. "We expose her publicly where it can't be refused. Unmasked in the centre of town so her reputation is destroyed. I'm still working on how to do that, but I'll come up with an answer once we know it's her."

"Can you distract her, detective?" Luna asked Knot.

"Monday evening, we've got a couple of routine calls to make. I'll give you her address and you can break in. Make sure that it isn't all of you. In fact, just one of you would be enough."

"Shamtile and I will do it," said Aurin confidently. "I know how to get in undetected."

Aurin explained his plan and although a few unconvinced looks were exchanged, everyone agreed to go along with what he said. The three tamers departed from Knot's house after checking the coast was clear and headed home.

Shamtile was briefed on his role in the plan as Aurin and Kyle returned to the ranch without Luna and Innogon. The masked lizard was enthusiastic to use his abilities for something other than battle, waving his arms erratically once Aurin had finished explaining what he had to do.

"You're sure you can manage that?" his tamer asked him.

"Blaaargh!" yelled the Minakai in his warbling voice.

"Kyle," said Aurin, unsure of whether he should bring up a lingering suspicion that he couldn't let go of.

"Yes?"

"How can we find Leo?" asked Aurin.

"He's probably in hiding."

"His Leo persona, yes, but not Frederick. As Frederick, he's a competitive battler so isn't it possible that we can track him down?"

"What for?" asked Kyle, eyeing his friend suspiciously.

"I don't think he's involved in any of these attacks. I think he can help us put a stop to them."

"No good can come from allying ourselves with a Zodiac member. Why would he help us? The second you tell him anything, he would betray us to his group, and we'd be worse off for it."

"I suspect that he's a firm believer in Zodiac's stated mission, to hunt down the cosmic Minakai and claim them for themselves."

"There's a big difference between their stated mission and what they actually do."

"Exactly, and I think Leo is one of the believers in that as opposed to the other opportunists who are looking for quick riches and easy power."

"I don't think it's a good idea," said Kyle. "You can't trust that man for a second. You don't even know what Zodiac want to use the cosmic Minakai for once they've found them."

"You're right about that," said Aurin. "And I don't trust him, but if my theory is correct, then we can make sure that these rogue members are purged of their usefulness once their identities are exposed to the world. That's something that would benefit both of us."

"That's a leap of faith that I'm not willing to take," said Kyle, refusing to participate in the discussion any further.

Chapter 46

"It's so stuffy down here," complained Aurin as he followed Shamtile. His Minakai ignored him and kept moving the dirt with a wave of one hand while holding the tunnel roof up with the other.

The duo was attempting to break into Detective Scarlett's house by way of a tunnel that the earth elemental Shamtile was digging. It had seemed like an easier idea in theory with Shamtile assuring his tamer that he could do it without a problem.

"Make sure we arrive in the garage, alright?" Aurin reminded him. "It's connected to the house so it's the stealthiest way. You can fix the stone after, so it doesn't need to be too pretty."

The longer he crawled through the tunnel, the stupider he felt. He wondered why Kyle and Knot hadn't questioned him more on this plan. Luna was the only one who insisted it was a bad idea, but even she reluctantly agreed.

"I wonder if anybody has ever tried to break into a bank vault this way?" pondered Aurin aloud. "My guess would be that they have Minakai in the vaults or it's reinforced with metal. Maybe a metal elemental could break through if you had one of those too?"

Shamtile gave a warbled yell, trying to make Aurin be quiet. The tunnel walls started to shake as the Minakai lost focus, so Aurin shut his mouth. Shortly afterwards, they had broken through the concrete floor of Scarlett's garage.

"Alright, we're in," he said, banishing Shamtile back to the ranch and replacing him with Chull. "It's time," he said to the undead bird. "Make sure that there are no security cameras, but if there are, nudge them out of the way so I can't be seen."

Chull flew through the house, awkwardly opening doors with his talons, but eventually returned satisfied that there were no cameras for his master to be concerned about.

"Good job," said Aurin, dismissing Chull and summoning Leonite. The lion roared upon appearing, but Aurin hushed him just in case there were any neighbours that may hear through the walls. "You're on guard duty, Leonite. If you hear or smell anybody coming too close, you signal me. Don't come into the main house unless you can help it because you'll shed your hair all over the floors and we don't have time to vacuum before we leave."

Aurin kicked off his shoes so as not to dirty the floor and walked into the bright kitchen. He had to give Scarlett credit for decorating it so nicely, presumably with her ill-gotten gains. The white walls were spotless and the golden wood varnish glistened in the evening sun that shone through the large windows.

As he explored, the young tamer kept low to avoid the windows. He couldn't risk being seen snooping about or Zodiac would be paying him a visit sooner rather than later. After a thorough search through all the cupboards and drawers, he was content in saying the kitchen was clear. He hadn't expected much from the kitchen anyway so he was content to move along without prying the bottoms out of the cupboards.

In the living room, he went even deeper, searching under the sofa cushions, beneath the rug, inside the fireplace, and every other nook and cranny that seemed like it could serve as a hiding spot for even the smallest trinket that would give away Libra's identity. There was nothing.

He searched each and every wardrobe, hoping to find the white leather jackets that Zodiac members wore, even a hat would do. He didn't think she would be foolish to keep the mask at home, but the jacket could be passed off as her own clothing if anybody ever stumbled across it.

Aurin moved from room to room, tearing it apart section by section and fixing it up again once he was finished. As he did so, his frustration grew greater and greater. He didn't find a thing, that is until he reached a bedroom that was being used as a storage room.

"What is this?" he said, examining a framed photograph that was stashed in the upper shelf of a walk-in wardrobe. Six individuals, four men and two women, were standing in a line. They were wearing casual clothes, but one of them was unmistakably Scarlett and another was Frederick. Libra and Leo together in a photograph; this proved Scarlett's alter ego beyond a shadow of a doubt.

"No uniforms," muttered Aurin, lamenting the fact that this wasn't usable evidence to anybody except those who already knew Leo's true identity. He took the photograph out of the frame, stashing it in his bag, and then placed the empty frame back where he found it. If it couldn't be used as evidence, at least it could be used to help him avoid the four Zodiac members that he didn't recognise.

Aurin moved along to the study and turned on the computer. "Of course...password protected," he said as Scarlett's login screen appeared. "Zodiac," he said as he typed his first guess. Password incorrect, two guesses remaining before ten-minute lockout. He tried Libra, but it wasn't correct either. In case the lockout flagged anything, he settled for moving on.

"Wait a second," he whispered to himself, pulling a book out from behind the computer screen.

He flicked through the pages and his eyes widened. He and Luna were correct the whole time, he now knew for certain how Zodiac planned to capture Ethruki. He decided that he had seen enough to form the next part of his plan and headed back to Leonite in the garage after double checking that everything except for the photograph was as he left it.

"What's that smell?" asked Aurin, as Leonite avoided eye contact. The tamer glanced at a few old cardboard boxes that were most certainly dry before. "Were you that desperate?"

Aurin hurriedly put on his shoes, dismissed Leonite and summoned back Shamtile along with his new Gorun to assist. "Okay, it's time to escape. Shamtile, you'll open up the tunnel again and close it behind us.

Gorun, you're to make sure the floor is smoothed over and then find somewhere to hide until we're out of here. I'll summon you, then send you back to the ranch right after that."

Gorun's central crystal glowed once, signalling that he understood what to do. Shamtile began waving his arms, tearing open the escape tunnel and guiding his tamer down and out. The way out was a lot smoother than the way in, and Aurin was itching to tell Luna and Kyle what he had learned.

"Well?" asked Knot, the second Aurin and Shamtile arrived at the ranch. Night had fallen and it was as cold in January as it had been in December. "Spit it out, boy."

Aurin furrowed his brow and Knot apologised for his impatience. "We were right, Scarlett is Libra," said Aurin, pulling out the photograph. "I think this is six of the twelve main Zodiac members, but I can't say for certain if the four I don't recognise are minions or anybody of importance."

"That confirms it," said Kyle, pointing at Frederick in the Zodiac lineup. "There's our good friend Leo. It's too much of a coincidence for both Scarlett and him to be in this photograph together. She hasn't ever mentioned knowing him before this?"

"Not once," said Knot, taking the photograph and looking at it with a furrowed brow. "It won't hold up in court, but plenty of eyewitnesses when she's unmasked in public will. I'll see what I can find on the rest of this sorry lot."

"Do you recognise any of these other people?" asked Luna, examining the photograph closely.

Knot shook his head. "I'm sorry to say that I don't but it shouldn't be too hard to find at least a little bit of information. How about any of you?"

Everyone else confirmed that they didn't know the four remaining mysterious individuals, but Aurin was convinced that a larger man with a ponytail was Sagittarius. "His build fits," he said, but Luna and Kyle weren't sure as his hair was always covered by a hat.

"What else did you find?" asked Knot impatiently. "If this was everything, it doesn't help us all that much."

"I'm getting to it," snapped Aurin. "The last important thing I learned was that Luna and I were right."

"About what?" asked Luna, not sure what she was supposed to be right about.

"Libra has been researching the Roche Berry," replied Aurin.

"Oh!" she exclaimed. "I thought it may have been a long shot, but they're really after one?"

Knot was nodding slowly. "I looked into it after you first brought it to my attention. It costs a ludicrous amount of gold to buy one."

"How much gold are you talking?" asked Kyle.

"Enough to buy you a couple of houses, easily. If you find one, you're probably set for half your life should you decide to sell it. It fetches a bigger sum than you would receive for winning the national championship."

"Ah, is it really that much?" laughed Kyle. "You're not going to find one low down in the tower anyway, so it's a stretch to assume that they've got one already."

"Why?" asked Aurin. "What if that's the reason they switched to selling Minakai on the black market? To raise enough money to buy one in case they weren't able to find it in the tower."

"I...hmm," said Kyle, thinking about it for a second. "To be honest, that's as good a guess as I've got."

"So now what do we do?" asked Luna. "How are we supposed to lure both Sagittarius and Libra...erm, Scarlett, out at the same time? We can't just pretend we have an Ethruki egg or a Roche Berry, can we? Who would believe that?"

"Why, I believe I can help you with that," came a familiar voice from the shadows, startling everyone.

Aurin, Luna, and Knot were shocked to see the blonde-haired Frederick standing behind the fence, having listened to everything they had been talking about. He had a rather sinister grin on his face, as though he had just been handed the keys to the kingdom.

Chapter 47

"What are you doing here?" asked Luna, readying her tamer glove while staring daggers at Frederick.

"I tracked him down and invited him," said Kyle, surprising everyone. Aurin was especially taken aback after their conversation two days before where Kyle had explicitly told him it was a bad idea. "I thought about it and...well, you were right again," the rancher told Aurin. "I need to stop coming to snap judgements and trust you. After all, you've had more dealings with the Zodiac Squad than any of us, especially Leo here."

"I would prefer that you call me Frederick when my face is exposed," said the Zodiac elite, walking through the gate so that everyone could see him clearly. "Hello," he added.

"What has Kyle told you so far?" asked Aurin,

clenching his fist in case Frederick made any sudden moves. He didn't believe that Frederick was a danger to them at this moment, but he wasn't going to take any chances. If there were any sudden moves, he would summon his whole team at once.

"You can relax," said Frederick, looking at Aurin's fist. "It would have been far more effective for me to attack you while you were unaware. Need I remind you already that your friend invited me here? My Minakai are elsewhere, and I am massively outnumbered by all of you. That should be enough to assure you that there will be no funny business from me."

"Fine," said Aurin, relaxing somewhat, but still watching Frederick carefully.

"I know everything, at least that's what I'm told," said Frederick. "You will indulge me a moment because I have a lot to say about our organisation, our ideals and particular members of the Zodiac Squad."

"The floor is yours," said Knot.

Frederick began. "Our organisation has not always been the way it is today. It began as solely hunting for the cosmic elemental Minakai. For what purpose, you will have to wait and see, but it was always our explicit goal. Each member must contribute in some manner to that task or they would be removed.

"I've been around for many years, far longer than most. As our leader's frustration with the lack of progress has grown, so has the discontent within the organisation. There have been those who have acted out and taken matters into their own hands and been reprimanded or excommunicated accordingly, but there are also those who have acted against us that we cannot simply get rid of.

"Sagittarius and Libra are big problems for us, as

they were the ones intent on increasing our criminal activities beyond that which helps fund our operations. It has worked well for it, at least at first, but now they're a thorn in our side. If you want to get rid of them, I assure you that I want that tenfold."

Aurin was finding some of what Frederick said hard to digest. "Sagittarius implied that your boss sent them here to burn this place to the ground. That doesn't fit well with what you've said about being a thorn in the side of the whole group."

Frederick shook his head. "I assure you that they acted independently. Sagittarius desires glory above all and getting rid of you, particularly after you cost him the chance at capturing an Ethruki, was his own intent. Frankly, I would rather we return to acting entirely in the shadows."

"What's it going to take for you to start naming names?" asked Knot.

The Zodiac elite laughed. "Do not mistake my being here for an act of betrayal. I am only here to help you ensure that the two individuals in question are exposed in such a way that they can be of no use to us. I want to clean house, so to speak."

"Why doesn't your boss fire them like any bad employees?"

Frederick shook his head and wagged his finger. "I am not here to tell you the ins and outs of the Zodiac Squad, was that not clear?"

"At least give us something," said Aurin. "You owe us that, don't you?"

"You will not be getting an exposé from me," frustrated by the constant questioning. "My interests and the interests of the Zodiac Squad come first. Now let me tell you what we're going to do."

"If he betrays us, you'll never hear the end of it," said Luna as she and Aurin sat at their favourite café. Shamtile and Innogon sat on the floor at her feet, each with three flavours of milkshake to pre-emptively quell their fighting.

"I know," sighed Aurin. "Kyle has to get some of the blame too because he's the one who made the call in the end."

"Oh, he won't hear the end of it either."

The pair of young tamers were waiting to enact the plan that Frederick had told them was a surefire way to draw out Sagittarius and Libra. Once the time turned eleven fifty, they would begin. They wanted the streets to get crowded shortly after they began.

"Alright," said Aurin, checking his watch. "Let's get moving."

Luna picked up a Minakai egg that Knot had given them and they walked along the street with Aurin, Shamtile and Innogon beside her. They moved into a back alley where it was quiet, and then they saw them. Three Zodiac minions blocked the far side of the alley.

"Hand over the egg," one of them said. "If you do, you can walk away." Aurin and Luna turned to run, but the other side was blocked by three more members.

"No way, it's Luna's egg," said Aurin defiantly.

"Then we'll do things the hard way," said one of the Zodiac members, as all six summoned their Minakai.

"Get us out of here," Aurin ordered, and Shamtile

raised the ground beneath their feet, delivering the group to the rooftops as the Zodiac members desperately tried to climb up.

Shamtile lowered them down at the other side and the two tamers ran back around and into the alley. The Zodiac members stopped trying to climb and all six ordered their Minakai forwards. Aurin summoned Steambot and he, along with Innogon, cast a wave down the alley, washing everyone away.

The duo turned and made to run back into the square, but their targets finally appeared. Libra and Sagittarius stood before them.

"Never send a grunt to do the work of a master," muttered Sagittarius. "Hand over the Ethruki."

"No," said Luna, clutching the egg tightly.

"Little girl, you're going to regret that," said Libra, summoning a Windjinn while Sagittarius summoned his Thundarun.

Luna sent Innogon back to the ranch as Aurin dismissed Shamtile and Steambot, summoning Leonite in their stead. "Let's go!" he called to Luna as they hopped on the lion's back and ran down the alley.

The Zodiac members jumped on their own Minakai and chased the young tamers, attacking with razor winds and lightning strikes that Leonite dodged. They all ran out of the alley, but Aurin flicked his wrist and conjured up Chull. The small bird darted at the Zodiac elites but was brushed aside.

The four tamers emerged in the town square, right as the clock struck twelve. It was lunchtime and people had started emerging from the surrounding buildings. Aurin ordered Leonite to stop and the pair dismounted as Luna summoned Spritzard.

People gathered as the Zodiac duo dismounted,

looking around nervously. They didn't like being exposed to the public eye, even while masked, but the prospect of an Ethruki egg was too great. "Attack!" they cried in unison, sending forth their Minakai.

Leonite battled the air serpent, while Spritzard fought the lightning unicorn. People backed off as the gusts of wind, water streams and lightning bolts were flung around the square. The tamers were focused intently on the battle, so much so that nobody noticed the black bird with the skull mask zoom past.

Aurin's Chull snatched Libra's mask with his talons, throwing it across the square. She tried to cover her face, but it was too late. Everyone in the square had seen her, and they all knew exactly who the Zodiac elite was.

Sagittarius realised what was happening, but it was too late as his own mask was swept away by the black bird. "Thundarun!" he called, hopping on top of his Minakai and the two sped off.

Spritzard chased, but the unicorn was too fast. She returned to the square as Leonite finished off Scarlett's Windjinn. As the detective raised her hand to summon another of her monsters, Spritzard pounced and restrained her hands. The water demon pulled her glove off and threw it away.

Scarlett was in a panic. Everyone was murmuring about her as Aurin and Luna watched on satisfied. "Give me the egg!" she cried hysterically.

"You can have it," said Detective Knot, walking into the square. "I bought it yesterday at Taming Solutions. It's a simple Cubtem egg. I'm sad to say that it won't do you a lot of good where you're going."

"Harvey!" she yelled, her eyes widening maniacally. "They set me up. They planted the mask; it was these two rats."

"Save it," barked Knot as a handful of police officers approached their disgraced colleague. "We've all seen who you really are. Dozens of eyewitnesses. My last piece of advice to you is to shut up. It's in your best interest."

Scarlett looked at Aurin and Luna, then glanced at Aurin's Leonite. The sight of the cobalt blue lion caused her to gasp. "It was Leo!" she yelled. "You're in cahoots with him. He gave us the false information about that egg. He's betrayed the Zodiac Squad!"

"I have no idea what you're talking about," said Aurin, stroking his Minakai's mane. "What I will say, however, is that you should never have messed with us. All I wanted to do was explore the tower, collect a few Minakai and enjoy exciting battles against tough opponents. It was you and your group that ruined that. This is a warning to the rest of them, including Sagittarius and Leo. Do not mess with me again."

Scarlett screamed as she was dragged away in handcuffs. Knot approached the two young tamers, a satisfied smile on his usually stoic face. "Good job, you two," he said proudly.

"We could have done better," said Aurin, pleased to have aided the unmasking and capture of Libra, but he felt as though the job was unfinished.

"What's going to happen with Sagittarius?" asked Luna nervously, voicing what Aurin was thinking. "He's far worse than Libra."

"I'll dedicate myself to catching him," said the detective. "I'll do whatever it takes to track him down and make sure that he's not a threat to anyone ever again. Mark my words."

After thanking the two once more, he headed back to the police station while Aurin and Luna left for the ranch to tell Kyle that the plan was a success. The town square was still abuzz with the Hazelton citizens. They were all gossiping about what had just occurred, excited that their lunch break had been so thrilling.

The man in the bull mask walked to the head of the table and sat down. He surveyed the nine Zodiac elites before him and then leaned upon the table, clutching his hands together. "Leo," he said, directing his eyes to the man in the lion mask.

"Yes, Master Taurus," said Leo.

"You know what it is that I am going to ask you, don't you?" said Taurus.

"I do, sir."

"Well?"

"It was as you suspected, and I have retrieved it. The Roche Berry that they kept from us." Leo removed a large pink, peach-like berry from his bag and set it on the table in front of himself.

The Zodiac members murmured amongst themselves. "So, it was true," said Virgo, aghast at the betrayal by his comrades. "They were trying to capture an Ethruki for themselves. Scum."

Pisces spoke up. "Perhaps they wanted to sell it and flee?" she contemplated aloud.

"That is not the case," said Leo. "I was able to retrieve this from Sagittarius before he escaped town. He won't be coming back to bother us again, I assure you."

Cancer looked unnerved. "Why's that then?" he asked.

Taurus shut him down. "I lent him one of my Minakai to take care of the problem and there shall be no more said about it. All written record of him will be scrubbed, but he will go down in Zodiac myth as a cautionary tale. Good work, Leo. I assure you that you will be highly rewarded for your efforts. I promote worthy replacements to their ranks in due course but, for now, we operate as the Council of Twelve with only ten members."

"What about the three troublemakers?" asked Virgo.

"We will leave them be for now," replied Taurus. "Let them enjoy their little victory. If we remain in the shadows as we should have done from the start, there will be no problem. I must confess to you all that my greed got the better of me and it must have rubbed off on Libra and Sagittarius. That ends today. We stick with the founding principles of Zodiac. Is everyone in agreement?"

"Aye," said the congregation of Zodiac elites. They were one step closer to obtaining their first cosmic Minakai and then they would start seeking out the rest.

Chapter 48

It was a beautiful April morning and the grass glistened with dew as Aurin walked out of Kyle's house, finally repaired after almost four months. He took a deep breath, ready for another day of preparation for the second Hazelton tournament that was right around the corner.

"It's going to be a good day," he said. Shamtile ran forward to greet him. He warbled and swayed back and forth, excited for what was to come. "We're all going to run laps around the ranch as a warmup. Assemble the team and I'll meet you by the gate shortly."

Kyle walked over as Shamtile disappeared into the pens. "Starting the morning right, are you?" he asked.

"Don't I always?"

"Yes, but I respect the commitment. You've

reaffirmed yourself since Zodiac went quiet."

"I take it there's still nothing from them?"

"Knot said there was a duo spotted in the tower a week ago, but they kept to themselves and didn't cause trouble. I'm not sure how reliable the information is, but it means they're still active. Perhaps they're going quiet because the bad publicity makes them a much more desirable target?"

"I don't think they fear the bad publicity as much as you think they do," said Aurin. "I think they're biding their time until they launch whatever their next scheme is. Probably something to do with Ethruki or whatever other cosmic elementals they can track down."

Kyle nodded slowly, but he wasn't sure if he agreed or not. "At least they can't track the other cosmics in Hazelton. Ethruki is the only one native to Harmony Tower as far as I understand, so perhaps we'll be lucky and they'll move along?"

Just then, Aurin's Minakai appeared, led by Shamtile. He greeted each of them one by one, Spikruption, Dolissile, Leonite, Desparee, Steambot, Chull and the recently evolved Gorungol. The Minakai were fired up and raring to go.

As Aurin was about to start the run, Kyle stopped him. "After you're done warming up, how about a battle?"

"Yes," said Aurin with a grin, "but only if you go all out."

"Fine," said Kyle, finally determined to give Aurin his best. "We'll make it interesting this time though. There's no point only testing three of your team, how about we do five different one-on-one matches?"

"You've got my attention."

"We each pick five team members, then one of mine

fights one of yours. Regardless of the outcome, both of those Minakai can't be used for the rest of the match."

"I'll think about who to choose during our warmup," said Aurin.

He and the Minakai ran around the ranch, all at vastly different paces. Dolissile and Chull had it easy, flying through the air as they tended to do. Gorungol stomped heavily, lagging far behind the rest. Once everyone was finished and had a moment to rest, Aurin lined them all up at the edge of Kyle's battlefield where he was already standing in wait.

"What's happening?" asked Luna as she wandered towards them from the ranch path. She was grateful to be able to come and go as she pleased again now that Zodiac wasn't a big concern.

"It's battle time," said Kyle, explaining to her the terms of the match. "Do you want the honours of being referee?"

"Yes!" she squealed gleefully, excited to see them both go all out. Innogon hopped off her back and sat on the grass, his eyes darting from Aurin to Kyle rapidly.

"When I give the word, you both summon your first Minakai," said Luna, pausing to let the tension mount. "Fight!"

Aurin sent in Spikruption to face off against Kyle's Hogannon. Neither had an elemental advantage against the other, both fire elementals, so it would come down to power and skill. Both tamers watched the other's Minakai intently, waiting to see who would strike first.

"Enough waiting," said Aurin. "Flatten that pig!"

Spikruption charged forwards as Hogannon took repeated shots at him. The dinosaur faced the attacks head-on, before rolling forward like a wheel and accelerating towards Kyle's Minakai.

"This seems familiar," said Kyle, remembering the time that he had used a similar technique with his own Spikruption in a battle against Aurin.

Hogannon stepped aside, but Aurin had expected this. "Whip!" he ordered.

Spikruption turned around and unfurled, slamming his tail into the cannon-armed hog and knocking it onto the grass. Spikruption followed up with a body slam, landing on top of Hogannon and crushing him with his enormous body.

Hogannon had stopped moving. "The first round goes to Aurin, giving him an early lead. Just what will happen next?" called Luna, trying to mimic the tournament announcer.

"Lucky," muttered Kyle, looking anxious. He did not want to lose this battle.

"Next!"

"Dolissile!" shouted Aurin, summoning his second Minakai.

"Snowlem!" cried Kyle at the exact same time.

Dolissile teleported in from the edge of the battlefield, while Kyle's Minakai warped in from the pens. The cybernetic dolphin blasted forward immediately, while Snowlem conjured a snowstorm, obscuring itself and blinding Dolissile, who veered off course.

"Sonar," ordered Aurin, and Dolissile detected his opponent's location through the storm. He charged forwards, but Snowlem grabbed him with his wooden arms and slammed him into the ground.

While Dolissile was dazed, Snowlem created a large block of ice in the air, and it fell on top of Dolissile. Aurin's Minakai burst through it, trying to carry on, but he fell to the ground again after moving only a few feet.

"It looks like Dolissile has torpedoed right out of this match," said Luna, while Aurin frowned at her. "Contenders, summon your third Minakai now!"

Aurin chose Desparee, while Kyle chose his Techwing, the evolved Techling that he had found in the tower with Aurin months before.

"When did you evolve him?" asked Aurin.

"A few weeks ago," said Kyle.

"I thought you were hitting me with your best."

"Let's see how this plays out then, shall we?"

Desparee immediately summoned roots from the ground that reached into the air and entangled the metallic bird, but Techwing sliced through the thick tendrils with his razor-sharp wings. He soared into the air and then accelerated towards Desparee, who lost a few of his leaves to the powerful opponent after a failed attempt to dodge.

"Use your signature attack," ordered Aurin. "Wild despair!"

Kyle was taken by surprise as Desparee began flailing wildly, crying and yelling with torment echoing in his voice. Trees and roots sprung up from the ground and retreated almost as fast. It was chaos and the battlefield was being torn to pieces. Techwing weaved in and out, but when he attempted to fly out of reach, he was caught by a root that grabbed his talon and pulled him to the ground.

As Desparee charged up his nature beam attack, Techwing shot a powerful laser from his eyes, finishing off the tree-like Minakai almost instantly. He dropped to the ground and the beam attack petered out before it had the chance to leave Desparee's hands.

Luna started performing an exaggerated announcer voice now. "Kyle has two points and Aurin has one. Will this next round be the decider? This battle is wild!"

"Shamtile, you're up," said Aurin, catching Kyle off guard. He had expected Shamtile to be saved for the final round, but he had already summoned his evolved Coldbat, Sanguice.

"Another new evolution?" asked Aurin.

"If I've trained them recently, they're ready to fight," said Kyle. "It's about my abilities as much as theirs."

"Let's show him that he can't compare to you, Shamtile," said Aurin. "Armour up!"

Shamtile conjured his stone armour as Sanguice shot icicles from her mouth. The masked lizard blocked each one with ease, then performed a ritual dance, shaking the earth. Rocks and stones rose from the ground, surrounding the Sanguice from all angles.

"Get out of there!" ordered Kyle, seeing that his large bat was trapped.

Shamtile pulled the rocks in at lightning speed, knocking the bat to the ground. She flapped her wings and returned to the air, but before she could gain any height, Shamtile had blown apart his rock armour and the largest chunk smashed into Sanguice's forehead.

"That was brutal!" exclaimed Luna. "But it's no surprise coming from the dreaded Shamtile. It all comes down to this final round. Tamers, summon your Minakai now!"

Kyle's Wingbloom and Aurin's Steambot both appeared on the battlefield. The large plant bird flapped its leaf wings, creating small gusts as it rose and fell. Steambot discharged little puffs of steam, ready to knock the air elemental out of the sky.

"You have the elemental disadvantage," said Kyle. "What were you thinking?"

"I'll tell you after the battle," said Aurin with a sly

grin.

The rancher didn't know what Aurin was up to, but it didn't matter. He had every confidence in his beloved Wingbloom. "Alpha manoeuvre," ordered Kyle.

Aurin didn't know what this meant, so he went with a more straightforward order. "Pressure cannon!"

Steambot shook violently, blocking his steam from leaving his pipes and building up pressure. Wingbloom had soared up high, out of reach of most Minakai. Suddenly, he dived, spiralling at an immense speed, and turning into a green cyclone.

"Release!" ordered Aurin, and Steambot fired a powerful blast of water that could knock a brick wall down like a domino.

Wingbloom was spinning too fast and protecting himself with his air technique. He forced his way through the stream, which poured down on the battlefield like rain. He collided straight into Steambot's shining blue eye, then rolled across the ground before springing up into the air again.

Steambot tried to move, but he was starting to malfunction. He took a couple of steps forward and then dropped to his knees, unable to control himself any longer. He was done for.

"The victory goes to the rancher with all the answers...Kyle!" called Luna. She ran onto the battlefield as the two battling tamers met in the middle.

"You know that doesn't rhyme, right?" said Aurin.

"Huh?" asked Luna.

"Rancher and answer."

"It's the closest I could get without spewing a complete nonsense phrase. I thought I did a pretty good job!"

Aurin laughed, not particularly downcast about the

results of the battle. He had expected to lose against Kyle but was very pleased that he had come so far. Had he lost earlier, he would have asked to finish all five rounds just to see what he was capable of.

"You did a great job, Aurin," said Kyle, offering uncharacteristically direct praise.

"Thanks," said Aurin, smiling proudly. "So did you for somebody so rusty."

"Who said I'm still rusty? Perhaps I've been secretly training while you were in town or off galivanting in the tower with Luna."

"You're a sneaky one," said Luna, wagging her finger at him.

Kyle shrugged and laughed it off. "Tell me then," he said. "Why Steambot for your final Minakai?"

Aurin laughed. "Honestly? I thought you were going to pull a switcheroo, so I moved Shamtile up a position. I was expecting Wingbloom versus Shamtile too."

"You tried to switcheroo because you thought I would switcheroo?" chuckled Kyle.

"Pretty much, yes."

Everyone laughed as Aurin and Kyle's remaining Minakai, plus Innogon, started playfighting nearby. Aurin was right, it had been a good day so far and he still hadn't gotten as far as breakfast yet.

"Who wants a classic Bretonian fry?" he said, jingling his wallet. "It's on me today."

"Only if you don't mention the tournament for the duration of the meal," said Kyle.

"What? Why?" said Aurin.

"You're going to ask me five different times if I think you have a shot at winning this year."

"That's not true at all," said Aurin. "I would ask you if you think I can make the semi-finals so I can qualify for the national championship."

"No tournament talk," said Kyle bluntly.

Luna shook her head in exasperation and walked ahead as the two men bickered frivolously about tournaments and talking about tournaments. Shamtile and Innogon left the other Minakai to it and scurried after their tamers, hoping to be treated to more milkshakes, unconcerned about the looming battles just around the corner.

End of Arc 4
Zodiac Hunters

Aurin's Team:

Luna's Team:

Other Books by Jordan Allen

Mutagenesis Series:
Mutagenesis: The New World
Mutagenesis: Human Regression

The tale of Jason Cooper, a young man raised in an idyllic walled town who is thrust into a wild world of bloodthirsty mutants, ruthless violence and post-apocalyptic adventure as he searches for his lost family.

The Hollow Realms Series:
Hollow Kingdom
Ashes of the Necropolis
Moonlit Soul
Hollow Empire

A dark fantasy series of largely standalone titles in a shared universe. Inspired by classic sword and sorcery, The Hollow Realms books are filled with action, adventure and horror as heroes fight against all manner of monsters and villains.